# The Arranged Ma
## Mafia L ...

Anna Braun

# The Arranged Marriage with the Mafia Boss

Anna Braun

Published by Anna Braun, 2024.

THE ARRANGED MARRIAGE WITH THE MAFIA BOSS

**First edition. November 19, 2024.**

Copyright © 2024 Anna Braun.

ISBN: 979-8230588238

Written by Anna Braun.

# Also by Anna Braun

Alessia Romano never imagined that fate would place her at the center of a war between families. Daughter of Lorenzo Romano, one of the most feared mafia leaders, she had always known her life would be marked by strategic alliances and unwavering loyalties. However, when she is forced to marry Matteo DeLuca, the feared boss of the rival mafia, she finds herself torn between hatred for him and an attraction she cannot control.

At first, Matteo is merely a pawn in his father's power game, an opportunity to expand the DeLuca empire. But as their marriage unfolds, hatred and attraction mix, creating a tense relationship filled with provocations and undeniable chemistry. Matteo, a ruthless man hardened by past tragedies, experiences vulnerability like never before with Alessia, though his pride and mistrust keep him from fully surrendering.

As secrets and betrayals begin to surface, Alessia discovers that her own family is involved in conspiracies that threaten the alliance with the DeLucas. Caught in a constant struggle between loyalty to her family and her heart, Alessia is dragged into a spiral of manipulations, treacherous alliances, and violence. When she finally rebels against her father's control, she becomes a traitor to her own family and a target for Lorenzo.

With war looming and the bond between Alessia and Matteo growing stronger, both are faced with impossible choices. What began as a marriage forced by the mafia evolves into a dangerous alliance, where love and revenge intertwine. But in a world where trust is a rare commodity, and loyalty is tested at every turn, can Alessia and Matteo build something real, or will they be consumed by the ghosts of their families?

"The Arranged Marriage with the Mafia Boss" is a story of passion and betrayal, where every decision could mean life or death, and where, even in the darkest moments, love may be the greatest danger of all.

# Chapter 1: The Relentless Contract

The clock marked the end of the night, and the first signs of a new day were emerging, but the heavy air in the Romano mansion made any hope of relief seem distant. Alessia Romano felt the weight of expectation in every cell of her body, as if she were trapped in a slowly tightening trap. She had always known that being the only daughter of Lorenzo Romano meant living under the will of her father and the empire he had built, but nothing had prepared her for what she was about to hear.

"Alessia, you will marry Matteo DeLuca," Lorenzo announced, his voice firm and cutting, leaving no room for objection.

Alessia felt a chill run down her spine, and for the first time, her body recoiled, revealing the shock she was trying to hide. She fixed her gaze on her father, hoping to see some sign of hesitation or regret. However, Lorenzo's face remained unwavering, a cold mask revealing nothing but determination.

"No. This is impossible," she whispered, her voice trembling. "I will not marry him, Father."

Lorenzo took a step forward, his gaze sharp as blades. "This is not about what you want, Alessia. You are a Romano. Marrying Matteo will secure peace between our families."

Peace. The word echoed in her mind like a cruel irony. He spoke of peace, but he was handing her over to a man who carried the blood of their enemies and had the power to destroy any shred of dignity she had left. Matteo DeLuca was the underboss of the DeLuca mafia, the family that had caused her so much pain over the years. A betrayal that still haunted her nights.

"So you're willing to sacrifice me to save the empire?" Alessia challenged, her chin raised and her eyes burning with resentment.

"Sacrifice? Don't be dramatic, Alessia," Lorenzo shot back, impatient. "What you are gaining is much more valuable. You'll have status, power, and a family to call your own."

Family. Another irony. He had no idea what that word meant to her, especially knowing that she was now destined to be the pillar of a union that suffocated her even before it began.

"Matteo DeLuca..." she murmured, almost to herself, and swallowed hard. The memories of her last encounter with him still burned in her mind like embers. Matteo was everything she despised: a cold, calculating man, with a thirst for vengeance fueled by the same hurts she carried. A man who, years ago, had nearly destroyed her with a betrayal he felt no remorse for.

Lorenzo watched her closely, and then, as if to make it clear what was at stake, added, "This marriage is also a contract. He won't just be your husband; you are obligated to give him an heir. Matteo needs a son to secure the DeLuca legacy."

Alessia felt as if every word was suffocating her chest, slowly crushing her. Giving herself to Matteo, becoming the mother of his child... The idea terrified her and made her stomach churn. But Lorenzo had already made his choice, and there was no escape. Resignation mixed with the hatred that began to boil in her veins. If this was the fate forced upon her, then she would do whatever it took to show Matteo that she was not a docile puppet.

She took a deep breath, trying not to reveal the storm of emotions inside, but Lorenzo seemed to understand every one of her reactions. He stepped closer and, in a tone almost condescending, murmured, "Accept your position, Alessia. Resistance will only make things harder for you."

She bit her lower lip, swallowing the bitterness. There was nothing more to say. There was no way to fight in that moment. Her mind was trying to process everything, but one certainty took shape: she would not let Matteo or Lorenzo break her.

As soon as Lorenzo left the room, she turned toward one of the large windows, seeking some escape in the distant and unreachable view. But any hope of freedom dissipated. She knew Matteo would come to her. He wanted to see her broken, powerless. And she would not give him that satisfaction.

When Matteo DeLuca crossed the threshold of the Romano mansion hours later, there was a coldness contained in every one of his steps. He wore a flawless suit, each detail meticulously calculated to convey power and control. Upon seeing him, Alessia felt her heart race, but she was overcome with a wave of determination. He would not see weakness in her eyes.

She was alone in the hall when he entered, and their gazes met in a silent exchange full of resentment.

"Alessia," he greeted her, his voice low and sharp, like steel.

She kept her chin up. "DeLuca. Did you come to reinforce the sentence my father already imposed?"

He smiled faintly, a smile devoid of affection. "It's not a sentence. But it's curious that you see it that way."

Alessia clenched her fists. "I have reasons to see it this way. We both know what this marriage means to you, Matteo. A way to exact your revenge. A form of control."

Matteo moved closer, his face just inches from hers. "Call it what you want. But in the end, you'll be by my side, and that's what matters." The proximity made him inhale her scent, a heady mix of delicacy and determination, and he couldn't help but feel satisfaction when he saw that her gaze remained firm, defiant.

"You can force me to be by your side, but you will never have my respect," Alessia whispered, her voice full of hatred and bitterness. She refused to give in, even knowing that he held all the cards.

"I don't expect respect, Alessia," Matteo replied, his tone almost dismissive. "But you will be mine. And soon, everything you think you despise about me will be exactly what keeps you by my side. Your hatred and pride are just parts of the game. And I intend to play it very well."

Those words echoed in her mind like a dark prophecy. Matteo DeLuca was dangerous, and now she was trapped in a web of lies and power she couldn't untangle. But Alessia knew she would never allow him to control her completely. Matteo may have the means, but he would never have her soul.

"You want a marriage? You'll have one. You want an obedient wife? Look elsewhere," she said, chin held high, as his gaze narrowed.

He smiled, but it was an icy smile. "We'll see, Alessia. In the end, everyone bends." He turned and walked out, leaving her alone with her anger and impotence.

When he disappeared, Alessia clenched her fists, feeling her pride and fury bubble up. She was willing to fight, and Matteo DeLuca had no idea what he was about to face.

Alessia remained alone in the hall, but her mind was far away. Her conversation with Matteo echoed in her head like a cold, inevitable threat. She felt the blood boiling in her veins, and the anguish gnawing at every part of her being. Matteo DeLuca, that arrogant, calculating man, now had control over her life and future. He represented everything Alessia despised: corrupted power, an insatiable thirst for dominance, and above all, the desire to see her submissive.

But what tormented her most was the fact that, despite how much she hated him, there was something undeniably disturbing in that proximity. Matteo had a dark magnetism that made her vulnerable in a way she couldn't control. He was dangerous, but also hypnotizing, and that infuriated her. The attraction she felt was a betrayal of everything she believed in, but she couldn't deny the effect he had on her.

When she saw her reflection in one of the room's windows, Alessia realized that her face was marked by tension and anguish. She straightened her posture, as though preparing for a battlefield. This marriage might be a sentence, but she promised herself that she wouldn't let Matteo control her. If he wanted war, she was ready.

Matteo, on the other hand, did not leave the mansion with a peaceful mind. Despite maintaining his unshakable expression, he felt a growing unease. He had known Alessia for years; he knew she was stubborn and difficult to deal with, but there was something in her, in that constant provocation and the way she challenged him, that fascinated him. She was not an ordinary woman. Unlike any other woman he had known, Alessia did not let herself be intimidated by him, and that both irritated and attracted him.

As he recalled her expression, a mixture of fear and hatred, Matteo smiled to himself. He knew she would try to resist at every turn, but that resistance only made everything more interesting. There was something intoxicating about the challenge of bending her, of making her the wife he wanted, a woman who belonged to him in every way. And while he knew this might be a difficult task, he was determined to win her over.

As the driver took him back to the DeLuca mansion, Matteo reflected on the implications of that marriage. He did not expect sweetness or submission from Alessia, and honestly, he did not want it. The truth was, Alessia was like fire, and he found himself yearning for that heat, even knowing he could get burned.

Later, when they met in the mansion's library to discuss the details of the wedding, the tension between them was palpable. Alessia stood with her chin held high, her posture rigid, and a sharp look in her eyes that seemed to challenge every word he spoke.

"So, Alessia," Matteo began, with that authoritative tone that irritated her deeply. "Tomorrow we'll be married. I think it's time you understood what this really means."

She crossed her arms, not hiding her irritation. "I understand perfectly, Matteo. I'm a pawn in your power game. But don't think I'll be a submissive wife. If you expect obedience, you've married the wrong person."

Matteo gave a half-smile, moving closer to her slowly, stopping just a few inches away. "You underestimate me, Alessia. I don't expect obedience... I demand it." He leaned in, his voice low and threatening. "And you'll understand that with time."

She raised an eyebrow, not backing down, and in an impulse, moved even closer. "I will never submit to you, Matteo. You may bind me to you with this contract, but my soul is free. And you cannot take something that doesn't belong to you."

Matteo smiled, but it was a cold smile. "Is that so? We'll see how long your freedom lasts." His hand brushed against her arm, a firm touch that made Alessia catch her breath. It was as if, even amid the hatred, there was a warmth enveloping them, something intense and almost impossible to resist.

He pulled away just enough to study her reactions, enjoying how Alessia's eyes challenged him, filled with restrained anger. That proximity, though charged with hostility, had something forbidden, intoxicating about it.

"You are truly arrogant," Alessia murmured, a little off balance. "You think you have control over everything, but what you don't realize is that you're playing with fire."

"I admit fire is dangerous, but it's also fascinating," Matteo replied, a provocative gleam in his eyes. "And, Alessia, you are the hottest fire I've ever seen. It will be a pleasure to tame it."

Her heart raced. Every word he spoke seemed designed to destabilize her, and she knew he was aware of that. But she wouldn't back down. She wouldn't let him see the effect he had on her.

"If you want a war, DeLuca, you'll get one," she whispered, staring straight into his eyes. "But don't expect me to surrender easily."

He laughed, a low, sarcastic laugh, and took a step back. "Great, Alessia. I like challenges. But remember, in the end, there's always a winner. And I'm not used to losing."

Alessia watched him leave the library with slow steps, leaving behind a trail of tension that seemed to fill the entire room. When he was finally gone, she exhaled the breath she hadn't realized she had been holding.

Alone, Alessia promised herself that Matteo DeLuca would never have power over her. But deep down, a part of her knew that this man was a danger to her resolve and perhaps even to her heart.

# Chapter 2: First Encounter as Enemies

The DeLuca mansion's hall was set for a formal meeting, but the atmosphere was far from cordial. Every detail, from the crystal chandeliers gleaming from the ceiling to the dark walls that seemed to absorb the light, gave the space a somber air. Everything there exuded the opulence and power that characterized the DeLuca family, and this was exactly the setting Matteo wanted for Alessia's arrival.

He awaited her at the center of the hall, his posture firm and imposing, with a slight smile that seemed more like a silent provocation. The tension in the room was palpable, as if even the furniture itself was tense, waiting for the imminent explosion. Matteo knew this encounter would mark the beginning of something unforgettable—a game between two forces, one he was determined to win.

Alessia entered the hall, her expression hard, her dark eyes fixed on Matteo with a contempt she made no effort to hide. She dressed with elegance and simplicity, but there was something in her posture that screamed rebellion, something he could not tame easily. She stopped a few paces from him, holding her head high, her lips pressed into a determined line. It was as if she wanted to show that, though he had forced her to be there, he would never have her obedience.

For a moment, their gazes met, and in that silent exchange, Alessia felt the weight of the past between them—the wounds he had caused and the revenge she knew he still harbored. Rage surged inside her, but at the same time, an overwhelming sense of attraction and contempt created an explosive mixture within her. Matteo seemed to feel it too, for the cold smile he wore took on an intense, dangerous gleam.

"Alessia," he began, breaking the silence, his voice low and loaded with irony. "Welcome to your future."

She furrowed her brow, her eyes flashing. "Spare me your fake hospitality, Matteo. I'm here because my father decided I'm a convenient bargaining chip to solidify his business deals."

Matteo tilted his head slightly, as though appreciating a performance. "Oh, don't underestimate yourself so much, Alessia. It's not just about business." He took a step closer to her, his eyes never leaving hers. "It's about power. About control." His voice dropped to a threatening whisper. "And, of course, about the revenge I've been waiting for, for years."

Alessia held her chin high, but inside, her heart was racing—a mixture of fury and an emotion she didn't want to acknowledge. He was so close she could smell the woody, cold fragrance he wore, a scent that matched his relentless personality.

"Revenge?" she questioned, sarcasm dripping from every word. "That's ridiculous. You want revenge for a war you started yourself, Matteo. If anyone should want revenge here, it's me."

He gave a slight smile. "You still don't understand, Alessia. This isn't just about the past. It's about making sure you know who's in charge. That you understand that by accepting this contract, you've handed me not just your name, but your freedom."

She clenched her fists, her chest burning with rage. "Do you really think you can control me? That you can make me obey your every command like a submissive doll?" She took a step toward him, unafraid of the proximity. "I am not your property, Matteo, and I never will be. No matter what you think you've conquered."

He raised an eyebrow, amused by her audacity, but also irritated by the challenge. "We'll see, Alessia. Because, in the end, this is the world your father chose for you. And you'll have to play by my rules."

She smiled, but the smile was acidic, laced with resistance that made her radiate strength. "I play my own game, DeLuca. And you have no idea what I'm capable of."

Matteo leaned in, his eyes locked on hers. "Be careful, Alessia. These dangerous games have consequences." He murmured, with a threatening undertone. "You may think you're strong, but do you know what happens when someone gets in my way?"

Alessia didn't back down, not an inch. On the contrary, she held his gaze with resolve, feeling the rage and disdain turn into a spark she could barely control. "Maybe you'll discover I'm an even bigger danger than you think."

A heavy silence fell between them. It was as if an invisible field of energy kept them close, entwined in a tension so thick it seemed impossible to ignore. The world around them seemed to fade away, and for a moment, Matteo saw not just the enemy he wanted to tame, but a strong, determined woman whose beauty challenged and provoked him at every turn.

He smiled, but there was no humor in that smile. "You have quite a big mouth for someone in your position, Alessia."

She returned the smile with an equally cold look. "And you're very arrogant for someone who expects loyalty through threats."

Matteo moved even closer, until their faces were mere inches apart. Alessia held her breath, but kept her posture, determined not to give in. "You know," he murmured in a low, almost hypnotic tone, "I can be arrogant. And maybe even cruel." He leaned in until his lips nearly brushed her ear, and whispered, "But you will learn to respect me, Alessia. You will learn that resisting me will only make everything harder for you."

She felt a chill run down her spine, and her body reacted, despite her mind screaming that this was a dangerous game. Without hesitation, she lifted her face, her gaze filled with challenge. "I will never surrender, Matteo. And I will never respect you."

His eyes gleamed with a mixture of admiration and irritation. There was something about her that made his blood boil, and it attracted him like nothing else. Matteo was used to receiving obedience without question, but Alessia... Alessia was like a storm he wanted to control, yet knew he could never tame.

He laughed, a low, cold laugh. "Well then, Alessia. Don't give in. But understand this—every act of resistance you make will only give me more pleasure. And in the end, you will have to submit. It will be inevitable."

She watched him walk away, but the tension lingered in the air, like a spark ready to ignite everything around them. When he left the hall, Alessia stood frozen, still processing every word, every provocation, and hating herself for feeling her body respond to his dangerous presence.

She swore she would never let herself be dominated. That Matteo DeLuca would never have power over her. But a part of her knew, deep down, that this clash between hate and attraction had only just begun.

**Matteo**

Matteo watched Alessia as she turned away. He knew that, though he tried to maintain a cold demeanor, something in her eyes betrayed the turmoil she was trying to hide. He felt a strange satisfaction in provoking such reactions from her, but there was something deeper that unsettled him. He should see her only as a tool in his revenge plot, a pawn in an old war. But Alessia wasn't an easy woman to categorize. She defied every expectation he had. Her resistance, her intensity... They were captivating in a way he couldn't admit.

As he made his way down the hallway, Matteo realized this marriage would be far more than a mere strategic alliance. There was a complexity in Alessia that made every encounter with her unpredictable and electrifying. He paused for a moment in the corridor, absorbing the impact her presence had on him, the undeniable desire to see her break, to control the fury she displayed.

**Alessia**

In the hall, Alessia remained frozen, her fists clenched. Rage mixed with something she refused to name. Matteo could make her blood boil like no one else. She was outraged by him, by his arrogance, by the way he spoke as if he controlled the world. But at the same time, something inside her responded in a way that confused her. There was an inexplicable attraction, as if the intensity of the hatred became, paradoxically, a spark of desire.

She knew it was dangerous. Matteo DeLuca was the enemy. The man responsible for the tragedy haunting her family. And now, instead of staying in the past, he was closer than ever, as if he wanted to possess her, consume every part of her resistance. She took a deep breath, fighting the urge to scream, to vent the rage he made her feel.

But at the same time, she knew Matteo wanted to see her lose control. He expected her to yield, to show weakness. And Alessia was determined not to give him that satisfaction. Matteo was cold, calculating, and every word he spoke seemed designed to break down her defenses, to manipulate her. But she would not bend. Not as long as there was breath in her body.

**The Unexpected Encounter in the Garden**

Later that same night, Alessia tried to calm herself in the mansion's garden. Her light steps on the wet grass were nearly silent as she allowed herself a few moments of reflection. But to her surprise, she noticed a familiar presence approaching. Matteo had followed her out there, and the intensity in his eyes was anything but friendly.

"I see the hall wasn't big enough for your pride, Alessia," he said, with his usual mix of provocation and disdain.

She lifted her eyes, already exhausted by so much tension, but still unable to ignore the provocation. "Don't confuse my pride with the need to breathe away from your control, Matteo. The air is much lighter without you around."

He smiled, closing the distance between them until they were standing very close. "Interesting, because you're the only one who still doesn't see the irony of this marriage." He leaned in until their faces were only inches apart, his eyes locked onto hers. "You think you're in control, Alessia? I think it's exactly the opposite."

She felt her face flush but didn't retreat. "And you think that with this little performance, you'll make me give in? Sorry, Matteo, but not everyone bends to your intimidation games."

The proximity between them was unexpected, but Alessia's heart raced faster with it, as if that fiery hatred was an energy that bound them together in a strange and intense way. Matteo smiled, a smile full of mystery and challenge. "We'll see, Alessia. The problem is, the more you resist, the more interesting this game becomes."

Without warning, he reached out and gently cupped her face, the tips of his fingers grazing her skin. The touch was soft, but Alessia felt as if an electric current ran between them. "This hatred you feel, Alessia," he murmured, his eyes deep in hers, "it's something I've never seen before. It's almost... poetic."

She tried to pull away, but Matteo held her firmly, not letting her escape. "Let me go, Matteo," she whispered, trying to keep her tone firm.

He studied her for a moment longer, then released her, but not without whispering, "This is just the beginning, Alessia. And I promise you, in the end, you won't have the strength to hate me anymore."

She glared at him, defiant. "I'd rather die than give in to you."

Matteo laughed, but this time the sound was dark, almost soft. "Hold on to that belief, Alessia. Because the more you resist, the more pleasure I'll get from making you change your mind."

The encounter in the garden only strengthened Alessia's resolve, but also confused her. No matter how much she wanted to hate him with all her strength, there was something in Matteo that disturbed her in a way she didn't want to admit. He made her feel challenged, and at the same time, he wanted her to become part of his power games. And in the midst of that darkness, Alessia wondered how far this battle would take them.

For Matteo, the encounter in the garden only reinforced how different Alessia was from anyone he had ever met. She was a woman he wanted to possess, to dominate, but who also awakened something deeper within him. He wasn't used to being attracted to someone who challenged him so, but he knew he wouldn't back down. He wanted to see that resistance break. He wanted Alessia to be his in every way, and to do that, he was willing to play every card.

Both of them knew they were at the beginning of a battle that could consume them both.

# Chapter 3: The Engagement Under Pressure

The ballroom was impeccable, decorated with imposing chandeliers hanging from the ceiling and arches adorned with white and red flowers. The night gleamed with the luxury and power of two of the most influential mafia families in the city, the night when Alessia and Matteo's engagement would solidify the union between the Romano and DeLuca families. For many, it was an occasion to celebrate the long-awaited truce between two rival families. For Alessia, it was a night of humiliation.

She entered the ballroom with Matteo by her side, his arm firmly wrapped around her waist, a possessive touch that made it clear to everyone present that she belonged to him. His touch was light, but the pressure on her skin was like an invisible chain, trapping her. Every time Matteo leaned in to whisper something in her ear, Alessia felt her body react in a mixture of revulsion and... a sensation that infuriated her for not being able to suppress it.

"Relax, Alessia," he murmured, his voice a dangerous purr. "We're not here for a war. Tonight is to celebrate our union."

She tried to pull away slightly, but Matteo only tightened his grip on her arm, pulling her closer as if mocking her attempt to resist. She forced a smile, her eyes scanning the people around them who were watching the couple with interest and approval. She knew everyone expected to see a harmonious union, a truce represented by the couple who, to her, felt more like a prison sentence.

"You can fake it much better than this, Alessia," he whispered again, his lips too close to her ear. "These people want to see a woman in love beside the man she chose to be with."

She turned slightly toward him, maintaining the smile, but her gaze promised challenge. "Choice is an interesting word, Matteo. Because the last thing I'd ever choose in my life is you."

He smiled, but his eyes grew colder. "Good thing it doesn't depend on you," he replied, with a calm arrogance that overflowed with possessiveness. "You belong to me now. And everything you do will reflect on me. Just like everything I do will reflect on you."

Alessia took a deep breath, feeling cornered and humiliated. She looked around the ballroom, where the guests' attentive gazes followed them, all waiting to see the happy couple that would unite two families and bring a false peace to the dark world they inhabited.

To increase the pressure, Matteo slid his hand down to her waist, the touch as subtle as it was imposing, and leaned in again. "Relax, Alessia," he continued, with a dangerous smile on his face. "If you behave well tonight, we might make this marriage more bearable."

She couldn't hold back a sarcastic laugh. "And what do you consider good behavior, Matteo? That I pretend to be completely enchanted by the man who destroyed my life?"

He held her gaze, the intensity in his eyes trapping her like a snare. "You don't know what destruction is yet, Alessia," he whispered, his voice low and threatening. "But if you keep this attitude, I can guarantee you'll find out."

Alessia stared at him, her look full of hatred and a hint of fear she struggled to hide. Matteo was a dangerous man, and she knew it better than anyone. But at the same time, she refused to let him see how vulnerable she truly was. She had to fight, she had to resist. He might have forced her into this marriage, but he would never have her submission.

As Matteo led her through the ballroom, Alessia felt suffocated by the forced dance of politeness. He smiled at the guests, conversed with family and acquaintances, while keeping her close enough for everyone to know she was his. With every exchanged glance with the people around them, she felt herself slipping away a little more, as if Matteo was slowly erasing who she was.

Suddenly, he pulled her aside, taking her to a more secluded corner of the ballroom, where the voices and curious glances wouldn't reach so easily. He pressed her against the wall, his arm blocking any attempt at escape. "You're doing very well," he commented, almost with disdain, but there was a hint of provocation in his voice. "Who would have thought Alessia Romano could be so convincing?"

She clenched her teeth, maintaining a firm posture even when he leaned in closer, their faces mere inches apart. "I'm not doing this for you, Matteo. I'm doing this because I have no other choice. But believe me, one day, you'll see what happens when I have one."

He chuckled softly, his hand still resting on her waist. "Ah, Alessia, you still think you have any control over your fate? That's what I admire most about you: that useless determination."

"You can enjoy yourself now, but I promise you one thing, Matteo," she said, her voice low but full of venom. "This game won't be so easy for you. I will fight. I will turn every damn rule you set against you."

He watched her, his eyes gleaming with a mixture of amusement and something deeper, an intensity he tried to hide. For a moment, Matteo stared at her as if trying to unravel every layer of resistance she had built. And in that moment, he saw more than just anger. He saw the strength, intelligence, and determination of a woman who was much more than a mere pawn.

Alessia seized the hesitation, stepping closer, her gaze defiant. "Enjoy it while you can, Matteo. Because I'm not like the submissive women you control so well. In the end, you'll be the one destroyed here."

He laughed again, but this time, the laugh was darker. "I admire your courage, Alessia. But you underestimate how far I'm willing to go to make sure you belong to me in every sense."

They stood in silence, their breaths mingling, the world around them fading as they continued their silent battle. It was as if, between hatred and attraction, there was an invisible electric current connecting them, something they both wanted to ignore, but couldn't deny.

Finally, Matteo pulled away, but not without making it clear that this was only the beginning of what he considered a long and inevitable conquest. He straightened his suit, his gaze still fixed on hers, and gave a slight nod, as if to say: "The game has begun."

Alessia watched him walk away, her muscles tense, her lips tight. She needed to get out of there. She needed air, space, anything that would remind her that she still had control over herself. She turned and left the ballroom, Matteo's words echoing in her mind.

Out of sight of the others, she breathed deeply and made a silent promise. This wouldn't end the way he expected. She would find a way to reverse the game, to destroy him the same way he seemed determined to destroy her freedom.

The engagement was sealed, but the war had only just begun.

In the garden, away from the party and the bustle of the ballroom, Alessia breathed in the fresh night air, trying to regain control of herself. But the echoes of Matteo's words kept ringing in her mind. Every provocation, every intentional touch, seemed to burn on her skin. It was a cruel game, but there was something perversely fascinating about the dynamic between them, something that made her heart beat faster than she would have liked to admit.

He knew how to affect her, and it infuriated her. Being beside him and feeling that mix of hatred and attraction was like a constant torture, but it wasn't something she could simply avoid. Matteo was the kind of man who filled the room with his presence, a natural leader who, despite how much she hated him, exuded undeniable authority.

Alessia didn't expect to be followed, but she wasn't surprised when she heard heavy footsteps behind her. Matteo appeared at her side, silent, but with that penetrating gaze that seemed to pierce through every defense she had. He was watching her, not hiding the interest in seeing her there, away from everyone.

"Running away from the party?" he asked, his voice low but laced with irony.

She turned to face him, crossing her arms. "Running away from you, if you want to know," she replied, sarcasm marking her words.

Matteo smiled, somewhat darkly, and took a step closer. "I told you, Alessia, running isn't an option. You're about to become my wife. You'd better get used to it."

She laughed, but it was a laugh without humor. "Your wife?" The word tasted bitter in her mouth. "Don't fool yourself, Matteo. This engagement is a play for you. I'm nothing more than a piece in your power game."

He raised an eyebrow, clearly amused by her contempt. "Maybe," he admitted, with a provocative tone. "But if you're a piece, you're the most valuable one. And whether you like it or not, now you belong to me."

Alessia felt a shiver run down her spine. The way he said those words disturbed her deeply. It wasn't just an assertion of power; it was almost a veiled promise, as if there was something more behind that controlled arrogance.

"You don't know anything about me, Matteo," she murmured, trying to maintain her cool.

He tilted his head, his eyes studying every detail of her face. "Oh, but I want to know," he replied, his voice low and full of intensity. "I want to know what goes on in that stubborn, proud head of yours. I want to understand what makes you resist so much. But in the end, Alessia..." He took another step closer, so near she could feel the heat of his body. "In the end, you'll realize it's pointless to fight."

She clenched her fists, feeling the warmth between them. Every word seemed heavy with a promise that she knew could be both a curse and an inevitable attraction.

"I'll never give in to you," she whispered, her voice full of challenge. "Never."

He studied her for a long moment, his cold smile softening slightly. "Never is a dangerous word," he replied, his voice almost gentle, but hiding a dark intent. "And that's where you're wrong, Alessia. Because, soon enough, you'll be in my arms, whether you like it or not."

Her heart raced. He spoke with such certainty, such conviction, that she almost believed it. Almost. But, as always, she refused to show any weakness. She remained firm, her eyes locked on his with an intensity that matched his.

"You're arrogant," she muttered, trying to ignore the tension that seemed to grow between them. "You think you can control everything and everyone, but I'll prove you wrong."

He raised an eyebrow, a low laugh escaping his lips. "Ah, Alessia, your spirit is what fascinates me the most. But remember... everything has a price."

She narrowed her eyes, feeling the hidden meaning in his words. "And I'm not something you can buy, Matteo."

He leaned in even closer, his voice now so low it was almost a whisper, but full of a promise that made her shudder. "We'll see, Alessia. We'll see."

For a moment, the world seemed to stop around them. He watched her, his eyes like flames seeking to consume every piece of resistance she offered. And, in that moment, Alessia realized that maybe this battle between them wasn't just a game of power. There was something deeper, darker, that connected them. Something that, despite the hatred, awakened in her a hidden desire she struggled to deny.

Matteo pulled away, but with a smile of satisfaction, knowing he had left his mark. Alessia stood there, in the garden, feeling both challenged and... attracted. She didn't want to admit it, but Matteo could break down her defenses in a way no one ever had.

# Chapter 4: Heart on Fire

The days following the engagement were a whirlwind of conflicting emotions for Alessia. Her mind was set on resisting, on planning strategies to keep Matteo from gaining any control over her. But with each encounter, something inside her began to unravel, as if the flame of hatred she felt for him had turned into an uncontrollable blaze consuming her. Matteo was no longer just the man she despised; he had become the center of a forbidden desire, something that made her feel torn and vulnerable.

She hated her own reaction. How could she let herself be affected by a casual touch, by an intense gaze that seemed to strip her soul and provoke feelings she would rather keep hidden? Matteo was her enemy, the man who had promised to control every aspect of her life, and Alessia knew that giving in to any temptation meant giving him even more power over her. But her willpower was being tested at every turn.

That morning, Alessia walked through the mansion's garden, trying to focus on a sense of calm that always seemed just out of reach. But the sound of firm footsteps behind her brought her back to reality. She turned and found Matteo watching her, his face impassive, but with that predatory gleam in his eyes.

"Lost in thought, Alessia?" he asked, approaching slowly, like a predator closing in on its prey.

She crossed her arms, trying to maintain a firm stance. "Not the kind of thoughts you'd understand, Matteo."

He smiled, an arrogant and provocative grin that made her heart race. "Oh, but I think I do. After all, you're not so different from me as you'd like to believe."

Alessia rolled her eyes, trying to hide the effect his words had on her. "Please. Don't waste your time trying to convince me we have something in common."

He took another step, closing the distance between them, until Alessia could feel the warmth of his body. "Denial is a beautiful distraction, Alessia. But I see in your eyes that there's more." He gazed at her intently, making it clear that he noticed every small reaction she had.

"Don't try to analyze me, Matteo," she murmured, but her voice came out low, almost a whisper.

"Why not?" he provoked, his tone soft but laced with intent. "I like seeing how much you fight it. How much you struggle to deny that there's something between us."

She wanted to pull away, but she felt as if she were enchanted. His words pierced through her defenses and unsettled her certainties. "You're wrong. There's nothing between us but a contract and an obligation."

Matteo tilted his head, a smile forming on his lips that suggested he didn't believe a word she was saying. "Then why does your body respond so... passionately to my presence? Why, when I get close, do you hold your breath?"

She opened her mouth to protest but realized there was no way to disguise the truth. He was right, and that angered her. "It doesn't mean anything," she whispered, as if trying to convince herself. "It's just... a reaction. Something physical, not emotional."

He laughed, a low laugh that made her stomach churn. "Then, if it's just a reaction, why are you trembling, Alessia?" he asked, moving closer still, until his face was inches from hers. "If it's just physical, why do you try so hard to resist?"

Her face heated, and a mix of anger and frustration took hold of her. "Because I hate you, Matteo," she murmured, her words laced with almost painful intensity. "I hate the way you make me feel..."

"Really?" he murmured, his lips dangerously close to hers. "Then hate me, Alessia. Because the more hate you feel, the stronger this flame between us will burn."

She knew she should pull away, that she needed to keep her head cool and push him away any way she could. But in that moment, it seemed impossible to fight the attraction that hung between them like an electric current. Matteo lifted his hand and gently touched her face, and the world around her seemed to disappear. She closed her eyes for a moment, allowing herself to feel his touch, even though she knew it was a small defeat.

"You hate yourself for wanting this, don't you?" he murmured, his fingers lightly tracing her face. "But it's no use fighting, Alessia. What's between us is inevitable."

His voice was soft, almost gentle, and for the first time, Alessia felt that Matteo was lowering his own defenses, showing something beyond arrogance and control. But as if regaining control, she pulled away abruptly, her gaze filled with a mixture of contempt and vulnerability.

"Don't fool yourself, Matteo," she said, her voice firm again. "What you call inevitable is just your desperate attempt to manipulate me."

He raised an eyebrow, the arrogance returning to his eyes. "Believe whatever you want, Alessia. But deep down, you know I'm right."

She glared at him with disdain, but as she turned to walk away, she felt her own resistance hanging by a thread. Matteo had touched parts of her she preferred to keep hidden, and the internal struggle between desire and hatred seemed bigger than ever.

As she walked away, his words echoed in her mind, a burning reminder of the power he had over her. And as much as she hated herself for it, Alessia knew that the hardest battle was just beginning—not against Matteo, but against herself.

After the intense exchange in the garden, Alessia returned to her quarters in the mansion, but her heart had not calmed. She felt suffocated by a rage and frustration that seemed to invade every fiber of her being. She hated herself for feeling her heart race when she remembered Matteo's touch on her face, the closeness of his lips that almost sealed a kiss, that electricity that ran through her skin. Matteo DeLuca was her enemy, someone she should only despise, but her own body betrayed her, responding to every glance and provocation from him in a way that defied her logic.

She ran her fingers across her forehead, trying to clear her mind. She needed to keep control; she needed to remember that every gesture from Matteo was calculated. He knew the effect he had on her and was using it as yet another weapon, a tool of manipulation. But no matter how many times she repeated those words to herself, his image remained burned in her mind, invading her thoughts and her heart.

On the other side of the mansion, Matteo sat in his office, a look of satisfaction mixed with introspection. He should have been focused on family matters, on his business, on maintaining control of everything around him, but his thoughts always returned to Alessia. There was something about her that he still didn't fully understand, a fire that intrigued him. He had expected her to be just another piece in the game, a part of a plan he would control easily. But Alessia was different. She challenged him, resisted, and at the same time, seemed to be drawn to him, even against her own will.

Sitting in his leather chair, Matteo allowed a smile to escape. He liked the game, the tension, the way Alessia looked at him with a mixture of disdain and desire. He knew that deep down, she was fighting her own feelings, and that only made everything more interesting.

Matteo decided to confront her again that night. With firm, determined steps, he walked to her quarters and knocked on the door. He knew he could simply enter, but the tension of waiting was part of the pleasure of this game they were both playing.

Alessia opened the door, her eyes narrowed, clearly irritated to see him there. "What do you want, Matteo?" she asked, her voice laden with exasperation.

He crossed his arms, studying her with an amused look. "We need to talk."

She raised an eyebrow, skeptical. "Talk? Since when do you care about what I have to say?"

He smiled, moving closer until she had to take a slight step back. "Since I realized that, no matter how much you say you hate me, you still open this door for me."

Alessia swallowed hard but refused to be intimidated. "Opening the door means nothing, Matteo. Don't confuse my manners with... interest."

"Manners? That's a new one." He let out a low laugh, watching her with that intense, penetrating gaze. "But I know it's more than that, Alessia. Don't pretend you don't feel something."

She rolled her eyes, trying to keep her composure. "What I feel is disgust, if you want to know. Disgust for your arrogance, for your controlling ways. You think you can manipulate everything and everyone, but I'm not one of your men, Matteo."

He moved even closer, and Alessia felt her heart race when he raised his hand, gently holding her face. "You don't know what you're saying, Alessia. There's a fine line between hate and attraction. And, from what I see, you're right on the edge of both."

She tried to pull away, but his hand on her face kept her in place, as if he wanted to make sure she heard every word. The intensity in his eyes disarmed her, and even though she hated admitting it, she felt more vulnerable in his presence than ever.

"I won't fall for your game," she whispered, trying to sound firm, but her voice betrayed a slight tremor.

"It's not a game," Matteo retorted, his voice soft but filled with undeniable authority. "I don't need to play to get what I want, Alessia. I simply take what's mine."

She felt her face flush, anger and confusion swirling inside her. "I don't belong to you, Matteo. I never have, and I never will."

He laughed, a low, almost affectionate sound. "We'll see, Alessia. We'll see what time does to your resistance." With that, he gently traced his thumb along her face before stepping back slowly.

Alessia felt as though she had just survived a storm, her heart pounding and her mind in a whirlwind of thoughts. She hated him, yes, but she also felt something far deeper, a force that seemed to pull her toward him, against all her promises and convictions.

Matteo watched her for a moment longer, as though savoring the end of a captivating dance. He knew that Alessia was unlike anyone he had ever met. She resisted, she fought, and that was exactly what made her so irresistible. Still, he was determined. He would make her understand that resisting him was futile.

"Good night, Alessia," he said, his voice almost tender, but heavy with a dark promise.

She watched him leave her room, feeling as though she was being dragged down an irreversible path. She closed the door, took a deep breath, and placed her hand on her face, where he had touched her, as if trying to erase the trace of that touch. But the truth was undeniable: Matteo DeLuca was inside her mind and her heart, and no matter how hard she tried, she knew she couldn't forget him that easily.

# Chapter 5: The Ring and the Promise of Revenge

The engagement ring glittered on Alessia's finger like a mark of ownership, a constant reminder that she was now part of Matteo DeLuca's calculated plans. He hadn't given her that ring as a symbol of love or commitment. To Matteo, it was an emblem of power, a piece of his cold game of revenge and control. Alessia knew this. Every time she looked at the ring, she felt the weight of an invisible prison, and her chest tightened with a mix of anger and helplessness.

Matteo, however, seemed delighted by the effect his presence and the ring had on her. During one of their discreet encounters after the engagement, he held Alessia's hand, his eyes fixed on the diamond he had placed there. His firm fingers tightened around hers in a possessive grip, and, with a hard expression, he whispered coldly, "This ring is not just a symbol. It's a reminder, Alessia. A reminder that, from now on, you belong to me."

She tried to pull her hand away, but he held it firmly, his eyes revealing a calculated coldness. Alessia shivered, but she raised her face, determined not to show any weakness.

"That's what you think, Matteo," she murmured, her tone defiant. "But I will never truly be yours. This ring may mean whatever you want it to, but for me... it's just a piece of metal."

He smiled, a cold smile, but there was something more in his eyes—a spark of challenge. Matteo leaned in until their faces were inches apart. "Oh, you'll change your mind," he said, almost in a whisper. "Because in the end, you'll realize that resisting me will be a lost battle."

Alessia held her breath, feeling his proximity like a blatant provocation. There was something magnetic about Matteo, something that made her want to pull back and move forward at the same time. But she refused to give in, refused to let him see the effect his presence had on her.

"You can try all you want, Matteo," she replied, keeping her voice firm, though internally, her resolve wavered. "But I won't be a piece you can easily manipulate."

He laughed, but it was a low, almost threatening sound. "You still don't understand, Alessia. This marriage isn't about love. It's about control. About revenge." He squeezed her hand tighter, his face darkening. "For everything your family did. For everything that happened in the past."

She felt the intensity of his words like a cold blade against her skin—sharp and lethal. Matteo's anger wasn't just a passing whim; it was something rooted in a deep wound, a resentment he seemed to have carried for a long time. But Alessia wouldn't be intimidated. If he was determined to see her as a trophy, she would show him she was a piece that would be difficult to control.

"If you think you'll destroy me, Matteo, you're mistaken," she murmured, her eyes locked on his. "I won't fall so easily."

He held her gaze, but the hand that had been gripping hers relaxed slightly, and a subtle smile appeared on his lips. "We'll see, Alessia. Because in the end, everyone gives in. Everyone finds their weakness." He let go of her hand, but the touch, even absent, seemed to still surround her, like an invisible chain.

Later, Alessia found herself alone in her room, staring at the ring on her finger. The soft light of the room reflected off the diamond, creating small beams that danced around the space. This wasn't just a piece of jewelry; it was a declaration of war. Anger bubbled inside her, but at the same time, she felt divided. There was something about Matteo that pulled her toward him—a dark, irresistible force. But she knew she couldn't allow herself to be swept away.

She closed her eyes, taking a deep breath. She had to be stronger than any attraction or spark that might arise between them. Matteo would not have the power to destroy who she was, and that ring, no matter how symbolic, would not define her life.

The next morning, when Matteo found her in the mansion's hall for another meeting between the families, Alessia decided it was time to confront him in a different way. She walked toward him with a serene face, but her eyes revealed a fire that he quickly noticed.

"Matteo," she called, without ceremony.

He looked up, surprised by the confidence she exuded. "Yes?"

She raised her hand with the ring, holding it in a way that allowed him to see every detail of the jewel. "You may think this ring means you have me under your control, but know this: for me, it will be a symbol of something different." She narrowed her eyes, her voice low and heavy with fierce defiance. "It will be my reminder that I need to tear down every plan you try to impose on me. It will be my reason to fight against you until the end."

Matteo observed her, a glint of amusement and something deeper in his eyes. "You're really fascinating, Alessia. So determined to fight against something that is inevitable."

"I make my own choices, Matteo," she replied. "You may see me as a pawn in your game, but you will never have my will."

He stepped closer to her, the proximity between them once again creating an electric tension. "Then let's see how far this determination of yours goes, Alessia. Because, like it or not, you're tied to me now. And I will make you understand what that really means."

She held her posture, her heart pounding unevenly. She wouldn't let him see any weakness. And though she felt the power of his presence, she was determined to show him that he wouldn't break her so easily. Matteo might have control in some areas, but he would never control her spirit.

When he pulled away, Alessia knew that the ring was more than just a symbol of revenge. It was the beginning of a battle—a battle she was ready to face, even if it meant putting her sanity and emotions at risk.

As Alessia made it clear to Matteo that the ring would not be her submission, something inside her vibrated with the same desire for revenge. She felt challenged, determined to resist the control he tried to exert, but at the same time, there was an intensity in his proximity that disturbed her. Matteo was a magnetic, dangerous force, and she knew that giving in would mean abandoning everything she believed in.

After the brief confrontation in the hall, Matteo watched Alessia walk away, the echo of her words still reverberating in his mind. He had always known Alessia would be a challenge, but she was surpassing his expectations. Every provocation, every attempt at resistance from her ignited in him a spark that was more than mere pride or thirst for control. It was something he tried to deny, but, like Alessia, he couldn't suppress it.

Hours later, at the family dinner, Matteo and Alessia found themselves face-to-face again. The atmosphere was charged with silent tension. The conversations around the table revolved around business and alliance plans, but Matteo's sharp gaze never let Alessia slip away for a second. He wanted her to know that her presence both challenged and captivated him, and she met his gaze with a mix of fury and veiled attraction.

At one point, he leaned toward her, ignoring the presence of others at the table, and whispered in a low voice, laden with sarcasm and authority, "I bet you're enjoying this little war between us, Alessia. Don't pretend that what we're experiencing is a nuisance."

She closed her eyes for a second, controlling the anger and shiver his presence caused. "Don't confuse my reactions with interest, Matteo. All you are to me is a stone in my path, and it won't be long before I remove you."

He gave a low laugh, a sound that made her stomach churn. "So much hatred... I admire that in you. But deep down, you know that this flame between us is inevitable."

She stared at him, her eyes blazing with fury. "This 'flame,' as you call it, is nothing more than disgust. And if you keep forcing me, you'll see just how far this 'flame' of mine will go."

He leaned closer, so that only she could hear his cold, calculated voice. "Then show me, Alessia. Show me how far you're willing to go."

She remained silent, the challenge echoing within her, as if every word Matteo said was a spark lighting something uncontrollable. As much as she hated him, each encounter with him seemed to leave her more vulnerable, more divided between disdain and attraction.

Later, when they were alone in the living room, Matteo approached Alessia again, his expression softer, but his eyes still carrying that predatory intensity. He observed her as if every movement she made was a puzzle he was determined to solve.

"You intrigue me, Alessia," he confessed, his voice almost a whisper, but still firm. "So much strength in resisting... but deep down, there's something else. I can see it."

She took a step back, trying to create some distance between them, but he grabbed her hand, stopping her. Their eyes met, and Alessia felt the weight of his gaze, as if Matteo were infiltrating her mind, trying to uncover every thought and every secret.

"Let go of me, Matteo," she murmured, her voice faltering slightly, but trying to keep an authoritative tone.

He pulled her closer, keeping his eyes locked on hers, a smile spreading across his lips. "Not until you admit that this isn't just hatred. There's something more, Alessia. Something you're trying to hide even from yourself."

She tried to break free, but he held her firmly, his face inches from hers. "You're really presumptuous, Matteo. You think everyone falls under your control like magic, but it won't work with me."

He smiled, a smile full of self-confidence and challenge. "Are you sure? Because every time you challenge me, Alessia, it seems like you're just getting closer to me."

She felt her breath quicken, her heart pounding with every word he said. She wanted to fight, to push him away, but that gaze, that touch... everything was contributing to the confusion that took over her. "I will never... never give in to you," she whispered, but her tone came out hesitant, betraying the certainty she was trying to convey.

He gave a faint smile, his thumb brushing gently across her hand. "That's what you say now. But I know that eventually, you'll realize that resisting is futile."

She stared at him, her gaze full of anger and confusion, but a part of her knew she was losing control. Matteo had a powerful influence over her, and every moment they spent together seemed to make it more difficult to avoid him. Hatred and desire mixed in a dangerous way, and Alessia knew she needed to be careful not to lose herself in this game.

Finally, Matteo let go of her hand, but not before casting one last look at her—a look that promised that their battle was far from over.

"Good night, Alessia," he murmured, with a touch of irony. "And think about what I said. This ring isn't just a symbol of control, it's a promise. And I always keep my promises."

She stood still, watching him walk away, feeling both challenged and frustrated. With every encounter, every exchanged word, she felt more tangled in that web of emotions and provocations that seemed impossible to escape.

But even with all the confusing emotions, Alessia promised herself that she would find a way to free herself from his control. Matteo might think he held all the cards, but she was determined to prove that he wasn't the only one controlling the game.

# Chapter 6: Bonds of Hatred

The forced coexistence between Alessia and Matteo felt like a minefield, where every word or gesture was a disguised provocation, every look a battle of power. Matteo made a point of marking his presence in every corner of the house, as if claiming territory. He moved through the space with the same arrogant confidence he always had, and Alessia felt she was being tested at every moment, challenged not to retreat.

That morning, while Alessia was in the living room, trying to distract herself with a book, Matteo entered and, without a word, sat in the armchair across from her, a cold smile on his lips. He watched her for a long moment, as if he wanted to pierce through every layer of her indifferent facade.

She tried to ignore him, keeping her eyes fixed on the pages of the book, but she knew it was impossible to remain unaffected. His presence was intense, suffocating, and no matter how hard she tried, she couldn't shake the tension that was building between them.

"Interesting choice of reading," Matteo said, breaking the silence. His voice had a casual tone but was loaded with sarcasm. "Thinking of escaping to a world where you still have control over your life?"

She snapped the book shut, her eyes locking onto his. "You really like hearing the sound of your own voice, don't you?" she retorted, her expression hard. "It must be the only thing that gives you any satisfaction."

He laughed, but it was humorless. "Ah, Alessia, you have so much courage in your words. But they don't change a thing." He leaned forward slightly, his eyes narrowing. "You're nothing but a pawn in this game, a pawn I intend to use however it suits me."

Her heart raced with anger, but she took a deep breath, determined not to show any weakness. "And you think you can control me with threats and provocations? I've told you before, Matteo: you have no power over me."

He tilted his head, a smile almost affectionate but laced with cruelty. "Ah, but I know I do, Alessia. Because, no matter how much you try to hate me, no matter how much you fight me, there's something you can't deny. This tension between us... this hatred that binds us."

Alessia scoffed, rolling her eyes. "You think you know me? You're just a selfish, cruel man, Matteo. You're incapable of caring about anyone but yourself."

The smile disappeared from his face, and something in his eyes shifted. He moved even closer, the intensity in his gaze becoming almost suffocating. "Maybe you're right, Alessia. Maybe I am incapable of love." He paused, his voice dropping to a darker, almost vulnerable tone. "But hatred... that's a real feeling. And what I feel for you is more real than anything else I've ever felt."

His words hit her like a blow. There was a raw truth in Matteo's voice that unsettled her. She felt a chill run down her spine but forced herself not to look away, determined not to show any vulnerability.

"You're pathetic, Matteo," she whispered, her voice trembling slightly. "If all you can feel is hatred, then you're emptier than I thought."

He stared at her in silence, and for a brief moment, Alessia thought she saw something beyond his usual arrogance—maybe a wound he was desperately trying to hide. But soon, Matteo returned to his mask of indifference, the cold smile back in place.

"Empty or not, Alessia, you're tied to me now. And I intend to savor every second of it."

She felt a wave of frustration and hatred burning inside her, like a flame Matteo seemed to feed with every word. But at the same time, that proximity, that defiant look, made her feel even more drawn to him, as if the hatred itself were fuel for something else.

"Don't underestimate me," she murmured, her eyes still locked on his. "I know how to play too, Matteo. And unlike you, I have real feelings, something that goes beyond your sick control."

He laughed, but it was dry, almost a sigh. "Feelings are a weakness, Alessia. Something I refuse to have."

She shook her head, incredulous. "Maybe that's why you'll never understand what it really means to be alive. Because living isn't just about control. It's about feeling, something you're incapable of doing."

Matteo watched her, his dark eyes fixed on her, and for a moment, the silence between them was almost palpable, as if they were both trapped in an invisible battle. Alessia wondered if there was something behind his mask of coldness, some trace of humanity he was trying to deny. But before she could think any further, Matteo stood up, pulling away from her with a calculated look.

"Believing in feelings is what makes you weak," he said finally, with a tone of disdain. "I survive because I don't let anything sway me except reason. And you, Alessia, will realize in the end that it's not love that wins. It's control."

She watched him walk away, her heart heavy and her mind confused. Matteo represented everything she hated, but at the same time, he was a force that challenged and consumed her, making her question just how long she could stay firm.

That night, Alessia was alone, thinking about Matteo's words. The hatred he felt seemed to come from a deep place, a place of pain he refused to admit. And as much as she wanted to hate him alone, as much as she wanted to see him only as a monster without feelings, something inside her prevented her from simplifying her emotions.

She realized that this shared hatred was more than just a destructive feeling. It was a bond, a connection that grew stronger with each confrontation. And even though she tried to deny it, Alessia knew she was trapped in a tie that she couldn't easily break, an attraction that, no matter how dangerous, seemed impossible to ignore.

After the intense confrontation in the living room, Alessia found herself walking through the vast garden of the mansion, trying to relieve the whirlwind of emotions Matteo had stirred inside her. The night was cold, and the wind seemed to whisper its own secrets, but nothing could calm the chaos Matteo brought into her life. He was like a storm that arrived without warning, shaking all her defenses, destroying every barrier she had carefully built. And the worst part was, the more she tried to hate him, her body reacted treacherously to his presence.

She stopped, watching the reflection of the moon on the still waters of the garden lake. Matteo wasn't just a threat; he was a force that pulled her in, against her will, and this attraction made her feel confused, fragile. She hated this vulnerability that came every time he was near. But no matter how much she tried, Alessia couldn't deny that there was an intensity in Matteo that captivated her, a mystery that challenged her with every look.

Suddenly, the sound of footsteps brought her back to reality. She turned around and found Matteo there, standing, watching her with that penetrating gaze that seemed to see every hidden thought. For a moment, the air between them became charged, as if his mere presence filled the space around them.

"Running away, Alessia?" he asked, his voice soft, but carrying dangerous sarcasm.

She raised her chin, determined not to show any weakness. "I don't run from anyone, Matteo. Especially not from you."

He took a step forward, moving closer, and Alessia felt her heart race. Matteo was like a predator, moving calmly, but with a gaze that revealed how much he enjoyed this game of provocation between them.

"It's curious," he murmured, his eyes locked on hers. "Because it seems like you're always trying to escape me. But I think, deep down, it's the opposite."

She rolled her eyes, trying to hide the intensity of what she felt. "You really believe everyone is fascinated by you, don't you? Your arrogance is pathetic, Matteo."

He smiled, a smile full of challenge. "Maybe it's arrogance, Alessia. But you can't deny the effect I have on you. Do you know why? Because deep down, you feel the same way."

She tried to protest, but the words caught in her throat. There was something in him that disarmed her, that left her defenseless, and he seemed to know exactly how to exploit it. She felt the heat rise through her body, and the anger and desire mixed, creating a confusion that left her at the mercy of her own feelings.

Matteo reached out, holding her by the chin, forcing her to look directly into his eyes. "That's what fascinates me about you, Alessia. You fight, you resist, but deep down, you're as lost as I am. And that's what makes us so alike."

She pulled away, stepping back from him with a sharp movement. "I'm nothing like you, Matteo. You're cruel, selfish, incapable of feeling anything real."

He laughed softly, but the expression in his eyes shifted, becoming darker. "Maybe I am incapable of love, Alessia. But I know what hatred is. And what I feel for you is the only real thing I've ever felt."

His words left her breathless. There was a hidden pain in every syllable, an involuntary confession from someone who had been marked by deep wounds. For a moment, Alessia felt compassion, but quickly pushed the thought away. Matteo was her enemy, the man who wanted to control her, and she couldn't allow herself to weaken.

"If that's what you feel, Matteo, then so be it. But know this: I will never be yours. This hatred of yours doesn't scare me, and no matter what you do, you will never have complete control over me."

He watched her in silence, his jaw clenched, and for a brief moment, it seemed as if her words had pierced something deeper. But in the blink of an eye, the mask of arrogance returned to his face, and he smiled, moving closer once again.

"I don't need your consent, Alessia. All I need is for you to keep feeling this intensity when you're with me. Whether it's hatred or desire... in the end, they both belong to me."

She stared at him, determined not to retreat. She knew he was playing a game, trying to break every resistance she had, and that made her even more determined to fight. But at the same time, there was something that felt inevitable, a bond forming against her will, an attraction pulling her toward him, no matter how hard she tried to resist.

Finally, Matteo released her chin, but his touch lingered on her skin, like an invisible mark she couldn't erase. He took a step back, but his gaze remained fixed on her eyes, and Alessia felt the air around her grow lighter, yet still charged with unspoken promises.

"Good night, Alessia," he murmured, with a soft voice that hid a dangerous intensity. "Sleep well. And try not to think too much about me."

She watched him walk away, and as she was left alone, she realized just how fast her breathing was, how erratic her heartbeat had become. Matteo was her enemy, the one who wanted to destroy her, but the more she tried to resist, the more the desire and tension he brought into her life consumed her.

Back in her room, Alessia sat on the bed, feeling that each encounter with Matteo left her more entangled, more trapped in a connection she didn't want to admit. She knew that, in some way, he was consuming her. And as her thoughts swirled around everything he had said, one certainty filled her mind: the hatred they shared was the strongest and most dangerous bond she had ever experienced.

# Chapter 7: Control and Restraints

Since the engagement, Matteo seemed to intensify his attempts to control Alessia. He established clear, rigid rules for her, a list of restrictions that included prohibiting her from leaving the mansion without his permission, limiting who she could talk to, and even dictating where she could go within the house. Each rule was a line Matteo drew between them, a constant reminder that he saw her as part of his domain, his territory.

Alessia, however, was not someone who easily accepted submission. With every new boundary imposed, she felt more determined to challenge him. Each rule seemed to fuel her desire to fight against him. The thought of being a pawn in Matteo's life filled her with indignation, and she refused to let him dictate her fate.

That night, after learning that Matteo was busy in a meeting in his office, Alessia decided to leave. She knew he had forbidden her from leaving the property without his permission, but she didn't care. She urgently needed to escape, to see the world beyond the mansion's walls, even if it was just for a few moments. She put on a coat, grabbed the keys to one of the smaller cars on the property, and silently walked to the garage, her heart racing.

However, before she could get in the car, a firm, familiar voice stopped her.

"Where do you think you're going, Alessia?" Matteo appeared in the doorway of the garage, his eyes flashing with a mix of irritation and something deeper. He was clearly furious, but he maintained a controlled posture, his voice low and threatening.

She closed her eyes, taking a deep breath to contain the frustration his tone caused. When she turned to face him, she raised her chin, determined not to back down. "I'm leaving," she replied simply, with a defiant tone. "I'm not your prisoner."

He took a few steps toward her, and Alessia felt the weight of his presence, the tension between them growing with each passing second. "I've made the rules clear, Alessia. You don't leave without my permission."

She narrowed her eyes, full of contempt. "Rules? I'm not a child to follow your orders, Matteo. And I'm definitely not your property."

He extended his hand, blocking her from entering the car. "While you're under my roof, Alessia, you belong to me. And yes, you'll follow every one of my orders."

Her blood boiled. "You're pathetic," she whispered, the anger pouring from her words. "You need to hide behind rules to feel powerful, to control something, because deep down you know you have no control at all."

Matteo's eyes narrowed, and he took another step, getting so close that Alessia could smell his scent, a dark and intense aroma that seemed as dominant as he was. "You like to challenge me, don't you, Alessia?" he murmured, his voice heavy with sarcasm. "But remember, I can be far more stubborn than you imagine."

She laughed with disdain, but the proximity made her shiver slightly. "Do you think that scares me? Do you think I'll bow to you?" She stared at him, her eyes flashing with defiance. "I'd rather live as a prisoner to a man I hate than give in to the control you think you have over me."

Matteo grabbed her arm, the touch firm but controlled, conveying a power that made her feel torn between hatred and something deeper. The pressure of his touch was a reminder of his strength, his ability to keep everyone around him under his control.

"You talk as if you could escape me, Alessia," he whispered, his lips dangerously close to her face. "But don't you see? You're already trapped, even if you don't realize it. I control every step you take, every movement, because you can't run away from me."

She tried to pull away, but Matteo held her tight, and at that moment, Alessia realized she was unable to deny the tension his touch provoked. "You control me physically, Matteo, but you'll never have my mind or my heart. I'm much more than you can reach."

He leaned in until their eyes met, his voice becoming a rough, possessive murmur. "If you want to hate me, Alessia, then hate me. But know this: that hatred, that resistance, only makes you draw closer to me."

Her heart raced, and for a moment, a spark of desire mixed with the anger. It was a connection that made her want to pull away, but it also drew her in, inexplicably. Matteo pulled her toward him, and at the same time, she wanted to get lost in the confrontation, in the struggle that seemed to consume both of them.

"You're sick, Matteo," she murmured, her voice trembling. "If you think this is love or some form of connection, you're more lost than you realize."

He gave a cold smile, one that sent a shiver down her spine. "I never said this was love, Alessia. But it's intense, and you feel it just as much as I do. Deny it, fight it, but you won't escape what's already between us."

She closed her eyes, trying to ignore his proximity, the heat that seemed to envelop them. She wanted to believe she could break free from this game, that she wasn't giving in to the power he had over her. But when she opened her eyes and met Matteo's dark gaze, she knew the line between hate and desire was becoming thinner by the moment.

In a burst of rage, Alessia pushed him back, freeing herself from his hand. "You can think whatever you want, Matteo. But you'll never see me give in to you. I'm stronger than this sick obsession you carry."

He laughed, a low, threatening laugh. "We'll see, Alessia. I like challenges, and you're my biggest one. But be sure of this: in the end, I'll be the one who dictates the rules."

Without saying another word, Matteo turned and walked away, leaving her alone in the garage, while Alessia tried to compose herself, her body still trembling from the intensity of the confrontation. He consumed her, challenged her in ways no other man had ever done, and it left her torn between the impulse to fight and the inevitable attraction she felt.

Back in her room, Alessia knew that, no matter how hard she tried, she was getting more and more entangled in Matteo's game. And no matter how much she fought, she couldn't stop that connection from growing stronger.

The door to her room closed behind her, and she leaned against it, breathing deeply, trying to calm her heart, which was pounding erratically. Matteo's proximity, the intensity in his eyes, it all affected her in a way she hated to admit. There was something dangerously addictive about that confrontation, that electric tension between them. Every time he got closer, it was like she was caught in a storm, being dragged into a whirlwind of emotions that left her confused and vulnerable.

She knew he saw her as territory to be conquered, a piece of his domination. And what infuriated her the most was how he made her feel so torn, as if the hate she felt for him was intertwined with something else, something she didn't want to accept.

Meanwhile, Matteo walked slowly back to his office, his steps firm and his expression impassive, but inside, he was far from calm. He forced himself to maintain control, to wear that mask of authority and coldness, but each confrontation with Alessia revealed a side of him he wasn't used to facing. She was fire, a constant challenge, and while he wanted to dominate her, he also found himself dominated by an irresistible attraction. Every time he saw her, it was as if her presence broke through any armor he tried to maintain.

When he reached his office, he poured himself a glass of whiskey, his thoughts still on Alessia. He couldn't exactly say what attracted him to her, but the fact that she resisted and challenged him made his desire grow. He leaned back in his chair, remembering the fierce look in her eyes, the sharp words she always used against him. She was different from anyone he knew, and that difference intrigued him.

Later that night, Matteo decided he wouldn't let Alessia's challenge go unanswered. He walked to her room, his face determined. Without knocking, he opened the door and found her by the window, watching the weak lights of the garden. Alessia turned quickly, surprised by the intrusion, but kept her chin raised.

"We need to clarify something," he said, his voice low and firm, closing the door behind him.

She crossed her arms, raising an eyebrow in defiance. "Then speak. I'm curious to know what your next order will be."

He approached slowly, his eyes locked on hers. "You don't understand, Alessia. This isn't about orders. It's about the way things should be. You're under my protection, under my responsibility. And as long as that's true, you will follow my rules."

She rolled her eyes, frustrated. "Protection? I don't need your protection, Matteo. And I definitely don't need your rules."

Matteo stopped just a few inches from her, his gaze dominating, but this time, there was something more. "If you really think you don't need me, Alessia, you're mistaken. Don't you see how involved you already are in all this? This marriage is much more than you think."

She looked at him, a mix of hatred and curiosity in her eyes. "And what exactly do you think this marriage is, Matteo? A power game? A way to subjugate me?"

He took a deep breath, his eyes never leaving hers. "I could answer yes. I could say this marriage is about control, about power. But that would be a complete lie." He paused, evaluating her reaction. "This marriage is about something that goes beyond that. About something you try to deny, but you know it's there."

She remained silent, his words echoing in her mind. She wasn't sure exactly what he was trying to say, but the proximity, the intensity of his gaze, left her confused and vulnerable. "You talk as if you know something I don't."

He reached out and held her face gently, the touch firm, but at the same time, carrying a strange tenderness. "I know, Alessia. I know that this tension between us, this hate, is a flame that consumes everything around us. And whether you like it or not, you feel the same."

She tried to look away, but he held her, forcing her to meet his gaze. "I will never... never give in to you," she murmured, but her voice came out hesitantly, as if even she doubted her words.

He leaned in a little closer, until their faces were inches apart, and Alessia felt her heart race even more. "You can say that as many times as you want, Alessia. But we both know that behind each word, there's a desire to give in, to lose yourself in what's between us."

She felt her face heat up, and for a moment, all she wanted was to close the distance, to forget the barriers she had placed between them. But quickly, she regained control and took a step back, freeing herself from his touch.

"That's what you want to believe, Matteo. Because you think you can conquer everything and everyone. But I'm different. I won't give in. I won't be a piece in your game."

He watched her, a smile appearing on his lips, filled with a mix of challenge and admiration. "I like your spirit, Alessia. I admire your strength. But in the end, you'll realize it's not about winning or losing. It's about how far we're willing to get involved."

She remained silent, trying to contain the whirlwind of emotions he awakened. She knew she was getting deeper and deeper involved, that the silent war between them was leaving marks that could never be erased. And even against her own will, she felt herself drawn further into the danger that Matteo represented, into that intensity that made her lose control.

When he left her room, Matteo gave her one last look, a look filled with promises and possessiveness that made her tremble. And when the door closed behind him, Alessia was left alone, trying to sort out her thoughts and feelings. Matteo DeLuca was a dangerous man, someone she should keep at a distance. But she knew that no matter how hard she tried, she was caught in a web of emotions that pulled her deeper and deeper into a game she knew, somehow, she could never win.

# Chapter 8: First Shared Night

The new mansion was luxurious and imposing, with its spacious corridors and furniture that exuded wealth and power. Alessia walked through the place with a sense of unease. She knew this would be her home after her marriage to Matteo, but the idea of sharing that space with him made her feel like a prisoner before even marrying him. The sound of his footsteps echoing through the hallways kept Alessia in a constant state of alertness.

Matteo seemed at ease, walking through the mansion as though he were the master of every inch of it. He watched her with an enigmatic smile, fully aware of the effect his presence had on her. There was something in Matteo's eyes that made Alessia nervous, as if he could see beyond her facade of indifference and self-sufficiency. The intensity of his gaze seemed to challenge her constantly, as if he knew she was trying, and failing, to resist him.

Later that night, Alessia took refuge in her room, trying to find some peace. She closed the door, leaning against it and taking a deep breath, as if trying to push Matteo's dominant presence out of her mind. But the calm was fleeting. A few minutes later, the sound of the doorknob turning brought reality back, and Matteo entered the room without hesitation, as if he had every right to be there.

"We need to talk," he said, his voice firm but carrying a hint of the provocation she knew all too well.

Alessia crossed her arms, trying to hide the discomfort she felt. "Do you know what privacy means, Matteo? I thought that was a basic concept."

He gave a half-smile, stepping closer. "Privacy? You still don't understand that, as long as you're under my roof, there are no... barriers that you keep trying to put up?"

She scoffed, irritated. "Barriers? What do you want, Matteo? I'm already here, following your rules, and now you think you have the right to invade my space?"

He stopped just a few inches from her, his gaze piercing. "Yes, Alessia. I want you to understand that from now on, every space, every moment... it all belongs to what we'll share." He leaned in a little, closing the distance between them until their faces were mere centimeters apart. "Running to your room won't keep away what's between us."

She averted her gaze, feeling her face heat up with his proximity. Matteo had a presence that left her vulnerable, and, as much as she hated to admit it, something inside her reacted to every word he spoke. But she wasn't willing to give in.

"You're arrogant, Matteo," she murmured, trying to keep her composure. "You think you can walk into my life, my mind, whenever you feel like it."

He smiled, a provocative grin that made her heart race. "It's funny you say that, because I'm already in your mind, Alessia. You think about me, you hate me... and still, you're always fighting against what you feel."

She stared back at him, defiant, even though she knew her resistance was weakening. "What I feel for you is contempt. That's something that will never change."

He gently cupped her chin, forcing her to look directly into his eyes. "Contempt? Are you sure that's all you feel?" He whispered, his voice low and thick with intensity. "Because what I see in your eyes is something much deeper than mere hatred."

Alessia tried to pull away, but his hand held her firmly, and the touch was almost hypnotic. Matteo was a master at provoking her, testing the limits of her resistance, and she could feel that with each passing moment, she was on the verge of surrendering. There was a part of her that wanted to fight, that wanted to keep up the façade of control, but his proximity shattered all her defenses.

"You're sick, Matteo," she whispered, almost breathless. "You think this is normal? You think you can manipulate everything and everyone?"

He smiled again, a smile that mixed amusement with a spark of something deeper. "I don't need to manipulate, Alessia. I just need to be present. The rest... what you feel... that comes naturally."

His words were a silent challenge, and she knew there was truth to them. No matter how hard she tried to deny it, Matteo had power over her—something that made her feel both vulnerable and drawn to him at the same time. It was a mix of hate and desire, a current pulling her in, one she couldn't resist.

He leaned in even closer, his lips just inches from hers, and Alessia felt her whole body tremble. There was something undeniably magnetic about his presence, something that made her unable to pull away, even when every fiber of her being screamed for her to run. Matteo was the man she hated most in the world, but he was also the one who could awaken feelings she couldn't understand.

"You hate me, Alessia," he murmured, his voice low and hoarse. "But I know there's more. Something you're trying to hide from yourself."

She remained silent, her gaze locked with his, and for a moment, all she wanted was to close that distance, to cross the line between hate and desire. But quickly, she regained control and took a step back.

"You're too arrogant, Matteo," she whispered, trying to mask the tremor in her voice. "And you're mistaken if you think you control me."

He watched her, a dangerous smile spreading across his lips. "I may be wrong about many things, Alessia. But about what's between us, I'm sure. And so are you."

Alessia felt a shiver run down her spine, and without another word, she turned away, leaving him in the room while she tried to regain her composure. She felt consumed by a mixture of rage and attraction, a tension that seemed to grow with each encounter. She knew she was in an internal battle, a silent war between desire and hatred, and that Matteo seemed to control every move she made.

That night, as she lay in bed, she could still feel his presence with her, like a shadow following her, a constant reminder that she was trapped by him, by his dominance, and by something deeper and more dangerous that she refused to admit.

# Chapter 9: Burning Gazes

The mansion's library was the only place where Alessia found some peace. She had always loved the old smell of books, the silence that surrounded her there. It was a refuge, a space where she could finally leave behind the constant pressure of living under the same roof as Matteo. However, tonight would be different.

She was sitting in a dark leather armchair, lost in a detective novel, when she heard the sound of footsteps. Her body stiffened. She didn't need to look up to know who it was; Matteo's presence was unmistakable. He stopped near the door, watching her with a sharp, confident gaze, as if he had every right to be there and to invade any space she thought was hers.

"Enjoying your reading?" he asked, with that slightly sarcastic tone, breaking the silence.

Alessia lifted her eyes from the book, slowly closing it and maintaining an indifferent expression. "More than I'm enjoying your presence."

He laughed, a low, controlled laugh that sent a shiver down her spine. Matteo moved closer, his eyes fixed on her, as if daring her to run. There was something predatory in his gaze, something that made her feel exposed.

"Impressive, Alessia," he continued, ignoring her sarcasm. "You know, I thought I'd come here looking for a survival book."

She raised an eyebrow, both irritated and curious. "Survival? I didn't know I needed help dealing with this mansion."

He smiled slowly, getting even closer. "Maybe I need a guide to survive a marriage to a woman so... hostile," he murmured, with a touch of irony. "Or maybe it's you who needs a book like that."

She rolled her eyes, but his smile unsettled her. "I certainly will, considering living with someone so egotistical is quite a challenge."

Matteo leaned over the armchair, his arms resting on its sides, trapping her there. His proximity was intense, almost suffocating. Alessia tried to look away, but her eyes were drawn to his lips, and for a moment, she lost herself in the thin line between hatred and desire.

"I see you're more distracted than you should be," he whispered, sensing her vulnerability. "Or is it... something else?"

Alessia felt her face flush, and as much as she wanted to keep her tone cold and defiant, her words came out hesitant. "You're mistaken if you think I'm... interested."

He smiled, a smile full of self-assurance. "Interested? No, Alessia, you're right. Interest isn't the word... but there's something here, between us, that you feel. And you don't need to deny it."

She felt her body tense, her heart race, but she refused to give in. "What I feel is contempt, Matteo. And the closer you get, the stronger that contempt becomes."

He didn't back off; on the contrary, he leaned in even closer, until their faces were mere centimeters apart. "Contempt can be a way to attract someone, Alessia. A winding road, but an effective one."

Alessia wanted to push him away, wanted to scream for him to leave and leave her in peace, but her hands were trapped on the armchair, and her body didn't seem to obey her mind. Matteo watched her closely, his gaze fiery and challenging, as if he was waiting for any sign that she was about to give in.

"You really think you know me, don't you?" she murmured, trying to regain control. "But you're wrong, Matteo. I'm not someone who gives in easily."

He raised an eyebrow, his smile widening. "I admire that about you. Your strength, your resistance. But we both know this battle is pointless. Attraction and hatred blur... and you're feeling both."

She stared at him, her face near his, and she felt as if she was about to break that line that separated them. The tension between them was so palpable that it seemed impossible to ignore. Matteo was dangerous, unpredictable, but at the same time, there was something about him that made her want to stay in this game, even if she was playing with fire.

Alessia finally released herself from the armchair, taking a step back, her eyes still locked on his. "You're mistaken, Matteo. I will never give in to your... arrogance."

He smiled, a smile full of provocation and something deeper. "Arrogance isn't what unites us, Alessia. What unites us is something you're fighting to deny, but that's becoming clearer with every passing second."

She shook her head, trying to regain her composure. "You can think whatever you want. But you'll never see the day when I..."

Before she could finish, Matteo pulled her closer, his eyes locked on hers. "I already see what I need to see, Alessia. You refuse to admit it, but you know you're just as trapped in this as I am."

His touch, his proximity, his scent—everything contributed to the chaos Matteo was creating in her mind. She wanted to push him away, wanted to keep her words sharp as a defense, but she felt the internal struggle growing more difficult.

"You're insufferable," she whispered, but the tone of her voice no longer held the same firmness as before.

He simply smiled, leaning in a little more until their lips were almost touching, but he stopped just millimeters away, keeping her trapped in that suffocating tension. "Maybe. But we both know that, insufferable or not, you're getting closer and closer to giving in."

She took a deep breath, the air caught in her lungs, feeling torn between the impulse to give in and the desire to fight against him. Then, in a decisive move, she pulled away from Matteo and quickly walked out of the library, not looking back. She knew she was running, but she needed that space, that moment to reorganize her thoughts and feelings.

As she left, her heart still raced, and her face burned with a mixture of anger and confusion. Matteo was an impossible force to control, and with each encounter, he seemed to break down a part of her resistance. She knew that, no matter how much she tried to deny it, there was something that connected her to him, something that went beyond everything she had ever known. But for now, she would stay strong, fighting against the desire and attraction that made her feel more vulnerable in his presence.

# Chapter 10: Alessia's Hidden Plans

Alessia felt she could no longer live as a mere puppet in Matteo's hands. Each moment under his control was like an unbearable weight crushing her independence, and she knew the only way to keep herself whole in this forced marriage was to fight, manipulate the situation to her advantage, and ultimately escape the shadow Matteo cast over her life.

She began to observe Matteo in a calculated way, analyzing his every word and movement, looking for any weakness she could use as a weapon. Matteo was confident, imposing, but Alessia knew even the most powerful men had weak spots. Amidst their conversations and challenging glances, she noticed something: Luca, Matteo's brother, was far too attentive to her, his gaze lingering just a bit longer than expected. Alessia saw this as an opportunity, a piece she could use in her game.

That night, during a family dinner, Alessia decided to put her plan into action. She feigned a friendlier demeanor with Luca, exchanging light laughs and discreet glances. She knew Matteo was watching her closely, but she deliberately ignored him, as if he wasn't there. Every word from Luca was met with a subtle smile, filled with hidden intentions. It was a risky game, but Alessia was willing to face the consequences.

Matteo observed her in silence, his eyes narrowed and his jaw clenched. He noticed the discreet flirting, the smiles and glances exchanged between Alessia and Luca, and something inside him ignited. It wasn't jealousy, he told himself, but rather a matter of control. Alessia was his, and watching her play with this idea in front of him made him lose patience.

After dinner, Matteo followed Alessia down the mansion's corridors, finally catching up to her in one of the empty rooms. With a swift motion, he grabbed her by the arm, turning her to face him. His eyes glowed with controlled fury, but his voice came out low and cold.

"What do you think you're doing, Alessia?" he murmured, his voice thick with tension. "Do you think you can challenge me like that, with Luca?"

She smiled, a defiant smile he had never seen before. "I'm simply enjoying your brother's hospitality. Or is even that against your rules?"

He clenched his jaw, controlling the anger bubbling within him. "You know exactly what you're doing. Do you think you can use Luca to manipulate me, to provoke me? You don't know who you're playing with."

Alessia looked at him, her eyes filled with a new determination, something that surprised Matteo. "Maybe you're the one who doesn't know who you're dealing with, Matteo. I'm not a chess piece you can move at your will. I make my own moves."

He let out a short, humorless laugh. "You're playing a dangerous game, Alessia. And in this game, whoever loses kneels."

She leaned slightly toward him, her face a mixture of anger and defiance. "Then let's see who kneels first."

For a moment, the air between them grew thick, as if the very hatred had turned into something physical, an electric current connecting them, even against their wills. Matteo, however, refused to give in, maintaining his usual control.

"You can fight as much as you want, Alessia," he murmured, leaning in closer, his eyes locked on hers. "But in the end, all your plans are useless. I already know all your moves."

She took a step back but kept her gaze steady. "You only know what I let you see, Matteo. That's your mistake: underestimating the people you think you control."

He raised an eyebrow, clearly intrigued by this new stance of hers. "And what do you think you'll achieve with this game? Do you want to irritate me? Make me lose my temper? Do you think I care about jealousy?"

She smiled, a smile that hid a calculated intention. "Maybe you're more affected than you'd like to admit. And maybe I'm more in control than you think."

Matteo observed her, his eyes dark and his expression serious, trying to read beyond her words. Alessia was a mystery, a woman who challenged him in every way. He couldn't tell if what he felt was anger or desire, but what mattered was that she was under his control, and he wouldn't allow her to escape.

"Let me make one thing very clear, Alessia," he said, his voice firm and threatening. "I don't care about the little games you're trying to play. But if you keep testing the limits, you'll find I can be much harsher than you imagine."

She stared back, defiant, and for a moment felt tempted to look away, but she knew she couldn't show weakness. Matteo was a man who used every opening to dominate, and Alessia couldn't allow him to see any vulnerability.

"Then go ahead and try, Matteo," she whispered, her voice laced with irony. "But remember: you're not the only one who can manipulate in this game."

He fell silent, watching her as if trying to gauge the extent of her resolve. For a moment, fury and desire mingled in his eyes, creating a tension that Alessia felt pressing down on her chest. It was a silent war, a battle of wills and desires that intensified with every word, every glance.

Finally, Matteo released her arm, taking a step back, but his gaze remained fixed on hers, heavy with a dark promise. "This isn't over, Alessia. We're only just beginning."

She held his gaze, though her heart was pounding in her chest. Matteo was an overwhelming presence, but Alessia knew she couldn't back down. Not now. This dangerous game of manipulation and power was her only way to maintain her independence, to preserve her essence amidst the control he tried to impose on her.

When Matteo left, Alessia took a deep breath, trying to compose herself. She knew the path she had chosen was risky, but deep down, she felt stronger. Each confrontation with Matteo strengthened her resolve. He might be a powerful adversary, but she was not a woman who was easily intimidated.

Alessia was willing to fight to the end, even if it meant facing the darkest sides of both Matteo and, possibly, herself.

# Chapter 11: The Temptation of the Forbidden

The night was quiet in the mansion's garden. A gentle breeze rustled the leaves of the trees as Alessia walked slowly, searching in the nighttime silence for some relief from the tension suffocating her. That mansion, so full of luxury and wealth, felt more like a prison with each passing day. The plans, the games of manipulation, the constant provocations with Matteo... all of it was exhausting. But at the same time, a part of her felt more alive than ever before. Matteo stirred a storm within her, something oscillating between hatred and desire, aversion and attraction.

Lost in her thoughts, she didn't notice when Matteo approached. He appeared beside her like a shadow, his steps soft but his presence imposing. When she noticed him, Alessia sighed in frustration, wishing he would leave. Yet his presence had the opposite effect; he seemed to anchor her, as if there were no escape.

"Lost in thought?" Matteo asked, with a slightly amused tone, as if he knew exactly the effect he had on her.

She glanced at him briefly, her face impassive but with irritation evident in her tone. "None of your business."

He smiled, ignoring the disdain in her voice. "Of course it is. Everything about you interests me now, Alessia."

She rolled her eyes, trying to maintain her façade of contempt. "Funny, I thought I was just another trophy to you, another piece in your game."

Matteo laughed, but there was something in his gaze that betrayed the casual tone of his words. "Maybe you're more than you think."

She stared at him, surprised by his response. Matteo wasn't the type to reveal feelings or intentions. He provoked her, toyed with her, but never made it clear if there was something beyond control and possession. Alessia felt her heart beat a little faster, and, unwittingly, her eyes locked onto his, trying to decipher what lay behind that dark gaze.

For a moment, the tension between them intensified, as if the very air around them had grown denser. Matteo took a step closer, and Alessia felt unable to move. He was so close that she could hear his breathing, and she could smell his woody cologne, something that left her inexplicably drawn to him.

"Why do you fight so hard against this, Alessia?" he murmured, his voice low and filled with intensity. "What's between us is inevitable."

She clenched her fists, trying to remember everything he represented—the control, the manipulation, the suffocating power he held over her life. "You're truly arrogant, Matteo. You think you can control even what I feel."

He smiled, but there was something dangerous and seductive in his gaze. "I think you already know it's not about control. It's something that just exists, Alessia. And denying it is a waste of time."

She tried to look away, but she felt trapped, as if the very desire invading her was an unstoppable force. Each time she looked at Matteo, it was as if the hatred she felt for him transformed into something deeper and more dangerous.

"I... I feel nothing for you, Matteo. Only contempt," she whispered, but her voice faltered, betraying the intensity of what she truly felt.

He took another step, closing the distance between them to mere inches. His dark eyes watched her with an intensity that made her feel naked, exposed. Matteo knew exactly what he was doing, and Alessia felt even more frustrated by the weakness he awakened in her.

"If it's only contempt, then why are you trembling?" He raised a hand and lightly brushed his finger across her cheek, a soft touch that sent a shiver through her entire body. "Why is your heart racing?"

She held her breath, unable to look away. That closeness disarmed her, and Alessia felt she was about to cross a line from which there would be no return. Matteo was so close that she could feel his warmth, and for a moment, she wanted to lose herself in that feeling.

"Don't... don't come any closer," she whispered, her voice full of anger, but also a vulnerability she was desperately trying to hide.

Matteo smiled, a smile that combined confidence and provocation. "Why? Because you're afraid to admit what you really feel?"

She swallowed hard, feeling cornered. No matter how much she wanted to push him away, no matter how loudly her pride screamed to resist that attraction, she couldn't deny that something stronger was pulling her toward him. It was an inner battle Alessia knew she was losing.

Then, in a surge of anger and desperation, she pushed Matteo, creating some distance between them. "You're insufferable, Matteo. I'm not one of your easy conquests."

He watched her calmly, his eyes gleaming with something that looked like satisfaction. "No, Alessia. You're anything but easy. And that's exactly why I can't stop."

His words left her breathless, and before she could respond, she turned and left, determined to leave that garden and the weight of that temptation behind. But as she walked, Matteo's face remained in her mind, his eyes burning in her memory like a brand.

Upon entering the mansion, Alessia felt a wave of frustration and anger wash over her. Anger at Matteo for destabilizing her so deeply, and anger at herself for allowing him to affect her that way. She knew she should remain cold, focused on her plans for resistance, but each encounter, each word he said seemed to pull her deeper into an abyss from which she wasn't sure she could escape.

Outside, Matteo watched her leave, a satisfied smile on his lips. He knew the tension between them was undeniable, and every time she fought against it, he felt closer to breaking down all her defenses. To him, Alessia was a challenge, a fire he couldn't control but wanted to dominate nonetheless.

As he watched her disappear into the night, Matteo knew this battle was far from over. Alessia was everything he'd never wanted—intense, resilient, defiant. And, as much as he tried to resist, Matteo realized he was increasingly ensnared by her, in a game of power and desire from which neither of them would emerge unscathed.

# Chapter 12: The Game of Seduction

Alessia spent the entire day crafting her plan. She knew she couldn't allow Matteo to keep controlling her every move, and the only way to change that was to reverse the roles. If he wanted to toy with her emotions and dominate her feelings, she was willing to retaliate. She would not hand him control over her on a silver platter. This time, she would be the one leading the game, provoking him, playing with her own attraction to him.

Dinner was set for that evening. The dining room was softly lit, with a perfectly arranged table. Alessia entered in a dark, fitted dress that outlined her silhouette with a boldness she knew would not go unnoticed. Matteo was already seated, but upon seeing her, he paused, his gaze fixed on her. There was something in his eyes—a mixture of surprise and admiration.

She smiled at him, a controlled, almost innocent smile that hid clear intentions. She sat down slowly, crossing her legs elegantly, and gave him a look that blended challenge with seduction. Matteo, always so unshaken, looked away for a moment—a subtle sign that her plan was beginning to take effect.

"Are you enjoying the dinner?" she asked, her voice soft and low as she picked up the napkin and placed it on her lap. There was an unusual lightness to her tone, though no less provocative.

He nodded, trying to keep his tone steady. "Everything seems... impeccable," he replied, his gaze returning to her. Alessia noticed a slight tension in his jaw and smiled inwardly. Matteo was unsettled, but he wouldn't back down so easily.

She raised her wine glass, her eyes locked onto his. "I'm glad you liked it," she murmured, taking a light sip of the wine without breaking eye contact. "After all, it's good to know I'm... pleasing."

Matteo raised an eyebrow, as if trying to decipher the true meaning behind her words. "I'm certain you know exactly what you're doing, Alessia."

She let out a light, provocative laugh and looked at him with a challenging gaze. "Maybe I do. Or maybe you're just imagining things," she whispered suggestively.

Matteo remained silent, but she could see the intensity in his eyes sharpen. He leaned forward slightly, his face close to hers, and his smile faded, replaced by an expression full of desire. "Don't play with fire, Alessia. You know very well how this game can end."

She bit her lip, feigning an innocence she knew would irritate him. "Maybe I like playing with fire, Matteo. Maybe the risk is part of the fun."

He let out a dry, humorless laugh, leaning back in his chair, watching her with an expression that combined amusement and exasperation. "You're determined to challenge me, aren't you? Do you think you're in control of this situation?"

She leaned forward slightly until their faces were just inches apart. "I don't think so, Matteo," she whispered. "I know."

He was silent for a moment, as if considering her words. Matteo wasn't the type to back down from a confrontation, and she knew that. But tonight, Alessia seemed to have found a new way to face him, to provoke a weakness he wasn't used to feeling.

Throughout the dinner, Alessia continued her game of seduction, her glances and smiles full of intentions she knew Matteo would understand. Every word exchanged was another step deeper into this dangerous game, where they both pretended to be in control but were, in reality, on the brink of losing themselves in each other.

At one point, Matteo took her hand across the table, his fingers firmly enveloping hers, and looked into her eyes with an intensity that made her heart race. "Don't think I'll surrender, Alessia," he murmured, his voice low, carrying a tone that bordered on a threat. "You can play all you want, but in the end, you know very well where this will lead."

She felt her skin tingle with his touch, and for a moment, her confidence almost faltered. But Alessia took a deep breath, regaining her composure. "Maybe I do know where this will lead, Matteo. But who said you'll be the one deciding when it ends?"

Matteo slowly released her hand, but his eyes remained fixed on her, filled with an intensity that unsettled her heart. Alessia knew she was risking a lot with this game, but at the same time, she felt more alive than ever before. He was a dangerous adversary, but by challenging him, she was also discovering a strength within herself, something that pushed her to continue.

At the end of the dinner, Matteo accompanied her to the door, his eyes locked on hers with a burning intensity. "Be careful, Alessia," he murmured, his voice heavy with desire. "You may think you're in control now, but know that I never yield without a fight."

She smiled provocatively. "Then let's see how far you're willing to go, Matteo."

He took a step closer, closing the distance between them even further, and Alessia held her breath, feeling the heat radiating from him. Matteo was close enough that she could feel his breath, and for a moment, she thought he would kiss her right there. But instead, he stopped just millimeters from her face, as if taunting her, as if waiting for her to cross the final boundary.

"Good night, Alessia," he murmured in a soft, dangerously seductive voice. "Dream of me."

She stood there, watching him leave, and felt the weight of desire and anger mingle within her. Each night, each confrontation, the line between hatred and attraction grew thinner, and Alessia knew that no matter how hard she tried to resist, she was becoming entangled in a game from which there would be no easy escape.

# Chapter 13: The Limits of Resistance

The night was cold and silent at the mansion, but Alessia felt like she was burning from the inside. Over the past few days, every interaction with Matteo had pushed her to a limit she didn't know she could bear. Her body seemed to act on its own, reacting to his presence with an intensity she refused to admit. It was a dangerous game of closeness and resistance, where desire and hatred blurred together, threatening to destroy her defenses.

Alessia stood on the balcony, gazing at the distant city lights, trying to find some relief from the turmoil Matteo had stirred within her. But he, as if guided by a sharp intuition, found her there, and his presence invaded her like an unwanted shadow. He approached slowly, his footsteps soft, his expression a mix of challenge and curiosity.

"Running away, Alessia?" he asked in a low, husky voice that seemed to echo in the cold night air.

She turned to face him, keeping her face impassive, although she knew her rapid breathing betrayed her. "From you? Never," she replied with a sarcastic smile.

He stepped closer, his dark eyes locked onto hers. "Are you sure? Because every time I try to get closer, you run. What are you trying to hide?"

She rolled her eyes, but felt a familiar warmth rising in her body. Matteo knew exactly how to destabilize her, and it seemed to amuse him. Alessia, however, would not give in. Not now. "Maybe I just want a little peace," she responded, her voice thick with sarcasm. "Something you seem determined to take from me."

Matteo took a step forward, until they were mere centimeters apart. She could feel his heat, the intensity of his presence, and her body reacted involuntarily. She tried to stay firm, but she knew he had already noticed. Matteo's gaze glimmered with a touch of amusement and triumph.

"Peace?" he murmured, leaning slightly toward her. "You know as well as I do, Alessia, that peace is the last thing you want when I'm around."

She held her breath but kept her defiant gaze. "You're too arrogant, Matteo. You think the world revolves around you. But I'll never surrender to you."

He laughed, a low, ironic chuckle, as if he knew her words were just an attempt to mask what she truly felt. "I don't need you to surrender. I just want you to admit what you feel. Admit that there's something between us."

She clenched her fists, trying to control the storm of emotions building inside her. Matteo was so close she could feel his breath, the warmth of his body, and his presence was so intense it made it impossible to think clearly. "There's nothing between us, Matteo. Just contempt."

He tilted his head, never breaking eye contact. "Contempt?" He took another step closer, until their faces were just inches apart, and Alessia felt her heart race. "Then why are you trembling?"

She bit her lip, trying to hold herself together, but his gaze was like an invitation she couldn't resist. "Because you're... unbearable," she whispered, her voice faltering, betraying the depth of what she truly felt.

Matteo smiled, a slow, dangerous smile. "You can keep saying that, Alessia, but we both know it's more than that. That there's something that draws you in, something that keeps you from walking away."

She was about to respond, to throw another provocation his way, but her words got stuck in her throat when he raised his hand and gently brushed her face with his fingers. It was a light touch, but it made her shiver. Every part of her screamed to push him away, but at the same time, something kept her from acting. She was trapped in that look, in that closeness, and she felt torn between the impulse to resist and the temptation to lose herself.

"Why do you fight so hard, Alessia?" he murmured, his voice low and laden with desire. "It's inevitable, you know that."

She swallowed hard, his face still close to hers, and she felt like she was about to break. Matteo was so close, and his touch, his look, everything made her feel vulnerable, exposed. But she couldn't give in. She wouldn't let him break her so easily.

"You're wrong," she murmured, her voice trembling. "You'll never see... me surrender to you."

He let out a short laugh, but there was something serious in his eyes. "We'll see, Alessia. Because every time you challenge me, every time you try to fight, I see you getting closer to giving in."

She pulled back abruptly, trying to regain her composure, still feeling her body tremble from the intensity of the encounter. "You really think you know me, Matteo. But you're wrong."

He watched her retreat, his eyes fixed on her, as if seeing beyond her words. "I know more than you think. And I know that what you feel is something you can't control."

She clenched her fists, her face flushed with anger and confusion. "That's what you want to believe. But you're nothing but an illusion."

Matteo took a step back but kept smiling, as though he knew that, despite her words, he had already planted a seed of doubt. "We'll see, Alessia. Because in the end, everyone gives in. And you're no different."

He walked away, leaving her alone, and Alessia felt as if she were on the verge of collapse. Matteo could break through her barriers, penetrate her mind in a way no one ever had. And no matter how much she tried to fight, she knew she was becoming more fragile, more likely to give in.

As she returned to her room, Alessia promised herself she wouldn't let herself be defeated. She was strong, and she wouldn't let Matteo have control over her feelings. But deep down, she knew that something inside her had already begun to change, and that made her even angrier—at herself and at him.

Matteo, on the other hand, felt triumphant. He knew Alessia was on the verge of breaking, and that excited him in a way he didn't quite understand. There was something about her that challenged him, that made him want to break every barrier she built. And as he watched the lights of the mansion from afar, Matteo knew the battle between them had only just begun.

# Chapter 14: First Cracks in the Armor

Alessia's resistance was beginning to crumble. No matter how hard she tried to maintain her defenses, small moments of vulnerability slipped through her emotional armor. Every glance from Matteo, every subtle touch, seemed to make her more aware of his presence. She found herself thinking about him more than she would have liked, remembering recent moments when the tension between them had brought them to the brink of something more intense. It was as though a shadow was constantly hovering over her, a force pulling her closer to him, even against her will.

Matteo, on the other hand, noticed every detail, every hesitation in Alessia's gaze, and every trace of doubt that slipped through her behavior. He saw the small cracks starting to form in her determination, and he knew that, if he played his cards right, he could finally break down her defenses. He decided to change his approach, swapping his usual arrogance for an unexpectedly tender demeanor that made Alessia question her perceptions of him even more.

One particularly cold night, Alessia was in the living room, sitting alone on the sofa in front of the fireplace. The soft light from the fire reflected on her face, giving her an almost ethereal look as she was lost in her thoughts. Matteo entered silently, and Alessia only became aware of his presence when he approached and placed a blanket over her shoulders, the gesture unexpectedly caring.

"I didn't know you cared about comfort," she murmured, pulling the blanket closer to herself, but not looking directly at him.

He sat next to her, his expression serious and focused. "There are many things about me that you don't know, Alessia," he said, his voice low, yet filled with a mysterious tone.

She hesitated, sensing that something was different about Matteo tonight, something that intrigued and unsettled her at the same time. "You act like I'm some kind of puzzle that you need to solve," she replied, her voice softer than she intended.

He gave a small smile, but his eyes held a depth Alessia hadn't seen before. "Maybe it's because I understand what it's like to hide behind an armor."

Alessia raised her gaze, surprised. "And you have armor, Matteo? I always thought it was just... a way to manipulate people."

Matteo looked away, as if weighing something before he responded. "I think, for someone who's been through what I've been through, armor is more than necessary. It's... vital." His voice took on a darker tone, filled with a pain Alessia hadn't expected to hear.

She studied him, curious. "What do you mean by that?"

He took a deep breath, as if preparing to reveal something he had never told anyone. "I lost someone very important to me," he began, his voice barely a whisper. "My sister. She was the only one who saw beyond what everyone else could. She was one of the few who knew my... human side." Matteo paused, looking away toward the fire, and Alessia could see a flicker of vulnerability in his eyes.

Alessia felt a tightness in her chest, an unexpected empathy. "I'm sorry, Matteo. I... didn't know."

He gave a small, sad smile but didn't look away from the fire. "Few know. And it's better that way. It's become easier to build this... armor, as you put it."

She fell silent, processing his revelation. Seeing Matteo in such a human, real way shook her defenses even more. It was as if, for a moment, she could see beyond the man she so despised, to see someone who, like her, had hidden scars.

"Sometimes, we build barriers to protect ourselves," she murmured, almost as if speaking to herself. "But deep down, those barriers end up imprisoning us."

He looked at her with a newfound intensity, as though he had seen a part of Alessia she was trying to hide. "And you know that better than anyone, don't you, Alessia?"

She turned away, feeling the weight of his words. "Maybe. But that doesn't change what I feel for you. Or rather, what I want to avoid feeling."

Matteo leaned in closer, his eyes fixed on hers, and the silence between them became almost unbearable in its intensity. "And what do you want to avoid feeling, Alessia? Hatred, or something more?"

She caught her breath, her heart racing, but held her gaze steady. "What do you want from me, Matteo? Why this game, this constant provocation? What are you really after?"

He smiled, but it was a smile filled with sincerity that unsettled her. "Maybe I'm looking for someone who sees me for who I really am. Someone who sees beyond the mask, beyond the... armor."

She felt a wave of empathy and confusion at the same time. Matteo was not the man she had imagined, at least not entirely. The revelation about his sister, his vulnerability, created an unexpected connection between them—something Alessia wasn't sure she wanted or could accept. There was a fine line between hatred and attraction, and every word, every gesture from Matteo seemed to pull her further toward the unknown.

"I won't lose myself in you, Matteo," she whispered, but her voice was weak, almost as if she were trying to convince herself.

He looked at her seriously and gently touched her hand. "And who said I want you to lose yourself? Maybe I want you to find yourself."

Alessia felt her heart race, and for a moment, she didn't know whether to pull her hand away or hold his more tightly. Matteo had a way of reaching places inside her that she didn't even know existed, and that left her vulnerable, exposed in a way she had never experienced before.

She quickly pulled her hand back, trying to regain control. "You don't know anything about me."

He smiled slightly, as though he knew she was trying to escape the truth. "I know enough to understand that you're fighting against something you can't control. And I know that, just like me, you hide behind armor."

His words struck her like a blow, and Alessia realized that once again, Matteo had managed to penetrate her defenses. He saw her in a way no one ever had, and no matter how much she wanted to run from it, something inside her kept her there, trapped in that moment.

By the end of the night, when Matteo stood and left, Alessia remained in the living room, staring into the emptiness. She felt as though she were on the edge of a precipice, a fall that could change everything. Matteo was not just an enemy; he was a man with scars, with pains and secrets that, in some way, reflected her own. And no matter how much she tried to deny it, she knew that connection was growing stronger with each passing day.

As the silence returned to the room, Alessia realized that if she continued down this path, she might end up losing herself in the tangled web of emotions Matteo was awakening within her.

# Chapter 15: The Forbidden Kiss

Alessia walked down the hallway with firm steps, rage boiling in every fiber of her body. Once again, Matteo had provoked her, tested her limits, crossed her boundaries. She refused to give in, to be manipulated by him, but every interaction made her emotions blur. He had a disturbing ability to stir something intense and uncontrollable within her, and that made her furious.

Without thinking, she opened the door to Matteo's office and entered, finding him by the window, hands in his pockets, with a calm expression that irritated her even more. He turned around when he sensed her presence, raising an eyebrow, as if he already knew the reason for her visit.

"Matteo, we need to talk," she said, her voice firm but carrying a tension he immediately noticed.

He smiled, a smile full of self-sufficiency that only fueled Alessia's anger. "Ah, Alessia, always so direct. What brings you here this time?"

She crossed her arms, trying to maintain her composure. "You're crossing the line. Don't you think it's time to stop these games?"

Matteo took a few steps toward her, his gaze never leaving hers. "Games? I think you're the one playing, Alessia. Insisting on pretending you feel nothing, that there's no attraction between us."

She laughed, a dry, humorless laugh. "Attraction? The only thing I feel for you is contempt. Or do you really think I'm going to fall for your little act?"

He stopped just a few inches from her, his gaze serious and challenging. "Contempt?" he murmured, his voice low and rough. "Then why are you always so close to me, Alessia? Why do you come to me every time I provoke you?"

Alessia felt her face heat up. It was hard to face Matteo's intensity so closely, but she refused to back down. "I'm here because someone needs to show you that your power is not absolute. That you don't control everything and everyone."

He leaned in slightly, until their faces were just inches apart. "You're right. I don't control everything, Alessia. But between us, there's something neither of us controls."

She opened her mouth to respond, but before she could say anything, Matteo pulled her to him, with a firm and decisive movement. His lips found hers with an intensity that stole her breath away. Alessia froze for a second, her heart racing, her mind blank, unable to process what was happening.

For a moment, she gave in to the touch, allowing herself to be swept away by the force of the kiss, by the urgency they both felt. It was as if all the provocations, all the tension had exploded at once, in a gesture that mixed hatred and desire. Matteo's hands slid down her back, pulling her closer, and Alessia felt her body respond, as if he were the only thing anchoring her in that moment.

But then reality hit her hard, and she pulled away abruptly, pushing him away with anger. Her eyes were wide, her chest rising and falling as she tried to catch her breath. "What... do you think you're doing?" she whispered, her voice trembling with indignation and confusion.

Matteo watched her, a satisfied smile on his face that made her feel even more vulnerable. "I'm just showing you what you refuse to admit, Alessia," he said, his voice low but firm. "What's between us is inevitable. Deny it all you want, but you know it's true."

She felt the rage bubbling up again, mixed with the frustration of having given in, even for a brief moment. "You're a manipulator, Matteo. An arrogant, insufferable manipulator. And never again... never again do that."

He took a step back, raising his hands in a false gesture of surrender, but the smile on his face showed that he wasn't the least bit sorry. "I can promise you many things, Alessia, but that... I won't promise."

She stared at him, trying to control the whirlwind of emotions the kiss had awakened. She felt betrayed by her own feelings, ashamed that she had given in, even for a second, to the desire he sparked in her. Without saying another word, she turned and left the office, leaving Matteo behind, still with that satisfied smile.

As she walked back to her room, Alessia's heart was racing, and the image of the kiss repeated in her mind, as if it were etched there. She hated herself for allowing him to affect her, for letting the desire consume her, even if for just a brief moment. She felt confused, torn between the hatred she had always felt for Matteo and the desire he seemed to awaken more intensely with every passing moment.

As soon as she entered her room, she closed the door and leaned against it, breathing deeply, trying to regain control. But the image of Matteo still haunted her, the memory of his touch, the heat of his body against hers. She felt weak, betrayed by her own emotions, and knew she needed to distance herself before she lost control completely.

The next morning, Matteo watched her with that intense gaze, full of ulterior motives, as if he wanted to remind her of the kiss, the weakness she had shown. Alessia avoided looking at him, but she felt his presence like a constant shadow, a reminder of the power he had to shake her.

He approached her during breakfast, leaning in slightly to whisper in her ear. "Still thinking about our kiss?"

Alessia felt her face burn, but she struggled to maintain a cold expression. "That meant nothing, Matteo. It was just a moment of weakness, and I don't plan to repeat it."

He smiled, amused. "If you say so. But you know it's a lie, Alessia. Deep down, you know you want more."

She clenched her fist, trying to control the anger and shame she felt. "You think you're irresistible, don't you? But let me tell you something: I'm not one of your easy conquests, Matteo. Never was, never will be."

He observed her with a look that mixed amusement and something deeper, something she couldn't quite decipher. "I don't want it to be easy, Alessia. I want exactly that... that resistance, that struggle. That's what makes me want you even more."

Alessia felt her heart race with his words, but she refused to give in again. She turned and walked out of the room, determined to keep control, not to let Matteo break down her defenses again. But deep down, she knew that the line between hatred and desire was growing thinner, and that every encounter with him brought her closer to crossing it.

As she walked away, Matteo stood still, watching her with the look of someone who had already foreseen the outcome of that game. He knew Alessia was a strong, determined woman, but he also knew that what was between them was inevitable, something neither of them could ignore for much longer.

# Chapter 16: The Impossible Distance

After the forbidden kiss, Alessia felt the need to distance herself to maintain control. Matteo played with her feelings and her mind in a way that made her vulnerable—something she refused to allow. Avoiding contact seemed to be the best strategy. She began to steer clear of the places he frequented, spending more time in the garden, the library, or any corner where she could pretend to be alone in that mansion. But Matteo, as if sensing her attempt to distance herself, always seemed to know where to find her.

He surprised her by showing up unexpectedly in the places where she sought refuge, with no warning. He was always there, shortening the distances she worked so hard to create. His gaze was always intense, watching her every move, every small reaction. This irritated her, frustrated her, but at the same time, secretly, she found herself longing for these unexpected encounters.

On one such occasion, Alessia was in the library, one of the few places where she could lose herself in her books and forget about Matteo's suffocating presence. However, her concentration quickly faltered when she heard the door open, and moments later, saw Matteo entering. He seemed at ease, but his gaze held the determination of someone who knew exactly what they wanted.

Alessia sighed, pretending indifference, but her voice came out colder than she intended. "Why do you insist on following me? Don't you have other places to be?"

Matteo walked toward her, a provocative smile on his lips. "Maybe I'm exactly where I want to be, Alessia. Or does my presence bother you that much?"

She rolled her eyes, trying to remain calm. "It bothers me that you don't seem to understand the concept of personal space."

He chuckled softly, leaning slightly toward her. "Personal space? I thought we'd already crossed that boundary," he teased, his tone light but heavy with ulterior motives.

Alessia felt her face flush, but she made an effort not to show the tension his words created within her. "Don't fool yourself, Matteo. The only thing I feel for you is contempt."

He raised an eyebrow, challenging her. "Contempt? Interesting. It seems you've been working hard to convince yourself of that lately."

She glared at him, her eyes filled with anger but also with something she couldn't name. "Maybe I just need a constant reminder that you're a despicable person."

Matteo laughed again, a laugh that irritated her deeply but strangely made her feel attracted. "Alessia, you can run away as much as you want, but we both know that the distance between us is an illusion. You can try to avoid me, but... in the end, we always end up meeting."

She bit her lip, trying to ignore the effect he had on her. "I have a choice, Matteo. And my choice is to stay as far away from you as possible."

He stepped even closer, reducing the gap between them to mere centimeters. "Then why can't you? Why are you always looking at me like you want to..."

She interrupted him abruptly, her voice trembling with frustration. "Don't confuse desire with hatred. What I feel for you isn't what you think."

He tilted his head, studying her intensely. "Then tell me what it is, Alessia. Tell me that what you feel is just hatred."

She opened her mouth to reply, but the words got caught in her throat. There was a mix of emotions inside her, a battle between revulsion and an attraction she couldn't ignore. Her gaze shifted for a second, but Matteo noticed, and a satisfied smile crept onto his face.

"I knew it," he murmured with a confidence that irritated her deeply. "You can't deny what's between us."

Alessia's heart started to race, and a rising fury overtook her. "What's between us, Matteo, is a war. A battle of wills. And believe me, I intend to win it."

He took a step back, still smiling, but his gaze was full of intensity. "Then, good luck, Alessia. But know this: in this war, you're the one losing."

She quickly walked away, leaving the library with her heart racing. The distance she tried to keep from Matteo was becoming impossible, and with each encounter, she felt her resolve weakening. He invaded her thoughts constantly, and the idea of staying away from him was slowly transforming into a frustrating need to be near him. She knew this game was dangerous, but the line between hatred and attraction was becoming thinner, and she feared the moment when she might cross it without even realizing.

Over the following days, Matteo continued to show up at the most unexpected moments, and Alessia couldn't escape the effect these encounters had on her. It was as if he were an inevitable presence in her life, someone destined to be there, breaking down her barriers and testing her resistance. And despite all her efforts to maintain control, she knew she was losing the battle against herself.

On one of these occasions, he found her in the garden at dusk, and the setting seemed to intensify the tension between them. Matteo approached slowly, watching her in silence, as if trying to decipher every detail about her. Alessia's heart sped up, but she kept her posture firm, determined not to give in.

"How long do you think you can keep pretending?" he asked, his voice low, but full of provocation.

She crossed her arms, looking at him with disdain. "What I feel for you, Matteo, is hatred. There's nothing else."

He tilted his head, his eyes locked on hers, and smiled. "Hatred and desire are two sides of the same coin, Alessia. And I think you already know that."

Alessia took a deep breath, trying to ignore the warmth rising in her body. His proximity, the intensity of his gaze—everything was destabilizing her. But she couldn't give in, she couldn't let him take control over her feelings.

"You're unbearable," she muttered, trying to pull away, but Matteo grabbed her arm, preventing her from leaving.

He pulled her gently toward him, bringing their faces so close that they were almost touching. "I may be unbearable, Alessia. But you know you can't stay away from me. No matter how hard you try, we always come back to each other."

She tried to pull her arm free, but Matteo's grip was firm. She felt her heart race, and for the first time, she couldn't avoid the impulse to look at his lips. He noticed, and a satisfied smile spread across his face, as though he knew he was getting closer to breaking her barriers.

"This... this doesn't mean anything," she whispered, but her voice was weak, lacking the firmness she intended.

Matteo smiled slightly, not breaking his gaze. "Keep telling yourself that, Alessia. But we both know the truth."

She finally managed to break free, but she knew something inside her had already started to shift. The battle between desire and self-control was becoming more intense, and the line between enemies and something more was growing increasingly indistinct.

# Chapter 17: Unplanned Touch

Alessia descended to the kitchen in an attempt to calm her thoughts, something that had become increasingly difficult since Matteo began to appear in every corner of the mansion, turning her attempt to distance herself into an unrelenting game of closeness. She held a glass of wine in her hand, her gaze lost as she tried to find some sense of peace in the quiet of the night.

The sound of firm footsteps echoing on the marble floor made Alessia quickly lift her eyes. There he was again, like an inevitable shadow. Matteo entered the kitchen with his usual confidence, his eyes fixed on her. Alessia felt her heart race, and an involuntary nervousness washed over her. He seemed to have the power to transform even the safest environment into a minefield.

"Can't sleep?" he asked, his voice soft but carrying a subtle provocation.

She took a deep breath, trying not to show the restlessness she felt. "I just needed a moment of peace, away from... certain unwanted presences."

He smiled, a smile she knew well, and one that only confused her further. Matteo walked toward her slowly, each step intensifying the tension that hung in the air. She averted her gaze, trying to focus on the wine in her hand, but his presence was overwhelming, and she knew he could sense the effect he had on her.

When Matteo stopped beside her, Alessia felt the scent of him mix with the air, and she tried to push away the whirlwind of emotions stirring inside her. She took a deep breath, focusing on maintaining a stiff posture, but then he took her hand in a gesture so unexpected that it disarmed her completely. His touch was firm, yet gentle, and Alessia felt warmth surge up her arm like an electric current.

"You're nervous," he said, not breaking his gaze, his voice low and captivating.

Alessia tried to pull her hand away, but he held it firmly. "Let go of me, Matteo," she murmured, trying to hide the tremor in her voice.

He studied her for a moment, and his fingers tightened around hers just slightly, as if trying to offer a reassurance Alessia wasn't sure she could accept. "There's no reason to run, Alessia. Not now."

She felt her body react to his closeness, and her determination to stay distant began to waver. Matteo lifted his other hand and, in an almost careful gesture, touched her face, his fingers brushing her skin with a tenderness that completely disarmed her. The intensity of his gaze seemed to penetrate every one of her defenses, and Alessia felt like she was on the brink of losing herself.

"Why do you fight so hard against this?" he whispered, his voice so close she could feel his breath on her skin. "What are you trying to prove?"

Alessia held her breath, her heart pounding in her chest, but his words brought her back to reality. With tremendous effort, she pulled away, breaking the touch and stepping back a few paces. "I don't need to prove anything to you, Matteo. And no matter what you do, you'll never control me."

He watched her silently, his eyes gleaming with something she couldn't quite place—a mixture of fascination and challenge. "Control is not what I want, Alessia. It never was."

She felt her face flush, his words echoing in her mind. "And what do you want, then?" she challenged, trying to regain control of the situation, though her voice came out more tremulous than she wanted.

Matteo stepped forward, his gaze still locked on hers. "I want you to stop lying to yourself. Admit that what's between us is more than you allow yourself to feel."

Alessia swallowed hard, anger mixing with desire, a whirlwind of emotions that left her vulnerable. "You don't know anything about what I feel," she murmured, looking away, trying to hide what he could so easily see.

He let out a soft laugh, but there was a note of tenderness in it that Alessia hadn't expected. "Your eyes say otherwise, Alessia. You want to run, but you know we always end up at this point. At this... connection."

She felt a growing fury—not just toward him, but toward herself for allowing him to get so close. "That's what you want to believe, Matteo. But I'm not yours. Never was, and never will be."

He studied her in silence, but his eyes carried an intensity that made her words lose their strength. "You don't have to be mine, Alessia. It's not about possession. It's about... feeling. Something neither of us controls."

She tried to repress the impulse to believe his words, but she knew her resistance was weakening. Matteo seemed to have a power over her that neither of them fully understood. Even with all the barriers she tried to put up, he always found a gap, a weak point.

Alessia took a deep breath, trying to control her emotions. "I need... I need to leave here," she said, her voice soft, trying to maintain her façade of indifference.

Matteo let her go, but his eyes followed her as she walked away, as if he knew that the moment of breaking was closer than ever. Alessia left the kitchen, her heart racing, her hands still trembling. His touch, though brief, seemed to have left an invisible mark on her skin, a sensation she couldn't shake.

When she reached her room, she leaned against the door and closed her eyes, trying to process everything she felt. Matteo was invading not just her life, but her mind, her thoughts. She hated the vulnerability he stirred within her, the desire she fought to deny.

But she knew that every touch, every intense glance, brought her closer to a surrender she had promised herself never to accept.

In the following days, Alessia continued to avoid Matteo, but his presence seemed to be everywhere, like a persistent shadow. She knew she couldn't keep running forever, but the idea of confronting her feelings and admitting what he provoked in her was terrifying. The battle between her reason and her desires was constant, and with each encounter with Matteo, she felt like she was losing a little more.

But, at the same time, she knew that this resistance was a matter of survival. Because deep down, Alessia felt that if she gave in completely to what Matteo awakened in her, there would be nothing left of the strong, determined woman she had always been.

# Chapter 18: The Trap of Jealousy

Alessia felt exhausted by the constant emotional battle she waged with Matteo. Each encounter, each accidental touch, each word filled with tension pushed her to a limit she didn't know how long she could sustain. However, as if the situation wasn't complicated enough, Luca, Matteo's younger brother, had begun to show an interest that, although surprising, brought Alessia an unexpected sense of relief. Luca was everything Matteo wasn't—lighthearted, relaxed, and capable of making her smile. He had an effortless charm that contrasted with Matteo's overwhelming intensity.

At first, Alessia thought Luca's approach was just a gesture of kindness, but soon she realized there was more to their interactions. He sought her out constantly, and the glances, always accompanied by a carefree smile, became more frequent.

One afternoon, Luca found her in the garden, where she liked to spend time to escape Matteo's presence. Luca approached with his usual calm and laid-back manner, and Alessia noticed the sense of peace he brought with him.

"Running from the tension in the mansion?" he asked with a half-smile, offering her a flower he had just picked from the garden.

Alessia laughed, taking the flower with a soft smile. "Let's just say, here I can breathe a little without feeling like I'm being watched... or controlled."

Luca nodded, sitting down beside her. "Matteo's always been... intense. A sort of hurricane who believes he has everything under control." He looked at her curiously, and Alessia noticed the spark in his eyes, a mix of admiration and interest.

She smiled, looking at him teasingly. "And you, Luca? How do you handle all this intensity?"

He shrugged, a mischievous smile playing at his lips. "I adapt. But I can see that, for you, dealing with Matteo has been... challenging."

She looked at him sincerely. "More than I imagined. And that's why I'm grateful for your good humor. I think I'd forget what it's like to smile if it weren't for these little interruptions."

As they conversed, Alessia noticed Matteo in the distance, watching them. There was a shadow in his gaze, something possessive and dark. Alessia saw that Matteo was tense, his fists clenched as he watched them. She felt a wave of satisfaction at seeing the jealousy in Matteo's features, and an idea began to form in her mind. If Luca was willing to get close, perhaps she could use him as a way to maintain control, to keep Matteo at a distance.

"You know, Alessia," Luca interrupted her thoughts, moving a little closer, "I enjoy spending time with you. There's something... refreshing about you."

She looked away for a moment, aware of Matteo's attention, then replied with a subtle smile. "I also enjoy your company, Luca. It's nice to be around someone... light."

Luca laughed, but Alessia noticed he understood the indirect jab at Matteo, and that provocation seemed to ignite something more in Luca. He leaned slightly toward her, his face just inches from hers, and Alessia felt her heart race, both from the proximity and the threatening presence of Matteo in the distance.

Suddenly, they heard heavy footsteps, and Matteo appeared, his expression pure fury. He stopped in front of them, his eyes fixed on Alessia, as if he were one step away from losing control.

"Luca," he murmured, his voice cold and cutting. "Could you leave us alone?"

Luca hesitated, but Alessia, with a provocative smile, touched his shoulder. "Don't worry, Luca. Matteo and I have... some things to sort out. But thanks for the company."

Luca looked from Matteo to Alessia, then gave Matteo a challenging smile. "I'll be around, Alessia," he said, clearly daring Matteo, and then walked away with calm steps, as if completely immune to his brother's intensity.

As soon as they were alone, Matteo stared at Alessia, rage evident in his eyes. "Do you think this is funny?" he asked, his voice low but filled with fury.

Alessia crossed her arms, defiant. "Maybe I've found more... suitable company," she replied, openly challenging him. "Luca is light, he doesn't try to control me, and... maybe he's exactly the kind of person I need."

Matteo took a step forward, closing the distance between them. "Luca's a fool if he thinks he can get close to you. You're mine, Alessia."

She lifted her chin, meeting his gaze with a sarcastic smile. "Mine? Funny. I didn't know I was an object to be claimed."

Matteo let out a cold laugh. "This isn't a game, Alessia. You're playing with fire by using Luca against me."

She felt his fury like a wave, but refused to back down. "I'll do what I want. And maybe Luca is a more sensible choice."

Matteo narrowed his eyes, his jaw clenched, and Alessia realized he was at his breaking point. The tension between them was palpable, and she felt a wave of satisfaction seeing how much she was affecting him. But at the same time, his possessive gaze pulled at her, like a current drawing her in closer.

Matteo took another step toward her, his face just inches from hers. "You're making a mistake," he whispered, his voice low and threatening. "Luca's not the man you need. And you know it."

She felt her heart race, but kept her gaze firm. "Maybe I need someone who respects me, Matteo. Someone who doesn't see me as... a possession."

He grabbed her arm, his touch firm and possessive. "You think Luca can offer you that? He has no idea what it really takes to be with you. He doesn't understand who you are... and what you feel."

Alessia remained silent, struggling with the emotions he stirred in her. Matteo was right in some ways, but she couldn't admit that. Not to him, and not to herself. "Maybe Luca sees me as a person, Matteo. Not something he needs to control."

He let out a cold laugh, but his gaze remained fixed on her, intense and unwavering. "And you think Luca will understand you better than I do? That he'll challenge you like I do?"

She bit her lip, unsure of how to respond. Matteo was an enigma, a mix of desire and frustration, and each word he said seemed to unravel her resistance.

But before she could answer, Matteo moved even closer, until his heat became almost unbearable. He whispered near her ear, his voice husky and laden with uncontrollable desire. "I know you hate me, Alessia. But I also know I'm the only one who can awaken what you feel."

She felt her heart race, and for the first time, she stepped back slightly, unable to hold his gaze. Matteo watched her, a satisfied smile spreading across his face, and she realized that, no matter how hard she tried, Luca would never be a barrier against Matteo's intensity.

She pulled away from him, trying to compose herself. "Don't think I'll surrender so easily. This... between us... is a war, Matteo."

He watched her leave, but Alessia could feel his gaze on her back, a reminder that, no matter how much she tried, staying completely distant was impossible.

# Chapter 19: The Declaration of the Possessive

Alessia was in the reading room, trying to distract herself with a book, but her mind was too restless to focus on any story other than her own. The tension between her and Matteo had reached a critical point. The past few days had been a constant game of provocations, where Luca had represented an outlet for her confused emotions and a clear challenge to Matteo. She knew she was playing with fire by getting closer to Luca, but each glance from Matteo calling her back, each possessive touch of his, only seemed to make her more determined to resist.

The sound of firm footsteps echoed through the room, and Alessia looked up. Matteo was standing at the door, his expression dark and intense. He observed her for a moment, as if deciding how to confront her, but then he began walking toward her.

"We need to talk," he said, his voice carrying an authority that instantly irritated her.

Alessia closed the book, looking at him without a hint of submission. "Oh, so you've decided we can talk now?"

Matteo ignored the sarcastic tone and came closer, until he was close enough for her to feel the weight of his presence. "What do you think you're doing with Luca?"

She rolled her eyes, feigning disinterest, though she knew Matteo could see beyond that façade. "I'm just talking to him, Matteo. Or are you going to tell me that's forbidden too?"

Matteo took a deep breath, trying to keep his composure, but she could see the tension in his expression. "This goes beyond a conversation, and you know it, Alessia. Luca may be my brother, but he has no right to get close to my wife."

Alessia felt her face heat up but kept her gaze defiant. "Your wife?" she murmured with a cynical smile. "Funny how you use that word like it's a possession. I am Alessia, Matteo. And I belong to no one."

He moved even closer, until their faces were mere inches apart. "In my world, Alessia, loyalty is the foundation of everything. And that includes you."

She raised an eyebrow, anger building inside her. "So you expect me to be loyal to a man who never gave me a choice? Who treated me like a pawn from the start?"

Matteo looked at her with a determined gaze. "I want you to understand what it means to be mine. And, yes, I expect you to accept that."

Alessia felt her heart race at his words, but anger was stronger than attraction at that moment. "Accept what, Matteo? Being a woman who lives in the shadow of a man who only wants to control me?"

He grabbed her arm, his grip firm but not painful. His eyes, however, were filled with a possessiveness that made her shiver. "Is that really what you think I am? That I only want to control you?"

She hesitated, feeling the intensity in his gaze, but didn't look away. "That's all you've shown me."

Matteo stepped even closer, his voice dropping to an intense whisper. "What I feel for you goes far beyond control or revenge, Alessia. And you know that."

She held her breath, feeling the warmth of his body near hers and the desire pulsing like a current between them. But Alessia refused to give in so easily. "No. You want me to surrender to this feeling, but I... I'm not that kind of woman, Matteo."

He smiled, a smile devoid of humor but filled with a disturbing certainty. "I don't expect you to be submissive, Alessia. But I do expect you to understand that, while you're by my side, there's a code, a respect. And that includes not provoking Luca just to get to me."

She pulled away from his touch, her breathing heavy. "Maybe Luca is a more viable choice. At least he treats me with respect, without this arrogance."

Matteo laughed, but it was a cold laugh, as if the idea of Luca was something he didn't even consider a real possibility. "You know as well as I do that Luca is not the man you want. He's a convenient distraction, Alessia. But you and I... we have something much deeper."

She tried to contain her anger, but the vulnerability he exposed left her defenseless. "And what is it that you think we have, Matteo? Hatred? Anger? Because that's all I feel."

He held her again, but this time he pulled her close enough that she was trapped in his arms, unable to escape. "You can call it whatever you want, but what exists between us isn't hatred. And as long as you keep pretending it is, you'll be fighting against something you've already lost to."

Alessia felt her heart beating hard, and her breathing became heavy. His words, his touch, everything pushed her to the edge of surrender, but she refused to give that power to Matteo.

"I will never yield to you," she whispered, her voice coming out weak, as if she were trying to convince herself.

Matteo slowly released her but kept his gaze fixed. "Maybe you still don't understand what it means to be mine, Alessia. But one day, you will."

She stared at him, furious and shaken at the same time, and without another word, left the room, leaving Matteo alone.

When she reached her room, Alessia closed the door and leaned against it, trying to catch her breath. Matteo was a storm, a presence that consumed her, and she knew that her control over her own feelings was hanging by a thread. She tried to push away the memory of his words, but they echoed in her mind, as if they were an irresistible challenge.

As she stood there, alone, Alessia realized that what she felt for Matteo was deeper than anything she had ever experienced. And as much as she wanted to fight it, she knew that something inside her had already begun to change.

# Chapter 20: The Silent Bond

Night had fallen heavily over the mansion, and the silence was interrupted only by the soft sound of rain against the windows. Alessia felt exhausted, her body weakened by a sudden fever. She had tried to ignore the symptoms, carrying on with her routine, but fatigue had won out. Leaning against the sofa in the living room, eyes half-closed, she tried to fight off the vulnerability that illness brought.

That's when Matteo entered the room, his footsteps firm and expression tense. He stopped upon seeing her, frowning, and Alessia noticed a shadow of concern that crossed his face. Matteo approached, and she saw how his eyes watched her attentively, assessing her as if she were something fragile.

"Alessia, you're sick," he said bluntly, his voice lower than usual.

She took a deep breath, refusing to show weakness. "It's just a passing fever. No need to worry."

Matteo, however, ignored her defensive tone and placed his hand on her forehead, feeling her elevated temperature. Alessia tried to pull back, but he held her firmly, his eyes locked on hers. "You need rest. I won't allow you to push yourself more than necessary."

Alessia looked up, feeling disturbed by the intensity of his care. "Since when do you care about my well-being, Matteo?"

He slowly released her hand but didn't look away. "When something is mine, I take care of it. And you, Alessia, are under my protection, whether you like it or not."

She felt the weight of those words, a statement that seemed to go beyond possessive pride. There was something almost vulnerable in the way he said it, as if the thought of losing her was unbearable. Confusion took over her, and Alessia realized she didn't quite know how to respond.

"I'm not one of your possessions, Matteo," she murmured, trying to keep her tone firm, but her voice faltered slightly.

Matteo simply watched her, and she felt his piercing gaze gradually disarming her. "That's what you think. But I see it differently."

Feeling weakened by both the fever and his words, Alessia sighed and closed her eyes for a moment. Matteo, noticing her exhaustion, softened his tone. "You need rest. I'll call the doctor."

She opened her eyes, surprised by the genuine concern he showed. "I don't need a doctor. It'll pass," she whispered, trying to show some resistance.

But Matteo seemed unconvinced. Without another word, he picked her up in his arms, lifting her from the sofa. Alessia protested, but she was too weak to put up a real fight. As he carried her to her room, her heart raced, taken by his closeness and the unexpected gesture of care. Matteo was an intense presence, but in that moment, there was something about him that disarmed her, a hidden gentleness that seemed to contradict everything she believed about him.

When they reached the room, Matteo laid her gently on the bed, arranging the covers around her. He knelt beside the bed, his gaze firm and protective, as if taking on an unexpected role.

"You think I don't care," he said, his voice low and hoarse, "but that's not true, Alessia. I'll always protect you, even if it means protecting you from yourself."

Alessia looked away, trying to process his words. There was something in that declaration that touched her deeply, a silent vulnerability that made her question what she really felt. Matteo irritated her, challenged her, but at the same time, he seemed to be the only one capable of seeing her completely. Even though she didn't fully understand, there was something there—an invisible, undeniable bond.

"Why are you doing this?" she murmured, still confused. "Why this sudden interest in taking care of me?"

He was silent for a moment, his gaze steady on her, before replying with a heavy sigh. "Because you're mine, Alessia. And I take care of what's mine."

She felt a shiver at the intensity of his words, a mixture of frustration and attraction that left her confused. "I didn't ask for this," she replied, almost in a whisper.

He touched her face, his thumb gently brushing her warm skin. "I know. But that doesn't change anything."

His touch was gentle, almost affectionate, and Alessia felt her heart race with that closeness. His hand on her face felt like it was burning, and she realized that the hatred she always claimed to feel for him was transforming into something deeper and far more dangerous. She was beginning to see a side of Matteo he hid under layers of pride and arrogance, but which now revealed itself bit by bit.

Alessia closed her eyes, letting herself be enveloped by his touch for a brief moment before opening them again. "This doesn't mean you can control me," she murmured, maintaining a tenuous resistance.

Matteo smiled slightly, but his gaze remained serious. "I'm not trying to control you, Alessia. I'm trying to protect you. And even if you don't understand it now, perhaps one day you'll realize that what I feel goes far beyond any word you could use against me."

She felt the depth of his words, a declaration that seemed to carry more than just a promise of protection. It was as if Matteo were admitting, albeit indirectly, that what he felt for her was more complex than he himself wanted to accept. And as much as she wanted to ignore it, Alessia knew that something was changing within her.

That night, as Matteo left the room, she remained lying down, her heart still racing. His figure by the door carried a silent intensity, and Alessia realized that something between them had shifted. Even without saying another word, Matteo had looked at her with a deep, enigmatic gaze before closing the door softly, leaving her alone with her confused thoughts and feelings.

Alone, Alessia reflected on what Matteo meant to her, on how much he challenged her but also protected her in unexpected ways. The idea that someone like him could care unsettled her, and gradually, she wondered if the real struggle was against the feelings beginning to grow inside her.

### Capítulo 21: The Game of Surrender

Alessia felt as if she were walking a tightrope. With every confrontation with Matteo, it seemed she was edging closer to crossing a line she had once considered impassable. But the intensity Matteo brought into her life surrounded her like a storm, challenging her to resist or surrender. Something within her urged her to test his limits, to see how far he was willing to go to keep her under his control. It was a dangerous game, yet Alessia couldn't stop.

She decided to adopt a provocative approach, hinting at her feelings through subtle gestures, then pulling back whenever he seemed about to respond. On one occasion, as they were in the dining room, Alessia brushed her hand lightly over Matteo's shoulder as she walked past him—a touch gentle but pointedly suggestive. He tensed immediately, yet kept his composure, his gaze fixed on her with an intensity that might have unsettled anyone else. Alessia, however, responded with a mysterious smile before returning to her seat, as if nothing had happened.

Of course, Matteo saw through her game. He knew Alessia was testing his patience, stretching the control he tried to maintain. Frustration simmered within him, yet it fueled something even more dangerous—desire. She was playing with fire, and he wondered how far she was willing to let it burn.

That evening, the tension reached a new peak. Alessia was in the library, her sanctuary of solitude. Matteo entered quietly, watching her from afar. She sensed his presence before she even saw him; it was as if the air had shifted, becoming heavier and denser. She looked up, a slight smile on her lips.

"Looking for a book, Matteo?" she teased, her tone light but laced with undertones.

He crossed his arms, leaning against the doorway, observing her in silence for a moment, his gaze piercing enough to make her almost shiver. "It seems you're the one seeking my attention, Alessia. Don't you think you've pushed these... provocations far enough?"

Alessia raised an eyebrow, feigning innocence. "I don't know what you mean. I'm simply living my life... or do you believe my very existence is meant to provoke you?"

Matteo smiled—a dangerous smile—and took a few steps toward her, each step making Alessia's heartbeat quicken. When he stopped mere inches away, the closeness between them became unbearable, a flame ready to consume everything in its path.

"You think I don't see what you're doing?" he murmured, his voice low and rough. "You want to test me. To see how far my patience will go. But, Alessia, this is a game you're not going to win."

She took a step back, trying to maintain her composure, but his intense gaze rattled her. "And what if I'm not trying to win? Maybe I just want to see how far you'll go."

He laughed—a dark, desire-laden sound. "So you want to see how far I'm willing to go to keep you by my side?" He took another step, and Alessia felt her back press against the bookshelf. "Perhaps it's time you admit what you truly feel."

She swallowed hard, her heart pounding. His closeness left her dizzy, yet she tried to keep her defiant facade. "You're so convinced I feel anything but contempt?"

Matteo leaned in until their faces were inches apart, his gaze locked onto hers. "Yes, Alessia. Because you wouldn't be trying so hard if it were only contempt."

She held her breath, captivated by his gaze. Matteo was right. There was something more, something she refused to admit but that showed in every provocation, every touch, every unspoken word. She felt lost between anger and desire, between resistance and surrender. And for the first time, she wasn't sure if she could resist.

But Matteo surprised her by pulling back. He watched her, his eyes still burning with a mix of frustration and restrained desire, but he didn't move any closer. "Think about this, Alessia," he murmured, his voice carrying an intensity that made her tremble. "Because one day, this game will end, and when it does, I want to know where you really stand."

He left her there, alone and lost in thought. Alessia felt both frustrated and relieved. It was as if Matteo had handed her the choice of how far she wanted to take this silent battle. But she knew the game between them was far from over, and that eventually, she would have to face the truth about what she felt.

Later that night, lying in bed, Alessia found herself dwelling on his words. Matteo had the power to shake her emotions profoundly, to dismantle her defenses. But now, Alessia began to wonder: was she resisting Matteo, or was she resisting her own feelings?

Deep down, she felt she was on the brink of an inevitable surrender, a path with no return. And as her heart pounded in her chest, she realized that what scared her most wasn't losing control over Matteo, but over herself.

As Alessia tried to process the whirlwind of emotions surrounding her, Matteo's image lingered in her mind. Every provocation, every exchanged glance replayed in her memory, as if it were etched into her body and mind. She was frustrated with her own vulnerability, yet there was a part of her that yearned for their next encounter, the next confrontation. Matteo was her greatest weakness and her greatest strength, the only man capable of challenging her, of awakening feelings she had always feared.

On his side, Matteo, though he maintained his cold and authoritative demeanor, was also in conflict. Alessia was different from anyone he had ever known, and that difference attracted him irresistibly. He admired her strength and her determination not to bow to his will, even though it irritated him profoundly. He realized that it wasn't just physical attraction that bound him to her, but a silent respect, a deep understanding, as if he saw in her a version of himself. Yet he refused to admit how much she affected him; for Matteo, surrender was not an option.

One night, they found themselves in the living room. Alessia was distracted, flipping through a book, but when she sensed Matteo's presence, she looked up, and their eyes met with an intensity almost tangible. He gave a slight smile, carrying a mix of challenge and curiosity.

"You're always so focused on denying what you feel," he murmured, approaching her slowly, as if expecting a reaction.

Alessia raised an eyebrow, keeping her defiant air. "And you're always so convinced you know everything going on with me."

He chuckled softly, a sound that made her shiver. "I know enough to understand that you're running from something inevitable."

She closed the book, facing him directly, her heart racing but her tone firm. "Maybe the inevitable is my determination to keep away from you."

Matteo leaned in, his eyes locked onto hers, and his voice came out in a rough whisper. "Alessia, the more you run, the stronger this becomes."

She felt the weight of his words and looked away, struggling to control her emotions. The truth was, Matteo was right, and it shook her deeply. He moved closer, until his hands softly brushed hers, and Alessia felt his touch like an electric current.

"You can try to run all you want," he murmured, "but we both know that what exists between us goes beyond any resistance."

Alessia held her breath, his touch enveloping her, and for a moment, she gave in. She felt his face close to hers, her heart racing as if it were on fire. But in a sudden motion, she pulled back, her eyes gleaming with a mix of desire and frustration.

"This will never work, Matteo," she murmured, but her voice was trembling, lacking the firmness she intended.

He only smiled, his gaze holding a silent promise. "Keep saying that, Alessia. Maybe one day, even you will believe it."

Matteo watched her leave, knowing her resistance was, in truth, a lost battle. He felt he was just a step away from breaking that last barrier between them.

### Capítulo 22: The First Fracture

Alessia paced the mansion's corridors, her thoughts swirling uncontrollably. Since her last confrontation with Matteo, something within her had started to unravel—a crack that widened with each attempt she made to escape her own feelings. The idea of surrendering to what she felt was unacceptable, yet she couldn't dispel the image of Matteo, the intensity of his gaze, the weight of his words. He stirred her in a way she never thought possible, leaving her in a constant state of vulnerability.

"I need to get out of here," she whispered to herself, trying to convince herself that escape was still possible, that there was a way to avoid the ending she feared. She attempted to focus on resisting the marriage, on finding a way out, but every thought of freedom inevitably circled back to Matteo, as if he were the gravitational center of her life.

As she walked down the corridor, Alessia saw him from a distance. He stood near a window, looking out with an expression she had never seen before. Matteo's usually firm and impenetrable posture seemed softened, almost melancholic, as if something weighed on him. She frowned, intrigued by this rare vulnerability.

Without thinking, Alessia approached him, her steps light but determined. Matteo turned as he sensed her presence, and for a brief moment, their intense gazes met, filled with silent questions.

"Why do you do this?" Alessia asked, her voice carrying a mixture of anger and curiosity. "Why do you insist on keeping me under control, as if I'm some possession that needs to be tamed?"

Matteo sighed, running a hand through his hair, revealing a tension she hadn't noticed before. "Because control is all I know," he replied, his voice lower and more honest than usual. "Hate, possession... it's part of me. It's the only way I know how to deal with what I feel."

Alessia stared at him, momentarily lost for words. He had always embodied coldness and dominance, yet that statement created a small opening, a fracture in his armor. Matteo seemed as trapped by his own past, as haunted by what had shaped him, as she was by hers. For the first time, Alessia glimpsed something beyond his arrogance and control.

"Is that it?" she questioned, trying to understand. "You control because you're afraid of losing?"

He watched her in silence, as if he were considering her words. "Yes," he finally admitted, a hint of sadness in his eyes. "And you challenge me in a way no one ever has. I don't know how to deal with that, Alessia. I don't know how to deal with you."

Those words struck something deep within her, a chord she had tried to keep unwavering but that now began to tremble. Matteo, the man who had always seemed unbreakable, was admitting she was his weakness, something he couldn't control. Alessia felt a mixture of compassion and attraction, an unexpected connection that threatened to crumble the walls she'd built around her heart.

She crossed her arms, trying to keep a firm stance, but her voice came out softer than she intended. "Then maybe you need to learn to see me as something more than a possession."

He let out a faint smile, a smile devoid of joy but filled with honesty. "Maybe you're right. But it's difficult, Alessia. I was taught to possess and control... and now you're showing me something I don't know how to handle."

They stood in silence, the weight of their words hanging in the air, creating a connection that went beyond any game of dominance. Alessia felt that something was shifting between them, a silent bond that grew with each glance, with every unspoken word. Matteo seemed vulnerable in a way she never imagined, and this vulnerability was slowly breaking down her own defenses.

She took a deep breath, feeling her heart racing. "Matteo," she murmured, looking at the floor before meeting his gaze again, "I don't know where this is going. But know that I'm not a piece you can manipulate forever."

He looked at her, and for a moment, a hint of softness passed through his eyes. "I know," he replied, his voice low. "But I'm not sure I can be different."

Alessia remained silent, her eyes locked on his. His vulnerability stirred something deep inside her, and she realized that the hatred she had sworn to feel was being replaced by something more complex. And, despite her resistance, she knew her heart was beginning to yield, that her attraction to Matteo was no longer a fleeting weakness but a reality she had to face.

Matteo slowly stepped back, but his gaze seemed etched into her mind, a silent promise that their battle was far from over. She watched him disappear down the corridor, aware that, although she wanted to escape, her heart was already bound to him in a way she couldn't deny.

As Matteo walked away, Alessia felt a wave of confusion and anxiety wash over her. No matter how hard she tried to control her emotions, every word he had said echoed in her mind, revealing a humanity she hadn't expected to find. Matteo, whom she had always judged as cold and calculating, had just shown her a vulnerability, a flaw in his absolute control. He had admitted that he didn't know how to deal with her, and that touched a part of her that had long been hidden, a part that yearned to break her own walls.

She wondered how she had reached this point. She despised Matteo's arrogance, his desire for control, but, at the same time, this vulnerable side made him irresistible. She knew she was involved but didn't want to admit it, even to herself, that what she felt was something beyond the simple desire for liberation.

For the first time, Alessia acknowledged that there was a connection between them, something beyond hatred, an attraction that defied her logic and intentions. The mixture of anger and desire left her disoriented, but, at the same time, a new desire arose within her—to explore this relationship, to understand who Matteo really was beneath his layers of arrogance and coldness.

Meanwhile, Matteo walked away, feeling the weight of his own words. He had never allowed himself to expose his vulnerabilities, never let anyone get so close to his fears and insecurities. Alessia challenged him in a way that made him question his own nature, a nature built on power and control. She was a storm, a force that shook his defenses and made him feel something he couldn't explain.

As he walked, Matteo found himself reflecting on each encounter, each provocation, each touch. He felt drawn to her in a way he had never experienced before. It wasn't just physical desire; it was something deeper, a desire to uncover every mystery, every resistance. Alessia was an enigma, and he wanted to unravel her, to see her surrender not out of imposition but because she desired him as much as he desired her.

Matteo stopped in the corridor, taking a deep breath. He realized that, for the first time, he was truly affected by someone. His control was beginning to unravel, and that both scared and intrigued him.

That night, unable to sleep, Alessia went down to the garden, where the nighttime silence and the scent of flowers helped calm her mind. But she was not alone. Matteo was there, seated on a bench, with an introspective air that made him even more enigmatic.

She hesitated, but before she could decide, Matteo saw her and gestured for her to come closer. Alessia walked over to him, her heart racing, a mixture of nervousness and excitement filling her.

"What are you doing here at this hour?" he asked, his voice gentle, almost kind.

"I needed some air," she replied, trying not to reveal the restlessness she felt.

Matteo watched her, his gaze intense. "It seems I'm not the only one trying to understand what's happening."

Alessia gave a sarcastic smile, but her tone came out softer than she intended. "Maybe it's because you insist on turning everything into a power game."

He stood up and took a step toward her, closing the distance until their faces were close. "Maybe it's the only way I know to deal with what you make me feel."

She shivered at those words but tried to keep her composure. "Then maybe you need to learn other ways."

Matteo took her hand, his touch warm and soft yet filled with intensity. "I'm trying, Alessia. You challenge me, make me want to be someone I'm not. And maybe, for the first time, I want that."

Alessia looked away, her heart racing. His honesty disarmed her, and she knew it was becoming increasingly difficult to deny what she felt. Matteo was a force that enveloped her, and now, without the walls of hatred, she realized that what existed between them was more complex than she could have imagined.

Sensing her hesitation, Matteo leaned closer until their breaths mingled. "Tell me you feel nothing, Alessia, and I'll leave you in peace. Tell me you hate me, that I'm just an obstacle... and I'll step back."

She looked into his eyes, feeling that she was on the brink of something inevitable. But the words wouldn't come. Matteo gazed at her with silent expectation, and, for the first time, Alessia didn't have the strength to push him away.

Then, in a moment of surrender, she closed her eyes and allowed herself to feel. Matteo's grip on her hand intensified, and he leaned closer. When their lips met, the world seemed to stop, and Alessia felt herself swept away by a flood of emotions—desire, challenge, and something she couldn't name. Matteo held her gently, yet the intensity of that kiss conveyed everything they couldn't express in words.

When they finally pulled apart, both were breathless, and the silence between them was filled with a new understanding. Alessia knew that something had changed; this was the first fracture in her defenses, a surrender that, though small, had bound them together in an irreversible way.

## Capítulo 23: Between Desire and Pride

Alessia was on edge. Since the kiss the previous night, a tumultuous mix of desire and anger had consumed her. Every time she thought of Matteo, her heart pounded faster, and she fought to rationalize everything. Pride and the instinct for self-preservation were her final shields, but deep down, she knew she couldn't maintain control around him. Matteo seemed to know exactly how to dismantle her defenses, how to access the parts of herself that she'd guarded so fiercely.

At the end of the mansion's corridor, she spotted Matteo. He was engaged in conversation, but as soon as he noticed her, his gaze locked onto hers, as if nothing else mattered. Their eyes held, and Alessia felt her heart quicken. She tried to keep a neutral expression, but the intensity of his look seemed to challenge her to confront the growing connection between them.

Finishing his conversation, Matteo began to walk toward her. Alessia stood her ground, but a part of her hummed with anticipation and apprehension. As he approached, the silence between them felt tangible, a weight that bound them in place.

"Alessia," he said, his voice low and intense. "Are you going to keep pretending nothing happened last night?"

She lifted her chin, determined to keep her composure. "There's nothing to pretend, Matteo. It was just... a moment of weakness. A mistake I don't plan on repeating."

He gave a slight smirk, that infuriating smirk that made her feel exposed. "A mistake? Funny, it doesn't sound like you really believe what you're saying."

She narrowed her eyes, defensive. "You think you know me that well?"

Matteo stepped closer, closing the distance between them until the air felt charged, his gaze holding hers with a fierce intensity. "I think I know enough to see that you're fighting what you feel, and that it's killing you as much as it is me."

Alessia's heart pounded even harder, but she held her ground. "You think you can control everything, Matteo, but I'm not a game piece for you to move at will."

"I'm not trying to control you, Alessia," he murmured, his voice filled with a sincerity that caught her off guard. "But what's between us is undeniable, and you know it."

She looked away, trying to regain her composure, but he didn't let her retreat. In a swift move, Matteo pinned her against the wall, his hands braced on either side of her face. The closeness, the warmth, his scent—everything made her breathless.

"Why are you fighting this?" he whispered, his voice thick with desire. "What are you so afraid to admit?"

Alessia felt stripped bare under his gaze, as if Matteo could see every emotion she tried to hide. "Because I don't want to lose myself," she murmured, barely aware she'd spoken aloud.

Matteo leaned closer until their faces were mere inches apart, his gaze dropping to her lips. "Maybe losing control isn't such a bad thing."

Her heart faltered, her breath uneven. The desire between them was palpable, and Matteo seemed to perceive every hidden feeling she couldn't bring herself to admit. But pride was her only remaining defense.

"You think you're the one in control, Matteo," she said, her voice trembling but resolute. "You think you can have me whenever you want, as if I'm just a prize to be claimed."

Matteo pulled back slightly, but not enough to break the tension. His expression shifted, and she saw a flicker of vulnerability in his eyes. "That's not what I want," he said firmly. "And that's not what you mean to me."

His words hit her like a shock. It was the first time Matteo had spoken with such sincerity, free from his usual arrogance and provocation. She fell silent, trying to absorb it, but his proximity, the intensity of his gaze—it all made her even more uncertain.

Sensing her hesitation, Matteo leaned in slowly, his lips barely brushing hers. "Tell me this is just hate," he whispered, his voice husky and filled with expectation. "Tell me you feel nothing, and I'll step back."

Alessia felt torn, her heart racing and her words caught in her throat. She wanted to maintain the facade, to tell him he was wrong, that it was all just a power struggle. But the truth was impossible to hide, even from herself.

In a surge of emotion, she lifted her face and kissed him, pouring all the tension and desire she had suppressed into that single moment. Matteo pulled her closer, his touch both possessive and intense, as if he needed to prove that this was real. The passion between them ignited, the kiss deep and charged with an intensity neither had known they could feel.

When they finally parted, both were breathless, and the silence that followed was filled with a new understanding. Alessia felt exposed, but also relieved, as if she were finally accepting a part of herself that she had long repressed.

Matteo looked at her, and in his eyes, she saw more than desire—she saw a silent promise, an acknowledgment that what was between them was more than mere attraction.

"Alessia," he whispered, his tone soft and deep. "I'm not giving up on you."

She swallowed, aware that, despite all the barriers she still tried to maintain, she was coming closer to surrendering completely. Between desire and pride, they would continue to struggle, but in that moment, Alessia knew that a part of her had already crossed the point of no return.

That kiss had changed everything. Alessia felt as if she had crossed an invisible line, one that could never be undone. She was torn between the exhilaration of finally giving in to what she felt and the panic of being left far too vulnerable. With her heart still racing, she pulled away from Matteo, attempting to regain her composure. But as she met those intense eyes, eyes that looked at her as if she were everything he wanted, she felt her resistance threaten to shatter all over again.

Matteo, on the other hand, watched her with a new intensity, a quiet resolve. He knew that this wasn't just any kiss; it was a silent confession, a surrender they had both resisted for so long. The way Alessia looked at him, torn between desire and pride, only made everything more exhilarating. He loved that she never made it easy, that she always challenged him, that she never fully gave in.

He took a step closer, closing the distance again, and Alessia found herself unable to back away. It was as if something pulled her to him, an irresistible force that kept her from moving. Matteo touched her face gently, his fingers brushing her skin with a softness that belied the fire in his gaze.

"Why do you fight this so hard, Alessia?" he whispered, his voice low and rough, filled with an emotion that made her tremble. "I know you feel the same as I do."

She looked away, struggling to regain control. "It's not that simple, Matteo. You... you're my opposite in every way. Controlling me isn't the same as loving me."

He smiled, but there was a vulnerability in that smile. "And who said I want to control you? I know you're fire, Alessia. That's what I admire about you. And maybe, for the first time, I don't want to control what I feel. I just want... to live this with you."

His words disarmed her in a way she never imagined. Alessia had always believed that Matteo saw her as a possession, something to conquer. But now, there was something deeper, something genuine in his voice and gaze, and it both confused and captivated her.

She sighed, still trying to maintain her defenses. "And what do you want from me, then, Matteo? For me to just give in? To ignore everything that's happened between us?"

He looked at her with an intensity that seemed to pierce through her barriers. "I want you to stop running, Alessia. I want you to face me without pride as your shield. I know you feel something... and I know you're afraid."

Alessia laughed, but there was a hint of nervousness in her voice. "I'm not afraid of you."

"No, not of me," he replied softly, a smile on his lips. "You're afraid of what you feel for me."

She opened her mouth to respond, but the words wouldn't come. Matteo was right. A part of her feared what she felt, knowing it could destroy her or leave her vulnerable in a way she had never experienced. She was used to protecting herself, to keeping her emotions in check. And now, he was challenging her to let down her guard.

Finally, Alessia lifted her gaze, looking at him with a mixture of defiance and vulnerability. "You're wrong, Matteo. This... this is just a moment. It means nothing."

He observed her in silence for a moment, his gaze softening, as if he could see beyond her words. Then, he leaned close, his lips near her ear, and murmured in a voice that sent shivers down her spine. "Say that while looking into my eyes. Tell me it means nothing, and maybe I'll believe you."

Alessia's heart began to race once more. She wanted to push him away, to shout that he was wrong, but the words were trapped. Matteo knew her too well; he knew how to reach her vulnerabilities, her hidden desires. And it frightened her as much as it thrilled her.

She closed her eyes, struggling to steady her breathing, and felt him pull back slightly, though not enough to break the connection between them. "Alessia," he said in a softer tone, almost tender. "I'm not giving up on us. I know there's something here... something worth fighting for. And no matter how hard you resist, I know you feel it too."

She opened her eyes slowly, looking at him with a blend of anger and attraction. Matteo had managed to disarm her in a way no one else had, and in that moment, she knew she was on the verge of a fall she couldn't stop.

## Capítulo 24: The Past Revealed

Alessia was restless; the kiss she shared with Matteo the previous night left her feeling unsettled. There was more to that man than his arrogance and desire for control. He was guarded, hiding a part of himself with extreme caution. Determined to understand Matteo's hidden depths, she started to observe him closely, quietly asking questions to Luca and Enrico, the few who might know the secrets he kept.

Initially reluctant, Luca eventually revealed fragments of Matteo's past. His expression changed every time he spoke about his brother, as though a shadow lay between them. "Matteo lost our mother far too soon," Luca confessed, his voice low and tinged with sadness. "And afterward, others close to him were taken too... tragically."

Enrico, listening intently, added in a somber tone, "Those losses changed him. Pain hardened Matteo, Alessia. Since then, he's shielded himself, believing any deeper connection would leave him vulnerable."

Those words stirred something within her. She began to see Matteo not just as an arrogant, controlling man but as someone bearing invisible scars, protecting himself from a world that had always seemed ready to take more from him. She felt torn between her desire to understand him and her reluctance to get too close. Yet something compelled her to keep looking deeper.

A few nights later, Alessia found Matteo standing in the quiet of the mansion's grand hall. He was by the window, gazing out into the dark night, his expression distant. Sensing this might be her moment to uncover more, she approached him cautiously.

"You always seem so alone, Matteo," she murmured, stepping closer.

He glanced away from the window, turning to face her with a guarded look. "And why would that matter to you, Alessia?" he questioned, his tone defensive.

Unfazed, she replied, "Because you challenge me constantly, but you never let me see beyond those walls. I want to understand what truly drives you, Matteo. What made you this way?"

He took a deep breath, his gaze hardening as if to shield himself. "You don't need to understand anything about me, Alessia. What I am has nothing to do with you."

"That's not how it seems," she replied, her courage unwavering. "You act like you're always protecting me, even when you claim to hate or control me. It's as if there's something you're trying to hide."

Matteo took a step back, visibly unsettled by her words. "You're stepping into dangerous territory, Alessia. Don't like what you find? Stay out."

"You think hiding everything from me protects you, but Matteo, I'm not your enemy," she said firmly, holding his gaze. "I'm not that girl you once saw as an adversary. I'm trying to understand you because, deep down, I think you need someone who will."

Matteo looked at her, his eyes intense and almost retreating, yet she stood her ground. Alessia could see he was fighting an internal battle, struggling to hold onto control even as his barriers seemed on the verge of breaking.

"And if I don't want to be understood?" he murmured, his voice dark and laced with bitterness. "What if I'm too far gone for any attempt at redemption?"

She stepped forward, ignoring the fear gnawing at her chest. "Then maybe it's time to accept that you don't have to face everything alone."

Matteo turned his gaze away, his jaw tight. Her words seemed to reach parts of him he'd kept buried for a long time. He took a deep breath, his hand clenching into a fist at his side, as though he were trying to contain something threatening to escape. At last, he murmured, "The people I loved... they were taken from me, one by one. Pain taught me to shut myself off, Alessia. To trust no one, to avoid getting close, because every bond could break, leaving only emptiness behind. That's what I've learned."

His words were harsh, but Alessia sensed the raw hurt underlying them. She took another step forward, close enough that he couldn't ignore her. "It doesn't have to be that way. Not every bond ends in loss. I don't know what the future holds, Matteo, but running won't protect you from anything."

He let out a bitter laugh. "Do you really think I can change? That I'm capable of giving up this control and allowing myself to feel something real?"

Alessia studied him in silence, his face reflecting the weight of the burden he bore. "I believe you're more than the walls you've built. And maybe, if you let me, I can help you see that too."

Matteo remained silent for a long moment, his eyes locked with hers, searching for something he hadn't dared to understand. Slowly, he lifted his hand and, with a gentleness she hadn't expected, touched her face. His touch was hesitant but full of a tenderness that felt utterly foreign yet profoundly genuine.

"You don't understand, Alessia. This... whatever this is between us... it's the closest thing to real I've felt in a long time. And at the same time, it's the thing I fear the most."

She placed her hand over his, holding it with strength, as though she wanted to convey the reassurance he needed. "Then maybe it's time to face that fear, Matteo. Not for me, but for yourself."

The silence that followed was laden with unspoken understanding. Alessia felt as though a new connection had formed between them, an opening toward something deeper. Matteo looked at her as if she were the only anchor in a sea of uncertainties, and in that moment, Alessia knew that, despite their intentions, both were irrevocably entangled.

Matteo's heart pounded as he held his hand softly against her face. He was not the type of man who allowed himself this level of vulnerability, especially with someone like her—a woman who challenged every one of his defenses yet brought him a strange sense of peace. Her presence shook him, and despite his struggle for control, her gaze disarmed him. In those intense eyes, he saw not just a bold woman, but someone willing to look beyond his armor.

Alessia, meanwhile, felt a mix of fear and yearning. Matteo represented everything she had been taught to avoid—danger, control, mystery. But now, as he touched her face, she sensed there was more. He was a man scarred by loss and trauma, and the vulnerability he revealed made her question everything she thought she knew about him. Every part of her was torn between the desire to protect herself and the urge to get closer, to be the one who might show him a different side of life, one where his scars no longer dictated his choices.

She placed her hand over his, feeling the warmth and strength in his touch. "Do you think shielding yourself from the world is the only way to avoid pain?" she murmured, her voice soft yet challenging. "Because I think you're just postponing an inevitable truth."

Matteo narrowed his eyes, a slightly ironic smile tugging at his lips. "And what inevitable truth would that be, Alessia?" he challenged, his voice laden with intensity.

She took a steadying breath, holding his gaze. "That you feel something. That, no matter how hard you try, you can't escape yourself. And that, perhaps, allowing someone in doesn't have to be a weakness."

He was silent for a few seconds, his eyes locked on hers, absorbing each word. "And you think you can show me that? That you can break through my walls?"

Alessia smiled, a playful glint in her eyes, as if accepting his unspoken challenge. "Maybe. But that depends on you, Matteo. I'm not the one who has to give in."

Matteo let out a faint chuckle, the sound as disarming as always. "You're stubborn, Alessia. And that's what intrigues me about you. This unbreakable will, this... audacity to confront me."

She stepped closer, their bodies almost touching, and looked directly into his eyes. "Because I know that behind all this coldness, there's more. I know that it's not just control you seek, Matteo. There's something deeper you're hiding."

He sighed, his fingers tracing gentle lines on her face. "You say that as if you know me better than I know myself, Alessia."

"Maybe I do," she replied, her voice firm yet kind. "Maybe I see what you don't want to see."

There was something in her tone that stripped away his defenses. Matteo knew Alessia was right; he had always known that beneath his rigid control and impenetrable facade, there was a part of him struggling against his own feelings. But looking at her now, he felt something that made him want to believe that perhaps this internal war could have a different ending.

Slowly, he leaned closer, his face inches from hers, and Alessia felt her breath catch. The closeness between them was electrifying, and although she knew this moment could change everything, she did not pull away.

"Maybe," he whispered, his lips barely grazing hers, "you're the only one who could make me see that."

And before she could respond, he kissed her. This time, the kiss was soft, different from the heated exchanges they had shared before. It was a kiss that spoke of unspoken promises, of a surrender they both feared but could no longer resist. Matteo's hands slid down to her waist, pulling her closer, and she felt his arms encircle her, as though he were both protecting her and allowing himself to be vulnerable.

When they finally parted, they remained in silence, still wrapped in each other's arms. Both were breathing slightly faster, but not from the intensity of the kiss. It was from the unspoken understanding that something between them had irrevocably shifted.

Alessia opened her eyes, finding Matteo watching her, his dark, enigmatic gaze softened by a newfound light. For the first time, she saw him stripped of all his defenses, and in that moment, Alessia felt she was facing a side of Matteo that no one else had ever known.

"I won't promise this will be easy," he whispered, almost as a confession.

She smiled, caressing his face tenderly. "I'm not expecting it to be. But maybe that's why it's worth it."

That final phrase lingered in the air, and for the first time, Matteo felt he had found someone willing to challenge him not out of power, but out of a desire to understand him. And it made him want, with an intensity he had never felt before, for Alessia to be the one to break down the barriers he had held up for so long.

## Capítulo 25: The Bond That Transforms

The night was calm, and the mansion's veranda was bathed in the soft glow of the moonlight, casting gentle shadows that created an atmosphere of peace—a rarity in Matteo and Alessia's turbulent lives. Sitting in silence, they gazed at the scenery, enveloped in an aura of mutual understanding that they both knew was fragile but, at the same time, felt increasingly real. This shared silence was new to them, a quiet moment that didn't demand words, only presence.

Alessia glanced sideways at Matteo. His profile, hardened by the life he had led, seemed less intimidating now. It was as if this moment had stripped away all the masks they held up between them. She saw a man who had suffered, who had built walls to protect himself but who, for the first time, seemed willing to lower his guard. Alessia felt a different warmth at that realization. An unexpected compassion washed over her, and she wondered when this feeling had begun to coexist with the resentment she had once held in her heart.

"You know I understand what you went through, don't you?" Alessia broke the silence, her voice gentle but firm, as though stepping into uncharted territory. "I know the things you've experienced haven't been easy, and I know they've shaped you in ways you might not even want to admit."

Matteo looked at her, surprised by her honesty. He had always seen Alessia as an adversary, someone he needed to subdue to maintain his dominance. But here, on the veranda under the moonlight, he began to see her differently. She was not just an imposed wife or a rival in his world of power plays. She was someone who, in a way, saw parts of him he had never shared with anyone.

"It's not that simple, Alessia," he replied, his voice low, almost hesitant. "I was taught never to show weakness. In the world I live in, any sign of weakness is used against you."

Alessia gave a slight smile, as if she had anticipated his response. "I get that, Matteo. But at the same time, you can't use what you've been through as an excuse to control everyone around you, including me."

Matteo frowned, but there was no anger in his expression, only contemplation. "Maybe you're right," he admitted slowly. "Maybe I've let my fear of losing everything take over. But, Alessia, you have to understand that control is the only thing I've ever had. If I let go of it, I feel like I'm risking everything."

She held his gaze, her eyes a mix of challenge and tenderness. "Control might feel like security, Matteo, but it's also a prison. And sometimes, letting go is the only way to find something more—something that goes beyond safety."

He fell silent, her words echoing in his mind. Matteo had always believed that strength resided in total dominance, but here, in Alessia's presence, he began to question whether that view was all he had to offer. Her gaze challenged him, yet it also seemed to extend a hand, offering something he didn't entirely understand but longed to explore.

"Why are you doing this, Alessia?" he asked, his voice softer than he intended. "Why do you keep trying to understand me?"

She shrugged, looking out at the horizon as if searching for the right words. "Because, somehow, I see something in you that maybe you don't see. I know that behind all that armor, there's someone who wants peace, who wants to be free. And if I can help, I... maybe I want to be there for that."

Matteo was momentarily speechless, a mix of shock and an unfamiliar emotion flooding over him. He had never imagined that anyone could look at him with such perspective, seeing beyond the layers of brutality and force. He had never thought someone would want to know him truly, especially someone like Alessia, who had always met him on equal footing.

In a gesture that surprised even himself, Matteo reached out and took Alessia's hand. She was startled for a moment but didn't pull away. His fingers were firm, yet his touch carried a tenderness she never would have imagined him capable of. For a moment, they remained like that, connected by a silent touch that seemed to communicate everything words failed to express.

"I can't promise to change overnight," he murmured, his voice low but filled with sincerity. "But maybe... maybe I can learn."

Alessia smiled, a genuine smile that lit up her eyes intensely. "I don't expect you to change, Matteo. I only hope that... that we can find a way to make this work, truly."

He nodded, still holding her hand, feeling vulnerable but, at the same time, surprisingly at peace. "For the first time, I see you as someone I can share more with than just distrust and power struggles. You're different, Alessia. And maybe I need that more than I realized."

She looked into his eyes, and the intensity of the moment wrapped them in a deep, almost reverent silence. Alessia knew that from this moment, there was something irrevocable between them—a bond that transcended any animosity or fleeting attraction. It was a connection that could transform them, for better or worse, but would undoubtedly change them forever.

As they continued to look at each other, Matteo leaned in slowly, until his lips met hers in a gentle kiss full of unspoken promises. It was a kiss that sealed the moment, a silent bond that grew stronger with every second. They were taking a risk—they both knew it—but they also knew there was no turning back.

Their world, full of risks and secrets, suddenly felt small in the face of the connection they were building. And as they pulled away, they both felt they had taken a step into the unknown but also into something that could, finally, bring them the peace they had both been searching for.

Standing there on the moonlit veranda, Alessia felt an unexpected calm. She knew her relationship with Matteo was a whirlwind of emotions, full of twists, fights, and provocations, but at that moment, everything felt silenced. Matteo, the man who had once been her greatest adversary, was now beside her, vulnerable and open in a way she had never imagined. Her heart beat strongly—not with fear or anger but with a mixture of feelings she was still learning to decipher.

Matteo watched her in silence, his eyes studying every detail of her expression. There was a growing fascination in his mind, as though Alessia were a puzzle he wanted to solve and, at the same time, a mystery he didn't want to fully unveil. Every provocation, every challenge between them seemed only to stoke the fire he struggled to control but now found impossible to ignore.

"You're very quiet, Alessia," he murmured, a slight smile forming on his lips. "That's rare."

She rolled her eyes but couldn't suppress a smile. "Maybe you finally left me speechless."

He raised an eyebrow, intrigued. "Oh, really? Tell me, what exactly silenced that sharp tongue of yours?"

Alessia let out a soft laugh, then turned to look at him, her expression serious. "Maybe it's the fact that you're finally being honest. You know, it's refreshing to see you without that cold mask."

He studied her for a moment, the intensity in his gaze sending a shiver down her spine. "Do you think I enjoy hiding behind that mask, Alessia?" His voice was low, almost a whisper, but it carried a weight he rarely revealed. "Maybe it's all that keeps me safe."

She fell silent, touched by the confession. Then, in a move that surprised even herself, she stepped closer and took his hand. "I think you're more than that mask, Matteo. And I'm willing to find out what lies behind it if you'll let me."

Matteo froze for a moment, his eyes fixed on their intertwined hands. It was as if her touch was stripping him of all his defenses. He lifted his gaze to meet hers, a glimmer of vulnerability in his eyes she had never seen before. "Are you sure you want to step into this part of my life? Because I can assure you, Alessia, it's full of shadows."

She gave him a half-smile, unafraid. "Shadows don't scare me, Matteo. I've lived among them myself. Maybe that's why I can see you."

A tense silence hung between them, and then, slowly, Matteo leaned closer, until their faces were so close she could feel his breath. His eyes locked onto hers, as if he were trying to read every thought, every feeling.

"You know that once you truly see me, there's no going back," he whispered, his voice deep and heavy with emotion. "I'm not the kind of man who loves lightly, Alessia. And I have a feeling you're not the kind of woman who settles for the superficial."

She held his gaze, her eyes shining with determination. "Then show me, Matteo. Show me who you really are."

He closed his eyes briefly, as though gathering courage, and when he opened them again, Alessia felt the full force of his gaze, a depth that nearly made her step back. Matteo then gently pulled her closer, wrapping her in an embrace that, despite its strength, was filled with a tenderness she never thought him capable of.

"You're a courageous woman, Alessia," he murmured, with a mix of affection and reverence. "And that courage is what attracts and disarms me at the same time."

She smiled, leaning into him until their lips met in a kiss that was soft but full of intensity. It wasn't just a kiss of desire; it was one filled with unspoken promises, a silent surrender. The world around them seemed to fade, and they both knew that from that moment, their relationship had changed forever.

When they pulled apart, Alessia looked at him with a mischievous smile. "Don't think that means I'll make things easy for you, Matteo."

He let out a low laugh, clearly enchanted by the gleam of challenge in her eyes. "I wouldn't expect anything else. In fact, I think that's why I'm so fascinated by you."

She shrugged, with a playful smile. "Well, someone has to challenge the 'all-powerful Matteo' every now and then."

He shook his head, but the smile on his lips revealed genuine satisfaction. "You're unbearably stubborn, Alessia. And that's precisely what makes you... irresistible."

Alessia's heart raced again, but she held her ground. "And you're unbearably arrogant, yet it seems I can't resist either."

They laughed together, and for a moment, it was as if all the conflicts, provocations, and fights had disappeared, leaving only the pure, profound connection growing between them. Even knowing the road ahead would be difficult and full of challenges, Alessia felt, for the first time, ready to face whatever came, alongside Matteo. And, as surprising as it was, he seemed ready to do the same.

From that night on, nothing would ever be the same.

# Chapter 26: A Revelatory Dinner

The Romano mansion was magnificently illuminated that night, every detail meticulously planned to showcase the family's wealth and power. The dining hall was decorated with luxurious floral arrangements and tables set with fine china, creating an atmosphere of unbreakable alliance in the eyes of the guests. But Alessia could feel the weight of every glance, every whispered word, every gesture that masked hidden interests and ambitions.

Sitting next to Matteo, she maintained an upright posture while he seemed completely at ease, as if that environment were his own territory. Matteo was a figure of strength and control by her side, and although Alessia was accustomed to this imposing presence, that night she felt a different connection. He was not just her fiancé for convenience; Matteo, in some way, was becoming her protector.

As the dinner unfolded, Alessia noticed how he responded coldly to the poisonous and deceitful comments of the guests, especially those who alluded to the troubled history between their families. Matteo kept a composed expression, but Alessia noticed the slight narrowing of his eyes and the tension in his shoulders every time a malicious insinuation was directed at her.

At a critical moment, one of the older men in the room, a distant associate, stood up with a cynical smile, clearly eager to cause embarrassment.

"Interesting how these alliances happen," he remarked, his voice laden with insinuation. "After all, not long ago, the Romanos and the DeLucas were on opposite sides. It's surprising to see how the wounds of the past can be forgotten so easily."

Alessia felt the blood drain from her face. She knew the man was about to touch on something her family had always tried to keep hidden—an old, painful story wrapped in secrets. The tension around the table was palpable, and all eyes turned to her, as if waiting for a reaction.

Before she could respond, Matteo spoke up. "There's a difference between forgetting and moving on," he said, his voice firm and authoritative. "Some of us understand that the past belongs to the past. And anyone who seeks to revive those shadows may need to reconsider their relevance in this environment."

Matteo's tone was cold and unyielding, and Alessia felt a mix of admiration and surprise. He hadn't hesitated to defend her, to set a clear boundary to protect her integrity and the alliance they were building. Matteo was no longer just an ally in that moment; he was a shield, someone who, despite everything, seemed willing to protect her from the venomous intentions of others.

After the dinner, as the guests dispersed, Alessia and Matteo finally found a moment alone. She pulled him into a more secluded corner, where the music and the other conversations couldn't reach them. Her heart was still racing, confused between gratitude and distrust.

"Why did you do that?" Alessia asked, looking at him, her eyes searching for an answer she could understand. "You... defended me, but you went beyond what I expected. I don't understand what that means."

Matteo looked at her intensely, his eyes darkened by something Alessia couldn't define. "I defended you because no one has the right to touch something that belongs to you," he said, his voice low but firm. "As long as you're with me, as long as you're mine, Alessia, no one will dare harm you without facing the consequences."

Alessia felt a shiver run through her body. Matteo's words carried something that went beyond mere protection; there was an intensity that spoke of possession, but also of a fierce loyalty, a silent commitment he might not even admit to himself. She knew it was a dangerous game to allow that kind of bond to strengthen, but she couldn't help the admiration she felt.

"And you think that makes me your property?" she provoked, her voice tinged with sarcasm. "Do you think that because you protect me, you have some right over me?"

He smiled, that enigmatic smile that always left her unsure of what to expect. "I think the right I have is something you're still trying to understand, Alessia," he replied, his tone challenging. "But I also know that this goes far beyond any alliance between families. Maybe you just need to accept that, despite all your resistance, something between us is undeniable."

She narrowed her eyes, but couldn't help a smile. "You're unbearable," she murmured, though the tone was softer than she intended.

He tilted his head, his gaze penetrating. "And you, Alessia, are as stubborn as anyone. But that's exactly what I admire about you."

The silence that followed between them was thick with tension, almost electrifying. Matteo, in an unexpected gesture, placed his hand on her face, his fingers tracing a soft line along her cheek. Alessia felt the touch like a spark, an electric current that connected her to him irreversibly.

"You'll never bow to me, will you?" he whispered, his voice rough and intense.

She raised her gaze, her eyes gleaming with a challenge he had come to admire. "And would you expect anything different?"

Matteo laughed softly, his hand still on her face. "No, Alessia. It's exactly what keeps me by your side."

They stayed like that for a few moments, connected by a silent understanding that defied the conventions of their world. The distance between them seemed to vanish, and before she realized it, Alessia found herself leaning in toward him, allowing herself to forget, at least for a moment, the barriers they had built.

When their lips touched, it was as if all the weight of that night disappeared, leaving only the reality that, behind all the provocations, there was an undeniable connection. Matteo pulled her closer, the kiss deep and possessive, as if he wanted to mark her, to show that, despite everything, she was a part of him.

When they pulled away, both were breathing heavily, but Matteo's gaze upon her was softer, and Alessia felt something shift inside her. He was no longer just the man she had been forced to accept. Matteo was her partner, someone who, in a strange and unexpected way, had become a part of her world in a way she could not deny.

That night, while the world around them continued with its games of power and control, Alessia knew that something inside her had changed. Matteo was no longer her enemy.

As Alessia tried to process what had happened at dinner, Matteo's presence still hovered over her like both a comforting and challenging shadow. His touch was still imprinted on her skin, and the intensity of his gaze continued to burn in her mind, leaving her unsettled. Matteo had this ability to lift her off the ground, to make her defenses crumble, but he did it in such an unexpected and mysterious way that she never knew what to expect from him. It was that which kept her attracted to him, even though, with each step, she tried to resist what she was feeling.

Matteo, on the other hand, felt a mixture of triumph and hesitation. By defending Alessia, he had realized that she was no longer just a piece in a power game. Alessia, with all her strength and audacity, was a woman who challenged him in ways he had never imagined. And he felt that it wasn't just his responsibility to protect her—it was his need, almost an obsession. Matteo knew that the moment he defended her publicly, he had made a silent promise of loyalty that went beyond any family alliance obligation.

He watched her, seeing the mix of surprise and determination on her face, and smiled faintly. Approaching her once more, with an intense and provocative look, he whispered, "Are you trying to figure me out, Alessia? Because if you are, good luck. I'm more complex than you think."

She rolled her eyes, trying to maintain composure. "Matteo, you're not as complicated as you think. You're too predictable, always needing to prove you're the strongest, the most impenetrable. I know there's something more beyond that."

He laughed softly, clearly enjoying the challenge. "You think you know me so well, huh? And what would you do if you found out you're wrong?"

Alessia lifted her face, staring at him closely. "Then prove I'm wrong. Show me you're not just this arrogant, controlling man."

Matteo gently took her chin, leaning in until their lips were mere centimeters apart. The proximity between them was electrifying, and both seemed to hold their breath, immersed in an almost unbearable tension.

"Be careful what you ask for, Alessia," he whispered, his voice low and intense. "Maybe I'll show you things you're not ready to see."

She felt her heart race but refused to back down. "Don't underestimate my ability to face the truth, Matteo. The question is: are you ready to show it?"

Matteo smiled, a smile that was both challenging and intrigued. He knew she was playing with him, challenging him in a way no one ever had. And to his surprise, he loved the challenge. Releasing her, he took a step back, watching her with a look that mixed admiration and provocation.

"You want answers, Alessia, but you also want to control this game. The question is: who controls who here?" His voice was deep, almost a whisper, and Alessia felt a shiver run down her spine.

She lifted her chin, her eyes shining. "That's something we may never know. But I'm willing to play, if you are."

He chuckled softly, extending his hand to her. Alessia hesitated but finally took his hand, feeling the comforting warmth of his palm against hers. For a moment, time seemed to stop, and the connection between them intensified, as if they were intertwined by something stronger than pride or attraction.

"Let the game begin," Matteo whispered, pulling her closer. His lips lightly brushed her face, in a gesture that felt both tender and a calculated mark of his claim.

And in that moment, Alessia realized that the lines between them were not just blurred—they were being completely redrawn.

# Chapter 27: On the Edge of Desire

The mansion was silent. The last guests had left, and now Alessia and Matteo were alone, surrounded by the dim light of the hall, where only a few soft lights remained on. The tension between them was almost tangible, as if the air was saturated with something they had both been desperately trying to avoid, but that now seemed inevitable.

Alessia felt her heart race as she tried to control the whirlwind of emotions consuming her. Since the moment Matteo had defended her at dinner, something inside her had shifted. He was no longer just the cold, calculating man who had tried to control her; Matteo had become an inescapable presence, a mixture of protection and desire, destabilizing her in every possible way.

Matteo watched her in silence, his intense and penetrating eyes fixed on her, as if he were trying to decipher every thought that crossed her mind. He took a step forward, and Alessia felt her body tremble at his proximity. Every word, every movement between them seemed charged with electricity, something both of them knew they could not control much longer.

"Alessia," he murmured, his voice low and full of intensity that made her hold her breath. "Tell me, why do you try so hard to resist what's happening between us?"

She looked away, trying to hide the tumult of feelings bubbling inside her. "Because I know exactly who you are, Matteo," she whispered in return. "And I know that giving in to this... to you... would be like losing all the control I still have."

He took another step forward, coming so close that she could feel the warmth of his body near hers. Matteo raised his hand and traced a soft line along her arm, a touch that was both gentle and possessive. Alessia felt a shiver run through her skin, every sense on alert.

"Maybe you're afraid to discover that this control was never really in your hands," he teased, a half-smile on his lips, though his gaze still burned with fierce desire. "And perhaps the only thing that keeps you here, by my side, is that attraction you refuse to admit."

She took a deep breath, trying to gather her strength to resist, but she felt her defenses crumbling. "You're impossible," she muttered, her voice breaking, trying to stay composed but knowing he could see through every crack in her armor.

Matteo moved even closer, until their faces were so close she could feel his breath against her skin. "Yes, and maybe that's exactly why you can't stay away," he murmured, his lips almost brushing hers, as if waiting for a response, a sign.

For a moment that felt like an eternity, Alessia struggled against the overwhelming pull drawing her to him, but at the same time, something inside her was surrendering, eager to cross the line she had drawn. And in that instant of hesitation, Matteo seized her waist, pulling her firmly against him. Their lips finally met, and the kiss they shared was an explosion of everything they had repressed until that moment—hatred, desire, anger, and an intensity that seemed to burn.

Alessia felt herself consumed, swept away by Matteo's passion, and for an instant, she forgot all the reasons she had tried to resist. His arms enveloped her tightly, as though she were something he feared losing. She clung to him, forgetting all logic, all consequences, and allowed herself to feel, for once, something that went beyond understanding.

When the kiss ended, both were breathless, their hearts racing, but still wrapped up in each other. Matteo looked at her as if he were hypnotized, but Alessia felt a wave of doubt and panic wash over her. She knew she couldn't let herself be carried away so easily, that there was still something insurmountable between them.

"This was a mistake," she murmured, pulling away, her voice trembling but trying to maintain her composure.

Matteo didn't let her go. "A mistake?" He raised an eyebrow, clearly irritated by her attempt to retreat. "If it was a mistake, then why did you give in so completely?"

She stared at him, trying to find the right words. "Because, no matter how hard I try, I can't ignore this attraction. But that doesn't mean I can just... surrender. Not to you, Matteo."

He sighed in frustration, but his eyes locked onto hers with even greater intensity. "Alessia, there are things between us that you might never understand. But what I feel for you... this connection between us... it's real, whether you want to accept it or not."

She closed her eyes for a moment, fighting the emotions threatening to overflow. The way he spoke, the weight of his words, made her question her own resistance. "But I can't just ignore everything you represent, everything this means for me."

He cupped her face in his hands, forcing her to look him in the eye. "Then what do you want, Alessia? Do you want me to pretend that I feel nothing for you? To step back and let you live in this illusion of control? Because if that's what you want, you're just fooling yourself."

She felt tears beginning to form, a mix of frustration and desire consuming her. "I don't know, Matteo. I don't know what to do with this."

He pulled her back into his arms, this time with a tenderness that surprised her, and whispered in her ear, "Then stop fighting, just once. Let yourself feel. Because, no matter how hard we try to resist, we know this between us is inevitable."

She closed her eyes, allowing herself to relax in his arms for a brief moment, surrendering to that shared moment of vulnerability. Matteo held her tightly, as if she were the anchor he had been searching for, and Alessia realized that, no matter how hard she tried to run, he was a presence that had already taken root in her heart in an irreversible way.

As silence enveloped them again, both knew they had crossed a line with no return. And though there were still doubts and fears, there was also a deep certainty—that, in some way, they were destined to face this whirlwind together, whatever the future held for them both.

Alessia felt the heat of Matteo's proximity, and it left her in a state of alertness mixed with a sense of surrender she had never imagined she would experience. It was a mix of adrenaline and peace, as if being near him was as risky as it was inevitable. She could not deny what he represented, not just in her life, but within herself. Matteo drew her in a way that transcended reason, touching parts of her she didn't even know existed. Every touch, every intense look he gave her seemed to disarm her and prepare her for battle at the same time.

Matteo, for his part, was also immersed in a whirlwind of emotions he didn't know how to control. Alessia had become his greatest provocation, a constant challenge that made him feel a spark he had believed was long gone. He knew she was independent and strong, and that strength attracted him. But at the same time, it was that resistance of hers that also challenged him the most. Seeing the spark of defiance in her eyes was a constant reminder that he had found someone who was his equal, someone who didn't bow to him—and that fascinated him.

"So, what will it be, Alessia?" he asked, his tone a mix of provocation and desire, keeping his gaze locked with hers, as if trying to read her thoughts.

She sighed, trying not to get lost in his stare. "I don't know, Matteo. That's what confuses me."

He leaned in, bringing their faces even closer, until she could feel the heat of his breath on her skin. "If there's one thing I can guarantee, Alessia, it's that I'm not the kind of man who gives up easily."

She lifted her chin, determined not to show vulnerability. "That doesn't surprise me one bit. You're stubborn, controlling, and... intensely irritating."

He smiled, a smile full of confidence, but also one that carried a softness only Alessia seemed to be able to see. "And you're no different. You're a woman impossible to control, unpredictable... and yet, exactly what I need."

His words surprised her, and she looked away for a moment, feeling her heart race. "And what does that mean, Matteo?" she whispered, unsure whether she truly wanted to hear the answer.

He gently held her face, forcing her to look at him. "It means that, no matter how much you try to resist, I'm going to stay here. And it's not to control you, Alessia. It's because I've finally found someone who understands what it means to fight every day. You're my strength and my challenge, and maybe you're everything I need."

Alessia swallowed hard, feeling a shiver run down her spine. Matteo wasn't the kind of man to make declarations lightly, and his words were like an unexpected confession, a vulnerability he was revealing only to her.

She gave a faint smile, regaining some of her composure. "So, you're saying that I'm the only one capable of challenging the great Matteo DeLuca?"

He laughed softly, brushing his thumb over her face. "You're the only one I allow to do that."

There was a moment of silence between them, a connection that transcended words. Alessia's heart was pounding, and she knew that, no matter how much she tried, she could no longer deny what she felt. Finally, with a defiant smile, she murmured, "I don't promise that it'll be easy. Not for you, and not for me."

He smiled, a sincere smile full of admiration. "I wouldn't expect anything less from you, Alessia. And that's exactly why you're the woman I've chosen."

In the face of that declaration, Alessia felt torn between the desire to run and the urge to surrender completely to him. Matteo was not just a powerful man; he was the man who, against all odds, had won her heart. In the end, she took a step toward him, closing the distance between them. The kiss that followed was soft yet intense, as if they were both finally accepting what they had been avoiding for so long.

As they pulled apart, Alessia realized that, for the first time, she was at peace with the surrender she had experienced. Matteo was her provocation and her passion, a man with whom she was willing to face any battle.

# Chapter 28: Matteo's Vulnerability

After the intense and unexpected kiss, Alessia found herself in a state of emotional confusion. She tried to convince herself that it meant nothing, that she was still capable of maintaining the necessary distance between herself and Matteo. However, the weight of the moment still lingered in her mind. She knew that Matteo was not someone who allowed himself weaknesses, and in that kiss, there was something deeper, something that shook all her convictions.

Matteo, on the other hand, was visibly different. He had spent the morning silent, with a distant, almost melancholic expression that Alessia had never seen before. He didn't address her with his usual provocative remarks nor adopt his usual imposing posture. Instead, Matteo seemed to be carrying an invisible burden, a weight that only he could understand.

By late afternoon, Alessia found him alone in the mansion's library, the soft light of the setting sun partially illuminating his face, highlighting the shadow in his eyes. Matteo was lost in thought, a glass of whiskey in hand, staring into the void. Alessia hesitated at the door, feeling as if she were about to intrude on a rare, intimate moment. However, the desire to understand what was going through his mind was stronger.

"Matteo?" she called, her voice low and hesitant.

He slowly lifted his eyes, as though awakening from a daydream. Upon seeing her, he tried to compose himself, but Alessia noticed the vulnerability in his gaze, a flicker of something undefinable, as if he had been caught off guard.

"I'm sorry, I didn't mean to disturb you," she said, about to turn away, but he stopped her with a gesture.

"No, stay," Matteo replied, his voice softer than usual. "Maybe... maybe I need someone here."

Alessia entered the library cautiously, unsure of how to behave. The distance between them felt smaller now, although neither of them moved. There was something in the air, a silent understanding, an improbable truce between two tired warriors.

"You seem... different today," Alessia remarked bluntly. "Like something is weighing on you."

Matteo smiled, but it was a tired smile, lacking the arrogance he usually displayed. "Maybe because it is. There are things, Alessia, that I can't control. And that's... new for me."

She fell silent, absorbing every word. Matteo rarely spoke about himself, and this moment felt as fragile as it was precious. Alessia felt a wave of compassion she had never expected to feel for him.

"It's hard for me to admit," he continued, looking away. "But as much as I try to keep everything under control, you... you affect me in a way I don't understand. And frankly, that scares me."

His words struck her deeply, and Alessia felt her heart tighten. Matteo, the man who had always been impenetrable, was now confessing a fear she herself carried, and it was impossible not to feel a connection to him.

"I don't understand what it means either," Alessia admitted, her voice trembling but honest. "But I know we're caught in something much bigger than us. And no matter how hard I try, I can't escape it."

Matteo looked at her with an intensity that made her catch her breath. He approached slowly, step by step, until he was mere inches from her. "The truth, Alessia, is that trusting someone is something I've always feared. And that hasn't changed. But with you... I feel that maybe, just maybe, it's possible."

She swallowed, unsure how to respond. Matteo disarmed her in ways no one else could, and now, as she watched him so close, she felt exposed yet somehow safe.

"I don't promise it will be easy," Matteo continued, his gaze fixed on hers. "Trust is something I lost a long time ago. And, to be honest, I don't know if I'm ready to trust anyone again."

Alessia felt the sincerity in every word he spoke, and it touched her deeply. Matteo, after all, was not just the controlled and calculating man she thought he was. He was someone who had been hurt, someone who carried invisible scars.

"I understand, Matteo," she murmured, her eyes fixed on his. "Believe me, I understand more than you think."

He studied her for a moment, as though seeing beyond her words, as if he were finally truly seeing her. Matteo reached out, gently touching her face, his thumb tracing a soft line along her cheek. It was a touch full of tenderness, a rare vulnerability he was allowing her to witness.

"Why don't you give up?" he asked, his voice low and almost inaudible. "Why do you stay here, despite everything?"

Alessia smiled softly, holding his hand against her face. "Because, somehow, I feel like it's worth it. And because I see something in you that maybe you don't see."

Matteo let out a deep sigh, as though he were finally releasing the weight he had been carrying. He moved closer, until their faces were mere millimeters apart, and Alessia could feel his breath against her skin. There were no words, only a silence charged with emotions they both understood without needing to express them.

He kissed her, and the kiss was different from all the others. There was no urgency or possessiveness, just a silent surrender, a request for understanding, and a gesture of trust. Alessia felt a sense of peace and warmth invade her, as though they had finally found a connection that didn't require words.

When they pulled away, Matteo still held her face, and she could see the transformation in his eyes, a tenderness he had never shown before. There was a new understanding between them, a silent bond that connected them on a deep and real level.

Alessia knew that this moment wouldn't solve everything, that Matteo's wounds wouldn't disappear overnight, but she felt that, for the first time, they had broken a barrier. Matteo had finally allowed her access to his true self, and she knew that from then on, nothing would be the same.

After the moment of sincerity they shared, Alessia felt her heart racing. She was confused, but at the same time, she felt an inexplicable serenity. Seeing Matteo open up like that, showing his vulnerability, revealing a side she never imagined existed, was like looking beyond the walls of a castle that seemed impenetrable. And as much as she tried to maintain her pride, Alessia couldn't ignore how deeply it moved her. Matteo was no longer just the arrogant, controlling enemy; he had become someone real, someone she wanted to understand and, perhaps, in a way she didn't yet fully comprehend, someone she wanted to help heal.

Matteo, on the other hand, felt inexplicably exposed. Showing his vulnerability to Alessia was something he had never imagined doing, yet here he was, vulnerable and unprotected, with her eyes fixed on him as though she could see all the scars he had buried so deep. But instead of feeling fear, he felt a strange peace, as if, for the first time in a long time, he was being understood. Alessia seemed to understand the shadows that surrounded him, and that made him feel a little lighter.

"So, you really think it's worth trying to understand me?" Matteo broke the silence, his voice soft, but with a hint of provocation, the old habit of hiding behind challenging words.

Alessia smiled slightly, her gaze firm and challenging. "Don't think I'm here to fix you, Matteo. I'm just curious to see what's behind that iron exterior of yours. Besides, someone needs to remind you that you're not as untouchable as you think."

He let out a low laugh, almost incredulous. "You really know how to test a man's patience, Alessia. Sometimes I think your purpose is just to challenge me."

She looked at him with a playful gleam in her eyes. "And isn't that exactly what you like about me, Matteo? That I don't bend, that I'm not intimidated by your supposed power?"

Matteo studied her for a moment, letting the truth settle in the silence. "Maybe you're right. Maybe that's exactly what draws me to you... and also what drives me absolutely crazy."

Alessia felt her heart race at those words but held her posture firm, not letting him see the intensity of her reaction. "So it seems we're at an impasse, Matteo. Two stubborn people who don't know how to give in."

He moved closer, his intense gaze locking onto hers. "Who said I want you to give in? Maybe all I want is for you to stay exactly as you are—an uncontrollable force, a challenge I never get tired of facing."

She held her breath, trying not to let him see the effect his words had on her. But Matteo was perceptive, and the smile he gave her told her he knew exactly what he was doing.

"This all sounds like a very well-crafted excuse to hide the fact that you're... in love with me, Matteo," Alessia teased, her words laced with sarcasm, but her eyes betraying the seriousness she truly felt.

Matteo raised an eyebrow, leaning in even closer, until their faces were dangerously close. "In love, Alessia? Do you think I'm that predictable? No. What I feel isn't love—it's something far more complicated... and, frankly, much more interesting."

Alessia swallowed, feeling herself drawn even closer to him, but unwilling to give in. She knew they were both caught in a dangerous game, a battle of wills and emotions that could either lead to uncontrollable passion or devastating war.

"Well, if you don't know what it is, I'm not going to explain it to you," she answered, in a challenging tone, trying to hold back the smile that was threatening to break through.

Matteo laughed, and the sound was deep and enveloping, a laugh that seemed to come from a very deep place. "Alessia, you're... insufferable," he said, but there was a warmth in his gaze that contradicted every word.

She rolled her eyes, but the smile was now impossible to hide. "And you're not much better, Matteo."

Before she could realize it, he grabbed her face with one hand, the touch both firm and gentle. The intensity of the contact disarmed her, and for a moment, both of them stood still, their breaths synchronized, their hearts beating in the same rhythm. He leaned in slowly, his lips almost touching hers.

"Tell me to stop, Alessia. Because if you don't, I won't be able to," he whispered, his voice rough, a final attempt at self-control.

She closed her eyes for a brief moment, allowing herself to feel the weight of that moment, the intensity of the connection between them. Finally, she opened her eyes and met his gaze, a look that said everything her words couldn't.

"I won't tell you to stop, Matteo," she replied, her voice barely audible, but filled with devastating sincerity.

And then, at last, he kissed her. A deep, intense kiss, filled with all the emotions they had both hidden for so long. In the softness of that night, in a moment of surrender, Alessia and Matteo found something stronger than pride, more intense than desire: a connection that, although still uncertain, felt more real than anything either of them had ever experienced.

# Chapter 29: A Secret Meeting

Alessia needed a breath, a moment to gather her thoughts. After the overwhelming kiss and all the confessions shared with Matteo, she felt lost, torn between the desire to maintain her pride and the overwhelming attraction that threatened to tear down her last defenses. She knew she couldn't ignore what was happening between them, but she also couldn't fully surrender. There was something dangerous in that path, a thin line that could lead to surrender or to the destruction of both.

The next morning, after ensuring that Matteo was busy in a meeting, Alessia quietly left the mansion. She met Serena, her childhood friend, at a discreet café in the city center. Serena was the only person Alessia trusted blindly, and she desperately needed her perspective.

"Serena, I'm drowning," Alessia confessed, holding the cup of tea with trembling hands. The warmth of the tea was comforting, but nothing seemed able to calm her heart at that moment.

Serena watched her with an expression of mixed understanding and concern. "Alessia, you knew that this arranged marriage with Matteo would bring complications, but it seems like there's more to it than just the forced alliance."

Alessia nodded, biting her lip as she reflected on the whirlwind of emotions Matteo provoked in her. "I wanted to hate him, Serena. I swear I did. But he... he's not what I thought. He's arrogant, controlling, and stubborn, but he's also someone marked by scars, someone who, in some way, seems to understand my own pain."

Serena looked at her seriously, leaning back in her chair and crossing her arms. "Alessia, you need to understand that opening yourself up to someone like him is risky. Matteo is a dangerous man, and I'm not just talking about his involvement with the mafia.

He lives by a logic of power and control. You need to be prepared for the consequences of getting emotionally involved with him."

Alessia sighed, confused. "I know that, Serena, but when we're together, everything feels so... real. I don't know if it's just desire or if it's something more. But I'm scared of losing control over my own life. I don't want to be just another piece in his game."

Serena took Alessia's hand firmly, her eyes filled with sincerity. "Then be cautious. Find out what you really want before making any decisions. Because, Alessia, getting emotionally involved with Matteo could be like stepping into a storm from which you may never escape unscathed."

Serena's words echoed in Alessia's heart, making her even more aware of the dangerous line she was crossing. They talked for a few more minutes, and then Alessia said goodbye, grateful for her friend's honesty, but also disturbed by the reality she had to face.

Returning to the mansion, Alessia felt exhausted, as if each step toward the entrance weighed a thousand times more than usual. Her mind swirled with Serena's warnings and the intensity Matteo exerted over her. She entered quietly, hoping to go unnoticed, but Matteo saw her as she climbed the stairs, his eyes following her inquisitively.

"Alessia, where were you?" he asked, his voice firm and laden with distrust.

She stared at him, gathering strength to hide her vulnerability. "I needed some air, Matteo. A moment for myself."

He raised an eyebrow, approaching with slow steps, his presence radiating warmth and tension that Alessia felt even from a distance. "You know I don't like surprises, Alessia. Disappearing without warning is a risk, especially with the circle of people we associate with."

Alessia snorted impatiently, trying to ignore the intense look in his eyes. "I'm not your prisoner, Matteo. I still have the right to breathe without you controlling every move I make."

Matteo narrowed his eyes, a flash of something deeper and darker crossing them. "Don't test me, Alessia. You know that if something happened to you, I'd never forgive myself."

His response caught her off guard. That brief moment of sincerity, that mention of his fear of losing her, stirred something inside her. Trying to deflect, Alessia crossed her arms and met his gaze with the remaining strength of her determination.

"You're really an enigma, Matteo. One day you push me away, the next you say things that make me think that maybe, just maybe, I'm more than just a piece for you."

Matteo fell silent for a moment, then moved closer until he was just inches away from her. The heat of his presence was so intense that Alessia could barely breathe. He raised one hand, gently tracing a line along her face, the touch both tender and possessive.

"Maybe you are, Alessia. Maybe you're the only piece in this game that truly matters."

His words left her speechless, and for the first time, Alessia saw something genuine and fragile in Matteo's gaze. She felt as though, in some way, they were both standing on the edge of an abyss. A wrong move, and they could both fall. Yet, she couldn't deny the desire growing inside her—the desire to get to know this man more, to decipher him, and to let herself be swept away by him.

Matteo leaned in, his lips just inches from hers, his breath softly brushing against her skin. "But be careful, Alessia," he murmured, his voice filled with a depth that made her heart race. "Entering my life is a one-way road."

She looked at him, trying to regain control, but Matteo's eyes were like an ocean pulling her under, impossible to resist. "Maybe it's a risk I'm willing to take," she whispered, barely recognizing the audacity in her own words.

Matteo's smile was light, but his eyes showed the intensity of a man who knew the power he wielded. He finally kissed her, and it was a kiss full of unspoken promises and a deep connection that bound them in a way both of them knew was inevitable.

The moment their lips parted, Alessia felt that there was no escape anymore. Matteo pulled her like a magnet, and she knew that, no matter how much she fought it, she was already trapped in their destiny, with all the complexities and dangers it entailed.

Alessia felt her heart pounding as though she were in an endless race. Each time Matteo drew closer, her barriers fell a little more, and it scared her. She knew that what she felt for him was more than mere physical attraction, and that realization threw her into a whirlwind of emotions. As much as she wanted to maintain distance, the connection between them was too strong to ignore. And there, after that intense kiss, she realized that, somehow, Matteo had already entered her life in a way no one else had.

"Alessia," he murmured, holding her close, his gaze fixed on her eyes. "You can deny it all you want, but I know you feel something for me."

She breathed deeply, trying to find some strength to confront him, to not give in to the intensity of the moment. "What if feeling isn't enough, Matteo?" she retorted, with a challenging look, as if she wanted to keep control of the situation. "You're used to getting everything you want, but I'm not something you can just have because you desire it."

He laughed softly, a deep and captivating sound that seemed to reverberate within her. "And that's what makes it all the more interesting. You're a strong woman, Alessia. Trying to conquer you is the only challenge worth facing."

Those words were like a shock. It was a declaration Matteo might not have made aloud if he were thinking rationally, but in that moment, Alessia saw that he was vulnerable, just as she was. It was as though they were both discovering hidden parts of each other, letting themselves be caught in a feeling neither of them had planned.

"Aren't you afraid of getting too involved, Matteo?" Alessia teased, raising an eyebrow as she watched him with a mix of challenge and curiosity.

He pulled her closer, their faces so near that she could feel his breath against her skin. "Fear has never been a problem for me," he replied, his voice low and husky. "But you... you leave me unsettled, Alessia. Maybe I'm more involved than I should be, but honestly, I don't care."

Alessia felt the weight of his words and realized that he was being completely honest. Matteo, the controlling and impassive man, was surrendering to her, even if he would never admit it directly. And, suddenly, she realized that she, too, was on a point of no return. She wanted to pull away, but something stronger held her there, and that duality between desire and pride made her vulnerable, yet filled with a new fervor.

"I'm not going to make it easy for you," she murmured, her voice breaking from the impact of their proximity. "If you want this so much, you'll have to deal with everything I am. I won't change for you, Matteo."

He smiled, a smile that showed the confidence of someone who accepted the challenge without hesitation. "I don't want you to change. I like exactly this woman who challenges me, who provokes me, and who never bends."

They both fell silent, the moment charged with a connection almost tangible, as if the world around them disappeared. Matteo leaned in slowly until his lips touched hers softly, in a different kiss from all the intense ones they had shared before. This one was delicate, almost reverent, as if he were exploring every nuance of that contact, absorbing everything she represented to him.

Alessia shivered as a chill ran through her body. That kiss was different, full of meanings she was still trying to decipher, but that made her feel deeply connected to him. When they pulled away, she looked at him, a mix of affection and challenge in her eyes.

"This doesn't change anything, Matteo," she whispered, in one last attempt not to give in completely.

He simply looked at her, the intensity in his eyes like a silent promise. "Then let's see how far this war of ours goes, Alessia. I'm willing to fight every battle if it means having you by my side."

And, in that moment, Alessia knew she was lost. She knew that resisting Matteo was like trying to contain a storm—something impossible and, at the same time, irresistible. He had become a part of her in a way no one else ever had. As they stared at each other in silence, with an understanding that needed no words, Alessia realized that, no matter what the future held, this man was irrevocably tied to her. And, for the first time, she allowed herself to accept that truth.

# Chapter 30: The Unexpected Alliance

Alessia entered the mansion in silence, the weight of her meeting with Serena still fresh in her mind. She felt more centered, but at the same time, she knew Matteo would not let her departure go unnoticed. As she approached the main room, she saw Matteo standing there, arms crossed, his expression tense, his dark eyes fixed on her.

He stepped forward as soon as she entered, his voice firm, one she already knew well. "Where have you been, Alessia?" The question was direct, but Alessia could sense the underlying tension in his expression.

She took a deep breath, determined not to hide. "I went to see Serena," she replied, keeping her tone calm. "I needed a different perspective on... all of this."

Matteo narrowed his eyes, his jaw tightening. "And you thought you shouldn't tell me? We're partners now, Alessia. You shouldn't just leave like that, without warning."

Alessia met his gaze with a defiant expression, aware that he expected an explanation. "Believe it or not, I went to talk about you. Or rather, about us," she admitted, crossing her arms as if to protect herself from the words that might follow. "And I decided I have nothing to hide. If we're going to continue with this arrangement, Matteo, you'll need to trust me."

Matteo fell silent for a moment, clearly surprised by her candor. It was as if Alessia's confession had disarmed him, and she could see the internal struggle reflected in his eyes. He was a man used to controlling everything and everyone around him, and here was Alessia, offering vulnerability that he didn't know how to accept.

"Trust," Matteo repeated, his voice almost skeptical. He walked towards her, staying close enough for Alessia to feel the intensity of his presence. "You want me to trust you, but you forget who I am, Alessia. Trust, for me, isn't something simple."

She nodded, understanding, but not yielding. "I know that, Matteo. And I'm like that too. But we can't keep playing this control game forever. If we want stability, if we're really going to form this alliance, then we need more than just tolerance."

Matteo watched her closely, and then a faint — almost imperceptible — smile appeared at the corner of his lips. "You really believe this alliance can be built without one of us trying to control the other?"

Alessia lifted her chin, standing firm. "I'm not saying it'll be easy. But if we're both willing to try... maybe we can find a balance. Maybe we can leave the past where it belongs."

Matteo crossed his arms, his gaze still intense, but less aggressive. After a long silence, he sighed and nodded. "Very well. Let's try."

Alessia blinked in mild surprise, not expecting him to agree so easily. Matteo rarely gave in, and here he was, proposing a truce.

"But," he continued, a challenging gleam returning to his eyes, "this doesn't mean I'll stop protecting you, Alessia. That's part of who I am. I can't just ignore what's at stake."

Alessia smiled, feeling a wave of relief mixed with a strange admiration for the man. "I don't expect you to change who you are, Matteo. But I want you to understand that I won't change who I am either."

He took a step closer, allowing the heat of his presence to surround her. "Then we have a deal, Alessia. A truce. But that doesn't mean the battle is over."

She gave him a slight smile, noticing the playful glint in his eyes. "I wouldn't expect anything less."

For a moment, they stood in silence, simply staring at each other, both aware that this agreement was a turning point. In an unexpected gesture, Matteo extended his hand to her. Alessia looked at it in surprise, but took it, feeling the firmness of his grip.

"If we're going to work together," he said, his voice softer, "we need to learn to trust. But know this, Alessia, I'm still a cautious man. And trust is something I take time to give."

She nodded, still feeling the touch of his hand. "I don't expect less, Matteo. But I believe that, if we're careful, we can find a way to make this work."

They slowly released their hands, but the contact left a mark. From that moment on, the tension between them felt different. There was something deeper, a fragile but real bond that tied them together in a way that went beyond the mere contractual alliance between their families.

That night, Alessia felt a newfound confidence rising within her, and Matteo seemed lighter, as if, for the first time, he had allowed someone to truly understand him. This silent pact was a beginning, an opportunity to look beyond the wounds and walls they had both built.

Though neither of them knew exactly what the future held, the newly-formed alliance was an important step. As Alessia climbed the stairs, she wondered if this agreement would be the beginning of a true partnership, or the prelude to an even more intense battle.

Alessia climbed the stairs in silence, but her mind was far from calm. What had just happened between her and Matteo seemed like an unexpected breakthrough, a silent truce that changed the course of the relationship they had been building. She found herself smiling involuntarily as she remembered the feel of his hand, firm and warm, offering a kind of security that surprised her. For the first time, she felt Matteo saw her as an equal, someone worthy of respect and not just a pawn in his game of power. But at the same time, the vulnerability he had allowed scared her, as if giving in to it meant losing control over her own feelings.

Still, the fear of losing control also drew her in. There was something about Matteo that challenged her in every way, something that made her want to uncover every hidden part of him, every layer beneath that cold façade. Alessia knew that giving in to that curiosity could be dangerous, but a part of her had already surrendered, albeit reluctantly.

While lost in her thoughts, she didn't notice when Matteo came up the stairs and stopped at her door. She felt her heart race when she heard his voice, low and provocative.

"Thinking of running away again, Alessia?" he asked, his smile bordering on sarcasm, but with an unusual softness in his expression.

Alessia crossed her arms, raising an eyebrow, determined not to give him the satisfaction of knowing how much his presence affected her. "I wasn't thinking of running away. Just wondering how your 'truce' will probably be broken the first chance you get to control every step I take."

Matteo took a step closer, his smile deepening, but his intense gaze never wavering. "Maybe, but I believe we understand each other now. Who knows, maybe we'll surprise each other with this alliance."

She rolled her eyes, but a soft laugh escaped her lips. "Matteo, do you really think someone like you knows what it means to yield? I bet you're just waiting for the right moment to take control again."

He watched her in silence for a moment, his face now inches from hers, causing Alessia to hold her breath. "You think I can't yield, Alessia?" He was challenging her, but his tone was almost vulnerable. "Then tell me, what do you want me to do?"

For a moment, Alessia lost the ability to respond. Matteo was right there, close enough for her to feel his scent, that intoxicating touch that made her forget everything around her. And he was offering her a choice, something she never imagined she would have.

"I want you to let me be who I am, Matteo," she replied, her voice soft but firm. "I want you to see me as your partner, not as a possession or an adversary."

He nodded slowly, absorbing her words with a seriousness that made her feel exposed but also strangely safe. Matteo reached up, lightly touching her face, his thumb tracing a soft line across her cheek. It was a touch full of affection and an intensity that Alessia had never seen before.

"I see that, Alessia. I'm trying," he whispered. "But you need to know... it's not easy for me. Being by your side forces me to deal with parts of myself I didn't even know existed."

Alessia felt a wave of understanding wash over her. This man, who seemed indestructible, had his own battles, and being with her seemed to be one of them. She reached up and touched his face, as if to reassure herself that this was real, that Matteo was truly allowing himself to be vulnerable before her.

"I'm not asking you to change, Matteo. I just want you to let me see who you really are," she murmured, her sincerity leaving them both in silence, trapped in a moment of mutual understanding.

Matteo leaned in, and this time, the kiss was gentle, filled with a tenderness they rarely shared. There was no urgency or tension like in their previous encounters, but a quiet understanding, as if this simple gesture was the answer to all the doubts they had carried.

When they pulled away, neither of them spoke, but the look they exchanged said more than any words could. Matteo took a step back, leaving her face with a gentleness that almost surprised him.

"Goodnight, Alessia," he said, a subtle smile playing at his lips as he turned to leave, but not without casting one last look over his shoulder, as if he knew that this moment would stay with them.

Alessia stood there, watching him disappear down the hallway, her heart still racing. She knew there was something both dangerous and fascinating in opening up to him in that way. Matteo wasn't just a man; he was a storm, a force of nature, and now she knew she was willing to face that storm, even without knowing what lay ahead.

# Chapter 31: The First Crack in the Truce

The days following the peace agreement between Alessia and Matteo brought a cautious coexistence. Both maintained the commitment to their alliance, but the tension still hung in the air, like a storm on the verge of breaking. For Alessia, staying submissive was impossible—it went against her determined personality. And Matteo, though he tried to give in, was constantly reminded of his deeply ingrained controlling instinct.

One evening, after returning from an outing with Serena without informing him, Alessia found Matteo waiting for her in the living room. His serious expression and dark eyes fixed on her made it feel like she had broken some sacred pact.

"Why did you leave without telling me?" he asked, his voice controlled but carrying an underlying frustration.

She sighed, tired of the constant discussions about the control he insisted on exerting. "Matteo, I'm free to come and go as I please. I don't need permission."

He narrowed his eyes, visibly irritated. "I'm not talking about permission, Alessia. I'm talking about safety. I'm the head of this house, and that includes making sure you're protected."

Alessia crossed her arms, defiant. "I thought we agreed on an alliance based on mutual respect. You can't demand submission and treat me like a possession."

"And I thought we had an understanding about the need for caution," he shot back, taking a step forward, his presence dominating the space between them. "I can't just ignore the danger around us, Alessia. If something were to happen to you..."

Alessia interrupted him, impatient. "Are you protecting me or controlling me, Matteo? Because to me, those two things look the same."

They both stood in silence for a moment, their heavy breaths filling the room. Matteo watched her, his hard gaze softening slightly. Part of him understood Alessia's point, but his instinct to protect her—to keep everything under his control—spoke louder.

"Is it too much to ask that you let me know where you are? So I can make sure nothing happens?" he asked, his tone wavering between an order and a request—something rare for someone so used to imposing his will.

She took a deep breath, trying to find the balance between giving in and preserving her freedom. "Matteo, I understand your concern. But you need to understand that I'm not an object for you to watch over all the time. If this alliance is going to work, I need you to trust me enough to know that I can take care of myself."

Matteo clenched his fists, visibly trying to contain his frustration. There was something about the way Alessia stood firm that both attracted him and challenged him to let go of his own pride. However, conceding to Alessia meant facing his own fears—and for him, that was harder than he cared to admit.

Finally, he let out a sigh and gave a small nod. "Alright, Alessia. If that's what it takes for you to feel respected, then I accept. But know that my concern won't just disappear."

Alessia gave a small, relieved smile, surprised by his agreement. She knew that for Matteo, that small gesture of trust was a big victory, a crack in the defenses he so carefully guarded.

"Thank you, Matteo," she said, softening her tone. "Believe me, I don't want to complicate our relationship further. I just want you to respect that I can make my own decisions."

Matteo stepped forward, getting so close that Alessia could feel the heat of his presence. He raised his hand and gently touched her face, tracing the line of her jaw with his thumb, his gaze softening as he looked at her.

"I respect your strength, Alessia," he murmured, his voice carrying a sincerity she rarely saw. "But know that this strength is what drives me crazy. It's a constant battle for me to understand that you're not someone I can simply... protect the way I want to."

She felt her heart race, the depth of his gaze revealing a vulnerable side of him he rarely allowed to show. It was as though Matteo was, for the first time, revealing his weaknesses, his fears—and that created an intimacy that drew her in inescapably.

"Maybe our alliance doesn't need protection, Matteo," she replied, her voice low and tremulous. "Maybe what we need is to find a way to... coexist, without one trying to dominate the other."

He nodded, his eyes never leaving hers. "Then that's what we'll do," he said, his voice firm but carrying a lightness that felt liberating. "I'll try... to trust you. But you need to know, Alessia, that this won't be easy for me."

She smiled, touching his hand still resting on her face. "I know. And I'll appreciate every small concession you make."

The silence that followed between them was thick with a deep understanding. In a rare gesture, Matteo pulled her into an embrace, holding her with a firmness that conveyed security. For Alessia, that touch was more than just physical closeness; it was a sign that Matteo was willing to go beyond his own limits to build something real with her.

"I don't want to lose you, Alessia," he murmured, the words slipping out like a silent confession.

She closed her eyes, allowing herself to sink into the feeling of being held by him, knowing that, for the first time, Matteo was truly being sincere about his emotions. And there, Alessia knew that, no matter how complicated their relationship was, there was a strong, unbreakable bond between them.

Both knew that any misstep could ruin everything, but for the first time, they felt ready to face this journey side by side.

Alessia felt Matteo's embrace wrap around her body, creating a sense of safety and connection that she hadn't expected to feel. At first, she had resisted the closeness, but seeing the sincerity reflected in his eyes and feeling the firm grip on her back, she allowed herself to relax against him, experiencing something she rarely allowed—vulnerability. His scent, the firmness of his arms around her, and the steady rhythm of his breath beside her face made her lose herself for a moment, allowing her to forget the constant conflict between them.

"This is getting complicated, isn't it?" Alessia murmured, her voice soft, almost fearful of breaking the moment they shared.

Matteo smiled lightly, his hand stroking her back in a tender, possessive gesture. "Complicated is our common ground, Alessia. Maybe we'll never know what's easy," he replied, his tone carrying a light provocation, but with a sincerity that touched her deeply.

Alessia pulled back just enough to look at him, her eyes a mix of challenge and tenderness. "And who said I wanted easy?" she retorted, with a mischievous smile, her eyes sparkling with provocation. "Easy was never in my vocabulary, especially when it comes to you."

Matteo chuckled softly, his fingers still on her waist, moving in gentle, almost absent gestures, as if exploring every inch of her came naturally. "Ah, I know that. You like a good challenge, Alessia. I see it every time you face me with that look of someone who isn't intimidated. And I confess, it's what keeps me here."

He leaned closer, his lips dangerously close to hers, but without taking the initiative, as though he were testing her. Alessia felt the tension rising with every second, the desire simmering between them, but she didn't want to give in completely. It was like a game of wills, where both wanted control, yet they were dangerously close to letting it slip.

"Do you think you can challenge me, Matteo?" Alessia asked, her tone provocative, daring him to make the next move. She knew what she was doing, feeling the heat rise through her body with his proximity, but her pride still held her back, like the last line of resistance.

He smiled, his eyes fixed on hers with an intensity that made her lose her breath. "Alessia, challenging you is what makes every second worth it. But you should also know... I always end up winning."

She laughed, shaking her head with a mocking smile that didn't hide how affected she was. "Winning? Oh, Matteo, I hate to inform you, but you've barely begun to understand how complicated it is to beat me."

They stood in silence for a moment, the mischievous smiles on their faces revealing the dance they were playing—a silent war where both wanted to come out on top, but at the same time, they were willing to lose, just to stay by each other's side.

After a few moments, Matteo raised his hand and, in an unexpected gesture, tucked a strand of her hair behind her ear, the touch gentle, filled with a tenderness that made Alessia's heart race. "I know it won't be easy, but I'm here, Alessia," he whispered, his gaze serious and deep. "And I'm willing to face every obstacle, every confrontation, if it means having you by my side."

She felt her throat tighten, the weight of his words sinking into her heart. Matteo wasn't just that controlling, dangerous man she had imagined. There, in that moment, he was someone who was risking it all, someone who might have found a reason to fight beyond his own interests.

Alessia reached out, resting her hand gently on his chest, feeling the strong beat of his heart. "I... I'm here too, Matteo," she whispered back, the surrender implicit in every word. "And, as difficult as it is to admit, maybe we really are on the same side."

They stood there, in silence, simply looking at each other, each absorbing the weight of the vulnerability they had revealed. The truce they had agreed upon now seemed more than just a peace pact; it was a promise to try, to explore what could be built between them, despite the pride and the scars.

The tension between them was still there, but now it came with a deeper understanding, a bond that defied logic. In that moment, Alessia knew that, no matter how stubborn they both were, no matter how much they provoked and challenged each other, there was something that united them, something neither was willing to ignore. And perhaps, just perhaps, that bond was strong enough to survive the battles still ahead.

# Chapter 32: The Confession That Brings Them Closer

The silence of the night enveloped the mansion as Matteo searched for Alessia, determined to share a part of himself that he had never allowed anyone to see. Something had shifted between them after their arguments, and despite both of them being driven by pride, Matteo felt he owed her an explanation—something that could justify the weight of his control, the almost obsessive need to protect and maintain everything under his command.

When he found Alessia in the library, sitting alone, he hesitated for a moment but decided that this was the right time.

"Alessia, I need to talk to you," he said, his voice softer and more hesitant than usual.

She looked up, surprised to see Matteo so serious. There was something in his expression that made her drop her usual defensive tone. She nodded and gestured for him to sit beside her. The room was filled with a quiet dimness, with only the soft light of the fireplace dancing on the walls, creating an atmosphere that felt intimate, almost confiding.

Matteo took a deep breath, as if he needed to gather all the courage he had. "I've never talked about this with anyone," he began, his deep voice wavering between determination and something Alessia recognized as vulnerability. "But I feel like, if we're trying to build something together, you deserve to understand... why I am the way I am."

Alessia remained silent, but her eyes were fixed on him, attentive, urging him to continue. Matteo looked away, focusing on the flames in the fireplace, and began telling the story he had kept hidden for so long.

"My mother was murdered when I was just a teenager. She was caught in an attack organized by a rival family... an attack that wasn't even aimed at her, but at my father. She was the kindest person I ever knew," he paused, his jaw tightening. "I remember thinking that if I had been stronger, if I had done something... maybe she would still be alive."

Alessia felt a pang in her heart as she heard the pain in his words. Seeing him in that way—so human, so affected by a past he tried to hide—made her realize that Matteo was not just the controlling and arrogant man she knew. He was someone who had closed himself off from the world, seeking protection in power and control.

Matteo continued, now looking directly at her, as if he wanted every word to be etched in her memory. "Since then, I swore I would never let anyone become my weakness again. Every time I trusted, every time I allowed myself to feel something... I lost someone. So, I built a shield. Control is my way of keeping people safe, even if it means becoming someone others despise."

Alessia felt her eyes sting, but she remained firm, absorbing every word. She knew what it was like to carry a burden, understood the weight of the emotional scars that shaped who they were. Without realizing it, she extended her hand and held his, a silent gesture of understanding.

"Matteo," she began, her voice soft, almost a whisper. "I understand this need for control. In a way, I've done the same. I closed myself off to protect myself, to prevent anyone from hurting me again. But that doesn't mean we have to live like this forever."

He looked at her with intensity, as if searching for a truth in her words. "It's easy to say, Alessia. But the scars are deep. I've learned to live this way. Sometimes, it's all I know."

She smiled faintly, a sad smile, but filled with empathy. "I know. And I don't expect you to change overnight. But... if we're trying something together, maybe we can find a way to help each other carry these scars."

They stood in silence for a few seconds, the sound of the crackling fire filling the room. Matteo squeezed Alessia's hand, feeling a genuine connection, something he never thought would be possible. Being with her, so vulnerable, brought him a mix of comfort and fear. He knew he was approaching a point of no return.

"Alessia, I never wanted to put you in danger. What I do... is to protect you," he confessed, his voice hoarse, laden with emotion. "But I understand that maybe I've overdone it. I need to trust that you're strong enough to protect yourself, and I need to learn to deal with that."

Alessia looked at him with a mixture of tenderness and determination. "Matteo, I know you want to protect me. And, in a way, I appreciate that. But, at the same time, I need my space, my freedom. Maybe we can find a middle ground."

He nodded slowly, his eyes never leaving hers. "I'll try," he said, the words heavy with sincerity that she rarely saw. "For you... I'll try."

They stayed there, still holding hands, aware that this moment sealed something deeper between them. It wasn't just a family alliance; it was a union of two broken souls who, somehow, found comfort in each other.

Alessia smiled, feeling closer to him than she ever imagined possible. Matteo was there, opening up to her in a way that required immense courage. And for a moment, she allowed herself to dream that, maybe, this man—the man she had learned to hate, but now understood—could be someone with whom she could build something real.

They moved even closer, and Matteo, without a word, pulled her into a silent embrace. There was no need for more explanations.

The warmth of the embrace said everything they needed to know: they were together, bound by something that went beyond power alliances and the dark pasts they both carried.

Alessia felt tears well up in her eyes, but she held them back, letting herself be carried away by the moment. Matteo was her strength and her weakness, the enemy who now seemed like an ally, and the man who, little by little, was beginning to win her heart.

As they pulled back slightly, he caressed her face, a tender gesture she never would have imagined coming from him. "No matter what happens, Alessia. You'll always have a part of me that no one else possesses."

She smiled, finally surrendering to this overwhelming feeling, and replied, "And you too, Matteo. I think, in some way, it will always be like that between us."

Alessia felt the weight of Matteo's gaze on her, intense and overwhelming. His presence seemed to fill the air around them, and although she had promised herself she wouldn't give in, her heart was beating wildly, betraying her intentions. She was so close to a man she had long considered her enemy, but now, with each revealed word, with each subtle touch, she was drawn into a connection she never imagined.

Matteo kept his gaze fixed on her, every line of his serious face softening as he saw her so close. He was a mafia boss, feared and ruthless, but there, with Alessia, there was a weakness that made him waver. Matteo was used to controlling everything around him, but she made him lose control in a way that both frightened and fascinated him. Being vulnerable in front of Alessia was a risk he had never thought he'd take, but for her, it was worth it.

"You know that playing with fire can burn you, right?" Alessia whispered, trying to mask her nervousness with a provocation. But her voice, though confident, trembled slightly, betraying the whirlwind of emotions he stirred in her.

Matteo smiled, a smile full of mystery and intensity. "And who said I'm afraid of getting burned?" he replied, his voice low and husky, full of a silent promise. "Alessia, I've lived surrounded by danger all my life. A little more intensity isn't going to push me away."

She rolled her eyes, but the soft expression on her face betrayed her. "You think you know everything, don't you?" she teased, trying to regain control over the situation, but Matteo's eyes reflected an unwavering determination.

He took a step closer, shortening the distance between them, and leaned in, bringing his face dangerously close to hers. "I don't know everything, Alessia. But I know enough to understand that you are the most unpredictable thing I've ever encountered," he confessed, leaving the words heavy with a mix of admiration and desire.

She felt her breath catch, as if the world around her had disappeared, leaving only the two of them in that moment. "You say that like it's a compliment," she said, trying to keep the teasing tone, but there was something deeper, something she couldn't control.

He raised his hand, brushing his thumb over her cheek in a soft gesture, a touch so tender that Alessia felt overwhelmed. "Maybe it is," he answered, his tone low and penetrating. "You challenge me in a way no one else has dared. And, no matter how hard I try to resist... with each passing day, you occupy more space in my life."

His words reverberated inside her, creating a heat that made her lose her voice for a moment. It was impossible to ignore the danger he represented, the man who ruled a criminal empire, whose hands were stained with secrets and power. But there, in that instant, Matteo wasn't the ruthless mafia boss. He was a man who, for the first time, seemed willing to lower his defenses for her.

"You're not easy to deal with, Matteo," she said finally, her voice barely a whisper. "But I admit, you make danger feel... tempting."

He laughed softly, a low laugh that seemed more like a promise than anything else. "For a woman who's always said she hates control, you seem to enjoy playing with danger, Alessia."

She felt a wave of heat rise through her body, her eyes fixed on him, defiant and at the same time vulnerable. "Maybe that's what attracts me," she admitted, with a sincerity that surprised her. "Maybe I just need someone who knows the value of a fight... someone who understands the pain of losing."

Matteo leaned in a little more, his voice a whisper full of meaning. "I understand, Alessia. And that's why you're the only one who can see who I really am. Underneath it all... underneath what the world thinks it knows about me."

They stood in silence, their gazes locked in a silent battle, where desire and vulnerability coexisted. She knew that by getting closer to Matteo, she was risking everything—her safety, her independence, and maybe even what remained of her heart. But the attraction to him, the silent understanding they shared, the strength he exuded, all of that made the risk seem worth it.

Finally, Matteo pulled away slowly, but not before holding her hand for a few moments, the touch laden with an unspoken promise. "One day, Alessia, you'll realize that I'm the only one who can protect you... and the only one who, no matter how hard I try, can't let you go."

She smiled, defiant, her heart racing. "We'll see, Matteo. Who knows, in the end, you might also discover that I'm your weakness, but also your salvation."

He released her hand, but his gaze stayed. They both knew they were playing a dangerous game, where there were no rules and emotions were powerful weapons. But at the same time, it was a game neither of them wanted to leave. Alessia knew that the love and hate they shared created a unique bond, a bond that tied them in a relationship that defied everything they had ever known.

And so, as the night fell and the dangers of Matteo's life remained as shadows around them, Alessia felt like she was exactly where she was meant to be—by the side of the man who not only challenged her limits but made her feel alive, even if it meant playing with her own fate.

# Chapter 33: A Night of Surrender

The night was shrouded in an unusual silence, broken only by the sound of soft footsteps on the marble floor. Alessia felt her heart racing as she walked down the hallway toward the main room, where she knew Matteo would be waiting. Since their last conversation, the air between them had been charged with something neither of them could ignore anymore, something that had become impossible to push aside.

Matteo had his back to her when she entered the room, but he seemed to sense her presence, turning slowly to look at her. Their eyes met, and in that instant, Alessia felt that all the walls she had built were about to crumble. There was something in his posture, an unspoken tension he seemed to carry along with the weight of everything he had confessed. And in that moment, Alessia felt she might finally be ready to abandon her own defenses.

"Alessia," he murmured, his voice low and laden with contained emotions. "Why do I feel like you're so far away and, at the same time, so close?"

She swallowed hard, walking slowly toward him, unable to look away. "Maybe it's because we've both been hiding, Matteo," she replied, her voice barely a whisper. "But I'm tired of hiding."

They stood in silence for a few seconds, a silence that spoke more than words ever could. Matteo raised his hand and gently ran his fingers down her cheek, the touch soft as a silent promise. Alessia closed her eyes, feeling her heart race as his hand slowly moved to hold her waist, pulling her closer.

"I don't want to hurt you," he murmured, his voice filled with sincerity. "But I can't let you go, Alessia. I never could."

She opened her eyes, looking deeply into his, seeing a vulnerability there she had never imagined in this man. "Then stop fighting it, Matteo. Stop fighting us."

The words left her lips before she could think, but in that instant, there was no more space for hesitation. They were so close, their bodies aligned in a way that the heat of their proximity seemed to envelop them completely.

Matteo held her face with both hands, his thumbs caressing her skin as he gazed at her with an intensity that made her lose her breath. "Alessia... you have no idea what you mean to me."

Before she could answer, his lips found hers, in a kiss full of desire and surrender. It was a kiss that asked for no permission; it was a claim, a silent promise that from that moment on, they would be together, body and soul. Alessia felt Matteo's strong arms around her waist, pulling her even closer, as though he wanted to protect her from everything while, at the same time, bind her to him forever.

They pulled away briefly, just enough to look at each other, both breathing quickly, hearts racing in sync. Matteo kept his gaze steady, as if every second of the moment was etched into his memory.

"I never thought this was possible," he confessed, his voice hoarse, the emotion clear in each word. "But you made me believe that maybe I also have the right to be happy... and to make you happy."

Alessia felt a wave of emotion rush through her. She wasn't just in love; she knew she had surrendered completely to this man who had so often challenged her and who, in that moment, seemed ready to tear down all the barriers for her.

The night went on, and in the warmth of the room lit only by the faint light of the stars outside, they gave themselves to each other in a way that went beyond the physical. It was a union of marked souls, of hearts that met at a point of surrender where love and desire merged, creating something deep and irrevocable.

Hours later, as they lay side by side, Alessia rested her head on Matteo's chest, feeling the steady beat of his heart. He ran his hand through her hair, in a gesture almost absentminded but filled with the intensity she now knew so well.

"You have no idea what you've done to me, Alessia," he murmured, his voice low, full of a mixture of admiration and respect. "I've never let anyone get this close."

She smiled softly, tracing a pattern with her fingers on his chest. "Maybe because deep down, you knew I wasn't just anyone. That, despite everything, I was always someone who could understand you."

Matteo nodded, pulling her even closer, his touch full of protective possessiveness. "And you're mine. No matter what happens. I know the world we live in is dangerous, but I swear... nothing will take you from me."

Alessia knew the world he spoke of wasn't just a figure of speech. Life with Matteo, the head of one of the most feared mafia families, would always be surrounded by risks, constant dangers. But at that moment, it seemed irrelevant. She felt safe, protected by him, and nothing in the world could erase that feeling.

"I trust you, Matteo," she said, her voice soft but full of conviction. "And I'm here, by your side. No matter what the future holds for us."

He looked into her eyes, their faces so close that Alessia could see the sincerity in his eyes, a silent promise that as long as he breathed, he would do everything to protect her. In that moment, she knew that the surrender was total, complete, and that, as much as she had tried to fight against her own feelings, there was no turning back.

Alessia was engulfed in a whirlwind of emotions. Still lying next to Matteo, she felt overwhelmed by a sense of safety and vulnerability, a combination she had never imagined possible with the man who, until recently, had been her greatest enemy. Every time her eyes met his, she saw not only the ruthless mafia boss, but a broken man who had built impenetrable walls around himself to survive the pains of his past. But now, beside her, Matteo was beginning to let those walls fall, revealing a side few had ever known.

She teased a soft smile, though her heart still beat rapidly. "So, this is how the feared Matteo DeLuca acts when he's vulnerable?" Alessia joked, a lightness in her voice that masked the intensity of the moment.

Matteo let out a low, raspy laugh, his expression filled with a familiar mix of challenge and tenderness. "You seem to forget that I'm still that Matteo, Alessia," he replied, keeping his gaze fixed on her, while his fingers slowly traced a soft pattern on her arm. "I just didn't think anyone would have the audacity to leave me so defenseless."

Alessia tilted her head, narrowing her eyes, but she didn't pull away from his touch. She felt incredibly vulnerable, but there was a strange freedom in that vulnerability. With him, she could be who she was—intense, challenging, free. She didn't want to lose that space they had built together.

"Do you think you can handle this?" she provoked, an ironic smile dancing on her lips. "Or do you prefer to return to being the tough, impenetrable boss?"

Matteo rolled his eyes, but she noticed the restrained smile he tried to hide. "I think the tough boss role is going to have to wait a little while," he murmured, holding her more firmly, as if he needed the touch to anchor his feelings. "But don't fool yourself, Alessia. I won't change who I am... maybe, just for you, there can be an exception."

This simple yet meaningful declaration sent a wave of warmth through Alessia's heart. It wasn't a common promise, nor was it a usual declaration of love. For a man like Matteo, admitting any weakness, any deviation from his implacable nature, was a rare achievement, a confession of deep feelings. And in that moment, she understood just how committed he truly was.

However, even with the growing intensity, they both knew the world they inhabited was filled with danger. Being with Matteo meant sharing his risks, living in the shadow of constant enemies, but in a way, it also made them stronger together. He represented the safety Alessia sought, but he also threatened her in ways she had never imagined. And still, she couldn't pull away.

"This is crazy," she murmured, more to herself than to him.

"Everything that's worth it always is, Alessia," he replied with a softness that didn't match his usual demeanor. "Do you think I wanted to feel this? Do you think I planned on letting anyone get this close? But the thing is, with you, the choices seem to dissolve."

Alessia looked at him, feeling even more drawn to him. "You have this way of making it seem like danger is the only path," she said, but her voice was soft, full of affection.

"Maybe it's because danger is the only path for someone like me. But with you... I've learned that danger can also be irresistible," he murmured, leaning closer, his lips just inches from hers, a hesitation laden with promise between them. "What we're doing is insane, Alessia. And that's exactly why I can't stop."

She felt her heart race again, and without thinking, she placed her hand on his face, feeling the rigid line of his jaw. Matteo leaned in even more, the tension between them almost palpable. Alessia knew that by giving in to what she felt, she was putting herself in a risky position, but at the same time, it seemed like the only place she wanted to be. He was the mafia boss, the hardest, most unyielding man she knew, but at the same time, he was the man who showed vulnerability, even if only for brief moments, for her.

"And I," she whispered, intertwining her fingers in his hair, pulling him closer, "won't ask you to stop."

Matteo pulled her closer, the kiss full of an unmistakable feeling. It wasn't just passion, nor was it just physical attraction. There was a need there, a deeper connection than Alessia could have ever imagined. In his arms, she felt complete, and at the same time, she knew they were stepping into uncharted territory, into a game that could lead them both to happiness or imminent danger.

"Alessia," he murmured against her lips, his voice hoarse and low, "The world out there doesn't understand what I feel for you. But that doesn't matter, because I will protect you, even if the whole world comes after us."

She smiled, a spark of provocation shining in her eyes. "I hope you're ready, Matteo. Because I'm not someone easy to have by your side."

He laughed, holding her tighter. "I never wanted something easy, Alessia. I wanted you, with all your strength and resistance."

And so, in that moment, they sealed a silent promise. They knew the challenges were still to come, that the world around them remained dangerous, but they also understood that, no matter how many enemies there were, no matter what barriers they would have to face, their bond was real. And Alessia, beside the most dangerous man she had ever known, felt that, at last, she had found a place where she belonged—even if it was with someone who, to the world, represented danger, but to her, meant home.

# Chapter 34: Alessia's Insecurity

The next day, Alessia woke up with a heavy heart. Matteo was still sleeping beside her, and even in repose, his expression was determined and rigid, as if he could never truly relax. She watched him for a moment, wondering if what they shared the night before meant something more than a fleeting satisfaction. Could he feel something genuine for her, or was she just another possession, another victory added to his endless list?

Rising quietly, Alessia walked over to the balcony of her room, letting the cool morning breeze calm her confused thoughts. The feeling of surrendering completely to someone like Matteo still disoriented her. Her heart seemed torn between vulnerability and the desire to resist. The truth was, falling for Matteo DeLuca meant accepting a man who lived in the shadow of danger and the dark obligations of the mafia. He was dangerous, unpredictable, and, above all, someone who had never been taught to express emotions in a normal way.

Lost in her thoughts, Alessia didn't notice Matteo approaching until he was right behind her. He observed her from the door, then slowly made his way over and placed a hand on her shoulder, pulling her back to reality. "Thinking at this hour?" he asked in a low, husky voice.

She looked at him, trying to hide the insecurity in her eyes. "Just thinking... about everything," she replied, attempting to keep her tone light. But Matteo knew her well enough to notice the tension.

"Are you regretting it?" he asked directly, his eyes intense, as if the answer meant more than he was willing to admit.

Alessia hesitated, surprised by the sincerity of the question. "No... but that doesn't make things easier, Matteo. Last night, I felt like maybe you could... maybe we could..."

Matteo moved closer, interrupting her by gently holding her face in both hands, forcing her to look at him. "Alessia, do you think this is simple for me? Do you think it's easy for me to deal with what I feel?" He exhaled a heavy sigh, as if words could not express what was between them. "I never wanted this to happen, but you came into my life like a hurricane. I don't know how to love the way you might expect, but this..." he gestured between them, "this is real for me."

She felt her heart flutter at his words. They were everything she wanted to hear, but at the same time, they caused a certain apprehension. Matteo was intense and complicated; loving someone like him meant facing the shadows that constantly surrounded him.

Later, still immersed in uncertainty, Alessia went to meet Serena. She needed to hear an outside perspective, someone who could offer a different view, especially now that she felt the weight of her conflicting emotions.

Serena greeted her with a warm smile and a concerned look, quickly noticing Alessia's restlessness. "Tell me what happened," Serena said gently.

Alessia sighed, feeling the tension ease a little in the presence of her friend. "I'm confused, Serena. Matteo isn't the type of person I imagined being with. He's dangerous, possessive... but at the same time, he makes me feel something I've never experienced before. Last night, he was... different. Vulnerable."

Serena looked at her with an understanding gaze. "And does that scare you?"

"Yes," Alessia admitted, looking down. "I'm afraid he'll go back to being who he was before. That I might just be deluding myself with this side of him."

Serena placed a hand on hers, squeezing it with affection. "Alessia, I don't think you're deluding yourself, but you also need to be realistic. Matteo is complex; he carries a dark past and a life that demands coldness. If you decide to get involved with him for real, you have to be prepared to accept those parts of him. But, from what you've told me, maybe he's trying to show you that he's more than just the mafia boss."

Alessia nodded, feeling a little calmer with Serena's words, but insecurity still hovered over her like a shadow.

When she returned to the mansion, she found Matteo in his office, buried in papers. He looked up as soon as he saw her enter, and for a moment, his eyes hardened, assuming the firm and authoritative posture she knew so well.

"Can we talk?" Alessia asked hesitantly, but determined to clarify how she felt.

He nodded, gesturing for her to sit down. She took a deep breath, trying to organize her thoughts. "I need to know, Matteo... what does this mean to you?" Her voice faltered, but she kept her gaze steady.

Matteo leaned back in his chair, interlacing his fingers and watching her with a calculated intensity. "Alessia, I've made it clear that I'm not good at dealing with these feelings. But I know that what we have is something I've never experienced with anyone." He paused, as if the next words were especially difficult to say. "But the world I live in demands strength, control. It's all I know. And having you by my side makes me feel... weak. And I can't afford that. Do you understand?"

She swallowed, feeling a wave of understanding mixed with sadness. He was trying to protect himself, as he always had. But at the same time, she knew he wanted to be with her, even if words failed him.

Alessia extended her hand and placed it over his. "Matteo, I'm not asking you to change. I just want to know that this is important to you, like it is to me."

Matteo covered her hand with his, squeezing gently. "You are more important than I'd like to admit, Alessia. And, no matter how hard I try, I can't keep this distance anymore."

They sat in silence for a moment, the connection between them deeper and more tangible than any words could express. Alessia felt that, despite all the insecurities and fears, there was something real here, a silent promise that, together, they would face whatever the future held.

Matteo watched Alessia in silence, as the weight of the words he had just confessed hung in the air. He had never imagined that a woman could awaken something in him so close to vulnerability. She was a constant presence, a flame that set him on fire and, at the same time, brought a strange peace, challenging all the defenses he had carefully built over the years. And no matter how much he tried to protect himself, it was useless; Alessia had managed to break through his barriers with the audacity of someone who didn't fear his dark side.

"Why do you look at me like that?" Alessia asked, breaking the silence, with a light smile, but a provocative look on her lips.

Matteo leaned in slightly, holding her gaze, and without losing his firm posture, replied, "Because you intrigue me, Alessia. It's like I'm constantly trying to decipher the most dangerous and fascinating puzzle of my life."

She raised an eyebrow, tossing her hair back with a graceful yet intentionally provocative gesture. "Maybe it's because you never managed to put me in one of your boxes. You think you can control everything around you, but with me, Matteo... you know things don't work that way."

The challenge sparked something in Matteo, and he moved a little closer, making it clear that he was accepting the challenge. "And you know, Alessia, that once you enter my world, you rarely get out unscathed," he said, his voice low and laced with a dangerous yet desire-filled tone. "You should be afraid, you know?"

She smiled, defiant, not backing down an inch. "Afraid? I thought I made it clear I'm not an easily intimidated woman."

This clash between them, this constant tension, was what made every moment so electrifying. Alessia felt her heart race, the adrenaline coursing through her veins, and at the same time, the exhilaration of being with someone who made her feel so alive. Matteo was not just a man; he was a storm, an uncontrollable force that pulled her closer, even when she tried to pull away.

Still holding her gaze, Matteo brought his hand to her face, his fingers tracing the line of her jaw possessively. "You talk too much, Alessia," he murmured, his voice soft yet intense. "If you weren't so challenging, maybe I could keep my distance. But you... you force me to want to break all my own rules."

She swallowed hard, feeling the weight of those words but refusing to pull away. "Maybe you're finally learning you can't control everything, Matteo. Sometimes, even the mafia boss has to surrender."

Matteo smiled, a rare and genuine smile that revealed how much her words affected him. "Surrender? To you?" He chuckled softly, but his gaze remained intense, signaling that the game was far from over. "Maybe you don't know, but in a way, I already have."

Alessia's heart raced even more, and for a brief moment, she felt exposed, as though she were treading in dangerous territory. The truth was, Matteo was not the only one who had surrendered; she too could no longer imagine her life without him, despite all the dangers and uncertainties their relationship brought.

They sat in silence for a few seconds, both submerged in the intense emotions surrounding them. She could feel the heat of his hand on her skin, and Matteo didn't seem willing to let her go anytime soon. He leaned in close, allowing their faces to almost touch, and their lips came together, hovering just a millimeter apart.

"You still have the chance to walk away," he murmured, his voice deep and intense, full of repressed desire. "You can still leave before you get trapped in this world."

She smiled, closing the gap until her lips brushed against his. "I think you underestimate how much I enjoy danger," she whispered, challenging him.

In that moment, the tension between them exploded, and Matteo pulled her closer in a kiss full of passion and surrender. It was a kiss that carried all the words they had not said, all the suppressed fears and desires. Alessia felt that, here, in his arms, she was safe, even knowing the world around them was filled with uncertainties and risks.

As they pulled away, they looked at each other in silence, both aware that something undeniable had shifted between them. He was still the most dangerous man she knew, the mafia boss who carried shadows and mysteries. But now, she also saw the human side, the vulnerability he tried so hard to hide from everyone.

"Promise you won't let me fall," Alessia murmured, her voice low and sincere.

Matteo held her hand firmly, his eyes darkened with intensity. "As long as I'm here, no one will hurt you, Alessia. I'll do whatever it takes to make sure of that."

And in that instant, even knowing the path ahead was uncertain, they both understood that, despite the dark and dangerous world around them, they had found something more valuable in each other than any power or security — something that made them feel alive and, paradoxically, vulnerable.

# Chapter 35: Proofs of Loyalty

Matteo and Alessia sat in their private room, where the tension felt almost tangible. The conversation with Lorenzo had deeply shaken Alessia, and the pressure from her own allies placed Matteo in an equally uncomfortable position. They knew that the changes in their relationship wouldn't go unnoticed, but the reality was even more relentless than they had imagined.

"My father wants me to choose the family above all," Alessia began, with a hard and determined look, though it hid the anguish she felt. "He made it clear that if I get too close to you, I could put everyone at risk. I have no choice, Matteo. He still controls much of the family's power."

Matteo watched her, feeling the same rising pressure from his own side. His allies had started questioning whether he was "softening," if Alessia's presence was eroding the strength he had built with such rigor. "And you think I'm not being pressured too? Alessia, some people think my closeness to you is a sign of weakness."

She shook her head, uncertain. "Matteo, I don't know if we can keep going like this. I feel that no matter how hard we fight, we'll always be at the mercy of our families."

He moved closer, taking her hands with a firmness that conveyed both authority and affection. "We need to show them that together we are stronger than apart. It's not weakness, Alessia; it's strategy. If we want to protect what we're building, we need to unite, to become unshakable."

She looked at him, surprised and touched by the clarity and determination in his eyes. The proposition was tempting, but Alessia couldn't ignore the weight it would bring. There, in front of Matteo, she felt a trust she had never experienced with anyone, but the fear still consumed her. "What if this is a mistake? What if we become the very reason for the destruction we're trying to avoid?"

Matteo raised an eyebrow, leaning a little closer to her. "You know what we have is dangerous. We've always known that. But what's wrong with fighting for what we want? With challenging the rules that have been imposed to keep us in line?"

Alessia took a deep breath, seeking security in his words. "I'm not afraid to fight, Matteo. I'm just afraid of losing everything I am. Of losing myself in the middle of this war."

He held her face gently, as if Alessia were something precious and fragile at the same time. "You'll never lose yourself, Alessia. Because now you're a part of me, and I won't let anything or anyone destroy you."

His words, spoken with a raw honesty, deeply moved her. Matteo was a man of few promises, but when he made them, they were unbreakable. There was something almost desperate in the intensity with which he looked at her, as though he was surrendering himself completely to her, breaking the reserves that had always protected him.

After a heavy silence, she shook her head, a decision taking form in her mind. "Then let's do this. Let's face it together, without secrets, without reservations." Alessia squeezed his hands, sealing the silent pact that would bind them even more intensely. "But, Matteo, you need to understand that I'm not just a pawn in your game. If we're going to walk together, it will be as equals."

He smiled, a shadow of amusement and challenge passing across his face. "Equality, Alessia? With me?" The provocation was clear, but soon his eyes softened. "Alright, we'll be partners. But know this—if it ever comes to it, I will give my life to protect our alliance."

His words were a shock to Alessia, and she felt a wave of emotion engulf her. It was more than just a pact of alliance; it was a promise of loyalty, of total surrender. Matteo was giving up something fundamental, risking his own security and control for her. It left her feeling both vulnerable and determined.

That night, the mansion felt like a different place, as if something new and powerful had been forged within those walls. Matteo and Alessia remained close, both aware that they had crossed a line. She rested her head on his shoulder, feeling the weight of responsibility and the comfort of safety by his side. Matteo wrapped his arm around her, his hands holding hers with a silent firmness.

He murmured, never taking his eyes off her: "From now on, anyone who stands between us won't just be challenging me or you, but both of us. I won't let anyone undo what we've built."

Alessia nodded, feeling a mix of fear and excitement pulse through her veins. She was standing by a dangerous man, the boss of a feared mafia, but he was also the man who had promised her protection and unconditional loyalty. She knew the battles were far from over, but at that moment, as Matteo's hands held hers, Alessia understood that her loyalty to him was stronger than any external threat.

The war against the world was no longer just Matteo's or Alessia's fight alone; it was their war, a battle they would face side by side. And while they knew the path ahead would be full of dangers and uncertainties, they had found, in each other, the strength to continue.

Matteo and Alessia remained silent after the unspoken pact, each processing the weight of what they had just decided. Matteo watched her closely, every detail of her etched in his mind like a promise he would make sure to keep. He knew she carried insecurities and fears, but at the same time, he felt captivated by the strength Alessia exuded, the resilience she never let fade, even in the face of the toughest challenges.

Alessia, on the other hand, felt her heart race. Being with Matteo was dangerous, like walking on a minefield. Every touch from him seemed to spark a fire in her chest, every word awakened emotions she could barely contain. No matter how hard she tried to keep her defenses up, he managed to break them down with an intensity no one had ever shown her. The feeling of being protected by Matteo was paradoxical. He was the mafia boss, the man she should fear, but strangely, it was by his side that Alessia found a safety she had never imagined feeling.

"You know this won't be easy, right?" she whispered, her eyes meeting his, as if seeking confirmation that he understood the implications of what they were about to face.

Matteo smiled, a crooked and dangerous smile, but it carried a hidden tenderness. "Nothing about us is easy, Alessia. But I think it's about time you understand that I don't shy away from challenges."

She laughed, teasing. "Challenges? I think I'm more of a complication in your life, Matteo."

He moved closer, his face so near to hers that Alessia could feel his warm breath on her skin. "A complication I wouldn't mind facing every day."

Her heart beat faster, and she felt her defenses falter once again. Matteo brought out a vulnerability in her that left her stunned, but she couldn't ignore the desire burning between them. This was the same man who, not long ago, she had sworn to hate forever, but now he was capable of stirring feelings she hadn't even known were possible.

He raised his hand and, with a gentle gesture, tucked a strand of hair behind her ear. "You worry too much," he murmured, his voice lower, filled with a tenderness she rarely saw in him. "You should learn to relax more."

She raised an eyebrow, challenging him. "Relax? By the side of the mafia boss? Do you think that's possible?"

Matteo smiled, that enigmatic smile that mixed danger and charm. "If it were up to me, I'd make you feel safe, Alessia. Maybe even to the point of forgetting who I really am."

She chuckled softly, but her expression softened when she saw the sincerity in his gaze. "I think that would be a bit difficult, Matteo. But... in a way, being by your side is the only place I really want to be."

Matteo pulled her closer, and Alessia let him wrap his arms around her waist, holding her as if she were something he would never let escape. There, in that moment, between the darkness of the night and the silence of the walls, they found a truce between danger and vulnerability. Alessia felt as though the world around them dissipated, leaving only the intensity that existed between them.

Matteo held her tightly, but with an unexpected gentleness, as if he knew that any sudden move could break that delicate moment. He whispered, his lips almost brushing hers: "Alessia, I never imagined someone could make me lower my guard. You manage to do it without the slightest effort."

She smiled, gently touching his face, feeling the contrast between the relentless man and the vulnerability he only allowed her to see. "Maybe you're starting to realize that having someone by your side isn't a sign of weakness, Matteo."

He laughed, but didn't pull away, responding in a low, confessional tone. "You're the exception to every rule I've ever made, Alessia. And I don't know if that's good for me or if it will destroy me."

Her gaze softened, and for a moment, Alessia felt they were both naked—not just physically, but emotionally. She knew that Matteo still carried the weight of the past and the dark choices that had been part of his life, but by his side, she found a unique comfort, as if, in some way, they completed each other in the scars and strengths they both held.

There, between kisses and whispered words, the couple understood that they were willing to face any threat. And for the first time, Alessia allowed herself to surrender without reservations, knowing that Matteo was also willing to take risks. Amidst provocations, secrets, and silent vows, they found the promise of something true and dangerous—a passion they both knew could either be their ruin or their salvation.

# Chapter 36: Family Secrets

Alessia felt increasingly uneasy as the pieces of her father Lorenzo's business web began to fit together. The thought that he was maintaining secret alliances with a family that had always been an enemy of the DeLucas not only troubled her but also enraged her. With each page of the documents Luca helped her decipher, Alessia realized the depth of Lorenzo's involvement in transactions that threatened not only Matteo's safety but also the future of the fragile alliance between the families. It was a double betrayal—against her and against Matteo—and Alessia knew she had to keep it a secret.

One rainy night, Alessia and Luca met in a secluded library at the mansion. The silence between them was broken only by the sound of rain against the windows, creating an atmosphere of tension and urgency. Luca handed her a folder containing the details of Lorenzo's most recent dealings.

— Alessia, are you sure you want to continue? — Luca asked, his expression showing genuine concern. — This is dangerous. If Matteo finds out, he might interpret it the wrong way.

Alessia sighed, her gaze fixed on the documents. — I know, Luca. But if he's in danger because of my father, I have to protect him. — She closed her eyes for a moment, trying to organize her thoughts. — Matteo has already been through too much because of me.

Luca nodded, respecting her determination. — I just ask that you be careful. Matteo... he's not a man who forgives easily.

Alessia smiled, a smile filled with irony. — I know that all too well.

However, Matteo was beginning to suspect something between Alessia and Luca. In recent days, he had noticed whispers and furtive glances exchanged between them, which created a growing discomfort in him that he couldn't quite name. A possessive feeling sparked every time Alessia mentioned Luca, and even though he tried to dismiss these suspicions, his need for control made him want to confront her.

That night, when Alessia returned to the mansion, Matteo was waiting for her in the office, sitting in his chair with a serious and impenetrable expression. Upon seeing her enter, he wasted no time and went straight to the point:

— Where have you been?

Alessia hesitated, surprised by his direct approach. She knew she wouldn't be able to lie, but she also couldn't reveal the truth without putting Matteo in danger.

— I needed some time for myself — she replied, avoiding his gaze.

Matteo stood up and walked toward her, his eyes intense and challenging. — Are you sure that's all, Alessia? Because I've noticed that you and Luca have been... very close lately.

His tone was sharp, and Alessia felt a chill run down her spine as she noticed the intensity of his gaze. Matteo moved even closer, and she could feel the tension growing between them, almost like a magnetic force.

— Are you doubting me, Matteo? — Alessia teased, trying to hide the fear and guilt consuming her.

Matteo narrowed his eyes, his face inches from hers. — I don't doubt you, Alessia, but I don't like secrets.

His reaction disarmed her for a moment. She knew that if she wanted to protect Matteo, she would have to keep this secret, but at the same time, she felt the weight of his disappointment growing. She sighed, trying to stay calm.

— What if I told you I'm doing this to protect you? — Alessia murmured, without revealing everything, but allowing her motivation to show.

Matteo looked at her, confused and intrigued. — Protect me? Alessia, what are you hiding?

Matteo's expression softened, and he reached out, gently touching her face. Alessia allowed herself to relax briefly, resting her face in his hand, feeling the warmth and security he exuded. Matteo continued to look deep into her eyes, as if trying to unravel every thought, every secret.

— Alessia, you know you don't have to face this alone — he said, his voice unexpectedly soft.

She closed her eyes, trying to suppress the emotions threatening to overwhelm her. — Sometimes, Matteo, some battles have to be fought in silence.

Matteo pulled her closer, enveloping her in a strong and protective embrace. — Trust me to be by your side, even if what you discover destroys me.

Alessia pulled back slightly, her gaze meeting his. In her heart, she knew that Matteo had become more than just a strategic alliance. He was someone who made her heart race, who brought to the surface her deepest and most contradictory feelings. She wanted more than ever to tell him everything, but at the same time, she feared what the truth might unleash.

— Promise me you won't act impulsively — Alessia whispered, a barely audible plea, a mix of fear and hope.

Matteo simply nodded, but they both knew that keeping that promise would be a challenge. The world they belonged to didn't allow for vulnerabilities, and the love between them was constantly being tested, threatened by intrigues and betrayals from every side.

Matteo watched Alessia with an intensity only he could maintain. She challenged him, was audacious, and this strength in her awakened both admiration and an overwhelming desire. He tried to understand why she stirred such conflicting emotions within him. Deep down, he knew the attraction he felt for Alessia went beyond the physical; it was something that corroded his defenses and made him question every decision. Still, Matteo remained rigid, masking his feelings with his usual coldness.

Alessia, in turn, felt the weight of Matteo's gaze, the intensity that always seemed to reveal more than he admitted with words. There was something about him that drew her in like a magnet, something that made her lose herself, even though her reason screamed at her to keep her distance. She tried to find strength in the memories of how he had treated her in the past, all the veiled threats and control imposed, but her emotional barriers were beginning to crumble.

— Are you trying to intimidate me again, Matteo? — Alessia murmured, trying to hide the nervousness while also provoking him, using sarcasm as her shield.

Matteo smiled, a barely perceptible smile that contained a mix of challenge and curiosity. He moved even closer, invading her personal space, and the proximity made the atmosphere even thicker, almost palpable.

— Intimidate you? — He tilted his head, his voice low, almost a whisper. — No, Alessia. If I wanted to intimidate you, I'd do something very different.

She lifted her chin, trying not to show how much his seductive and dangerous tone affected her. It was a constant internal struggle: to hate the idea of giving in and, at the same time, to desire each provocation, each implicit touch from Matteo. He was the mafia boss, the most dangerous man she had ever known, but paradoxically, he was also the only one who could make her feel alive in a way no one else could.

— Do you think you can just bend me to your will, Matteo? — She challenged, holding his gaze, trying to hide the tremor inside her.

He looked down at her, his face serious, but his eyes gleaming with amusement and something more. — No, Alessia. I know you're untamable. — He paused for a second, as if carefully choosing his words. — But I also know that, deep down, you're as trapped in this as I am.

Alessia felt her heart race, her self-control faltering. He had just admitted something she never thought she'd hear from him. She tried to maintain composure, but her feelings were already written all over her face. The silence between them became a silent confession, a moment when everything seemed about to explode.

She took a step back, trying to regain her balance. — You're wrong, Matteo. I'm free, and nothing will bind me to you.

He smiled, but this time it was bitter, as if he knew a truth that she had not yet accepted. Moving even closer, Matteo gently brushed his thumb along her jawline, his touch soft and unexpectedly protective.

— If that's what you need to tell yourself to sleep at night, Alessia, then keep repeating it. — He tilted his face until it was mere centimeters from hers. — But we both know that this whole freedom story no longer makes sense between us.

The warmth of his touch, the proximity, the vulnerability she felt... all of it combined to create a storm of emotions Alessia could barely control. She hated him for being so dominating, for tearing down every barrier she tried to build. And at the same time, she hated herself even more for secretly wishing he was the only one to break through those barriers.

They stood in silence, Matteo's touch still burning on her skin, and Alessia finally understood that, in this game of power and desire, they were both equally lost.

# Chapter 37: A Risky Discovery

Alessia's heart raced as she flipped through the documents hidden in her father Lorenzo's office. She could hardly believe what her eyes were reading: a meticulous sequence of steps, each detailing how the Romano family planned to infiltrate the DeLuca business and destabilize Matteo's organization from within. She recognized her father's precise handwriting on every page, and the cold calculation that terrified her. Lorenzo didn't see her marriage to Matteo as an alliance, but as an opportunity for infiltration and destruction.

The pain of betrayal washed over her like a tidal wave. Alessia felt like a puppet, a pawn in Lorenzo's power game. Matteo, whom she was beginning to see beyond his ruthless facade, and who was finally showing some vulnerability, had become a victim of a calculated scheme. Guilt overwhelmed her, but at the same time, she knew she had to act cautiously. Matteo would never forgive her if he knew the truth, but withholding the information could break the fragile peace between the families. If Matteo found out, he wouldn't hesitate to destroy the Romano family.

Determined, Alessia went to confront Lorenzo. When she entered his office, her father looked up from a thick pile of papers and smiled that calculating smile.

"Is there something I can help you with, Alessia?" Lorenzo asked, his voice laced with sarcasm.

She glared at him, her hands shaking with anger and disappointment. "I found your plans, Father. This whole alliance... It's just a game to you. A way to destroy Matteo and the DeLuca family."

Lorenzo furrowed his brow, his expression quickly shifting from disdain to absolute coldness. "I see you've been meddling too much, Alessia. You should remember that your loyalty is to the

Romano family, and what's at stake here is far bigger than you and this sham marriage."

"I'm your daughter!" Alessia's face flushed with rage. "Not a chess piece for you to manipulate!"

Lorenzo stepped toward her, his eyes hard, filled with a cruelty she had never seen so clearly. "You've always been my chess piece, Alessia. And you always will be. That's why I raised you to obey. Matteo isn't your husband, he's an opportunity. And now, you're going to play your part."

She swallowed hard, feeling the weight of his words. For the first time, Alessia realized how far her father was willing to sacrifice everything in the name of power. He had no love or consideration, just a ruthless ambition that seemed to consume even family ties.

"What if I refuse?" Alessia whispered, challenging him.

Lorenzo laughed, but the laughter sounded hollow and threatening. "Don't be naive, my daughter. Any resistance from you will be crushed. You know what happens to those who turn against the family? They don't survive." He grabbed her by the chin, tilting her face until their gazes met. "You belong to me, Alessia, and you'd do well not to forget that."

Alessia managed to pull away from his grip, stepping back as she tried to process the coldness of her own father. The weight of the secret was almost unbearable. She would need to protect Matteo while concealing her intentions from Lorenzo. With her heart in pieces, she left the office determined not to let her father's dark plan come to fruition.

When she returned to the room she shared with Matteo, she found him going over some documents. He lifted his gaze when she entered, and the look of concern that flashed across his face didn't go unnoticed.

"Is something wrong?" he asked, his voice heavy with suspicion.

Alessia felt a tightness in her chest. The man who provoked and challenged her at every turn was now someone she needed to protect, even though he would never understand—or know—this.

She took a deep breath, fighting to maintain her composure. "It's nothing. Just... had an argument with my father. Family stuff."

Matteo nodded, but the intense look he gave her made it clear that he didn't fully believe her. "Between Lorenzo and family business, you'll never have peace, Alessia. And neither will I."

She hesitated for a moment, feeling an impulse to tell him everything she had discovered, but the risk was too great. Instead, she moved closer to Matteo, trying to hide her anguish. "Maybe not everything has to be as it always was, Matteo. Maybe we can redefine what loyalty means."

He stared at her, his eyes sparkling with an unexpected curiosity. "And what would you do, Alessia, if you had to choose between loyalty to your family and loyalty to me?"

The question left Alessia speechless. The intensity between them seemed to grow by the second, and she knew that for Matteo, this was a matter of life and death. She looked away, unable to answer, but a part of her already knew the truth.

At that moment, Alessia realized she was willing to do anything to protect Matteo—even if it meant defying her own family.

Alessia felt the weight of the secret she carried on her shoulders, tightening around her heart with each passing moment. Discovering Lorenzo's intentions had left a mark that she was trying with all her might to hide from Matteo. But as she saw him sitting on the bed, that serious look he always used to try and decipher her thoughts made something inside her falter. Matteo was everything she had sworn to hate, but now, as she got to know him and saw beyond his hardened exterior, she felt a deep—and dangerous—connection forming between them.

Matteo was watching her, noticing the unease in Alessia's movements. There was something different in her behavior, a subtle vulnerability he couldn't ignore. He moved closer, gently touching her face, his thumb tracing a delicate line across her skin. It was rare for him to express gentleness, and Alessia felt her heart race at the unexpected touch.

"What are you hiding from me, Alessia?" he asked in a low, almost hypnotic tone. The question seemed simple, but it carried a dangerous intensity.

Alessia looked away, struggling against the urge to open up, but at the same time, knowing that any poorly chosen word could ruin everything. "I'm not hiding anything, Matteo. I can't tell you everything about my family, just like you don't share the DeLuca secrets."

He narrowed his eyes, distrust clearly visible on his face. But instead of confronting her, Matteo smiled enigmatically, a smile that left her unsettled and vulnerable. "Maybe you don't tell me everything, but know this: I always manage to find out what I need to know." The proximity between them was palpable, each word seeming like a challenge, an attempt to discover how far she was willing to go to keep that secret.

Alessia felt torn. On one hand, she wanted to trust him, to tell him everything about Lorenzo's dark plan. On the other, she knew that any sign of loyalty to her family could put them both in danger. Deep down, there was something else holding her back: the fear that by confessing, Matteo would see her as an enemy again.

"Matteo..." she whispered, her voice barely audible. He moved closer, as if every syllable Alessia spoke was a veiled promise, something he wanted to uncover.

He tilted his head, his lips dangerously close to hers. "Why do you seem so... scared?" he whispered, his voice laden with a mix of desire and curiosity. She felt the warmth of his breath, every word enveloping her and breaking down her defenses.

"I'm not scared, Matteo. I'm just... confused." Alessia hesitated, but couldn't pull away. The power he exuded pulled her in, as if Matteo were a force from which she couldn't escape, even if she tried.

"Then stop running from me, Alessia." He held her chin, lifting it gently so their eyes could meet. "Stop running from what you feel."

At that moment, everything around them seemed to disappear. Alessia felt Matteo's body so close to hers, the emotional walls crumbling little by little. She tried to resist, but seeing the intensity in his eyes, she knew he was inviting her to surrender completely.

When their lips finally met, the kiss was filled with all the repressed emotions, the tension between love and hate that defined their relationship. Alessia felt the weight of the past and the distrust between them fade for a brief moment, as if in that moment, all that mattered was the touch, his presence, and the connection they shared. Matteo deepened the kiss, and Alessia, for the first time, allowed herself to give in.

When they pulled apart, Matteo looked at her with a half-smile, the same smile that both provoked and charmed her. "That's as close as I've ever come to vulnerability, Alessia. Enjoy it."

She laughed softly, trying to hide the whirlwind of emotions that flooded her heart. But she knew that after this moment, nothing would ever be the same. With each touch, each word, Alessia found herself more involved, closer to abandoning the defenses she had fought so hard to maintain.

The danger, however, didn't disappear. Being with Matteo was like walking on the edge of a cliff: any mistake could lead to their destruction. But for a moment, Alessia put the fear aside and surrendered to what she felt, to the man who, despite everything, knew how to awaken her like no one else.

# Chapter 38: Pressure and Betrayal

Alessia felt increasingly cornered, as if she were being crushed by a silent and relentless pressure. Lorenzo was a master of manipulation, and with each veiled threat, he made Alessia feel that any wrong move would be fatal, not just for her, but for Matteo as well. Her father's cold, calculated tone echoed in her mind as she walked through the mansion, lost in thought. Every word Lorenzo had spoken reverberated with crushing weight.

"You think he'll trust you once he knows?" Lorenzo had said, a cold smile playing on his lips. "I'll do whatever it takes to make sure our family isn't betrayed. Either you act according to plan, or he'll be the target of my next move."

She knew Matteo, with his own mafia instincts, already suspected something. There was a look of questioning, almost hurt, that she could see every time their gazes met. That night, when she saw Matteo across the room, Alessia felt like a prisoner of her own loyalty. She approached him with her heart pounding, but a forced calm on her face.

Matteo looked at her intently, his dark eyes revealing a whirlwind of emotions. He didn't need to say anything; the silence between them was so heavy that Alessia knew he was waiting for an explanation. She opened her mouth to speak, but the words seemed to betray the loyalty she still felt for her own family.

"Is there something you want to tell me, Alessia?" Matteo broke the silence, his voice low, but filled with distrust and something more—perhaps pain?

Alessia swallowed, averting her gaze. "I don't know what you're talking about, Matteo."

He narrowed his eyes, as if trying to read every thought she kept buried deep inside. "Don't lie to me, Alessia. I know you're hiding something. And I can feel it's about your father."

She hesitated, feeling torn between duty to her family and the growing feelings for Matteo. "What can I say?" she whispered, trying to hide the tremor in her voice. "It's complicated."

Matteo stepped closer, gently holding her arm, as if trying to convey that he was willing to understand. "Complicated is what we do here. There's no easy or simple. There's only truth and betrayal. Which one will you choose?"

Her heart tightened. Matteo was laying it out so plainly, and she knew he accepted nothing less than transparency. However, what he didn't know was that telling the truth would lead them both down a path that could ruin everything they had built together.

"Matteo, there are things... things you wouldn't understand." Her voice faltered, and she tried to control the emotion welling up in her throat. "If I could tell you everything, I would."

Matteo let out a bitter laugh, his eyes filled with a pain Alessia had never seen before. "Alessia, when are we going to stop playing these games? I'm here, trying to protect you, trying to trust you, but you keep pushing me away. What else has to happen for you to realize that I'm not the enemy?"

His declaration completely disarmed her. For a moment, Alessia forgot the tension and felt an almost visceral desire to embrace him, to surrender to the moment. But the fear of what Lorenzo might do kept her bound. It was an invisible prison, but she felt every wall around her heart.

"I want to trust you, Matteo. But my father... he..." She stopped, realizing the weight of the revelation she was about to make. She knew any word could be used against her.

"What is Lorenzo planning, Alessia?" he insisted, holding her firmly, his eyes locked onto hers with an intensity that bordered on desperation. "I've heard whispers, suspicions. Don't make me find out from someone else. Please, tell me the truth."

His plea broke her, but she held back, pressing her lips together to avoid saying more than she could. "Matteo, I... I don't want to hurt you." Her words were a broken whisper.

Matteo released her arm, frustrated. "Then maybe you should start realizing that silence hurts even more. I'm in the dark, Alessia, and every secret you keep is like a weapon aimed at me."

She felt the weight of his words, each one piercing her heart. They stared at each other in silence, both exhausted from the constant battle between loyalty and love. Alessia knew, deep down, that she was making a decision—one that would define whether she would follow her father or her heart.

Matteo sighed and stepped back a few paces, leaving a cold emptiness between them. He took one last look before leaving the room, leaving Alessia alone with her choices and regrets.

In that moment, Alessia realized that if Lorenzo went through with his plan, the bond that had started to form between her and Matteo would be forever corrupted. She closed her eyes, wishing there were a way out, a way to stay true to herself and protect the man she had learned to love, even if she could never admit it aloud.

However, deep down, she knew that the next night would bring even more challenges, and the confrontation between love and loyalty was just beginning.

Matteo moved away from Alessia with contained intensity, a mixture of frustration and desire visible in his gaze. He tried to maintain a firm posture, but his feelings for her were starting to break through every layer of his self-control. Deep down, he hated his own vulnerability in front of Alessia. And that infuriated him as much as it fascinated him. For Matteo, the mafia was not just a life; it was the only way to protect himself, the only path to keep anyone or anything close to him. But with Alessia, everything seemed to fall apart.

Alessia, in turn, felt her heart race every time she found herself alone with Matteo. Even amid the suffocating tension surrounding them, her heart could not deny how much he affected her, even when he cursed each of her words with arrogance. The man, with all his power and authority, made her feel as if she were challenging gravity itself. But at the same time, every step toward him felt like a mortal risk, and the idea of giving in to such a controlling man made her falter. She knew his family, the mafia itself, was the battlefield of their lives, but the closeness to Matteo stirred feelings that threatened her sanity.

Sitting on the sofa, Alessia stared at the door Matteo had just walked through, her mind flooded with almost unbearable unease. Determined to clarify what she was feeling, she followed him down the corridor and found him in his office, his face a mask of hardness and control.

"Matteo, why is it so hard for you to believe that, even amid the chaos, I don't want to hurt you?" she asked, her voice broken but firm.

He raised his gaze and observed her in silence, as if trying to decipher her. For a few seconds, Alessia saw a glimpse of something beyond the hardness, a tenderness he struggled to hide. Stepping closer, Matteo let out a sigh, a rare gesture for someone always so contained.

"Because, Alessia, you put me in a position of risk," he murmured, his voice low and hoarse. "You're the only one who can make me let my guard down. And that's the most dangerous thing someone like me can do."

Alessia felt an unexpected warmth in her chest with this confession. The tension between them was palpable, and no matter how much they wanted to pull away, both of them knew they were trapped in a connection that only intensified.

"Maybe... you just need to learn to trust," she said, the light provocation behind her words, though a silent plea was hidden there. "I'm not a threat to you, Matteo. Unless you make me be."

He pulled her closer, holding her waist firmly, yet with a surprising softness. The dark, intense look in his eyes made her shiver, but she didn't look away, making it clear she was willing to face him, even if it meant losing control.

"I don't need anyone to show me my own weaknesses," he said, a challenge-laden smile playing on his lips. "You're like poison, Alessia. And still... I can't stay away."

She gave a small smile, leaning in just enough for their faces to be a few centimeters apart. "Then, maybe, you've found someone who understands your own chaos."

The kiss that followed was filled with the repressed passion they had both held onto for so long, like combustion finally igniting. Matteo's hardness softened for a moment as he surrendered to the moment, and Alessia felt complete, as if she had finally found something real in the midst of the storm.

But at the same time, there was a sense of danger. She knew that loving Matteo meant being ready to face the shadows of the mafia, the constant threats, and the weight of a past he carried. She knew it wouldn't be easy, but in that moment, all that mattered was that he wanted her as much as she wanted him.

As they pulled away, he whispered, still holding her firmly, "I'll never let anyone hurt you, Alessia. But if you play with my feelings, I'll be the danger you'll fear."

Alessia smiled, feeling the power of the threat and the warmth of protection mixed together. "I think I can handle that... if you can handle me."

Matteo smiled, the same dark smile that hid both desire and a promise. "I wouldn't expect anything less from you, mia dolce."

# Chapter 39: A Desperate Alliance

Alessia took a deep breath as she met Luca at the agreed location, a discreet café far from the cameras and the watchful eyes of the mafia. Each step toward the place made her question her own choices, yet the weight of what was at stake pushed her forward. She knew she was stepping into dangerous territory, but there was no other option. If Lorenzo discovered her efforts to sabotage his plans, the fragile peace between the families could crumble, and Matteo would never forgive her for hiding something so grave.

Luca waited for her with a serious expression, his eyes examining her with intensity as she approached.

"Alessia, I thought you wouldn't show up," he began, his voice low and heavy with the seriousness of their meeting.

Alessia pulled out a chair and sat down across from him, meeting his gaze steadily. "I had no choice, Luca. Lorenzo... my father is planning something that will destroy everything. He wants to bring down your family from the inside, and I can't let that happen."

Luca nodded slowly, his expression hardening. "And you think I'm the right person to help? This will test my loyalty... especially with Matteo."

She swallowed, aware that Luca was right. "I'm not asking you to betray Matteo. I'm asking you to protect something bigger. If this war breaks out, none of us will come out unscathed."

Luca watched her in silence for a few moments, his eyes searching for something in her features. "Alessia, I might agree to help, but I need to know... what do you really feel for my brother?" His voice was filled with intense curiosity, and she realized that this question came from the heart.

She looked away, biting her lip as she considered her words. Finally, she decided to be honest.

"I entered this marriage out of obligation, thinking I would hate every second with him. But..." she hesitated, feeling the weight of the revelation. "But things changed. Now, I feel something I never thought I would feel. Matteo challenges me and makes me question everything. He is chaos, but it's a chaos that pulls me in and..." Alessia stopped, her eyes shining with the intensity of her emotions.

Luca observed her closely, a shadow of disappointment crossing his face, but he nodded. "That's enough for me. I'll help you, Alessia. But I want you to know, if anything happens to Matteo, I hope you can trust me. That I can be the one you lean on."

Luca's request caught her off guard. There was a raw honesty in his words, something that Alessia knew placed him at risk of being hurt. She nodded, trying to ignore the guilt rising in her chest.

"Alright, Luca. I trust you," she replied, trying to sound more confident than she really felt. "And I appreciate your help. I know this won't be easy."

From that moment on, the two of them dedicated themselves to gathering evidence against Lorenzo. They spent nights reviewing documents and confidential information, growing more aware of the gravity of what they were uncovering. Alessia felt a growing urgency with each new detail revealed, fearing what it meant for Matteo and the delicate balance of power between the families.

During one of the late nights, Matteo began to notice Alessia's constant absence, and a pang of distrust settled in his chest. She was acting strangely, avoiding questions, keeping her distance. His distrust quickly turned into jealousy and silent concern, and he decided to confront her.

"Alessia, you've been absent a lot lately. Do you think I don't notice?" Matteo looked at her with intensity, searching for some explanation.

Alessia knew she couldn't tell him the truth, but his words disarmed her, and she tried to stay calm. "Matteo, I'm dealing with personal matters. Things that involve my father, and they're complicated to explain."

"Complicated?" Matteo stepped closer, his voice tinged with veiled jealousy. "Or maybe you don't want to explain because you're with someone else... someone closer to you?"

The accusatory tone stung, and Alessia felt a tightening in her chest, but she held her ground. "Matteo, I'm not cheating on you. I'm trying to protect you, even if you don't understand it now."

"Protect?" Matteo grabbed her arm, his eyes darkened with frustration and doubt. "If you think you can play with my trust, Alessia, you're very wrong."

She looked at him, her eyes burning with a mixture of anger and sadness. "Matteo, if you knew everything that's at stake, you'd understand that what I'm doing is for the good of both of us. But, apparently, trust is something you expect from me without ever offering it in return."

The two of them stood in silence, their breathing heavy as their gazes remained locked on one another, each battling with what they were feeling. Matteo was torn between his desire to protect her and the need to understand what she was hiding. And Alessia, aware of the risks she was taking, knew her secret could ruin everything between them.

Still, seeing the wounded look in Matteo's eyes, Alessia stepped closer and cupped his face, a rare and tender gesture that brought a moment of silent peace between them.

"Matteo, I need you to trust me," she whispered, with a sincerity he had never heard before.

Matteo closed his eyes, and Alessia realized that he was struggling to put aside his distrust. The barrier between them kept them vulnerable, and though he felt betrayed, Matteo held her hand and pulled her close, whispering in response:

"I'll try, Alessia. But know this, if something comes to light and I realize you've played against me... there will be no safe place in the world where you can run."

Alessia watched Matteo in silence as he stared out the window, his expression grim. He seemed lost in thought, his face hardened, but his eyes carried an intensity that made her feel trapped. Being with him was like navigating dangerous waters: alluring and frightening. She knew there was a thin line between the ruthless mafia man and the man who, somehow inexplicably, showed a subtle care for her.

Feeling bold, Alessia moved closer, her steps silent in the stillness of the room. Matteo noticed her presence and slowly turned, his gaze full of mystery and challenge. Without hesitation, he pulled her by the waist, holding her close in a possessive gesture. His touch was firm, sending an electric current through Alessia's body, as if he could set every part of her on fire with a simple touch.

"I still don't understand why you insist on testing my patience, Alessia," he murmured, his voice low and rough, as his fingers traced a light path along her waist, almost as if marking the moment.

She lifted her chin, meeting his gaze with determination. "Maybe because you test mine too," she teased, letting a faint smile play on her lips.

Matteo let out a short laugh, but his eyes remained serious, as if he wasn't fully relaxed, as though he was constantly torn between his desire to protect her and his fear that she might betray his trust. He tilted his head, studying her, and finally, his face softened a little.

"It's hard for me, Alessia, to lower my defenses," he confessed, something rare in his voice. "I'm not used to caring about anyone other than myself or the power I've acquired."

His words hit Alessia deeply. It was a raw confession, a glimpse of vulnerability that Matteo almost never allowed to show. She looked at him with affection, but still with that touch of defiance that was so characteristic of her.

"You don't have to worry about me, Matteo," she whispered, trying to show confidence, but her voice betrayed a fraction of the emotion she really felt. "I can take care of myself."

He let out a dry laugh, still holding her firmly. "And it's exactly that self-sufficiency that drives me crazy. How you insist on doing everything alone, risking your safety."

The intensity of the moment made Alessia's heart race. She knew that what he felt for her was real, but the circumstances surrounding them made everything complicated, dangerous, as if a bomb were about to explode at any moment. Alessia knew that Matteo, despite his coldness, desired her in a way that bordered on possessiveness. And that both scared and attracted her.

He lowered his face, bringing his lips closer to hers, but stopped just before they touched, letting the warmth of his breath heat her skin. "Tell me, Alessia, what am I to you? An ally, an enemy... or something more?"

She took a deep breath, trying to stay calm, but her heart was racing at that question, and the answer that came to her mind was as confusing as it was intense. "Maybe you're all three things, Matteo. But if I'm your weak point, you're also mine."

That confession seemed to catch Matteo off guard. He didn't expect to hear something so vulnerable and truthful from her. He closed his eyes for a moment, struggling with something inside him that seemed to roar to come out.

Alessia seized that moment of hesitation, and with a soft touch, slid her hand to his face, tracing the outline of his strong and determined jawline with her fingers. Matteo opened his eyes, and without waiting any longer, let their lips meet in a kiss that was both possessive and tender, as if he wanted her to know that, in that instant, she was his — in every way possible.

They both knew the dangers that this feeling represented, the risks each of them faced by getting closer. But in that moment, the questions of power and control dissolved, leaving only two souls who, even within the shadows of the underworld, had found something genuine.

# Chapter 40: A Dangerous Game

Matteo found himself on the edge of fury. Every fiber of his being seemed to vibrate with the mix of betrayal and jealousy gnawing at his heart. He looked at Alessia, trying to recognize in her the woman he thought he had begun to trust, but the doubts and the feeling of being manipulated clouded any remaining clarity. Finally, he broke the silence, his voice laced with rage.

— *So, that's it?* — he said, his tone cold and cutting. — *All this time, you've been with my brother, conspiring with him. Pretending... pretending that you were on my side, that you felt something for me, while using all of this against me?*

Alessia, feeling the weight of the accusation, tried to approach him, but he stepped back, his gaze filled with bitterness. The pain in her chest was almost unbearable; she knew that if she couldn't explain everything, she might lose Matteo forever.

— *It's not like that, Matteo!* — she exclaimed, her voice growing desperate. — *I did what I did to protect us. To protect you!*

He looked at her with disdain, his eyes narrowing with a mixture of distrust and pain.

— *Protect? Don't come at me with that pathetic excuse, Alessia. All I see here is a woman who played me, who toyed with my trust to get information. You're just like everyone else... no different from Lorenzo, manipulative and treacherous.*

Alessia felt his words like knives, each one striking her heart with precision. The pain of seeing Matteo so blind, unable to see her intentions, was devastating. But she wouldn't give up; she needed him to understand.

— *Listen to me, Matteo. I know it looks bad, I know it seems like betrayal, but I never wanted to hurt you.* — She struggled to keep her voice steady, but the tremble in her hands betrayed her. — *I got close to Luca to find out my father's plans, to stop him from destroying*

*what we have. My father never accepted this alliance, Matteo, and I...
I chose you.*

Matteo remained silent, but his gaze stayed hard and relentless. He crossed his arms, but something in his eyes suggested that her words had hit him in some way, even though he was reluctant to admit it.

— *Chose?* — He shook his head, the bitterness evident in his voice. — *You talk about choices, Alessia, but the truth is I no longer know what's real and what's an act coming from you. I don't know if I can trust you, I don't know if I want to.*

Those words made Alessia feel a coldness seep into her body. She had exposed her feelings, her loyalty, but she could see that Matteo's pride and hurt were beyond her understanding, locking him in a fortress of distrust.

— *You may not trust me now, but I will prove to you that I'm by your side. I'm not your enemy, Matteo. If I had meant to betray you, I would have done it differently, without involving my own feelings.* — Alessia felt her heart race with the weight of the words she had just spoken.

Matteo stood motionless for a moment, but soon his expression softened, just a little. He lowered his arms, as if he were too tired to keep up the anger. The silence hung between them, thick and tense, as he searched for an answer that made sense of it all.

— *I really hope you're telling the truth, Alessia. Because if I find out you're lying... there will be no forgiveness. Not for you, not for Lorenzo, not for anyone who's played with my heart and my trust.*

Alessia stepped back, her breath shaky, but determined. She knew that any mistake now would be fatal for what they had, or for what they could still build.

Matteo remained standing there, unyielding and distant, his eyes locked on Alessia. Yet behind that steel facade, his heart was at war. He knew that his life, governed by unforgiving rules and an incessant desire for control, had never allowed anyone to get this close to his vulnerable side. Still, Alessia, somehow, had pierced through that armor, and it terrified him.

Alessia felt the weight of his gaze, and although she knew he was deeply hurt and distrustful, there was a palpable tension between them that transcended the conflict. She tried to contain the trembling of her hands, the internal confusion mixing with the desire to embrace him, to make him believe in her intentions. But Matteo's pride, his need to keep control over his own vulnerability, prevented any possibility of an easy reconciliation.

She took a deep breath, approaching him with a courage she knew could be her ruin.

— *Matteo,* — she began, her voice softer now, almost a whisper. — *I know all of this sounds like a betrayal to you, but I need you to understand...* — Her words faltered, the rising emotion thick in her throat. — *I need you to understand that what I feel for you is real.*

Matteo, hesitating, looked away, as if absorbing each word from her was a sign of weakness. But his heart was pounding, torn between fury and the irresistible attraction he felt for Alessia. Finally, he looked at her again, his eyes fierce with intensity.

— *And you expect me to just... trust you?* — he asked, the words laden with irony and anger, but also with repressed pain. — *Alessia, this world, our world, doesn't allow for mistakes. Trust is a luxury we can't afford, not now.*

She stepped a little closer, her hand rising to his face, hesitant but firm. Matteo tensed at her touch, but he didn't pull away. Alessia's soft touch seemed to dissolve, even if only for a brief moment, the hardness he carried.

— *I know it's not easy, Matteo, but you're not alone,* — she murmured, her eyes shining with a sincerity he couldn't ignore. — *We both have darkness inside us... but maybe together we can find something more. Something that gives us peace, even if just for a moment.*

Matteo's heart raced as he watched her lips move, each word cutting through his defenses. Without thinking, he slid his hand to her face, his palm cupping her delicate skin. There was a moment of hesitation, where they both knew they were crossing a line they couldn't uncross, but neither of them stepped back.

— *You're a danger to me, Alessia,* — he murmured, a bitter smile on his lips. — *More dangerous than any enemy I've ever faced.*

She smiled back, a defiant grin that mixed pain and affection, her eyes locked on his.

— *And you, Matteo DeLuca, are the chaos I never knew I wanted.*

Before he could react, Matteo leaned in and kissed her with an intensity that combined rage and desire. It was a kiss that revealed all the passion he had been holding back, all the pain of someone who had never allowed themselves to feel something so overwhelming. Alessia kissed him back, surrendering completely, letting all the doubts and insecurities be absorbed in that moment.

When they pulled apart, both of them were silent, their breath coming in short gasps, their gazes filled with something inexpressible. Matteo brought his hand to Alessia's face, lightly caressing her as if trying to memorize every detail.

— *I don't know where this will take us,* — he said, his voice rough and almost vulnerable. — *But I know that if you betray me... Alessia, there will be no redemption.*

Alessia nodded, her eyes conveying a silent promise of loyalty.

— *If you ever lose yourself, Matteo, I promise I'll be the one to find you.*

# Chapter 41: The Weight of the Choice

Alessia felt more torn than ever before. With every step she took towards her plan to confront Lorenzo, the feeling grew stronger that she was drifting away from her own family and diving headfirst into a new life—one that now included Matteo in a way she had never imagined.

She met Luca in an isolated spot, an abandoned warehouse near the port, where the salty smell of the sea mixed with the scent of rusted steel, creating an almost suffocating atmosphere. Luca was waiting for her, leaning against a wall, his serious expression and watchful eyes revealing the internal conflict he also carried.

"Are you sure you want to do this, Alessia?" Luca asked in a low tone, concern clear in his voice. "Betraying your own family... This isn't an easy decision, and I don't want you to do this on impulse."

Alessia took a deep breath, looking at Luca with a determined gaze. "It's not impulse, Luca. My father has made it clear he doesn't care about me; to him, I'm just a pawn, a weapon to achieve his own goals. Matteo is the only person who's shown me anything close to loyalty, even with all the doubts. I... I can't just turn my back on that."

Luca fell silent for a moment, absorbing her words. He knew Alessia was fully committed to the decision, but he himself felt the weight of betraying his own father. However, the depth of Alessia's feelings for Matteo was evident, and he didn't want her to face this battle alone.

"Then let's do this," Luca finally replied, his tone one of acceptance. "I'll help you gather all the evidence against Lorenzo. But you know, Alessia... Matteo may not accept it so easily, even with all the evidence. His pride... his distrust."

Alessia nodded, feeling a sharp pang at the thought of how Matteo would look at her when he found out about Luca's involvement. There was a good chance he would see it as another betrayal, and that broke her heart.

"I know, Luca," she murmured, her voice thick with emotion. "But I have to try. I need to show him that, even though I've made mistakes, I'm willing to sacrifice everything to protect what we've built."

Luca watched her in silence, recognizing the passion in her eyes, an intensity that reminded him of Matteo. He realized that Alessia was willing to face any storm for that man, even knowing the risks. And though he felt something special for Alessia, he knew he would never stand between her and his brother.

At the end of the meeting, they exchanged few words, but Alessia left with a determination stronger than ever. With every step she took away from the warehouse, the weight of her choice seemed to multiply, but her resolve didn't waver. She knew the path she had chosen was irreversible.

**When she returned to the mansion that night, Alessia found Matteo waiting for her in the living room. His expression was tense, his eyes dark and filled with a distrust that Alessia knew well.**

"Leaving without telling me again?" he asked, his voice cold and cutting. "Or is it that you no longer have to answer to anyone, Alessia?"

She hesitated for a moment but then lifted her gaze, meeting his eyes with courage. "I needed some time to think," she replied, trying to keep her voice steady. "And no, Matteo, I'm not running away. Not anymore."

Matteo narrowed his eyes, taking a step toward her. "Where were you? Who did you meet?"

Alessia felt her heart race, but she stood firm. She knew the answer could destroy the little trust that was left between them. But now, more than ever, she knew she couldn't hide. Even without telling him everything, she knew her loyalty had to be proven through actions, not words.

"With someone who can help me protect you," she murmured, her eyes shining with intensity. "Someone who understands that the greatest danger isn't within these walls, but out there, where my father conspires against us."

Matteo frowned, surprised by the directness of her statement. He took another step closer, just inches away, his gaze almost fierce. "And why should I believe a word you say?"

Alessia felt the sting of his distrust like a blow, but she didn't look away. "Because, despite everything, I chose you, Matteo. I could just close my eyes and let my father destroy everything, but I won't do that."

For a moment, silence stretched between them, heavy with tension and unspoken feelings. Matteo seemed to be struggling with his own emotions, and Alessia, vulnerable, wished he could see the sincerity in her words. She felt that every moment they spent together was a step deeper into that dangerous abyss, but one that was impossible to resist.

Finally, Matteo let out a heavy sigh and, without saying a word, gently brushed his fingers along her cheek in a hesitant, tender gesture. "I hope you don't make me regret this, Alessia," he whispered, his voice hoarse, laden with emotions he was trying to suppress.

Alessia closed her eyes for a moment, allowing herself to feel his presence, that unexpected touch that made her forget all the betrayals, all the dangers surrounding them. In response, she placed her hand on his chest, feeling the steady beat of Matteo's heart, a reassuring sound amid the chaos.

"I won't disappoint you," she murmured, her voice soft but determined.

Matteo pulled her closer, and in that silent moment of intimacy, Alessia felt that, even surrounded by dangers and shadows, there was something true between them—something worth fighting to protect.

**Matteo watched Alessia as she gazed out the window, her reflection outlined by the soft light of the moon. He knew that, as much as he tried to control his emotions, the fact that Alessia was risking herself for him struck something deep within him. She, the woman who had entered his life as an imposition, was now the one he didn't want to let go of, despite all the distrust and the anger that sometimes still filled him.**

"You don't have to do this, Alessia," he said in a grave, almost hesitant tone, finally breaking the silence. "Getting involved in all this will only put you in danger... and that's something I can't tolerate."

Alessia smiled faintly, a smile full of irony and perhaps a touch of bitterness. "You talk like you're capable of protecting me from everything, Matteo. But even though you're the most feared man in this city, there are things you can't control."

She turned to face him, her eyes defiant, but there was something more—a glimmer of vulnerability she rarely showed. Matteo took a step closer, the intensity in his gaze making it clear that he wasn't willing to back down in this moment.

"Yeah, but that doesn't mean I'm going to stop trying," he replied in a low voice, but with firmness. "I don't like seeing you put yourself in danger, especially with Luca involved. I don't trust him like I trust you."

Alessia raised an eyebrow, letting out a soft, ironic laugh. "Trust? Since when do you trust me, Matteo? I don't know if you've noticed, but everything we've built is hanging by a thread of distrust and a million misunderstandings."

He moved even closer, until only inches separated them. She could feel his dominant presence, the heat radiating from him, and it made her heart race in a way that both unnerved and attracted her. Matteo gently cupped her chin, leaning in slightly, his eyes locked on hers, and murmured, "Trust may be a small word, but I'm trying, Alessia. And you know that if I didn't trust you, even a little, we wouldn't be here."

She felt a wave of emotion course through her body, a mix of indignation and surrender. Alessia tried to pull back, but he pulled her back toward him, his fingers firm on her waist. He looked at her as if no one else existed, as if the world around them didn't matter.

"Why do you do this to me, Matteo?" she murmured, almost a whisper. "Why can't you just... be the cold, distant man I first met?"

"Because you changed me," he replied, without hesitation, his tone deep and full of sincerity. "Since the moment you entered my life, Alessia, everything I thought I knew about myself started to fall apart. That's the problem. I should hate you. And in some ways, I do. But at the same time, I can't imagine my life without you in it."

Alessia felt a lump in her throat. Matteo's words hit her with a force she wasn't expecting. There was danger in his eyes, but also something deeply honest. She knew she was playing with fire by getting this involved, but in that moment, it seemed impossible to retreat.

She cupped Matteo's face with both hands, allowing herself a moment of vulnerability too. "So maybe we should stop fighting this, Matteo. Maybe we should accept that... what we have is something unique, no matter how complicated it is."

Matteo tilted his head, and slowly, his lips met hers in a deep, intense kiss, filled with silent promises and unspoken secrets. It was a kiss that seemed to seal an invisible pact, an agreement between two hearts broken and hardened by the world around them.

When they finally broke apart, both breathless, Alessia looked at him with a soft smile, but her eyes carried a spark of challenge. "But don't think I'll make it easy for you, Matteo. I'll still challenge you every chance I get."

Matteo chuckled softly, a rare sound, almost surprising coming from him, but it lit up his face. "I wouldn't expect less from you, Alessia," he replied, pulling her closer. "After all, it's that courage of yours—and your stubbornness—that made me... want you."

With that, they stood in silence, embracing, aware of the dangers that surrounded them. There, entwined in a moment of surrender, Alessia and Matteo knew that, despite everything, they were ready to face whatever challenges fate had in store for them, even if it was a dangerous and uncertain game.

# Chapter 42: Traps and Distrust

With a heavy heart, Alessia realized that Matteo was growing more and more suspicious. With every gesture, every look, she felt his eyes on her, searching for any proof of her supposed betrayal. And even though the love she was beginning to feel for him was genuine, Alessia knew it wasn't enough to dissolve the doubts that kept him on constant alert.

That night, the tension between them grew during a gala dinner, where both had to maintain the appearance of normality. The hall was illuminated by imposing chandeliers, and the light reflected in Matteo's intense eyes, which were watching her with an almost devastating intensity. Alessia kept a diplomatic smile on her face, but inside, she felt the weight of his scrutiny. Every move she made, every brief conversation she had with other guests, was being analyzed in minute detail.

After the dinner, Matteo pulled her into a private room, away from the curious gazes of the other guests. He closed the door behind him and moved closer, each step making Alessia's heart race faster. She knew what was coming and, at the same time, feared the words he was about to say.

"I want the truth, Alessia," Matteo began, his voice low and sharp. "Are you really with me, or is all of this a facade to cover up Lorenzo's manipulations?"

She lifted her gaze to meet his, seeing the internal battle reflected in his eyes. "Matteo, I've already told you... I'm on your side. My loyalty is with you, not with my father."

But Matteo didn't seem convinced. He moved even closer, reducing the distance between them to almost nothing. "Words, Alessia. Just words. And words can be lies."

She felt the weight of his words, as if each one were a knife piercing through her defenses. There was so much she wanted to say, so much she wanted him to understand, but she knew that in that moment, nothing seemed enough.

"If you don't trust me now, then what do you want me to do?" Her voice came out as a whisper, almost a plea for help.

Matteo ran his fingers along her jawline, holding her firmly, but in a way that showed both strength and rare vulnerability. "I want something that proves it, Alessia. Something that shows me that you are truly mine."

She held his gaze, feeling the heat of their closeness and the pain of the challenge he was placing before her. Her heart raced, as if it were about to be torn into pieces, but her determination only grew. Alessia knew she couldn't lose Matteo, not now that she realized how much he meant to her.

"If you want proof, then I'll give it to you. I'll show you that I'm yours, that my loyalty belongs to no one else," Alessia whispered, her voice firm despite the insecurity bubbling within her.

Matteo leaned in even closer, his eyes flashing with a mix of desire and distrust. "I want to see it, Alessia. Because if I find out you've been lying... there will be no forgiveness."

She swallowed hard, feeling the palpable threat in his words, but also the confusion he was trying to hide. Alessia knew him well enough to understand that Matteo was being consumed by the conflict of whether to trust her or give in to his suspicions. And that hurt her, because it meant the bond they had built was at risk of crumbling.

Slowly, Alessia placed one hand on his face, tracing the outline of his beard, feeling the roughness against the warmth of his skin. "I know what you're risking by letting me into your life, Matteo," she murmured, her words laced with both tenderness and determination. "But even if you don't believe me now, I'm willing to prove to you, day after day, that I'm by your side."

Her touch seemed to soften the hardness in Matteo's gaze, even if just for a brief moment. He intertwined his fingers with hers, squeezing her hand with intensity. The simple gesture left her defenseless, almost surrendered. It was a moment where words were unnecessary, where silence spoke louder than any justification.

"I won't disappoint you, Matteo," Alessia whispered, feeling the weight of the promise she was making. "Even if I have to face everything I know, everything I've been, I'll prove you can trust me."

And with those words, Alessia sealed the promise, making it clear that despite the obstacles and distrust, she was ready to face whatever came her way to win the love and trust of the man who was becoming more entrenched in her heart.

That night, they both left that encounter with a renewed bond, even though it was filled with uncertainties and challenges. Alessia knew the journey would be dangerous, that by Matteo's side, the risks would only grow, but she also understood that she was exactly where she wanted to be.

Matteo watched Alessia from across the room, where she was speaking with a few trusted allies. His gaze was fixed and full of an intensity that mixed contained admiration with persistent distrust. The conflict inside him was evident, but he was a master at hiding his emotions. Alessia, on the other hand, tried to concentrate on the conversation, though she felt the weight of Matteo's stare every second. She knew he was studying her, looking for any sign that would confirm his suspicions, but at the same time, there was something more. He wasn't just the cold, calculating mafia boss; there was a spark in his eyes, something she barely dared to decipher, but that made her heart race.

Matteo walked slowly toward her, his steps calculated and silent. When he got close enough, Alessia felt the air around them change, an electricity hanging between them. She turned to face him, keeping her posture firm, but her eyes betrayed a mix of challenge and curiosity.

"Don't you ever get tired of analyzing me so much, Matteo?" she teased, lifting her chin in a gesture of defiance.

He smiled wryly, that arrogant smile she knew all too well, but now it made her shiver. "I'm just trying to understand the intentions of my wife," he replied in a low voice, full of tension. "After all, you always surprise me."

Alessia raised an eyebrow, leaning slightly in his direction. "And since when do you like surprises, Matteo? I thought you preferred absolute control."

He moved even closer, invading her personal space with a proximity that made them both aware of the magnetism between them. "Normally, yes," Matteo admitted, his voice almost a whisper, as his eyes locked onto hers with penetrating intensity. "But you seem to have a special talent for challenging each of my rules."

Alessia felt her heart race. Even though she tried to keep control, the effect he had on her was undeniable. "And why don't you just admit that it intrigues you?" she whispered, feeling her own voice tremble.

Matteo raised his hand to her face, his fingers gently touching her skin as he traced the outline of her face. The touch was both gentle and possessive, and Alessia couldn't help but close her eyes for a moment, surrendering to the sensation.

"You forget, Alessia..." he murmured, his voice deep but full of something almost vulnerable. "In my world, vulnerability is weakness. And you make me feel things that... that I shouldn't."

Alessia opened her eyes, meeting his gaze. There was a rare honesty in his words, something that made her see beyond the ruthless boss and into the man Matteo was hiding. "Maybe not everything is weakness, Matteo," she replied, holding his gaze. "Maybe you're just afraid to feel."

He let out a short laugh, but the smile on his lips didn't reach his eyes. "Afraid? Alessia, I don't know what it means to be afraid."

She let out a soft laugh, moving even closer until their faces were mere inches apart. "Then why are you always so close and, at the same time, always pulling away?"

The provocation in her voice seemed to strike something deep within Matteo. He tilted his face, his lips almost brushing hers, and whispered, "Maybe, Alessia, you're the one thing I've never been sure I could control."

What started as light teasing turned into an intense exchange filled with emotions. They were in a game of attraction, where each word felt like a promise and every glance, an invitation. Matteo moved closer, but before he could take any definitive action, Alessia stepped back, leaving him with an expression of surprise and dissatisfaction.

"Control that, Matteo," she said with a provocative smile. "Because I'm not the kind of woman you can control."

As she walked away, Matteo watched her, struggling against the impulse to follow her. He knew this woman was different from all the others, someone who challenged him, who dismantled his defenses with a simple look. But at the same time, she was the greatest risk he'd ever allowed into his life. And in that moment, he realized that maybe, just maybe, he was willing to take the risk.

# Chapter 43: The Plan to Overthrow Lorenzo

Alessia stood in the quiet room, where the dim lights cast shadows on the walls, reflecting the weight of the decisions to come. Luca stood by her side, his expression serious. Both knew the risk they were about to take. The evidence against Lorenzo was carefully organized—documents revealing his plans, secret alliances, and, most importantly, his betrayal of Matteo's trust and the Romano family itself. It was a dangerous game, where any misstep could cost them their lives.

"Are you ready?" Luca asked, his tone grave, but there was mutual understanding between them.

Alessia nodded, but her heart tightened. Even though Lorenzo was her father, that man had long stopped being a father figure to her. Now, in the face of the harsh truth about his intentions, Alessia saw clearly that loyalty by blood was a burden she had to abandon in order to protect what truly mattered. She thought of Matteo, the intensity in his eyes, the way he challenged her and, at the same time, enveloped her in a dangerous passion. Alessia knew that the only way to prove her worth was to follow through with the plan, even if it meant severing all ties with her past.

"Luca, I need you to understand..." Alessia began, hesitating. "Matteo... he's important to me. More than I ever imagined anyone could be."

Luca sighed deeply, looking away for a moment. He knew there were complex feelings involved and, even though he felt something for Alessia, he respected the bond she shared with Matteo.

"Alessia, I just want you to be safe. I'll help because I know what Lorenzo is capable of, and if this plan is your chance for freedom, I'll be by your side," Luca replied sincerely.

Alessia felt a wave of gratitude, but also a heavy weight. She knew that Luca's involvement put him in danger, and the fact that he was willing to go against his own father for her was something she would never forget.

For days, Alessia and Luca worked in silence, crafting the strategy with precision. Alessia secretly met with old friends and allies—people who still held genuine loyalty to her and wanted to see the Romano organization freed from Lorenzo's cruel grasp. Every meeting was held in caution, in isolated locations, and every word was carefully chosen to ensure nothing leaked.

Meanwhile, Matteo noticed Alessia's absence. His heart, usually wrapped in a controlled coldness, began to show cracks. He saw less and less of her every day, and the distance made him uneasy, making him question if, in the end, she was involved in something more. On impulse, he entered the office where Alessia was organizing documents in the darkness of the night; the only light was from a lamp casting a soft glow on her face.

"Did you think I wouldn't notice your absence?" Matteo said, his voice low, but filled with suspicion mixed with a vulnerability he hated to show.

Alessia looked up, surprised, but kept calm. She knew this moment was crucial to dispel any doubts Matteo still had.

"Matteo, I'm... taking care of things that need to be dealt with before it's too late," she replied, trying to balance sincerity with the need for protection.

He approached, his steps soft but deliberate, stopping just a few inches from her. His eyes analyzed every detail, as though searching for a clue in Alessia's face that could confirm or deny his suspicions.

"And do these 'things' involve my safety or your loyalty?" Matteo's question landed like a blow, and Alessia felt the urgency to reassure him that she was on his side.

"Matteo, everything I'm doing is to protect what we have. I know it's hard to believe, but..." She paused, looking him directly in the eyes, letting him see the raw sincerity in her heart. "I'm on your side. Even if it means losing my own family."

For a moment, Matteo's expression softened, and he took a deep breath. Even though he was a man hardened by life, there was something in Alessia's gaze that disarmed him. He extended his hand and cupped her face, gently running his thumb along her jawline as if trying to etch that feeling into his memory.

"Just give me a reason, Alessia, to believe in you," he whispered, his voice low and intense, filled with a mixture of desperation and desire.

"I'm giving it to you, Matteo," she answered, her voice almost a whisper. "The risk I'm taking, the people I'm defying... it's all for you."

They stared at each other, and the tension between them seemed to grow stronger, evolving into something even more intense. Matteo pulled her into a kiss, one that mixed anger, passion, and a desperate need for reassurance. His touch was possessive, as if sealing what she had just said, while Alessia responded with equal intensity, allowing herself a moment of complete surrender.

When the kiss ended, they remained silent, their gazes locked. Matteo, despite all his layers of control, knew there was something in Alessia that disarmed him, and he hated the power she had over him.

"Prove it to me, Alessia," he murmured, still with his fingers tracing her face. "Because if this is another betrayal, there won't be another chance."

She nodded, knowing that this moment was pivotal. Now, all that was left was to follow through with the plan and show him, not with words, but with actions, that her loyalty belonged to him.

As Alessia stepped away from Matteo after their intense confrontation, she felt a whirlwind of emotions swirling inside her. The weight of Lorenzo's threats and Matteo's distrust seemed to form an insurmountable barrier, but still, she knew that, despite all the risks, something deep inside kept her by his side. Matteo wasn't just the cold, calculating man the world saw; he was someone who, in small moments, showed a vulnerability that few were privileged to witness. And it was precisely this complexity that attracted her, even knowing the dangers involved in loving someone like him.

Matteo, on the other hand, watched Alessia as she left the room. He felt the strength of his distrust pulling him in one direction, while the undeniable attraction to her pulled him in another. There was a silent anger, a frustration he could barely understand. He had always been a man of calculation, someone who knew what he wanted and controlled every aspect of his life. But Alessia, with her defiant presence and vulnerable demeanor, shattered that security. She disarmed him, and he hated that feeling, hated that someone could have so much power over him. Yet, at the same time, he couldn't resist.

That night, Matteo found himself standing in the hallway, his fists clenched as he thought about all the ways Alessia left him unstable. He knew she was keeping secrets, but he also knew that, no matter how hard he tried, he couldn't just see her as a threat. Decided to confront her once more, he walked toward her bedroom, his footsteps firm and echoing through the silent mansion.

When he entered, Alessia was standing on the balcony, gazing out at the city lights. She heard his footsteps and turned, her face showing a mix of surprise and expectation. Matteo approached slowly, stopping just a few inches from her. The intensity of his gaze made the air around them feel thicker.

"What do you really feel, Alessia?" Matteo asked, his voice low but firm, as though demanding a confession.

Alessia felt her heart race. She knew she needed to be careful with her words, but in that moment of vulnerability, something inside her gave way.

"Matteo... I feel like I'm caught between two forces that are going to destroy me," she whispered. "Between my duty to my family and something... something much deeper for you."

He stepped closer, his eyes darkening, as though those words had struck something deep inside him. His finger traced her face, outlining her jaw before stopping at her chin, making her look directly at him.

"Alessia, you know that in this world, trust is a rare weapon, and you're playing with it in a way that makes me question everything," he said, his voice rough, laden with a mix of desire and anger.

Alessia breathed deeply, feeling his presence so close and the heat radiating from his body. Even knowing the risks, she found herself unable to pull away.

"I never wanted it to be this way, Matteo. I never planned on feeling something for you, but..." Her voice faltered for a moment. "But I can't control what I feel."

Matteo, unable to resist that confession, pulled her into a possessive kiss, their lips meeting with intensity, as if trying to resolve their frustrations through that contact. Alessia responded with the same intensity, feeling every barrier between them melt away. For a brief moment, they were both vulnerable, with no need to hide anything.

After the kiss, he kept her in his arms, looking into her eyes with an expression that mixed desire and something deeper, perhaps a silent admission that, against his will, he was as involved as she was.

"Alessia, you affect me in a way I hate to admit. And if you're lying to me... I don't know if I can forgive you," he whispered, keeping his eyes on hers.

"Then give me a chance to prove I'm not," she answered, challenging him, knowing that this was the only way for him to see her for who she truly was.

Matteo slowly released her, taking a step back, but his gaze remained fixed, showing that even as he tried to pull away, he was drawn back to her. He knew that any mistake could cost him everything, but in that moment, the possibility of believing her seemed more tempting than any revenge or control.

Both knew that this was only the beginning of a dangerous game, where every move carried the risk of destroying them. However, for the first time, they felt willing to take the risk.

# Chapter 44: A Confrontation with Danger

On a bitter winter night, Alessia quietly stepped out, determined to face Lorenzo, her father, in a remote and isolated location. The atmosphere was suffocating, shrouded in shadows and silence, reflecting the tension she carried in her chest. She knew this meeting would be decisive, a line drawn that would leave no room for return. When Lorenzo finally arrived, the sound of his footsteps echoed through the emptiness, carrying a weight that seemed to reflect the dark intentions behind each step.

Lorenzo, with his penetrating, unwavering gaze, approached, his eyes narrowed in a mix of disdain and distrust. Before he could speak, Alessia met his gaze with resolve, her voice laced with an unexpected courage.

"I know everything, Father. I know your plans against Matteo, the alliances you've formed in the shadows to destabilize him and destroy everything he's built." Her voice didn't falter, even though her heart was in a storm.

Lorenzo flashed a cold smile, full of sarcasm.

"So, this is it? You, my daughter, turning against your own family? All because of a man who should be your enemy?" He let out a dry laugh, his tone dripping with contempt. "I expected more from you, Alessia. I thought you were smarter, less... sentimental."

Alessia swallowed hard, but didn't look away.

"If being sentimental means wanting to choose my own path, then yes, I am guilty. I won't allow you to manipulate my life any longer, Father. I know what you've done, and I won't let you destroy the only man who truly cares about me." She threw the words like blades, piercing the impenetrable armor Lorenzo had always shown.

The fury on Lorenzo's face intensified, his eyes burning with rage. He took a threatening step toward her.

"You don't understand, Alessia." His voice dripped with venom. "Everything I've done was to strengthen the family, to ensure that we Romans remain untouchable. You're just a pawn in this game, and your place is to follow orders, not question them."

Alessia lifted her chin, her eyes reflecting a firmness he had never seen in her before.

"I'm no one's pawn anymore. I will fight for what I believe in, even if that means facing you. I won't betray the one person who showed me some truth, someone who, despite everything, showed me that I can be more than a tool. I am more than your puppet, Father, and I am ready to pay the price for it."

Lorenzo laughed bitterly, but there was a gleam of threat in his eyes.

"You think he'll protect you, Alessia? That this man, Matteo, truly cares for you?" He leaned in, his voice a sharp whisper. "You'll learn the hard way that in our world, loyalty is a treacherous currency. He'll destroy you before you even realize it."

Lorenzo's words sank deep, leaving Alessia breathless for a moment. But as he turned to leave, threatening to leave her alone with her choices, she felt a flash of certainty. She couldn't go back, even if she wanted to.

When she arrived home, every step seemed to carry the weight of that decision. Matteo was waiting in the hallway, his expression dark and filled with questions. He didn't know exactly where she'd been, but his face was a mixture of concern and suspicion. Upon seeing Alessia, he moved closer, his eyes scanning her face for answers.

"Where were you?" he asked, his voice cold, hiding the worry in his gaze.

Alessia took a deep breath, feeling tired but determined to face whatever came next.

"I was where I needed to be." She answered with the same firmness, unafraid to provoke him.

Matteo studied her, his eyes analyzing every inch of her expression. There was something different about her, something that both challenged and drew him in.

"And I'm supposed to believe that without any further explanation?" His voice was cold, but for a second, his eyes seemed to beg for a justification, a reason to trust.

Alessia stepped forward, closing the distance between them, as if daring that mistrust. Her eyes met his, and she felt a wave of conflicting emotions stir within her.

"I don't need you to trust me, Matteo. I just need you to see that I'm doing everything I can to protect what's important to me." Her voice softened slightly. "And that includes you."

Matteo fell silent, feeling the weight of her words. Each one seemed to pierce the armor he had built over the years, challenging him to believe, to yield, to lower his defenses. He raised a hesitant hand, gently touching her face with a softness Alessia hadn't expected.

"If you betray me, Alessia, there will be nothing left but ruins for both of us," he whispered, his voice laced with a hidden fear, a vulnerability he rarely revealed.

Alessia placed her hand over his, pressing it against her face.

"Then don't doubt me." She replied in an almost inaudible tone, but full of emotion.

They stood like that, in silence, their hands intertwined, their gazes locked on one another. It was a silent truce, a moment of peace in the chaos that surrounded them.

Matteo watched Alessia in front of him, his eyes scanning every detail of her face, as if trying to decipher something beyond her words, something she hadn't yet revealed. He felt the weight of his distrust, but at the same time, an irresistible urge to trust her. The feeling of allowing himself to depend on someone again made him uneasy, almost as if he were lowering his guard to an enemy. He, who had always maintained absolute control, now felt his heart waver in her presence.

Alessia, on the other hand, was fighting an avalanche of emotions. Being so close to Matteo, touching him and feeling his breath near her stirred something inside her that she hadn't imagined. Even knowing the dangers it represented, a part of her wanted to continue this game of tension. She wanted to provoke him, to make him fight between anger and desire, a silent battle that seemed to spark something intense between them.

"You know, Matteo," Alessia murmured, with a challenging tone. "You're always so controlled, but I see the truth. Behind those cold, distant eyes, you're vulnerable too." She raised an eyebrow, her gaze intense.

Matteo smiled, but there was something dark in his smile, a mix of arrogance and desire.

"Vulnerable?" He whispered, his voice low, laced with sarcasm. "Do you really think you have that effect on me, Alessia?"

"I think I've already proven that I do, Matteo." She took a step closer, reducing the distance between them, letting the provocation hang in the air.

Matteo's gaze hardened, but there was a gleam in his eyes, something Alessia had only glimpsed on the rare occasions he let down his guard.

"Be careful what you wish for, Alessia. You might end up caught in the same game you're trying to play against me," Matteo murmured, gently but firmly holding her chin, as if daring her to back down.

She didn't back down. Instead, she leaned in slightly, just enough to feel the warmth of his breath on her face, the touch of his fingers against her skin. Alessia's heart raced, but her expression remained firm.

"I'm not like the others, Matteo. I'm not afraid of you." Her words were resolute, but deep down, she knew there was an internal conflict within her. With each provocation, the thin line between desire and hatred blurred, making it harder to distinguish.

Matteo released her chin, but didn't pull away. His gaze remained fixed on her, and for a moment, they stood in silence, trapped in a suffocating tension. Finally, he spoke, his voice almost like a confession.

"And that's why you're dangerous, Alessia." His words were harsh, but his tone revealed an unexpected vulnerability. "Because you make me question every decision, every limit I've set for myself. And that... that I cannot allow."

Alessia smiled, a defiant smile, but her eyes revealed the internal battle she was also fighting.

"Maybe it's time for you to allow yourself a little more, Matteo. What are you really afraid of?" she asked, her voice laced with provocative sweetness.

He suddenly pulled her in, his gaze now overwhelming. Matteo held her face, his touch both delicate and possessive.

"I fear losing myself in you, Alessia. And in this world, that could cost us everything." The words were whispered, almost like a confession he didn't want to admit.

She felt the impact of those words, the way he was opening up, even if just a little, showing the man hidden beneath layers of coldness and hardness. Alessia raised one hand, gently touching his face, feeling the warmth of his skin under her fingers. Matteo closed his eyes for a moment, surrendering to the touch, as if that brief moment of peace was something he'd longed for.

"What if losing yourself is the only way to find yourself, Matteo?" she whispered, her voice soft, almost a caress to him.

Matteo opened his eyes, and for a moment, his gaze was purely human, without the mask of the mafia boss, without the weight of being the most feared and impenetrable man. He leaned in and kissed her, a deep kiss that carried all the repressed intensity, the desire they both tried to control.

When they pulled apart, both were breathing heavily, but Matteo's eyes remained fixed on hers.

"Alessia, if you go down this path, there will be no turning back for either of us," he said in a grave tone, but his gaze was different. It was a warning, but also a promise.

Alessia took a deep breath, feeling the weight of his words, but knowing that with him, she was ready to face whatever came their way. They were playing with fire, but in that moment, the danger only intensified the attraction between them.

# Chapter 45: The Final Revelation

Alessia crossed the door of the mansion with the overwhelming sensation of loss. Her confrontation with Lorenzo still lingered in her mind, mixed with the fear of what this final break could mean. Upon seeing Matteo waiting for her, she felt the weight of the distrust he still held, even after all the sacrifices she had made. Their eyes met, and she realized he was ready to question her, ready to demand answers.

Taking a deep breath, Alessia walked toward him and handed over the documents, her fingers trembling slightly as she gave them to him. Matteo accepted the package in silence, opening it and reading each page, his face changing as the information sank in. With each word, he began to understand what Alessia had faced, the danger she had risked, and the weight of the decision she had made when she betrayed him for the last time to protect him.

"Why did you risk so much?" he murmured, still not looking up from the papers. "Why not just go back to your family, where you would have power, safety?"

Alessia felt the pain of his words like a blow. But despite the implied accusation, she knew this was her chance to open her heart, to show him that, despite everything he expected from her, she chose to stand by his side.

"Because... I'm not that person anymore—the one who submitted to what Lorenzo planned. Because, despite everything, I see who you are, Matteo," she replied, her voice softer than she intended. "I knew the risk I was taking by doing this, but it's what my heart told me to do. Maybe it's too late for you to believe it, but... you are my choice."

Matteo finally lifted his gaze, his hardened face softening. Alessia's words seemed to echo in his mind, a mix of relief and regret crossing his eyes. He took a step closer, close enough for her to feel the warmth radiating from his body.

"You risked your life for this alliance... for me?" he asked, his voice low, almost a whisper.

Alessia nodded, hesitant but determined. "Yes. I wanted you to know that I'm on your side, Matteo. Even if it means losing everything."

He raised his hand and touched her face with tenderness, his thumb gently tracing a line across her cheek, which immediately grew warm under his touch. "You risked everything for us," he murmured, his voice carrying a vulnerability he rarely allowed to show.

That touch, so unexpected and delicate, brought a torrent of emotions to the surface. Alessia's heart raced, a mix of relief and love flooding through her. It was as if, for a brief moment, all the barriers between them had fallen, leaving them only with the raw and sincere truth of their feelings.

"Matteo..." Alessia murmured, trying to hide her own emotions, but knowing he could see right through her.

He moved closer, his gaze locked on hers, and whispered, "I want to leave the past behind too. Maybe... maybe it's time to start something real."

His words hung in the air, and for the first time, Alessia allowed herself to believe that this moment could be the beginning of something she never expected to find amidst the chaos and danger of their lives.

Matteo looked at Alessia with an intensity she could barely bear, as if he was seeing every piece of her soul. He was the head of one of the most powerful and dangerous mafia families, a man hardened by power and violence, but here, in front of her, his eyes revealed something beyond the calculated coldness he usually wore. For the first time, Alessia felt she could see the man behind the mask of the ruthless leader.

Alessia, for her part, was struggling against a whirlwind of emotions. She felt vulnerable and exposed, but also inexplicably safe in his presence. Despite all the dangers Matteo represented, the control and authority he wielded over everyone and everything, she sensed a tenderness hidden beneath his brusque gestures, a subtle, but palpable care.

"Alessia," Matteo murmured, his voice firm, but carrying a rare note of hesitation. "You... challenged me like no one ever has." He took a step forward, closing the distance between them, while his hand found her chin, gently lifting it so their gazes met. "You entered my life like a whirlwind, and I've never been able... to stop myself from being swept away by you."

She felt the heat rise in her cheeks, and her response came out almost as a whisper, filled with emotion. "I never wanted any of this, Matteo. I was forced into this marriage, but... I couldn't help what I feel now. Even though I hated you at first, now I can't imagine my life without... you."

He smiled, a rare smile that softened his otherwise hard expression, and lowered his face, coming so close that Alessia could feel his breath mingling with hers. It was the kind of closeness that made her heart beat unevenly, a mixture of desire and nervousness that she hadn't felt since the beginning, when it was all just a game of provocation and resistance.

"Do you know what this is, Alessia?" Matteo asked, his voice deep and low, almost a whisper laced with emotion. "It's danger. Being with me is dangerous, standing by my side means your life will always be at risk. I have enemies who would do anything to strike at me, and you... are my most vulnerable point now."

Alessia didn't look away, remaining firm. "I know the risk I'm taking. And, despite that, here I am. I'm not going anywhere, Matteo."

He hesitated, as if considering her words, searching for any sign of doubt in her eyes, but all he found was determination. Alessia wasn't just an imposed wife; she was his partner. That understanding, that acceptance, seemed to strengthen them both, while also carrying an inevitable vulnerability.

Matteo pulled her closer, finally letting down his guard as their lips met in a deep, intense kiss, laden with all the emotions they had been holding back. Alessia felt his warmth, the possessive and protective touch that scared her so much, but at the same time, made her feel whole.

When they finally broke apart, he held her firmly, as if fearing she might disappear. "I'm a man who commands through fear and respect, Alessia," he confessed, his eyes dark and honest. "But with you... it's different. With you, I'm just Matteo."

Alessia smiled faintly, touching his face gently. "And that's why I'm here, Matteo. Because, despite everything, you let me see that side of you."

They stood there, in silence, understanding that, no matter how much their worlds were marked by darkness and violence, they had found each other, and that, no matter how dangerous it was, it was something worth protecting.

# Chapter 46: The Price of Betrayal

Throughout the night, Alessia and Matteo remained in the library, where the shadows of the tall shelves cast a somber, austere air around them. Matteo was silent, watching the flickering flame of a candle, reflecting the gravity of the situation they were facing. For Alessia, the room, usually a refuge, now felt like a place of waiting, restlessness, and preparation for the inevitable. She felt the weight of the betrayal on her shoulders, but when she looked at Matteo, her heart calmed.

He broke the silence, his voice deep and steady. "Alessia, by choosing to stay by my side, you know you can never turn back." His hand found hers, gripping tightly, like a protective ring. "Lorenzo is merciless. He won't hesitate to destroy everything we have."

Alessia looked up at him, determined, and replied firmly, "I know, Matteo. But by your side, I feel I've finally made the right choice. The price of betrayal is high, but I'd rather face any danger than live under his control."

Alessia's response made Matteo's gaze soften for a moment, revealing a mix of admiration and respect. He brushed his hand across her face, his thumb gently tracing a line down her cheek. "You're stronger than I imagined, Alessia," he murmured. "And I... I won't let anything happen to you. You have my word."

She smiled softly, feeling the warmth of that touch, as if all the fear and tension of the situation dissolved in Matteo's firmness. Despite knowing they were surrounded by enemies and threats, it was in that touch, in that look, that Alessia found an unprecedented sense of peace. Still, they both knew that Lorenzo wouldn't let his daughter's act of defiance go unpunished.

Matteo stood up and looked out the window, which overlooked the mansion's dark gardens. He knew that from this moment on, he had to stay alert, for Alessia's betrayal meant an open war with Lorenzo and his allies. The air around them seemed thick with the tension of what was to come, and he turned to Alessia with determination.

"I'll reinforce security at every entry point. Lorenzo will come prepared to attack where we're most vulnerable. He knows what we're doing, and he won't rest until he's seen us destroyed."

Alessia moved closer, standing by Matteo's side. She felt closer to him than she had ever felt to anyone else. "Matteo, you've already done so much for me... for us. I don't want to be just someone you need to protect. I want to fight by your side, to be beside you not as a burden, but as a partner."

He looked at her, surprised by her determination. Matteo knew Alessia was strong, but this strength went beyond what he had imagined. Without a word, he pulled her into an embrace, holding her tightly, almost as if sealing a silent vow between them. For Matteo, Alessia had stopped being just a forced wife or a pawn in a power game. She had become his equal, someone who had chosen to stand by him, even at the bitter cost of betrayal.

"Alessia," he whispered into her ear, his voice heavy with emotion. "You have no idea how much this means to me. But know that by choosing this path, you're choosing to live in danger, in uncertainty... always in the shadow of enemies and dubious allies."

She smiled faintly, her eyes shining with fierce intensity. "That's the price I'm willing to pay, Matteo. I chose you... I chose us."

The bond between them felt stronger than ever, a connection forged not just by need or circumstance, but by the mutual choice to face the storm together. They knew nothing would be easy, that Lorenzo would not rest until he destroyed what they were building, but they also knew that, in this moment, they had something precious: each other's trust.

That night, Matteo and Alessia shared something more powerful than words or promises. It was a silent pact, a decision to face whatever the world could throw at them together. And as they prepared for the imminent battle, they were both aware that, despite the uncertainties, there was no safer place than by each other's side.

Matteo sat in his office, alone, immersed in heavy thoughts about the situation with Lorenzo and Alessia's decision to turn against her own family. He knew she had lost much, and as he remembered the courage she had shown confronting Lorenzo, he felt something deeper than admiration. It was a feeling he hadn't allowed himself to experience in a long time. That woman, whom he had once considered an adversary, had become the person he trusted most and wanted to share the darker, more vulnerable parts of his life with.

As Alessia entered the room, Matteo looked up and saw her standing at the door, her expression one of someone carrying the weight of the world. She hesitated for a moment, but then stepped into the office and approached him, the silence between them heavy with meaning and unspoken words. Matteo noticed the shadow of uncertainty in her eyes, and before she could speak, he stood up, closing the door with a firm gesture, signaling that this would be a moment for just the two of them, away from the prying eyes and intrigues of the outside world.

"Are you sure about this, Alessia?" Matteo asked, his voice low, but full of intensity. "I won't let you go back. Not after what you've faced... and what you've sacrificed to be here."

Alessia lifted her gaze to him, and in her eyes was a mixture of challenge and vulnerability. "I've never been one to back down, Matteo. I chose this path. I chose you." She stepped closer, her fingers grazing his, almost by accident, but it made both of them hold their breath. "But... I'm afraid. Not of Lorenzo, or what he might do, but of everything this means. We both know this life is a high-stakes game."

Matteo watched her with an intensity that made her shiver. The usual banter between them had transformed into something deeper and more intimate, as if the resistance and desire that had always been present were now impossible to ignore. "I've never been a man of grand gestures, Alessia," he said, his tone almost a whisper. "But what I feel for you... it's different. I can't see you anymore as just a business partner or an arrangement. It's more than that."

She sighed, trying to maintain her composure, but feeling her defenses breaking. "Then prove it, Matteo. Prove that this is more than just an arrangement. That I'm not just another name on your long list of alliances."

Matteo stepped closer to her, so close that he could feel the heat of her skin. He cupped her chin, gently lifting her face so she would meet his gaze. "Do you think I haven't proven enough by defying Lorenzo at your side?" He pulled her even closer, his lips almost touching hers. "I don't need alliances without meaning, Alessia. I need you. With all your choices, and all the consequences they bring."

At that moment, the silence between them became unbearable. Alessia couldn't resist anymore and closed the space between them, pressing her lips to his. The kiss was fiery, a mix of repressed desire and silent promises, a complete surrender without words. Matteo held her tightly, his arms enveloping her possessively, almost as if he wanted to protect her from all the danger surrounding them.

When they finally broke apart, both were breathless, but with renewed certainty. Matteo looked at her, and with a slightly arrogant smile, whispered, "So, now do you believe me?"

Alessia let out a soft laugh, still feeling the warmth of the kiss and the intensity of the moment. "Maybe I need more proof," she replied with playful provocation. "But for now... maybe I'll give you the benefit of the doubt."

They stared at each other, both smiling, both aware that their relationship was built on challenges, provocations, and, above all, an attraction that defied all logic and rules of the world they lived in. At that moment, though, none of it mattered—the danger, the betrayals, or the secret plans. It was just the two of them, caught up in something bigger than any conspiracy or alliance.

# Chapter 47: Attack in the Dead of Night

The silence of the night hung heavily over Matteo's mansion, like a dark promise on the verge of being broken. The darkness spread across the stone walls, making everything even quieter, the air dense, charged with a tension that felt alive. Matteo knew that the peace in his life with Alessia was fragile. Even when they were together, something in their gazes confessed that the truce between them and the world was far from complete.

He patrolled the hallways alone, his thoughts on the upcoming meeting with his allies the next day. His senses were always on alert, trained to catch any strange movement, any sound that might indicate a threat.

Suddenly, the distant sound of heavy footsteps reached his ears. Matteo stopped, his body tensing, eyes narrowing. Then, a sharp crack came from outside, followed by an explosion that shook the walls and shattered the silence of the mansion like glass being crushed. Matteo didn't need another second to understand: they were under attack.

He rushed to Alessia's room, where he hoped to find her safe, but the explosions and the sound of breaking glass in the distance made it clear that Lorenzo Romano had sent henchmen to storm his house without mercy. The shouts of his men echoed through the mansion, and gunfire quickly began flooding the corridors with overwhelming intensity. Matteo knew they were at a disadvantage. The Romanos weren't here to negotiate; they were here to kill.

In Alessia's room, the silence was abruptly broken when she heard the sound of the first gunshot. Adrenaline started coursing through her as her heart raced. She knew that, despite all the bravado she pretended to have, she wasn't prepared for the kind of war her own family had brought to her doorstep. She ran to find cover, but before she could hide, the door swung open forcefully, and Matteo appeared with a determined expression, his eyes fiercer than ever.

"Alessia!" he called, his voice low and sharp. "Stay behind me."

She hesitated, but the fear in her eyes didn't go unnoticed by Matteo, who grabbed her arm firmly, guiding her to a safe corner of the room. The intensity of his touch brought her security, and for the first time, Alessia allowed herself to trust that, by his side, maybe she would survive whatever Lorenzo had planned.

Matteo pulled out a gun, his eyes scanning the hallway, alert to the sounds of footsteps and harsh commands from his men.

"Alessia, listen," he murmured, without taking his eyes off the door. "We need to get out of here, but you have to follow every order I give, without questioning. Understood?"

She nodded, her face tense. Matteo made his way down the hall, and she followed closely behind, her eyes wide open, trying to prepare for what was to come. The hallway had already become an improvised battlefield, the echoes of gunshots filling the air and the scent of gunpowder permeating everything. One of Lorenzo's henchmen lunged toward them, but Matteo was faster, shooting him down before he could cause any harm.

The steps echoed on the marble floor as Matteo and Alessia moved through the hallways. Suddenly, they heard a closer explosion, and Alessia was thrown to the side, falling to her knees as dust and debris filled the air around them. Matteo immediately crouched beside her, wrapping his arms around her tightly, protecting her from the impact of the shrapnel.

"Are you hurt?" he asked, his voice low, but his concern evident in his eyes.

She nodded, still gasping for breath, and when she tried to get up, she felt a sharp pain in her side. Matteo immediately noticed the bloodstain appearing on the sleeve of her blouse and clenched his fists, his eyes turning dangerous.

"This won't go unpunished, Alessia," he murmured, his voice dark with fury. "Lorenzo dared to attack us like this, and he's going to pay dearly for it."

His words echoed in Alessia's heart, and though she was injured, she felt strangely protected in that moment. She saw the fierce determination in Matteo's eyes—a man willing to do anything to keep those he loved safe.

"Matteo, you don't need to do this for me," she whispered, trying to hide the emotion in her voice, though she knew he could see through what she was trying to mask.

He stared at her intensely, his eyes burning. "Don't underestimate what I'm willing to do, Alessia. Neither you nor anyone else is leaving this situation unprotected, not while I'm still breathing."

When they managed to stand up, Matteo held her firmly by the arm, guiding her down an alternate path that would lead them downstairs, where he hoped they could find shelter until reinforcements arrived. But just as they were about to reach the exit, they were ambushed by more of the Romano's henchmen. Chaos erupted again, with Matteo firing while trying to cover Alessia, and she, overcoming her panic, grabbed a fallen weapon at her side.

"Watch out!" he yelled as he saw her wielding the gun for the first time. Alessia hesitated, but the determination to survive made her pull the trigger, hitting one of the men approaching. Matteo looked at her with something akin to pride, as adrenaline took over both of them. She was no longer just a woman trying to survive; she was becoming a warrior, someone fighting alongside him.

When they finally reached a safer point, both of them were out of breath, Alessia's face marked by tension and exhaustion, but her eyes shining with newfound strength. Matteo pulled her to him, his strong arms enveloping her, as he took a deep breath, trying to recover and assess what they had just faced.

"You fought well," he murmured, his voice a little softer. "I didn't know you had it in you."

She managed a smile despite the pain. "I didn't know I'd have to fight for my life in my own home," she replied with a bitter tone, but still grateful to be alive.

Matteo cupped her face in his hands, forcing her to meet his gaze, his eyes intense, as though he were trying to memorize every detail of her in that moment. "This will never happen again. I won't allow anything or anyone to hurt you again, Alessia. I promise."

His touch was firm but gentle, and Alessia found herself yielding to his fierce yet protective gaze. It felt like a new, deeper connection had been forged there, in that instant, amidst the chaos and danger. For a moment, everything around them disappeared, and the only sound left was their rapid breathing, still marked by the adrenaline.

After the attack, Matteo took her to his office, where he could tend to her injuries with a minimum of privacy. Alessia sat on the edge of an armchair, watching him as he grabbed a first-aid kit. The attentive way he prepared the materials made her realize that, beneath his cold and powerful exterior, Matteo hid a sensitive side that he rarely allowed anyone to see.

He carefully cleaned the wound, his fingers touching her gently, almost as though handling something too fragile to rush through. Alessia watched him in silence, his eyes focused on her arm, his face concentrated and filled with intensity that made her lose herself.

"You didn't have to protect me like this," she said, breaking the silence. "I would have found a way out."

He sighed, a faint smile tugging at his lips. "Don't say nonsense, Alessia. I promised I'd take care of you, and that's what I'll do, whether you like it or not."

Her eyes met his, and Alessia felt that, in that moment, there was something more between them than words could express. She felt safe, protected, as if no harm could touch her as long as she was there with him. For the first time, she realized that Matteo was not just a ruthless man; he was a warrior, willing to risk everything for her.

She reached up to touch his face, feeling the roughness of his stubble, and a shiver ran through her body as she saw the look he gave her. "Matteo... thank you," she whispered, the words heavy with a vulnerability she rarely allowed herself to show.

He took her hand in response, bringing it closer, until the distance between them was nonexistent.

Matteo remained close to Alessia, the silence between them heavy but strangely comforting. He had never allowed himself to show this much to anyone; in fact, he never imagined himself in this position, caring for the wounds of a woman who not only challenged him but, in some way, completed him. His hand still held hers tightly, a current of something unknown flowing between them. He studied every feature of her face, as though the intensity of his gaze could keep her safe forever.

Alessia felt the warmth of his touch on her skin, and although she knew that Matteo was a man capable of indescribable brutality, that gaze conveyed a promise of care and protection she never imagined receiving from someone like him. Still, it wasn't easy to accept her feelings. There was fear, distrust, but there was also desire and something even deeper, something she didn't dare name. For a moment, Alessia wanted to surrender, let that moment be just theirs.

"You're... insufferable," she murmured, her voice hesitant, but her eyes still locked with his, as if something invisible was stopping her from pulling away.

He smiled, this time with an intensity that made her catch her breath. "Good to know," he replied, the tone teasing, but his eyes filled with an unexpected softness. "Because you're the same. And I wouldn't change a thing."

They remained like that, in silence, their bodies close, both feeling the intensity of that moment. Matteo knew that by keeping Alessia close, he was putting her in danger, and that scared him in a way he never imagined. He had power, strength, control, but with her, those concepts crumbled, and he found himself exposed. For her, he would do anything. And although he knew their world was dark, that night, in that instant, he felt at peace by her side.

"I know it's not easy," he said finally, his voice carrying a rare hint of vulnerability. "But if there's one thing I'll never do, Alessia, it's leave you behind. I won't let anyone take you from me. We're in this together, no matter how insane it seems."

She smiled, a genuine smile, feeling that even amidst the chaos, by his side, she was home.

# Chapter 48: The Peace Proposal

On the night before the meeting, the air in the mansion felt dense, and the shadows seemed darker than usual, as if anticipating what was to come. Matteo and Alessia were discussing the details of the plan, and the tension between them was palpable. Sitting in front of a table covered with maps and strategic plans, Matteo's serious expression showed that he knew exactly how risky this move was. Alessia, on the other hand, tried to suppress her nerves. She knew that facing her father in a situation like this would require more than just strategy; it would take courage.

"Let's clear this up," she said, breaking the silence that had lingered for long minutes while Matteo reviewed documents in front of him. "What's your real goal with this meeting, Matteo? I don't believe for a second that you really think peace with Lorenzo is possible."

Matteo lifted his gaze, his eyes penetrating hers like a sharp blade. He knew he couldn't fool her, and maybe he didn't want to. "Alessia, I know it's hard to believe, but if there's a way to avoid a bigger bloodshed, it's this meeting. If Lorenzo commits to a true truce, we can minimize the losses."

She watched him silently, her shoulders relaxing just slightly. Deep down, she wanted to believe his words, but she knew her father well enough to understand that he never accepted an agreement without hidden motives. "And what if he decides it's easier to eliminate you once and for all?" she asked, her voice low but filled with genuine concern.

Matteo reached out, placing his hand over hers. His touch was firm, warm, and conveyed a security that only he could inspire in her. "Alessia, I'll be ready for anything. I'm going with the intent to propose peace, but don't expect me to hesitate in ending Lorenzo if he crosses the line." His voice was filled with a dark determination, an unspoken promise that he wouldn't hesitate to protect her and everything they had built together.

She looked at him, feeling the truth in his words, but a chill ran down her spine as she thought about the consequences of such a meeting. "Promise me you won't risk your life unnecessarily, Matteo," she murmured, her eyes shining with an intensity filled with emotions she no longer tried to hide. "I... I can't lose you."

Matteo cupped her face, his touch warm and comforting, yet still filled with a strength that calmed her. "I promise you, Alessia. I won't risk myself beyond what's necessary. But I know this is the only chance we have to live without this constant threat."

They stared at each other for a moment that felt eternal, a silent understanding flowing between them. Alessia saw in him the firmness of someone who never backed down, even in the face of danger, but she also saw a man who, in some way, had surrendered to her—someone who had learned to put her well-being above his own ambitions.

The day of the meeting, the tension was thick in the air. Matteo and Alessia prepared in silence, each aware of the responsibility that this encounter carried. Matteo wore a dark suit, his demeanor even more rigid than usual. He knew he was about to face one of the most calculating men in the criminal world, a man who wouldn't hesitate to break any agreement if it served his own interests.

Alessia accompanied him, and as they entered the car, she felt a chill. She knew her father was unpredictable, and the peace meeting could easily turn into a deadly trap. Matteo looked at her, noticing the unease on her face, and took her hand in his.

"Trust me," he said, with a gentleness few had ever heard from him. "I know exactly what I'm doing, and I won't let him deceive us."

She nodded, trying to keep her heart steady. Matteo's presence, the security in every gesture he made, helped her feel stronger. Still, she couldn't ignore the fear growing within her. It was as though she knew this meeting wouldn't bring lasting peace, but rather an uncertain truce.

The car drove them to an abandoned building on the outskirts of the city. The place seemed deliberately chosen for any eventuality: silent, deserted, and without witnesses. Matteo got out of the car first, his eyes scanning the area before extending his hand to Alessia, who took it without hesitation. Beside him, the Romano family mansion seemed smaller, as if it were waiting for the exact moment to rebel against Matteo's control.

As soon as they entered, they were greeted by Lorenzo, who awaited them with a stern face and a calculated smile. Upon seeing Alessia beside Matteo, his frown deepened, his eyes flashing with a mixture of surprise and contempt. "I didn't expect my own daughter to ally herself so deeply with my enemy," he said, each word dripping with venom.

Alessia, however, kept her gaze steady. "You forced me into this, father. Your obsession with power has always been greater than any feelings for me."

Lorenzo smiled bitterly, his face contorting. "Feelings are for the weak, Alessia. That's why I always knew you were destined to fail if you let your heart guide you."

Matteo interrupted the exchange between father and daughter, his voice cold and controlled. "Lorenzo, I'm here to discuss a truce, but if you intend to insult Alessia, this meeting ends now."

Lorenzo let out a dry laugh, regarding Matteo with a disdainful expression. "You've always been so impulsive, Matteo. You shouldn't let this girl interfere with your plans."

Matteo moved closer, each movement calculated, his eyes fixed on Lorenzo. "I'm here for her, Lorenzo. And I'm also here to give you a chance to avoid a war that will destroy us both. Agree to a truce and allow your daughter to have the life she deserves. Or continue this war and face the consequences."

Lorenzo fell silent, his eyes narrowing as he assessed each word, weighing the risk of the agreement. Finally, he smiled, but there was a dangerous gleam in his eyes, a look Alessia knew all too well. It was the look of a man who never admitted defeat.

"I can accept a truce, Matteo," he said slowly, each word laced with an unspoken threat. "But know this—I don't trust you. I know that at any moment, you could try to turn the game in your favor."

"Just as you would do with me," Matteo replied, without hesitation, a cold smile spreading across his face. "But if Lorenzo Romano is the intelligent man you claim to be, you know this is better for all of us."

The tension in the air was thick, but Lorenzo nodded slowly. "Very well. We'll end this war... for now."

Alessia saw the gleam of revenge in her father's eyes. She knew he didn't accept this as a defeat and that Lorenzo wouldn't let this situation go unpunished. She squeezed Matteo's hand beside her, feeling the comfort of his presence, even though she knew the future was still uncertain.

As they left the building, she turned to Matteo, her eyes reflecting the uncertainty she tried to mask. "Do you really believe this truce will last?"

He pulled her close, his arms enveloping her protectively. "I know Lorenzo is a dangerous man, Alessia. I'm not naïve enough to believe this truce is forever. But as long as it lasts, we'll be ready for anything. And I promise you, I won't let anything or anyone hurt you."

She smiled, a smile that carried both relief and the worry she couldn't avoid. "I know what we have is fragile, Matteo, but maybe it's enough. We're together. And that's what matters."

Matteo leaned in, his touch as soft as the promise of protection he had made. They both knew the danger was constant, that the truce was merely a pause. But in that moment, nothing else mattered but the strength they shared.

As they left the building where the peace meeting had taken place, Matteo and Alessia found themselves enveloped in a heavy silence, filled with tension. The car waiting for them was parked under the dim light of a streetlamp, and on the way to it, Matteo kept his hand firmly over hers, as if the simple gesture was a silent promise of protection. His hand was warm and strong, and Alessia felt inexplicably safe. Even after the intense confrontation, Matteo's presence was an anchor for her.

When they entered the car, he closed the door behind him and let out a long sigh, before looking at her with a mix of relief and caution.

"I won't lie, Alessia," he said, with a small smile. "You scared me in there, with that deadly look you gave your father. I thought you were going to rip his head off right then and there."

She smiled, a little surprised by his light tone, but she couldn't resist the teasing reply. "I did consider doing that, I admit. But I decided it's better for this war to have you as the mafia boss instead of me. You seem to handle betrayals and deals well, while I... well, I'm just a betrayed daughter."

Matteo looked at her with admiration, the intensity in his gaze capturing her in a way she couldn't ignore. "I prefer you exactly as you are," he murmured, his voice deep, carrying a sincerity that disarmed her completely. "That strength, that courage... I never imagined I'd find someone so... resilient."

She looked away for a moment, trying to hide the blush rising in her cheeks. Matteo always knew what to say to disarm her, but the way he complimented her now, so far from the teasing remarks from when it all began, made her feel vulnerable and, at the same time, desired in a way she had never experienced before.

"I know it sounds crazy," he said, as if reading her thoughts, "but since you came into my life, I realized that despite everything, there's something here." He placed his hand on his chest, right where his heart beat fast. "Something only you awaken."

She remained silent, feeling his words echo in her own heart. She knew that from the beginning, Matteo had represented everything that should have been dangerous and forbidden. But, paradoxically, he was the only person who truly understood her, who saw beyond appearances and the blood that united them as enemies.

"Matteo," she whispered, trying to find the right words, "I know we're trapped in this world of darkness, of constant danger. But... by your side, no matter how contradictory it seems, I feel a peace I never imagined feeling."

He smiled, and the smile, which had once carried arrogance and challenge, was now soft and full of tenderness. Matteo moved closer, his face just inches from hers, as his strong hand gently cupped her face.

"And I... never thought anyone would make me want to leave this darkness," he murmured, his voice soft but filled with emotion. "But, Alessia, with you, I see a path that was once impossible."

She took a deep breath, feeling his touch against her skin. "Then, promise me you'll stay by my side. That no matter what happens, we'll face it together."

Matteo leaned in even further, until their lips were so close she could feel his breath mixing with hers. "I promise you, Alessia. That whatever happens, I'll be by your side. And if necessary, I'll face the whole world to keep you safe."

They kissed, a kiss that carried all the promises words could never express. Matteo held her tightly, as if assuring that nothing, not even the constant danger surrounding them, could tear her from him. It was a kiss that spoke of surrender, of desire, but above all, of love.

When they pulled apart, Alessia sighed but kept her face close to his. "I still think you're annoying," she murmured, with a smile that revealed how that teasing was just part of a game that had become vital for them both.

"Great," he replied, with a low, deep laugh. "That way I know the Alessia who made me lose my head is still here."

The car took them back home, but in that small space, isolated from the world and its dangers, they shared a moment that was just theirs. They knew the peace was fleeting, that their world was filled with betrayals and risks. But as long as they were together, they were stronger than any threat.

And, for the first time in a long time, Matteo felt that, amid the chaos, he had found something worth protecting at any cost.

# Chapter 49: Secrets of the Past

Night fell silently over the mansion, but Alessia felt restless, as if the air around her was charged with secrets. The meeting with Lorenzo had brought up memories and suspicions she had buried, but now, by Matteo's side, something pushed her to seek answers, to uncover every fragment of the past her father had tried to hide. She knew that digging into the past could be dangerous, but she couldn't ignore the feeling that something was missing, that an essential piece of the puzzle was still hidden.

Sitting in her room, Alessia opened an old box of documents that had belonged to her mother. Those papers hadn't seen the light of day in years, but she knew that among the notes, letters, and clippings, there was something that could lead her to the truth. Matteo was in his office, reviewing plans to ensure the mansion's security after the attack. She knew he trusted her, but she also knew that revealing what she suspected about Lorenzo and his mother's death would carry a devastating weight.

As she flipped through the papers, one letter in particular caught her attention. It was a correspondence from Lorenzo to Matteo's father, full of vague promises and, in parts, veiled threats. The tone was cold, and one phrase stood out: "The agreement will only be fulfilled if each of us does our part. There is no room for mistakes." Alessia felt a shiver as she imagined what that could mean. Matteo's mother's death, which occurred shortly after the signing of that agreement, now took on a new perspective. Her hands trembled slightly as she tucked the letter into her pocket, knowing she had to tell Matteo what she had discovered, even if it meant opening an old wound.

Matteo was in his office when Alessia entered, her footsteps light but her face tense. He noticed her gaze, the shine of uncertainty and anguish in her eyes. "What's wrong, Alessia?" he asked, sensing the growing tension.

She took a deep breath, trying to calm the agitation in her chest before speaking. "Matteo, I... there's something you need to know." She moved closer, pulling the letter from her pocket and placing it on the desk. "I found this among my mother's old documents. It's a letter from my father to yours... just before your mother's death."

Matteo took the letter, his eyes quickly scanning the paper, the lines imprinted in his mind like a bitter revelation. When he finished reading, he closed his eyes for a moment, struggling to control the fury and sadness that flooded his heart. He had suspected a larger plot, but he never imagined that Lorenzo was so directly tied to the worst moment of his life.

"So this is it..." he murmured, more to himself. "My mother wasn't just a random victim of an attack. She paid the price for a dirty deal between our families." He raised his gaze to Alessia, his eyes filled with deep pain. "Everything in my life has been manipulated, every decision, every loss... it's all been calculated by your father's whims."

She felt her chest tighten as she saw Matteo's suffering laid bare. She approached him, taking his hand in a gesture that mixed support with regret. "Matteo, I'm so sorry. I... I never knew the extent of everything Lorenzo was capable of. But I'm here now, by your side, and I promise we'll uncover every detail, every secret he tried to hide. I won't let this story end like this."

He squeezed her hand, a silent thank you in his touch, but his expression revealed the anger that was growing inside him, a flame that refused to be extinguished. "Alessia, I don't know what this path will cost us, but I know I can't let this story die. I need to know the truth, and I need to get justice for my mother. Lorenzo will pay for every pain he caused, and not just to me."

She nodded, her gaze determined. "Then we'll do this together. I'll help you uncover every secret, expose everything. I'm willing to face Lorenzo, even knowing how dangerous he can be. There's no turning back for me. And if that means fighting by your side, then that's exactly what I'll do."

He pulled her close, enveloping her in an embrace that was both a promise and a silent plea for support. "You don't know what that means to me, Alessia. My whole life, I fought alone, hiding every pain and every secret. And now, for the first time, I feel like I'm not alone anymore."

She tightened her embrace, feeling the weight of the mission they now shared. Matteo's pain had become hers too, and she knew nothing would stop them from seeking the truth. After a moment, she pulled back slightly, looking at him with a mix of strength and tenderness. "I know it's difficult, Matteo, but there's something else I need to ask you... Are you prepared for what we might find? For the fact that, in the end, it might be me who has to confront my father?"

Matteo held her face, his eyes shining with an intensity that disarmed her. "Alessia, I know it's unfair to ask you to choose between your loyalty to your family and the truth. But you've already made that choice, and I don't know how to thank you for it. Together, we are stronger than any dark past they try to hide."

She smiled, a soft and determined smile. "Then we're in this together... to the end."

The next morning, they began the investigation, analyzing documents, making contacts, and seeking information that could confirm their suspicions about Lorenzo's involvement in Matteo's mother's death. With every discovery, they felt closer to a terrible and inevitable truth, but also closer to each other. Alessia saw in Matteo a strength that went beyond his role as the mafia boss;

he was a man driven by love and loyalty—qualities he had never abandoned, despite everything.

One night, while discussing the information they had gathered, Alessia watched him in silence, noticing the weight he carried on his shoulders. Without saying a word, she moved closer and placed her hand on his face, caressing him softly.

"Matteo, you don't have to carry this burden alone. I'm here, and together we'll get to the end of this story, no matter how painful it may be."

He took her hand against his face, closing his eyes for a moment. "Alessia, I don't have the words to express what this means to me. The thought that you're by my side... it's something I never thought I'd have."

She smiled, moving even closer, until their faces were inches apart. "Then don't say anything. Just know that for you, I'll face anything. And now... you'll never be alone again."

They kissed, and in that moment, all fears and uncertainties seemed to disappear. Matteo and Alessia were united not only by the past but by the promise of a future, no matter how dangerous it might be. And although they knew the road ahead was filled with challenges and risks, their love and determination made them stronger, making them unbeatable.

That night, they decided they would not rest until the truth was revealed, until Lorenzo and all those responsible for the pains of the past paid for their actions. The bond between them had become stronger than any agreement or alliance forged by their families. They were now an unbreakable alliance, driven by love and justice.

In the quiet of the office, as the shadows of the night enveloped them, Matteo and Alessia stood side by side, immersed in the quest for truth and settling accounts with the past. The tension between them was thick, but not in the way it had been before, when they saw each other only as obstacles, veiled threats. Now, each shared glance, each touch, carried a deep meaning, as if the weight of their stories had united them in an irrevocable way.

Matteo watched Alessia as she read a document, her eyes focused and serious. He couldn't help but smile, admiring her courage in standing by his side, even knowing the risks. She was no longer just a pawn in this game; she was his partner, his accomplice, and that was more than he had ever expected to have.

"You're staring at me," Alessia murmured, not looking up from the papers, but a subtle smile forming on her lips.

He gave a small laugh, leaning back in his chair, relaxed, but his eyes still fixed on her. "It's hard not to stare when you're so determined. And besides..." He leaned in a little closer, lowering his voice. "I admit, I've got a thing for your stubbornness."

She rolled her eyes, but a light blush colored her cheeks. "I think you're losing focus, Matteo. We're not here to flirt."

"If you distract me like this, maybe you're not as focused as you claim," he teased, smiling with that mischievous glint that always managed to disarm her.

Alessia put the papers down and looked at him, arms crossed. "You're unbearable, you know that? How can you stay so calm when we're in the middle of a storm? As if nothing is enough to shake you."

He looked at her with intense eyes, the smile replaced by a more serious expression. "Nothing scares me anymore when I'm with you. With you, I feel invincible. And that, Alessia, is something I've never felt before."

She blinked, surprised by the raw sincerity he shared. Matteo was known for his hardness, his coldness, and his ability to keep everyone around him in the palm of his hand. But there, he was stripping away his defenses, revealing a vulnerability that made her feel special.

"Matteo... you know this is crazy," she whispered softly, her voice tinged with emotion as she looked into his eyes. "If I were the Alessia of before, I'd still be trying to destroy you, to see you fall."

He nodded but a slight smile appeared at the corner of his lips. "Maybe that's why I fell for you, Alessia. Because you were the only one who challenged me, the only one who wasn't afraid to face me." He slid his hand to hers, holding it gently, fingers intertwined. "And now, together, we're stronger. Stronger than any threat from the outside."

She squeezed his hand, feeling the warmth and strength of his touch, as if it were an anchor keeping her connected to him. "So, Matteo, promise me that no matter what happens, we'll face this together. That you won't back down."

He pulled her even closer, their faces inches apart, and whispered, with an intensity that took her breath away: "I'll never back down, Alessia. Not for you, not for anyone. And if anyone tries to come between us, I'll do whatever it takes to protect us."

She smiled, a smile full of provocation and admiration. "I should be scared of you, you know?"

He raised an eyebrow, leaning in to whisper in her ear, his voice low and husky: "Are you?"

She stared at him, her smile becoming even more playful. "No. I think I'm more attracted to you than I should be."

Matteo laughed, a low laugh full of desire. "Good. Because you're the only one I want by my side, through all of this. You're the only danger I'm willing to face."

Alessia felt her heart beat faster, the tension between them building. Matteo pulled her toward him, and their lips met in an intense kiss, filled with everything they had tried to ignore. It was a kiss of surrender, a silent pact, a promise that they would face every battle, every danger, together, against everything and everyone.

When they pulled away, Matteo's gaze was softer, but still determined. "You're my weakness, Alessia," he murmured, caressing her face. "But you're also my strength."

She touched his face, running her fingers gently along his strong jawline, and smiled. "And you're the most stubborn and dangerous mafia boss I've ever known. I think we're destined for this madness together."

Matteo pulled her even closer, and in that moment, they both knew that, no matter how many secrets and promises of revenge the past held, the future would be faced side by side. What they had was stronger than any family agreement, stronger than any fear. It was a love built in tension, in danger, and it grew stronger with every moment they spent together.

In the midst of the chaos surrounding them, they knew they had found something worth fighting for, and even if the world collapsed around them, nothing would be able to tear them apart.

# Chapter 50: Justice and Vengeance

The morning was gloomy, reflecting the heavy burden that Matteo and Alessia carried. They had passed the point of hesitation, and now they were immersed in the pursuit of the truth about his mother's death and Lorenzo's dark role in it all. Matteo's determination was unshakable, and Alessia, standing by his side, felt a mix of pride and fear. She knew the truth would bring them even closer, but she feared what vengeance might do to Matteo if he allowed himself to be consumed by his fury.

That morning, they met with one of the former members of the Romano organization, a man named Vittorio, who was now in Matteo's custody. Vittorio had once been a close ally of Lorenzo, but as threats and loyalties shifted, Matteo knew he could use the man to get the answers he sought.

The office where the interrogation took place was dim, the heavy curtains blocking the sunlight, creating a dense and oppressive atmosphere. Matteo and Alessia stood, while Vittorio, his hands bound, looked at them with a mixture of defiance and resignation.

"I'm only going to ask once, Vittorio," Matteo began, his voice firm but controlled, as though keeping his anger contained behind a thin layer of self-restraint. "I want you to tell me everything you know about Lorenzo's involvement in my mother's death."

Vittorio hesitated, but Matteo's gaze was that of a predator about to strike. Alessia observed in silence, her hands slightly trembling, but her gaze sharp, ready to support Matteo in every decision.

"Do you really think Lorenzo is going to forgive anyone who talks about this?" Vittorio retorted with a nervous laugh. "He'd kill me before he'd consider any kind of truce."

Matteo stepped closer, his eyes cold, his voice low. "And do you think I can't do the same? You lost your loyalty a long time ago, Vittorio. So speak. The truth is the only path left for you now."

Vittorio swallowed hard, his gaze wavering as he understood the seriousness of the situation. "Alright, alright," he murmured, his voice tense. "Yes, Lorenzo was involved. He benefited from the deal, Matteo. Your mother... she was an obstacle, a weakness that Lorenzo used to get what he wanted. The deal with your father... it involved more than you think. Money, control, influence. And her death was a consequence of that."

Matteo clenched his fists, every word from Vittorio fueling the rage he struggled to contain. Alessia, noticing how deeply it was affecting him, touched his arm, trying to convey some calm. But the truth, once revealed, was like acid, corroding every fiber of control Matteo still had.

"The deal... so it was all about power," he murmured, his voice heavy with dark resentment. "My mother was sacrificed so these bastards could keep their alliances?"

Alessia looked at him, her eyes full of silent understanding. She knew that beneath the anger, Matteo was shattered, crumbling inside as he realized the extent of the manipulation that had involved his own family.

"Matteo," she whispered, trying to pull him back before he got lost in that abyss. "I know it's hard to hear all of this, but we need to think about what we're going to do now. We can't let this vengeance consume you."

He stared at her, pain evident in his gaze, as though every part of him was falling apart. "Alessia, my mother was killed for greed, for an alliance that destroyed any sense of dignity. How do you expect me to control the rage when I know Lorenzo benefited from her suffering?"

She cupped his face in her hands, forcing him to focus on her. "Matteo, you have every right to seek justice, to demand that Lorenzo pay for every repulsive act. But I will be by your side, and I can only do that if you promise that we will act together, calmly. I don't want to lose you to this vengeance."

His eyes softened slightly as he looked at Alessia, and he placed his hand over hers. "I won't lose you, Alessia. But Lorenzo needs to pay. And he will."

The next day, Matteo and Alessia organized a meeting with remaining members of the Romano organization who had lost faith in Lorenzo. Every word they uncovered about the patriarch's actions made it clear the level of corruption and manipulation he had imposed on his own alliances. Matteo knew that, to bring an end to it all, he would have to destroy Lorenzo completely, dismantle his influence, and expose every secret.

As they planned their next steps in his office, Alessia watched Matteo with a mix of apprehension and admiration. He was the figure of an unyielding leader, someone willing to sacrifice everything for justice. But at the same time, she knew this was the man who, in moments of calm, looked at her with tenderness that no one had ever seen.

"Do you really think he will give in?" she asked uncertainly. "Lorenzo isn't the type of man who's easily defeated."

Matteo looked at her, a dark smile forming on his lips. "No, Alessia, Lorenzo is stubborn and proud. But I will dismantle every piece of power he's built. He will lose everything before he falls."

Alessia breathed deeply, feeling the weight of the plan unfolding before them. "Matteo... you know this won't be easy. And I know it will consume you until the last second."

He took her hand, his gaze softer now, as the rage gave way to a tenderness reserved only for her. "None of this is worth it if I don't have you by my side. This war, this vengeance... it's for justice, but it's also so we can live in peace."

She smiled, a smile full of love that went beyond words. "Then, we're in this together until the end. I'll be here to remind you of who you really are. You're so much more than this anger."

He pulled her to him, holding her tightly, as if he needed that closeness to stay grounded. Matteo knew the road ahead was treacherous, but Alessia was his light, his refuge amid the chaos.

"Alessia, you are all that's good in my life," he murmured against her hair. "I don't know what I'd do without you."

She pulled back just enough to look into his eyes and smiled. "You don't need to know. Because I'm here. And together, we'll face whatever comes."

They stayed there, in that moment of complicity and love. Deep down, they both knew the war wouldn't end anytime soon, but the bond between them made them invincible. Matteo and Alessia were a force that even Lorenzo couldn't foresee, a union forged in pain, but held together by love and the determination to finally put an end to the cycle of betrayal their families had created.

As they prepared for the next step, they both knew that fate had brought them together for something greater. The justice they sought wasn't just vengeance; it was the freedom they both longed for, and together, they would do whatever it took to achieve it.

In the stillness of the night, Matteo and Alessia were alone in the office, the room bathed in a soft yellow light casting shadows around them. The silence between them wasn't uncomfortable, but laden with an intensity that almost seemed palpable. After everything they had uncovered about Lorenzo, the weight of it all felt heavier, and yet, in that moment, Matteo could only think of Alessia.

He watched her as she flipped through some documents, her face focused, her eyes shining with a determination he admired.

There was something so profound about her, a mix of strength and vulnerability, that made him feel incapable of resisting. When Alessia looked up and noticed him staring, she couldn't help but smile, raising an eyebrow in challenge.

"Are you going to stand there staring at me like a hungry wolf, or are you going to say something?" she teased, her tone daring in a way that always made his heart race.

He smiled back, that slow smile full of intensity that always made her breath catch. "I can't help it. You fascinate me, Alessia. Every detail, every part of you. And you know it."

She rolled her eyes, but couldn't hide the blush spreading across her cheeks. "Maybe I've just gotten used to being the center of attention. Especially when there's a certain mafia boss involved," she replied, trying to sound casual, but his gaze made her feel disoriented.

Matteo took a step closer, closing the distance between them until he could feel her presence overwhelming. "You know, Alessia," he said, his voice low and laced with an unspoken promise, "in the midst of all this chaos, you're the only thing that makes everything make sense. No matter how many enemies, how many betrayals... as long as I have you by my side, I'm willing to face anything."

She felt her heart race, each word of his touching her in a way that made her question everything she believed about love and who she was. He wasn't just an unrelenting mafioso; with her, he was simply Matteo, the man willing to risk everything for someone he loved.

"Don't think I'm going to make things easier for you," she responded, still trying to keep the playful tone, but her voice cracked slightly with the emotion she felt. "I'm your partner, Matteo, but that doesn't mean I'm going to follow you without questioning every decision you make."

He smiled, his face drawing closer, until his lips were a hair's breadth from hers. "That's why I fell for you, Alessia. Because you never feared challenging me. You never tried to mold yourself into what I wanted. And maybe... maybe that's what makes me completely yours."

The intensity in his gaze was almost overwhelming, and Alessia couldn't resist any longer. With a mixture of desire and emotion, she placed her hands on his face, her fingers trailing along his jawline before pulling him into a kiss that wasn't just physical, but charged with everything they felt for each other. It was a kiss of surrender, of unspoken promises, and of a love that refused to be tamed.

When they pulled away, Matteo's eyes still burned with that fierce intensity. He cupped her face, his thumbs gently caressing her cheeks, and whispered, with a tenderness that contrasted his usual hard tone: "I never imagined I could feel something this deep. You transform me, Alessia. And I don't care if that means being weaker... as long as it's for you."

She smiled, but her eyes were misty. "You're not weak, Matteo. And being by your side... makes me stronger, too."

Alessia realized that, no matter how dangerous and uncertain the world around them was, in his arms, she felt safe. As if nothing could break what they were building together.

She teased, with a light smile, "So, mafia boss, are you finally going to admit you can't live without me?"

He laughed, that low, husky laugh that made her melt, and pulled her closer. "Yes, Alessia. I admit it without reservation. And I hope you're ready, because I'm willing to face hell and back... just to have you by my side."

Those words struck deep within Alessia, and she looked at him as if he were the only man who mattered in the world. "And

I'm ready to go wherever you go, Matteo. You're not alone in this anymore. Whatever comes, we'll face it together."

They stayed there, in the comfortable silence, feeling the weight of the promises they had made. Matteo knew that, no matter how hard he fought against a past full of pain, with her by his side, he could finally see a future where there was more than vengeance. A future where there was love, and maybe even peace, something he had never dared to dream.

And Alessia, looking at him, knew that, despite all the threats and dangers, there was no place in the world she'd rather be. Matteo was her home, her north. And with him, she was ready to face whatever came their way, because now, more than anything, she understood what it meant to love a man like him.

In that moment, both of them realized that the love they shared was the most powerful force they had.

# Chapter 51: The Treacherous Discovery

The darkness of the office enveloped Matteo as he flipped through the yellowed papers he had found in a secret safe. Each line, each word of the letters and messages burned in his eyes like a flame, fueling the rage that grew relentlessly inside him. The letters between Alessia and Lorenzo were ambiguous, but they revealed a closeness and an understanding of the marriage plot he had never imagined. The idea that Alessia, his Alessia, knew more than she had let on was like a sharp knife cutting through his chest.

Matteo couldn't control the thoughts flooding his mind. He remembered every moment when Alessia had sworn loyalty, every vow of love, every time he had believed he had found someone he could trust completely. Now, every memory became a shadow, a reflection of betrayal and manipulation.

When Alessia entered the office, she immediately noticed the tense and dark expression on Matteo's face. He stared at her as though he didn't recognize her anymore, as if she were an enemy instead of his ally and lover. His cold gaze made her shiver.

"Matteo... what happened?" she asked uncertainly, stepping forward.

He held the papers in his hands, her eyes immediately falling on the familiar letters. She felt her heart sink when she realized what they were.

"What happened?" Matteo repeated, his voice low but each word laced with venom. "I think it's me who should be asking that, Alessia. What happened between you and Lorenzo? Because, it seems, you knew far more about our marriage than you let me believe."

Her eyes widened, taking a step back, pain crossing her face as she saw the coldness in his eyes. "Matteo, I can explain... these letters don't mean what you think."

"Don't mean what?" he retorted, laughing bitterly. "And what exactly do they mean? Because what I see here is an Alessia who was involved in your father's plan from the beginning, who knew everything and still pretended to be my ally, pretended to love me. Tell me, Alessia, what was real all this time?"

His voice sounded bitter, the words cutting her deeply, as if each syllable were a cold blade. She felt her chest tighten, her throat dry as she tried to approach him, but Matteo's cold gaze stopped her.

"I never wanted to deceive you, Matteo," she murmured, her voice trembling. "These letters... my father used me like a pawn, like he always does. He knew I would never agree to such a dark plan, so he manipulated everything. Made it look like I was part of the game, but Matteo, I fought for you... for us!"

He laughed again, but without humor, his eyes narrowing in distrust. "Fought? And let me believe, all this time, that we were equals, that you were different. Now I see that you are just as manipulative as he is."

"No, Matteo, you're wrong!" Alessia exclaimed, tears welling in her eyes. "I never wanted this, I never wished for things to turn out this way. When I realized what was happening, it was too late! I tried to pull away, I tried to resist, but then you appeared... and I... I fell in love."

Her words seemed to hang in the air, but he absorbed them with an expression of pain and disbelief. "Love? You think that matters now? Alessia, you broke my trust. And there's no going back from that."

He turned away, his back to her. Alessia, desperate, stepped forward, grabbing his arm. "Don't push me away, Matteo. I know it looks like betrayal, but I never deceived you on purpose. Everything I did after that was for you, to prove I'm loyal, that what I feel is real."

He turned around, his face full of rage. "Unspoken truths are lies too, Alessia! How can I trust you now? How can I believe that all those moments were real?"

She felt the tears fall but didn't wipe them away. She knew she had to fight, she knew she couldn't let him think everything was a lie. "You know my heart, Matteo. You know every corner, every truth. If you just stop for a moment and look beyond this pain, you'll know that my love for you is real. It always has been."

Matteo looked at her, his face torn between rage and pain. For a moment, she thought he might relent, that her words might break through the wall of distrust. But he stepped away, his gaze growing colder.

"Maybe one day I'll believe you again, Alessia," he murmured, his voice hoarse. "But today... today you're just another lie that I need to fix."

She felt her heart break hearing those words, but she didn't retreat. "I won't give up on us, Matteo. I know you're hurt, but I know the man I loved is still there. You want revenge, but you're just distancing yourself from the truth that's right in front of you."

He stared at her, a mixture of desperation and anger in his eyes. "Then prove it, Alessia. Prove that I can trust you. But don't expect me to open up again. You broke me, and now that pain will follow you too. We'll see how much you can fight for what you say you feel."

She nodded, determination burning in her chest. "If that's the condition, then I accept it. I'll prove it to you, Matteo. I'll show you that my love and loyalty are real."

Matteo watched her in silence, and at that moment, Alessia knew they had returned to square one, but with much more at stake. She was willing to go through hell to regain his trust. And even with the pain of rejection he was imposing on her, she knew she wouldn't give up. After all, Matteo was everything to her—and the love they shared, though wounded, was the only thing worth fighting for until the end.

In that moment of thick silence, Alessia felt the weight of the world on her shoulders, but also the intensity of what remained between them. Even with Matteo's cold gaze, she saw traces of pain, of hesitation—as if, no matter how hurt he was, he still couldn't completely detach from her. Every part of her wanted to scream, to break the distance he was putting between them, but she knew words wouldn't be enough; she would have to show, through every gesture and sacrifice, how much he meant to her.

Matteo was torn. There was a part of him that wanted to believe Alessia, that longed to hear her voice confirm that all of this was a misunderstanding. But the betrayal weighed on his chest like a burden, and he fought the urge to surrender, to give in to the irresistible force that always pulled him toward her. When he looked at her, he saw the woman who challenged him, who loved him with an intensity he had never known existed. And that was exactly what made the pain even deeper.

He sighed, breaking the silence. "You say you love me, Alessia, but all I see now is a chain of lies. How do you expect me to forget all of this? How do you expect me to trust again?"

Alessia took a step forward, her eyes steady, her voice soft but full of determination. "I don't expect you to forget, Matteo. I know I've hurt you, and maybe I'll never be able to erase that pain. But give me a chance to prove that what I feel is real, that every word of mine, every touch, was true. I don't want you to forgive me easily. I just want the opportunity to show you that I'm on your side, that I will fight until the end for us."

He looked at her, hesitant. Reason told him to step back, to keep that safe distance. But his heart seemed incapable of obeying, and Matteo felt control slipping through his fingers. He knew he loved her, that what was between them was much stronger than wounded pride and distrust.

"Do you really think one chance will be enough?" he murmured, his voice low, almost a whisper.

She smiled faintly, a hidden sadness in her eyes, but a flame of determination burning even brighter. "I don't think I have another option. And I know you're the most difficult man in the world, but I fell in love with you precisely because of that. Because I know that, behind this armor, there's someone worth fighting for."

Matteo couldn't help but smile bitterly, but his eyes softened. "You know, Alessia, you always throw me off balance. You've always been the only person who could make me question my own rules. And maybe... maybe that's what makes me hate you and love you with the same intensity."

She felt her heart race, as if that moment, that fragment of surrender from him, was proof that there was still something between them. She moved closer, touching his face with a near-reverent softness. "Then hate me if you need to. But know that what I feel for you will never change. I'm here, Matteo, and nothing will push me away."

He took her hand, pressing it against his face while closing his eyes. That touch, that presence, was still a comfort he couldn't find anywhere else. Finally, he opened his eyes, looking at her with an overwhelming intensity. "This is madness, Alessia. Everything between us is madness. But I can't help it... you're the only person who makes me want to face any hell."

She smiled, a smile full of tenderness and unshakable love. "Then let's face it together. I'll go through everything with you, Matteo. I promise I'll prove to you, with every act, that I never wanted to hurt you. And I'll be by your side, even if it means fighting against the world."

Matteo pulled her closer, his arms wrapping around her possessively, as if he needed that contact to push away all the doubts. When their lips met, it was a kiss full of urgency, desperation, but also an unbreakable connection. It was as if, in that moment, both of them had given up any doubt, any pride. All that mattered was what they felt for each other, the raw truth that existed between them.

When the kiss ended, they stayed close, their foreheads touching, breathing together as if they were synchronizing their broken hearts. Matteo held her even tighter, as if he never wanted to let her go again.

"This isn't forgiveness, Alessia," he whispered, his voice still rough with emotion. "But it's a beginning. And I promise I'll watch you, every step you take, every gesture. I'll demand every proof you want to give me."

She nodded, her eyes sparkling. "You can demand it, Matteo. I'll show you that, despite everything, we're real. I'll never give up on us."

In that moment, both knew they had taken a step toward redemption, a step toward rebuilding the love that, though wounded, still burned between them with the intensity of a flame that would never go out.

# Chapter 52: Cold Revenge

In the days that followed, Alessia noticed that the Matteo she once knew seemed to be disappearing, replaced by a colder, more calculating version. Matteo ignored her in every significant aspect of the organization, making decisions without even mentioning them to her, as if the trust and partnership they had built were nothing more than an illusion.

That morning, Alessia found him in his office, engaged in a conversation with two of his trusted men. When she entered, Matteo didn't even lift his gaze. She waited for him to notice her, but he ignored her completely, until Alessia finally found the courage to speak up.

"Matteo, we need to talk about the next steps," she said, trying to keep her voice steady despite the pain she was feeling.

He finally lifted his eyes, but the look he gave her was icy, devoid of the tenderness she had once known. "Talk to someone who cares, Alessia," he replied dismissively, before turning his attention back to his men. "We're in a meeting. Your presence isn't necessary here."

That rejection hit her like a knife in the chest. Alessia felt her blood boil, her pride wounded, fighting against the pain. "I thought we were partners, Matteo. I thought you trusted me enough to discuss this together."

He let out a short, cold laugh, not even bothering to look at her. "Trust you? I think I made that mistake once, and I won't fool myself again. Maybe I was a fool to believe in your promises."

Alessia took a deep breath, trying to hold back the tears threatening to spill. She wanted to scream, to make him see how deeply his words were cutting her, but she knew that would only feed the bitterness he felt. Instead, she decided not to give him that satisfaction.

"You're making a mistake," she murmured, her eyes fixed on him, silently pleading for Matteo to see beyond the cold mask he was wearing. "I never lied about what I feel for you."

"You want to believe that, Alessia," he retorted, his voice devoid of emotion. "But we both know that, deep down, you've always been loyal to him. To Lorenzo." He stood up, walking toward the door without giving her another chance to explain.

Matteo left her alone in the office, her heart tight and a sense of emptiness settling over her. She tried to follow him, but he constantly avoided her, and what hurt the most was realizing he made a point of showing off with other women at organizational events. It was as if he wanted her to notice his indifference, to see just how much he was rejecting her.

One night, during a party organized for allies, Alessia watched from a distance as Matteo conversed intimately with a woman, his hand sliding down her arm, a smile effortlessly playing on his lips. He glanced at Alessia for a brief moment, but his gaze was empty, almost as if he didn't recognize her. Alessia felt her heart shatter, but she knew she needed to confront him.

Later that night, after the guests had left, she finally found an opportunity to speak to him. Matteo was sitting on a couch, relaxed, but with a lost look in his eyes. Alessia approached, her breath heavy, her feelings overflowing with pain and anger.

"Is this what you want, Matteo?" she asked, her voice thick with emotion. "To hurt me, push me away, destroy me?"

He lifted his eyes, and for a brief moment, Alessia saw a flicker of pain in his gaze, but he quickly regained his cold composure. "I just want you to understand what it feels like to be betrayed, Alessia. And know how much it hurts."

"So it's cold revenge, is that it?" she whispered, her heart shattered. "You want to punish me for something you never even tried to understand fully?"

"Maybe I do," he said, his voice harsh. "Maybe I want you to feel what I felt when I discovered I was just a pawn in Lorenzo's game. A whim of your father's."

She closed her eyes, trying to absorb the blow. Matteo was distancing himself from her as a form of protection, but she knew his revenge was also hurting him. Alessia moved closer, her gaze filled with tenderness and sadness, and knelt before him, holding his hands despite the disdain he radiated.

"Matteo, I know you're hurt, and I know it won't be easy to forgive me. But I was never loyal to my father. I've always been on your side, even if you don't see it now."

He stared at her, his eyes unreadable, but his face filled with pain. "How can I trust you, Alessia? How can I believe after everything?"

She gripped his hands, pulling them to her chest, where her heart was beating desperately. "I can't erase the past, Matteo. But I can promise you that my love for you is the only real thing I've ever had. And I'm willing to fight for you, for us, until the end."

He withdrew his hands, his gaze heavy with anguish. "Fight for us? You don't understand, Alessia. I can't bear this doubt anymore. Every time I look at you, I see your father's shadow, I see betrayal. And I don't know if I'll ever get past this."

She felt the tears fall, but didn't look away. "I know you love me, Matteo. And I know this revenge won't bring you peace. It will only destroy us further."

He looked at her, the internal struggle clear on his face. He wanted to stay cold, he wanted to keep her away, but every word she said made the wall he'd built around himself tremble. Matteo knew that, as much as he wanted to punish her, he was also destroying himself with every cruel word, with every distant gesture.

"Then tell me, Alessia," he murmured, his voice filled with pain. "How do I trust you again? How do I believe that this isn't just another illusion?"

She brought her face close to his, her gaze filled with determination. "You don't need to believe all at once. I'm here to show you, day by day, that what I feel for you is stronger than any hurt. And if that means suffering, then I accept it. But know that I won't give up on you, even if you reject me."

Matteo took a deep breath, her words touching parts of him he preferred to keep dormant. Finally, he murmured in a low, hoarse voice, "Then prove it, Alessia. Prove that I can trust you."

She nodded, determined. She knew it would be a difficult battle, but she was ready to face any storm, as long as she could regain Matteo's love.

Silence settled between them, but it was a dense silence, filled with conflicting emotions that almost seemed tangible. Matteo and Alessia were close, their eyes locked, and even in the whirlwind of hurt and distrust, they could feel the intensity of what they shared. He still felt the need to distance himself, to keep a wall around his heart, but her presence was a stubborn flame that refused to go out.

Alessia took a deep breath, feeling the weight of his gaze, which, even filled with doubt, showed traces of the man she loved. "You want me to prove my love, Matteo? I accept," she whispered, her voice soft but full of conviction. "But you need to allow me to be by your side, to show you, every day, how loyal I am."

He looked away, still conflicted, but he took her hand, pulling her closer. "And what happens when I can't forget?" he murmured, his voice filled with vulnerability. "What happens if this pain never goes away, Alessia?"

She raised her hand, gently placing it on his face, her fingers caressing his tense jaw. "The pain might not disappear all at once, Matteo, but I don't expect that. I want to be by your side, even if it means seeing you fight that pain every day. I want every part of you, even the dark and painful parts."

That delicate touch felt like a caress that broke through his defenses. Matteo closed his eyes, feeling the softness of her hand against his skin, the closeness of the person he so badly wanted to push away but couldn't. When he opened his eyes again, his emotions were overflowing, and he spoke with an intensity that surprised even him.

"I don't know how you can forgive me so easily, Alessia," he said, almost in a whisper. "I pushed you away, hurt you, treated you like you were nothing. And yet, you're still here. Why?"

She smiled, a soft smile full of tenderness. "Because I see the man you really are, Matteo. Not the mafia boss, not the ruthless man everyone fears. I see the man who loves me and who, despite everything, fights to protect me, even if he won't admit it." She leaned in closer, her eyes locked on his. "And I love you, Matteo, with everything I am. I knew this journey wouldn't be easy, but I still choose you."

He took her hand to his lips, holding it with a touch that mixed gentleness and possession, as if he was finally allowing himself to feel that love, though reluctantly. "You're unbearably stubborn," he murmured, a light smile playing on his lips. "You've always been, from the beginning."

She laughed softly, a sound that enveloped him and reminded him of the good moments, the ones when she challenged him, when they provoked each other until one of them gave in. "And you think it's easy for me, mafia boss?" she teased. "But we're in this together. And that's all that matters."

# Chapter 53: The Return of Lorenzo

Alessia was alone on the balcony of her room, lost in painful thoughts about the conflict with Matteo. The cold night breeze seemed to echo the pain she felt inside. The man she loved, the one for whom she had risked everything, was now a distant shadow, consumed by hurt and doubt. She was exhausted, but her determination to prove her love kept her standing firm. Yet in moments like this, she questioned whether all the sacrifice would be worth it.

It was then that she heard soft, deliberate footsteps approaching. Even before turning around, she recognized the sound. Lorenzo, her father, was there. The man who had manipulated her for much of her life, the one who had pulled her away from Matteo. She felt her heart tighten; his presence was the last thing she needed in that moment.

"Alessia," he began, his voice surprisingly gentle. "I'm here to give you a choice."

She slowly turned around, her face unreadable, though the disgust in her eyes was evident. "And what choice would that be, Father? I thought my options were always defined by you."

Lorenzo didn't seem at all intimidated by her coldness. He stepped forward, a calculated smile on his face. "I know you're hurt, my daughter. Matteo is a ruthless man, and the way he's treating you... it's disgraceful. You deserve a better life, Alessia. A life of dignity and safety, far from this madness of revenge."

She let out a small, humorless laugh. "And you really believe you have something to offer that could save me from this 'chaos'? Because, if I recall correctly, it was you who threw me into this dirty game."

Lorenzo raised his eyebrows as if her response had caught him off guard, but he continued with his calm, almost hypnotic voice.

"You know that, with me, you will have the safety you'll never find with Matteo. He's consumed by rage, willing to destroy anyone who threatens his pride—and that includes you. Why insist on fighting for someone who will never fully believe in you?"

Lorenzo's words seemed to penetrate every crack in Alessia's heart. The hurt was still there, fresh and throbbing, from Matteo's cold treatment and the feeling of betrayal that had come between them. A pang of doubt crept in, an uncertainty that Lorenzo exploited mercilessly.

"What do you want from me?" she asked, her voice hesitant. "Why come back now, after all this time, using me as a pawn in your game?"

He took another step closer, his voice smooth as poison. "I want you to come back to where you belong, Alessia. With your family. By my side, you'll have a full life, free from the suffering and uncertainty that Matteo brings to you. But for that, I need you to help me destroy him. Matteo is a threat, a shadow over our name. If you want, together we can erase that shadow forever."

Alessia felt a chill run down her spine. What Lorenzo was asking wasn't just betrayal, but complete surrender to his manipulation. She knew that if she accepted, she would lose any trace of freedom she had ever dreamed of. She would be, once again, a pawn in his game.

"Do you think I'm that weak?" she whispered, struggling to control the anger rising inside her. "Do you think I would come back to you after everything? You're offering me a 'dignified' life, but I know what that means: a life of control, of submission. There's no freedom by your side, Lorenzo."

Lorenzo watched her, a dark expression forming on his face. He knew she was strong, that she wouldn't be manipulated easily. But there was one more card he could play, one last touch that he knew would shake her resolve.

"If you don't come back with me, Matteo will be the one to suffer the consequences," he said, his voice cold. "You know my power. You know I can end him once and for all."

The ground beneath Alessia seemed to falter. Threatening Matteo was the final move that Lorenzo knew would rattle her. She found herself at a crossroads: give in to her father, returning to his web of control, or stand by Matteo, knowing it would put him in danger.

"You don't really care about me," she murmured, trying to keep her emotions in check. "You've always seen me as a tool, a piece you could use for whatever you wanted."

"Alessia," he replied, impatience creeping into his voice. "This is your last chance to make the right choice. Come with me, and everything will be as it was. A safe, ordered world, free from the chaos of the DeLuca mafia. Refuse, and you'll lose him forever."

She took a deep breath, feeling the weight of the decision she was about to make. She knew that no matter what, there would be pain, but there was something deep inside her that urged her to resist, to fight for the love she had for Matteo, even if he didn't believe in her now.

"My place isn't with you, Lorenzo," she replied, her voice firm. "Even if Matteo doubts me, even if he rejects me, I would rather fight by his side than surrender to your control."

Lorenzo stared at her, his eyes narrowing with suppressed fury. "You're making the wrong choice, Alessia. And you will regret it."

He stepped back, the shadows darkening his expression. "If you won't come back, then it's only a matter of time before Matteo falls. And I guarantee that, when that happens, you'll be alone."

She kept her gaze steady, though inside, his words hit hard. "Maybe I'll be alone, but I won't betray who I am, or what I feel. And know this: when all of this is over, the one who will be alone is you, Lorenzo."

He laughed, a dry, cruel sound, before turning away and walking off, leaving her to her thoughts. As soon as he was gone, Alessia felt a heavy weight settle on her shoulders, but the certainty of her decision remained firm. She was ready to face whatever came her way, even if Matteo would never know the sacrifice she was making.

That night, Alessia went to find Matteo, determined to fight by his side, even if it meant facing his contempt and rejection. She found him in his office, his expression hardened and his gaze cold, but she wasn't intimidated.

"Matteo," she said, her voice firm yet carrying a softness that betrayed her vulnerability. "I know you don't believe in me now, but I won't give up. I'll fight by your side, and I'll prove that what I feel is real."

He looked at her with an unreadable expression. "You're still trying, Alessia? After everything that's been revealed, you think there's anything left to save?"

She held his gaze, her determination unwavering. "There is, Matteo. And even if you don't see it now, I will keep fighting because I know, deep down, you feel it too."

Matteo watched her for a moment, and for a brief instant, Alessia saw the shadow of the man she loved. But he quickly turned his gaze away, his expression hardening. "Do whatever you want, Alessia. Just don't expect me to believe your intentions so easily."

She smiled, a sad smile but one full of hope. "You may doubt me, but I'm here to prove every word. I'll fight by your side, even if you see me as an enemy. Because, to me, you are everything."

Matteo didn't respond, but when she left the office, he was left alone with his thoughts, his expression wavering. He knew there was something deeper between them, something that even bitterness couldn't erase. And deep down, the thought of seeing her leave haunted him more than any revenge.

In that moment, both knew the battle wasn't just against Lorenzo, but against the walls they had built between each other.

# Chapter 54: A New Threat

Tensions were at a boiling point. The DeLuca mansion, once a symbol of power and security, now felt like a place on the brink of war. Alessia could sense that the attacks against Matteo's family were intensifying, and with the coldness Matteo was showing her, she knew he refused to see the real threat Lorenzo posed. To him, she was just a manipulative pawn, infiltrating his life to destabilize him.

One evening, Alessia found him in his office, strategizing with a few of his men. When they left, she entered, feeling the weight of Matteo's icy stare on her.

"We need to talk, Matteo," she started, her voice steady. "Lorenzo is making a move. These attacks aren't random, and he won't stop here."

He leaned back in his chair, arms crossed, a cynical smile on his lips. "Ah, so now you care about the safety of my family?" he mocked. "Interesting, considering you're part of it. To me, Alessia, it's just a convenient disguise."

She stepped closer, unwavering. "I came here to warn you. I know what Lorenzo is capable of, and I'm trying to protect you."

He laughed, but it was cold, devoid of humor. "Protect? Let me guess, you want to protect the position you still hold here, while serving your father from the shadows."

"You're blind, Matteo!" she exclaimed, emotion heavy in her voice. "Don't you see that he won't stop until he destroys you? I'm here, fighting alone, trying to stop him from getting to you, but you refuse to see the truth!"

"And what's the truth, Alessia?" Matteo stood, walking toward her, his gaze filled with fury and pain. "The truth is that I loved you, trusted you, and you betrayed me. That's what matters. So don't come with this loyalty act. I'm tired of it."

She felt his words like a knife in her chest, but she didn't back down. "If you truly believed I was here to manipulate you, then why keep me around, Matteo? Why not just kick me out for good? Tell me!"

He hesitated, just for a second, but that brief moment of uncertainty didn't go unnoticed by her. His eyes held deep pain, a battle inside him he refused to admit. "Because I want you to feel it, Alessia. I want you to know what it's like to stand by someone and have your trust shattered. I want you to feel every piece of the pain you caused me."

Alessia closed her eyes, trying to hold back the tears. "So, that's it? That's all I am to you now? A target to unleash your rage on?"

He stared at her, his lips pressed into a thin, tense line. "If that's what you think, then yes. Because trusting you now would be a weakness. And weaknesses are fatal in this world."

She took a deep breath, feeling crushed by his coldness, but determined not to give up. "You don't want to believe me, Matteo, but what I'm doing is for you. Lorenzo gave me a choice—betray you or be exiled forever. And I chose to stay. I chose to fight, because you mean more to me than anything."

"Empty words, Alessia," he murmured, without looking at her. "Nothing you say can erase the past. Go and do what you want, but don't expect me to care about your decisions."

With that, he left the room, leaving her alone. Alessia felt the weight of rejection and pain pressing down on her, but something inside her refused to give in. She knew Lorenzo was advancing, and if Matteo wouldn't listen to her warnings, she would have to act alone.

In the days that followed, Alessia started investigating Lorenzo's movements on her own, using the few contacts who still trusted her to intercept information and plans. Each night was a solitary battle, each discovery a reminder of the risk Lorenzo posed.

She intercepted messages, dismantled schemes, all without Matteo knowing.

One night, while observing a secret meeting of Lorenzo's thugs, Alessia overheard part of a conversation revealing the next target: Matteo would be ambushed at an event the following day. The plan was to take him down and ensure no one would suspect the Romano connection. She knew she had to act fast to prevent a tragedy.

However, when she arrived home, Matteo was waiting for her in the entrance hall, dark and angry. He watched her approach, suspicion heavy in his gaze.

"So, Alessia," he began, his voice dripping with disdain. "Where have you been all night? Off on another mission for your father?"

She sighed, exhausted, but determined not to lower her head. "I've been trying to stop his next attack. Lorenzo plans to ambush you tomorrow, during the event."

He let out a bitter laugh. "And you expect me to believe that? Is this your last attempt to gain my trust?"

"If you want to believe I'm lying, then go ahead," she replied, her tone controlled. "But know that I'm risking my life to protect you, even if you don't believe me."

"Risking your life?" he interrupted, stepping forward in a threatening manner. "Who do you think you're fooling, Alessia? You're part of this, and the rest is just a show."

She stared back at him, her anger finally spilling over. "I'm fighting to save you, Matteo! To save the man I love, even if he's pushing me away, even if he treats me like an enemy! And I will keep fighting, because my love for you is greater than any hurt!"

For a brief moment, he fell silent, his breath quickening, his gaze fixed on her. There was an obvious internal struggle in his eyes, but he quickly regained his cold composure and stepped back.

"Then continue your little act, Alessia," he said, his voice low and icy. "But know that when the truth finally comes out, there will be no room for forgiveness."

She felt his words like a blow, but she didn't look away. "I don't need your forgiveness, Matteo. I just want you to live, to see the truth, even if it costs me everything."

In the days that followed, Alessia continued to intercept Lorenzo's attacks. Without Matteo knowing, she dismantled ambushes, convinced some of Lorenzo's men to give up, each time risking her own safety. Matteo watched her from afar, still distrustful, but even without admitting it, something in his heart began to waver. He saw the exhaustion on her face, the scars of a solitary fight.

Finally, after yet another night of returning home exhausted, he found her sitting on the balcony, her eyes fixed on the sky. He approached, saying nothing, simply sitting beside her. Alessia felt his presence, but didn't say anything, just took a deep breath, hoping he would leave.

"Why do you keep going?" he asked, finally, his voice softer than she had expected.

She looked at him, surprised by the tone. "Because I love you, Matteo. And because, no matter how much you see me as a traitor, my love is real. I don't need you to believe it now. But I'll fight until the end for you."

He stayed silent, his gaze thoughtful, and for the first time, Alessia saw a flicker of understanding in his eyes. He didn't say anything else, but as he left, he felt that, for the first time, he may have glimpsed a trace of truth in her words.

At that moment, the war between them began to ease, and both silently hoped that the coming day would bring more answers than wounds.

# Chapter 55: Test of Loyalty

The sound of gunshots echoed through the walls of the abandoned warehouse, and Matteo could hardly believe what was happening. The ambush had been meticulously planned, and he knew Lorenzo wanted him dead. But what he hadn't expected was to see Alessia emerge among the armed men, her eyes fixed with determination, her expression resolute, as if she was willing to risk everything.

Matteo paused for a moment, surprised, but quickly his instincts took over. He ran toward Alessia, pulling her to safety, but she anticipated him, positioning herself directly in the line of fire, protecting him with her own body. Matteo barely had time to react before seeing the flash of a gun in one of Lorenzo's men's hands and hearing the shot that cut through the air.

The gunshot echoed in the sudden silence that followed, and Matteo felt his heart stop for an instant as he saw Alessia collapse, wounded, blood spilling from her blouse. Without a second thought, he knelt beside her, rage and desperation mixing in his chest.

"Alessia!" he shouted, his voice filled with an emotion he had tried to deny for so long. "Why did you do this? Why did you put yourself in front?"

She was breathing heavily, her face pale, but her eyes met his with a tenderness that disarmed him. "Because... Matteo," she whispered weakly, "because I... never lied about how I feel. And I'd rather... I'd rather die than see you suffer."

Matteo felt his chest tighten, overwhelming guilt flooding through him as he held her hand tightly. He tried to hold back the tears, but each of her words felt like a blade piercing through his defenses. How could he have been so blind? How could he have doubted someone who was willing to sacrifice her life to protect him?

His men had finally managed to push back the rest of Lorenzo's thugs, and one of them approached to help carry Alessia to the car waiting to take her to the hospital. Matteo held her the entire time, refusing to let go of her hand, as though the mere touch could preserve the bond that, now he realized, was the only true and unshakable thing in his life.

At the hospital, while Alessia was being taken into surgery, Matteo paced back and forth, tormented by guilt and pain. Every memory of her replayed in his mind—every moment he had pushed her away, every cruel word he had said, all of it came rushing back to haunt him. He realized he had treated her like an enemy, as though she were part of Lorenzo's plan, but she had always been by his side, facing her own father to protect him.

Hours passed before the doctor came out, informing him that Alessia was out of immediate danger, but would still need constant monitoring over the next few hours. Matteo entered her room, and upon seeing her there, lying so vulnerable, something inside him broke. He pulled up a chair and sat beside her, holding her hand gently, almost reverently.

"Alessia..." he murmured, his eyes fixed on her face. "I was a fool, a blind fool. I thought I was protecting myself by pushing you away, but now I see that all I did was sink deeper into a revenge that made no sense."

She slowly opened her eyes, still weak, but with a soft glow upon seeing that he was there. A fragile smile appeared on her lips, and she squeezed his hand slightly. "I... just wanted you to know... that I never lied," she murmured, her voice soft but full of sincerity. "Everything I did was... for you."

Matteo felt his heart tighten, each of her words a reminder of the loyalty and unconditional love she had shown him. "I know that now," he replied, his throat tight. "I realize now that, while I treated you like a traitor, you were always by my side, sacrificing everything for me. I was blind, Alessia, and I don't deserve your forgiveness."

She looked at him, her eyes shining with emotion, and with great effort, she whispered, "Matteo... I didn't do this to earn forgiveness. I did it because I love you. Because... I can't imagine my life without you."

He lowered his head, closing his eyes, feeling the tears escape. It was rare for him to feel vulnerable, but there, with Alessia fighting for her life, all the coldness he had built up came crashing down. Matteo lifted his face and looked directly into her eyes, with a determination he hadn't known still existed within him.

"Alessia, if you give me a second chance, I promise I will do everything to make things right," he said, his voice thick. "I want you to trust me, just as I need to learn to trust you again. I was a fool, but you deserve more than this... you deserve more than I've been so far."

She smiled softly, a smile that, though weak, showed the depth of her love. "I just wanted... you to see the truth, Matteo. To understand that I've always been by your side."

He moved closer, his lips gently brushing against her hand. "I see it now, Alessia. And I swear, with everything I am, I will never doubt you again. From now on, we will face everything together, as we should have from the beginning."

She closed her eyes, exhausted, but peace was reflected on her face. Matteo stayed by her side, feeling the weight of his guilt transform into fierce resolution. He knew he had much to prove, but he was determined to make every promise count. He held her firmly, feeling that, for the first time, he was ready to protect what mattered most in his life.

The following days were ones of recovery for Alessia, and Matteo was there every step of the way, watching over her, caring for her, and slowly starting to rebuild the trust he had destroyed.

Each word of gratitude he spoke to her, each careful gesture, was his way of trying to mend the damage he had caused. He knew the emotional scars would need time to heal, but for the first time, he felt that there was hope.

One night, when Alessia had finally managed to get up and walk around the room, Matteo helped her sit in an armchair by the window. He knelt in front of her, holding her hands between his, his gaze intense and sincere.

"Alessia, I can't change the past, but I want a future by your side, a future where we trust each other without fear. I want you to know that every cruel word I said... was the result of my own pain and blindness. But today, I see you, and I'm just grateful for every sacrifice you made."

She looked at him, feeling the weight of his words, and nodded, her smile gentle. "I forgive you, Matteo. Because the love I feel for you is greater than any hurt. And because, deep down, I knew you would understand one day."

Matteo closed his eyes, relieved, and pulled her into an embrace, his heart racing with an emotion he never thought he could feel. There, together, they both knew they were finally ready to build something real, a love that, even marked by pain, was unbreakable.

# Chapter 56: The Return of Desire

The morning dawned silently, and in the hospital room, Alessia slowly opened her eyes, feeling the weight of exhaustion in her body. The soft morning light bathed the space, creating an almost peaceful atmosphere, as if the chaos around them had been temporarily suspended. By her bedside, Matteo sat, his eyes fixed on her with an intensity she wasn't used to seeing. There was something in his gaze—a mixture of regret and tenderness, a trace of vulnerability she never imagined witnessing on the face of the mafia boss.

"Alessia..." he whispered, his voice hoarse, as if he had stayed awake all night.

She looked away, still trying to absorb what had happened, the conflicting emotions filling her chest. There was love and hurt mixed together, and as much as she had fought by his side, she feared that Matteo might still doubt her.

"Why are you still here, Matteo?" she murmured, trying to hold back the wave of emotions threatening to overflow. "After everything... after how you treated me, I thought... I thought I was just a pawn to you."

He lowered his head, gently squeezing her hand between his. "I was a fool, Alessia," he confessed, his voice low and filled with pain. "I let pride, anger, and revenge blind me. I wanted to punish you, push you away... but the only one who got hurt was me. Now I see that my revenge was aimed at the wrong person. You've always been by my side, even when I treated you like an enemy."

Her heart quickened, a mix of surprise and hope stirring inside her. Matteo had never been one to admit mistakes, and seeing him there, so vulnerable, was like witnessing a silent surrender, a crack in his defenses.

"Do you know how much you hurt me, Matteo?" she asked, her voice faltering, but her eyes locked onto his, as if she wanted to see just how far his sincerity went. "I loved you, sacrificed for you, and still... you chose to see me as a traitor."

He closed his eyes for a moment, breathing deeply, as if her words were a direct blow to his soul. When he opened them again, his gaze was filled with regret. "I know, Alessia. And if I could go back, I would never have doubted you. I was blind, I let my pain control me, but... all I want now is a chance to make things right. I know I don't deserve your forgiveness, but I want you to know that... my love for you never stopped existing, even when I tried to bury it."

She looked at him, surprised by the depth of his confession, and felt a wave of intense emotions. The love for him had never disappeared, no matter how much the hurt tried to drown it. Matteo leaned in slowly, approaching her with a hesitation that was unusual for him. His eyes fixed on hers, seeking permission, a silent answer.

"Alessia... let me show you what I really feel," he whispered, his voice heavy with desire and vulnerability.

She didn't answer in words, but her gaze, full of emotion and contained forgiveness, was enough. Matteo leaned in even more, until their lips met in an intense kiss, full of everything they had repressed. It was a kiss of surrender, of unspoken apologies, and of a love that refused to survive the scars. She felt the warmth of his hands cradling her face, as if he feared she might disappear.

The passion that arose between them was overwhelming, like a flame that had been lit long ago and was now finally finding space to break free. The kiss deepened, and each touch, each sigh between them was a declaration of everything they had hidden from each other. Matteo held her with reverence and repressed desire, as if he wanted to engrave himself into her soul, as if he wanted to prove, without words, how much she meant to him.

Alessia, for a moment, forgot about the physical pain. All she felt was Matteo, so close, so completely surrendered. The hospital room disappeared, and all that mattered was that moment, that connection that transcended any distrust or hurt.

He pulled away slightly, his gaze still fixed on hers, his breath heavy. "Alessia, I know my pride and anger almost destroyed us. But I want you, I want this love without reservations, without fear. Let me show you what you mean to me."

She nodded, wordlessly, simply wrapping her arms around him with an intensity that reflected everything she felt. The night that followed was a moment of redemption, where they both allowed themselves to fully surrender, leaving behind the weight of doubts and wounds. Matteo held her with a tenderness that contrasted with his usual personality, as though she were too precious to be treated with anything less than reverence.

Hours later, still in the dim light of the room, he held her in his arms, her body nestled against his. Alessia, with her eyes half-open, felt the warmth of Matteo's breath against her face, and a soft smile formed on her lips. For the first time, she felt that they had finally found solid ground, a foundation they could rebuild.

"Matteo," she whispered, breaking the silence, "this doesn't change the past, but... I'm willing to move forward, to start over, if you are."

He gently caressed her face, his fingers lightly gliding over her skin, while his gaze reflected a tenderness she never imagined she'd see in him. "I want this more than anything. And I promise you, Alessia, I'll never let doubt come between us again. You are everything to me."

She sighed, finally feeling at peace. "I just hope the past doesn't come back to haunt us. Lorenzo is still out there, and we know he won't give up."

Matteo held her tighter, a fierce determination in his eyes. "This time, we're in this together. He can try, but as long as we're side by side, nothing will tear us apart. I promise."

Alessia closed her eyes, allowing herself to believe those words, feeling that, despite the shadows of the past, they had finally found a light.

The soft darkness of the hospital room enveloped Matteo and Alessia as they stayed close, sharing that comfortable silence, where words weren't necessary. Matteo watched her, his gaze capturing every detail of her face, as if he wanted to keep every expression, every smile. He felt a peace he hadn't known, a sense of belonging beside her, something his turbulent life had never allowed.

Alessia gazed at him with a mix of tenderness and challenge. She felt vulnerable, yet safe in his arms, but she didn't want to let go of the opportunity to tease him, to keep the playful tone that had always surrounded them, even in the midst of danger.

"So, mafia boss," she murmured, raising an eyebrow, "have you confessed that you're sorry, shown your sensitive side, even asked for a second chance. What else are you hiding, Matteo?"

He chuckled softly, a rough sound that made her smile. "You already know too much about me, Alessia. And, unlike everyone else, you know that I'm dangerous... but also vulnerable with you." He lightly squeezed her waist, his eyes playfully meeting hers. "Besides, you know you can provoke me as much as you want, but now the question is: can you handle it?"

She laughed, tilting her head back slightly. "You think I'm afraid of you? Oh, Matteo, you should know I love a good challenge."

He smiled, moving closer until their faces were just inches apart. "I love your challenge, Alessia. And do you know why? Because you made me feel alive, in a way I never thought possible."

Her heart raced at those words. Matteo, the tough, relentless man, confessing how much she transformed him. It touched her in a way she couldn't even describe. Without resisting, Alessia brought her hand to his face, her fingers caressing his stubble as she kept her gaze locked on his dark eyes.

"I want to be by your side, Matteo. Even knowing how difficult you are, how dangerous our world is. I want this. I want you," she whispered, her voice full of sincerity.

He pulled her even closer, his hand sliding down her back as he murmured, "You're the only one brave enough to say that to me, looking me straight in the eye. And that's why I'm yours, Alessia, even if I never admitted it."

The kiss he gave her was a mixture of desire and tenderness, as if he wanted to show how much she meant to him, as if each touch was a silent promise that, this time, he wouldn't let her go.

When the kiss broke, they stayed close, their foreheads touching, breathing together. Alessia smiled, running her fingers through his hair, while whispering, "Does this mean you finally admit you can't live without me?"

He chuckled, the sound low and deep, and replied, his voice full of humor and desire: "You're insufferable, you know that?"

"And you're impossible," she retorted, laughing too, and they both knew that this playful banter was what kept them connected, a spark that would never fade.

The night continued, and Matteo stayed by her side, holding her hand, sharing stories, secrets, and glances that spoke more than any words could. They both knew the danger was always lurking, that living by the side of the mafia boss meant choosing a life of uncertainty and risks, but none of that mattered as long as they were together.

For Matteo, Alessia was a mix of chaos and peace he had never known he needed. She made him want to protect and surrender at the same time, and now, with her by his side, he felt complete. As for Alessia, Matteo was the storm she had always been drawn to, but now, in the midst of it all, she felt she had found her home.

# Chapter 57: The Return of a Dark Past

The return to the mansion brought a sense of calm and normalcy to Alessia and Matteo, an almost surreal contrast after the intense revelations and nights spent between threats and secrets. The house, with its imposing atmosphere, seemed to welcome the new alliance between them, as if the walls had witnessed the growth of the connection that now strengthened them.

While Alessia was in the garden, Matteo walked through the mansion's hallways, reviewing some old documents and letters left there by generations of DeLuca family heads. It was then that he found an old letter, yellowed and carefully folded, with handwriting he immediately recognized. It was a letter from Alessia's mother, addressed to Lorenzo.

With his heart racing, Matteo opened the letter and began reading, feeling intrigued. The letter had a desperate tone, almost a plea. Alessia's mother was asking Lorenzo to keep her daughter away from the dark world of the mafia. She spoke of a dark secret, something Lorenzo seemed determined to hide, and that Alessia should never find out.

As he read, the weight of Alessia's mother's words began to form a knot of worry in his chest. There was something in between the lines, something suggesting an old agreement, something that involved both families in a much deeper and darker way than he could imagine. He felt compelled to uncover what Lorenzo had planned for Alessia and what role she would play in all of it.

Some time later, Matteo found Alessia in the garden, sitting on a bench surrounded by the flowers she loved so much. She looked up when she saw him approaching and immediately sensed something was wrong; Matteo's expression was serious.

"We need to talk, Alessia," he said, his voice firm but with a softness reserved for her. He sat beside her and held her hand, placing the letter between them.

"Matteo... what is this?" Alessia asked, her voice heavy with hesitation, her eyes fixed on the letter.

"It's a letter from your mother to Lorenzo," Matteo began, his voice steady. "She asks him to keep you away from all this... away from the mafia world. But there's more. Something about a secret that connects our families, something she seemed to beg for you never to find out."

Alessia took the letter with trembling hands, reading each word carefully as her face transformed from surprise to pain and, finally, to shock. "She... she really asked for this?" Alessia murmured, her heart racing. "I never knew my mother tried to protect me from all this. I thought... I thought she was in agreement with Lorenzo on everything."

Matteo watched her every expression, every reaction, feeling his own heart tighten as he saw how much it was affecting her. "Alessia, there's more here, something Lorenzo kept hidden even from you. He had a plan, something that went beyond you and me, beyond any alliance between our families. We need to figure out what it is."

Alessia sighed, still processing the idea that her whole life could have been a game manipulated by her father. "Do you think... do you think I was never really a daughter to him?" she murmured, her voice cracking, as if she was finally beginning to understand the depth of Lorenzo's control over her fate. "Was everything he did just part of a plan?"

Matteo held her firmly, his eyes locked on hers. "I don't know what Lorenzo's goal is, Alessia, but I know you're not just a pawn in his game. I know you're real, true... and I know that together, we can uncover the truth."

She looked at him, pain and confusion reflected in her eyes. "Matteo, if all this is true... if Lorenzo always saw me as just a piece to get what he wants... then what am I, really? A daughter who never had a real family?"

He gently touched her face, trying to calm her. "You're more than any plan Lorenzo could have had. You're the woman who made me realize what really matters, the woman who defied her own father to protect the ones she loves. Nothing Lorenzo could have planned will change the fact that you're an extraordinary person, Alessia."

She held his hand against her face, absorbing the comfort his words brought, yet still feeling the weight of the discovery. "But what if this affects what we're building, Matteo? What if there's something in my history that destroys the trust we've finally rebuilt?"

He pulled her closer, his eyes fixed on hers with overwhelming intensity. "It doesn't matter what we uncover, Alessia. The only thing that matters is that we're together now, and I promise you, nothing and no one will change that."

Alessia felt tears welling up in her eyes, but she held them back, determined to be strong. "Then let's uncover the truth, Matteo. Let's face this, whatever it is. I don't want to live in the shadow of secrets anymore."

He nodded, his face determined. "We'll do it together. And this time, there will be no more lies, no more secrets between us."

That night, Matteo and Alessia began searching for information about their families' pasts, analyzing old records and speaking with people who had worked for both clans. With each discovery, the ties connecting the DeLucas and the Romanos seemed deeper and darker. There was an old alliance, a pact involving more than just money and power—something that involved sacrifices and broken promises.

As they investigated, Matteo couldn't help but notice Alessia's strength, her determination to uncover the truth, even knowing each answer could reveal an even darker past. He watched her, his heart aching with the certainty that, no matter what came, he would do everything to protect her.

In one of the documents they found, they finally came across a crucial clue. There was a recorded pact between the families, and Alessia seemed to be mentioned in one of the paragraphs. Her heart raced as she read her own name in an agreement made even before her birth. The text spoke of a "union that would bring peace, a sacrifice that would guarantee the families' strength."

Alessia turned to Matteo, her eyes wide. "This... this means I was always destined for this, right? That Lorenzo already saw me as part of a plan before I even knew what was happening."

He pulled her close, holding her with protective firmness. "It doesn't matter what Lorenzo planned, Alessia. You are more than any destiny imposed by him. We have the power to change that, to write our own future."

She nodded, hugging him tightly, feeling safe and strong for the first time amidst all the uncertainty. Matteo held her as if he would never let her go, and Alessia, wrapped in his embrace, knew she would face any shadow of the past by his side.

From that moment on, Alessia and Matteo were determined to unearth every secret, to face every challenge, and to destroy any plan Lorenzo had created to control them. They knew the next discoveries would be intense and, perhaps, painful, but now, side by side, they felt invincible.

Silence stretched in the room, where only the soft light of the night illuminated Matteo and Alessia. The recent discovery of the dark past of their families seemed to cast a new and deep shadow between them, but at the same time, it created an even stronger connection. Matteo couldn't take his eyes off Alessia, admiring her strength, the way she faced the dark secrets without losing her determination.

He watched her in silence, admiring her strength and beauty, and despite all the doubts, he knew he didn't want anyone else by his side. "You know, you surprise me every day, Alessia," he said, his tone soft and filled with admiration he rarely let show. "I always thought you were stubborn, unbearable... but I never imagined you'd be so brave."

She rolled her eyes, smiling at the teasing tone he always used. "Brave? No, Matteo. I'm just stubborn enough not to let you push me away," she replied, a spark in her eyes. "And frankly, dealing with the most stubborn and proud mafia boss already takes more courage than anything else."

He laughed, a low, rough laugh, leaning in a little closer until he was right next to her. "Stubborn and brave," he murmured, his eyes fixed on hers, his voice filled with intensity. "You're a danger, Alessia. A danger I can't stay away from."

Her heart sped up, his words echoing in an overwhelming way. Matteo, the cold and calculating man, was there, vulnerable, with a gaze full of emotion, allowing himself to lower his defenses. With a gentle touch, Alessia placed her hand on his face, tracing the line of his strong jaw. "Then stop trying to pull away," she whispered, her voice carrying a subtle challenge. "You know we're bound to each other, Matteo."

He held her hand against his face, closing his eyes for a moment, absorbing the touch that somehow made him feel complete. When he opened his eyes, Matteo stared at her with an intensity Alessia had never seen before, as if he were seeing his own soul reflected in her eyes.

"Alessia... you're the only one who can throw me off balance, who can make me forget who I am and, at the same time, remind me of who I really want to be," he said, his voice thick with the confession. "With you, I feel like I can face anything, but I also feel a huge fear of losing you."

She smiled, a soft smile that hid a mix of relief and passion. She moved a little closer, pressing her lips softly to his in a light kiss, but one filled with silent promises. When she pulled away, she whispered, "Then stop fighting it, Matteo. Stop fighting us."

He pulled her closer, his arms wrapping around her with a possessive protectiveness. "I'm not fighting anymore, Alessia," he said, his voice low and filled with desire. "I just want you to know that, even in the middle of this war, with everything we will face, I'll be by your side, no matter the cost."

She rested her head against his chest, feeling the steady beat of Matteo's heart. She felt safe, something she never thought possible amidst the chaos surrounding their lives. Every word from him was a promise she knew was true, even with the uncertainties and dangers that surrounded them.

"I trust you, Matteo," she said, her tone soft but resolute. "And I know that together, we can face anything, even the worst that Lorenzo can throw at us."

He held her tighter, as if he wanted to protect every part of her from the dangerous world surrounding them. "If Lorenzo thinks he can use us, he has no idea of the strength we have together. He may be a master of manipulation, but we're so much more than any plan of his."

She lifted her gaze, a mischievous smile on her face. "So, boss, what do we do now? Are you ready to fight alongside the most stubborn person you've ever met?"

He laughed, his eyes shining with passion and determination. "Stubborn or not, Alessia, you're the woman I want to face whatever comes. And together, we're unstoppable."

# Chapter 58: The Truth About the Arranged Marriage

Alessia walked through the grand halls of the Romano mansion with steady steps, though her heart was heavy. The confrontation she was about to have with Lorenzo was inevitable. The weight of the revelations she had begun to uncover made her anxious, but she knew it was necessary to confront the truth, even if it meant shattering everything she had believed about her father.

Entering Lorenzo's office, she found him sitting behind his mahogany desk, his cold, calculating gaze watching her with a faint trace of curiosity. He did not show any surprise at her arrival, but his eyes indicated he knew this moment would come. Alessia took a deep breath, gathering all the courage she had.

"I came here to get answers, Lorenzo," she began, her tone firm. "I want to know the real reason behind the arranged marriage with Matteo. I want to know what I am to you."

Lorenzo remained silent for a few seconds, his eyes fixed on her, as if calculating his next words. Finally, he sighed, and a weary expression appeared on his face. "I always knew this day would come, Alessia," he said in a low, almost melancholic voice. "But knowing the truth won't change the past or the agreement we made."

"That doesn't interest me," she replied, her anger barely contained. "I want the truth, Lorenzo. I want to understand why I was always treated like a pawn, like a piece in this dirty game. I was never a daughter to you, was I?"

He looked away, but his expression hardened. "You were never just a daughter, Alessia. From the moment you were born, you carried something much greater with you. You were... are an essential part of our family's survival."

Alessia felt her heart tighten, but she refused to let him see her vulnerability. "Essential?" she repeated bitterly. "So I was never anything more than a bargaining chip, was I? Someone you could use to get what you wanted."

Lorenzo took a deep breath, his face impassive. "Our arranged marriage with the DeLucas was more than just an alliance, Alessia. It was a way to keep the Romano name intact, to protect our finances. You were destined for this from the start. There was a hidden inheritance, something your mother and I have kept secret for generations. You've always been... special, but you couldn't know."

She felt a mix of disbelief and pain upon hearing her father's words. The man she had spent her life trying to understand, and perhaps even love, was now revealing that she had been raised only to fulfill a role— a duty he had imposed upon her from birth. "So, I was never important to you as a person? Just as an asset?" Alessia whispered, her voice barely audible.

He looked at her, and for a moment, it seemed like he might say something, but then he withdrew. "Important, Alessia? What's more important than keeping an entire family alive? What I did was necessary. Sacrifices need to be made."

Those were the same empty speeches she had grown up hearing. Words from a man obsessed with power, incapable of understanding the meaning of affection or family. Alessia stood up, bitterness welling up inside her. "You never loved me for real, Lorenzo. I was just a resource, something you could use in your struggle for power."

Lorenzo remained silent, watching her leave with the same calculating gaze he had always had, incapable of showing any emotion. For him, that conversation was over, and all that remained was resignation.

When Alessia returned to the DeLuca mansion, she went straight to the office where Matteo was waiting for her, his concerned gaze searching her face, which was filled with pain and vulnerability. She approached him, her hands trembling as she recounted what she had discovered. Her voice faltered at times, and the weight of the truth seemed to threaten to crush her.

"Matteo, I was never anything to him," she whispered, tears filling her eyes. "I was always a coin, something he could use for his own purposes. All the love I thought he might have had for me... it was all a lie."

Matteo held her firmly, his eyes filled with both compassion and fury for what she had gone through. He wiped away a tear that slid down her cheek and, in a serious tone, said, "Alessia, I will never let Lorenzo hurt you again. He doesn't even deserve the loyalty you gave him. From now on, you have a new family, and I will fight to make sure you never feel that pain again."

She collapsed into his arms, allowing herself to cry for the first time in a long time. Matteo held her with a strength and tenderness that made her feel protected, and she knew that, right there, she finally had someone who loved her for who she was, not for what she could offer.

After a few minutes, she pulled away slightly, wiping her tears. "I'm sorry," she murmured with a sad smile. "I never wanted you to see me like this."

He cupped her face in his hands, looking deeply into her eyes. "Alessia, you don't need to be strong all the time. Not with me. I'm here for you, and I want you to know that you will never be alone again."

She smiled, a spark of gratitude and affection in her eyes. "I don't know what I would have done without you, Matteo. I think I've never felt so... so safe, even with everything falling apart around us."

He leaned in and kissed her gently, a gesture of care and devotion. "As long as we're together, no one can tear us apart. We'll face all of this, all the secrets, all the challenges. I won't let anything hurt you again, Alessia."

She hugged him, feeling that, for the first time, she had found her true home. Matteo was her refuge, her support, and now, with him by her side, she felt she could face the world, confront all the secrets and lies Lorenzo had built.

Alessia knew the road ahead would be hard, but she also knew that with Matteo beside her, there would be no more secrets or loneliness.

The weight of her conversation with Lorenzo still pressed on her heart as she remained in Matteo's arms. He was her anchor, the calm in the storm of revelations that were shaking her certainties and her past. In the silence of the room, the closeness between them was the only thing that could quiet Alessia's thoughts, and Matteo seemed to understand this, holding her firmly, without haste.

Matteo watched her face, studying every detail, every shadow of pain that passed through her eyes. He knew Alessia was strong, that she faced everything with a determination that fascinated him, but at that moment, he saw something deeper, a vulnerability that she rarely allowed to show. It was as if all the layers she used to protect herself had fallen away, and he could see her true heart—one he wanted to protect at any cost.

Alessia, noticing Matteo's intense gaze on her, smiled faintly, trying to mask the pain with a little teasing. "Are you going to keep looking at me like that? It's starting to get a little weird, you know?"

He let out a low laugh, but his eyes remained fixed on hers, filled with a mix of desire and tenderness. "You know, Alessia, it's funny how you try to be strong and sarcastic all the time... but I know you better than that. And no matter how much you try to hide it, I know how hurt you are."

She rolled her eyes, but couldn't disguise the smile that formed on her lips. "Always thinking you know everything, huh, DeLuca? You think you know me so well?"

Matteo cupped her face with one hand, gently caressing her skin with his thumb. "I know you're stubborn, Alessia. I know you won't admit how much you need someone to support you. And I also know that behind all that strength, there's someone who just wants to be loved for real, with no games, no conditions."

She looked away for a moment, feeling his words break through all the barriers she had built. No matter how hard she fought to hide it, Matteo saw her like no one else, and that made her feel incredibly vulnerable, but at the same time, safe.

"You have this annoying habit of always being right, Matteo," she murmured softly, her words contrasting with the tenderness in her tone. "And maybe that's what attracts me to you."

He leaned in, bringing his lips to hers, stopping just a millimeter away. "Then admit it, Alessia. Admit you need me, that you want this as much as I do."

She sighed, trying to resist his intensity, but it was impossible. Matteo was like a force of nature, impossible to ignore. Finally, with a defiant smile, she whispered, "I need you as much as you need me, Matteo. Don't fool yourself into thinking I'm the only one involved in this."

He kissed her with a contained passion, as if each touch was a silent promise, a guarantee that he wouldn't let her face this alone. The kiss was a fusion of emotions, of pain and a desire to protect that transcended everything. When they pulled away, both were breathing heavily, still connected by their gaze.

"Promise me you won't hide anything from me anymore," he whispered, his voice grave, almost an order, but with a hint of vulnerability. "I know you think you can face the world alone, but we're in this together now. I won't let you carry everything by yourself."

She smiled, gently caressing his face, finally feeling understood. "I promise, Matteo. I'll trust you. And I know that with you by my side, I can face anything."

He pulled her closer, a satisfied smile on his face, and teasingly murmured, "That's the woman I know. Stubborn and difficult, but mine."

Alessia laughed, feeling the lightness return. "And never forget that, Matteo DeLuca. I'm yours... but I'm equally stubborn, and I'll fight with you, no matter what comes."

They stayed there, embraced, enjoying the moment, as if they had finally found the balance between strength and vulnerability. And as the world continued to spin around them, they both knew that together, they were unbeatable.

# Chapter 59: The Price of the Truth

The meeting room was filled with a heavy, dense atmosphere. Matteo had called together the most loyal and trustworthy allies of the DeLuca family—men and women who had shown unquestionable loyalty over the years. Alessia, sitting beside him, felt a mixture of tension and determination; she knew that what they were about to discuss could shake the foundations of both the Romano and DeLuca families forever.

Matteo opened the meeting with a direct speech. "We are at a critical point, and everything we believed about this alliance between our families was built on lies and manipulation. Lorenzo never wanted peace. He never wanted the benefit of both families. What he wanted was absolute power."

The tension in the room increased as he exposed the secrets they had uncovered, mentioning Alessia's mother's letter and her involvement as a "pawn" in Lorenzo's strategies. The glances exchanged among those present revealed disbelief and growing anger. Many had invested their lives in loyalty to an alliance that now seemed like a farce.

It was at that moment that the door opened, revealing a familiar but unexpected face. Angelo, a former member of the Romano organization, entered the room. Matteo narrowed his eyes in suspicion, but he allowed the man to speak with a slight nod.

Angelo looked around, aware of the underlying hostility. "I know my presence is a surprise, but I'm here to tell you something you need to hear. Lorenzo entrusted me with secrets, secrets he never shared with anyone because... he knew they were too dangerous."

Alessia and Matteo exchanged a tense glance, and she felt a chill run down her spine. Angelo continued: "From the beginning, Lorenzo never intended to form just an alliance with the DeLucas.

In fact, the arranged marriage was only the first step in his plan. He intended to use Alessia as bait. The idea was to make Matteo trust her, but in the end, Lorenzo planned to manipulate both of you to take control of the DeLuca organization and then eliminate Matteo."

Alessia brought a hand to her mouth, shocked, while Matteo clenched his fists, his anger growing. He looked at Alessia, and the suffering in her eyes hit him like a blow. She now saw her own father as a man who had, from the beginning, used her in a cold and calculating way.

"Does this mean that..." Alessia whispered, her voice weak, "my father always wanted to sacrifice me, always saw me only as a tool for his own goals?"

Matteo touched her hand, trying to offer reassurance. "Alessia, you're not a pawn, not to me. You never were."

But Alessia, lost in thought, murmured, "I spent my whole life believing he cared, that he saw me as a daughter, even if it was in a twisted way. But now, seeing that everything was manipulation, just a way to get what he wanted..."

Angelo continued, looking at both of them with seriousness. "I knew Lorenzo was capable of a lot, but even I was horrified when I discovered the extent of his plan. He believed that by eliminating Matteo, he would gain absolute power over all the operations, using you, Alessia, as the key to his strategy."

Matteo felt a silent rage bubbling in his chest. He squeezed Alessia's hand more tightly, looking at her with a determined gaze. "If Lorenzo thinks he can keep playing with you, he's completely wrong. I won't allow him to hurt you any more. I won't let him use you against me, or against yourself."

She looked at Matteo, her eyes shining with emotion and gratitude. "I never imagined I would find someone willing to fight for me like this, to see me beyond what Lorenzo built around me.

Matteo, I trust you, and if that means confronting Lorenzo and everything he represents, I'm ready to do that by your side."

Matteo nodded, and for a moment, the intense look they shared was enough to strengthen his resolve. He turned to the allies in the room, his voice firm and filled with conviction. "Lorenzo may think he has control, but he underestimated what we have. He never imagined that, together, we would be stronger. From now on, Lorenzo Romano is our enemy, and we will do whatever it takes to bring him down."

The allies nodded, some murmuring words of support, while others exchanged determined glances. Matteo knew he had put everyone in a dangerous position, but he also knew it was the only way to protect Alessia and ensure both their safety.

Later, in a moment of privacy, Alessia and Matteo were on the mansion's balcony, looking out at the city at night. The cool breeze seemed to calm Alessia's restless heart, still processing everything she had discovered.

"Do you think we can do it?" she asked, her voice soft but filled with uncertainty. "Challenging Lorenzo means more than just facing one person... it means facing the very shadow of our history, the lies, the manipulations."

Matteo moved closer, putting an arm around her and pulling her nearer. "We can, Alessia. Because now we're not alone. We're together, and that's something Lorenzo never understood. He thought he could manipulate you, that he could divide us, but he underestimated something he never knew: trust."

She smiled, still a little shaky, but with a new strength in her eyes. "You talk as if it's easy. As if facing my own father is something I could do without hesitation."

He lifted her chin, his gaze filled with understanding and affection. "It won't be easy, Alessia. But I will be by your side every step of the way, every moment. And if you need to hesitate, hesitate. I will be your support, your strength."

Alessia couldn't help but feel her heart race at his words. Matteo wasn't just a mafia boss, nor a man hardened by power. He was the man who saw her true self, who understood her vulnerabilities and accepted them.

She hugged him tightly, feeling safer than she had ever felt. "I couldn't do this without you, Matteo. And, no matter how dark the road ahead is, I know that by your side, I can face anything."

Matteo held her firmly, his voice low and filled with promise. "We'll defeat Lorenzo together, Alessia. He may have manipulated you, but he won't hurt you again. Now you are under my protection, and I won't let anything harm you."

They stayed there, together, watching the night, both knowing the battle wouldn't be easy, but ready to face whatever came. For Alessia, Matteo was her strength; for Matteo, Alessia was his reason. Together, they were unbeatable, ready to expose the truths and destroy all the lies that had kept them apart for so long.

# Chapter 60: The Last Test of Loyalty

Tension hung in the air as Alessia and Matteo put their final plan into motion against Lorenzo. Every step was calculated, every move made with precision and caution. Matteo, who had once hesitated to delegate such important responsibilities, now trusted Alessia fully. He looked at her with a respect and admiration that were hard to hide, but behind his dark eyes, there was a mixture of pride and apprehension.

"Alessia, this mission... it's risky," he began, holding her hands between his as he looked at her seriously. "I need you to be prepared for anything. One slip-up, one overlooked detail, and Lorenzo will have the advantage over us."

She nodded, her eyes determined. "Matteo, you can count on me. I know what's at stake, and I'll do whatever it takes. He won't have a chance to escape this time."

He smiled, a brief and tense smile, but still a smile. "You know, I've always admired your strength, but now... it's different. You're really by my side, Alessia. And that... is something I never thought I could have."

Alessia felt her heart race upon hearing those words. Despite Matteo's hardened exterior, he was revealing a vulnerability he rarely showed. And knowing that he trusted her in this way filled her with an indescribable feeling.

"Then don't worry, Matteo," she replied, her usual teasing tone softened by a touch of affection. "I can handle this. After all, I'm a Romano and a DeLuca, aren't I?"

He laughed, shaking his head. "Yes, and you're also stubborn and impossible to control." He leaned in and whispered, his lips almost touching hers, "But, in the end, that's what I love most about you."

She laughed softly and moved closer, sealing the moment with a kiss that carried with it the intensity and depth of all the feelings they had built together. Then, with her eyes still shining with emotion, Alessia prepared to play her part in the plan.

During the raid on one of Lorenzo's offices, Alessia felt the weight of the danger, but also the adrenaline of knowing that every document, every piece of evidence she collected, brought them one step closer to destroying her father's manipulative empire. Rummaging through drawers and old files, she searched for anything that could directly link him to the frauds and conspiracies.

It was then that she found a folder hidden at the back of a cabinet. When she opened it, she froze. There, smiling in black and white, was her mother, very young, standing next to a man whose presence was as imposing as it was familiar: the original head of the DeLuca family, Matteo's grandfather. Alessia felt a chill run down her spine, as if she had uncovered a lost piece of her own history.

"But... what does this mean?" she whispered to herself, trying to understand what that connection suggested. This changed everything she knew about her own lineage. Did her mother also play a part in a plan involving both families from the very beginning?

She quickly returned to the mansion, where Matteo awaited her anxiously. When she entered the office, he noticed the disturbed expression on her face and immediately approached, his eyes filled with concern.

"Alessia, what happened? Is everything okay?" He pulled her closer, his eyes searching her face for answers.

She took a deep breath and handed him the photograph. "Matteo, look at this. I found it hidden among Lorenzo's documents. My mother... she knew your grandfather. This means our connection goes far beyond what we thought."

He took the photo and examined it silently, his eyes fixed on the image as he processed what it might mean. "This... this means our history was intertwined even before we were born. Alessia, you're part of a much greater legacy than any of us could have imagined."

She nodded, still trying to absorb it all. "I think Lorenzo knew this all along, Matteo. Maybe he manipulated this alliance because he knew about the connection. Maybe I... maybe I was always meant for this."

Matteo grabbed her by the shoulders, forcing her to look at him, his eyes intense and determined. "Listen, Alessia. It doesn't matter what Lorenzo planned or what the past of our families holds. What matters is what we decide to do from here on out. What we've lived together, what we've built... that's real. And no one, not even Lorenzo, is going to take that away from us."

She took a deep breath, his words comforting her, bringing back the sense of security she needed. "Then let's do this together, Matteo. Let's face Lorenzo and all the secrets he tried to hide."

He smiled, a dark and resolute smile. "Yes, let's. And this time, he will pay for everything."

Later, as they prepared for their final assault on Lorenzo, Alessia and Matteo found a moment of peace together. Sitting side by side on the sofa in the office, he held her hand, and both gazed out at the city skyline, silent but united.

"You know this is dangerous, right?" he said, his voice soft but filled with concern. "What we're about to do... it could change everything. And if something happens..."

She interrupted him, squeezing his hand tightly. "Matteo, we've already made this decision together. And I don't want to think about what might go wrong. I want to think that, by your side, I can face anything."

He smiled, his heart warmed by her firmness. "You're everything I never knew I needed, Alessia. And no matter what fate has in store for us, we'll come out of this together."

She looked at him, her eyes sparkling with a mixture of love and defiance. "Then stop trying to protect me all the time, DeLuca. I can fight too, and you know that."

He laughed, shaking his head. "Yes, I know. And that's exactly why I fell in love with you. Because, despite everything, you never gave up on us."

With a mischievous smile, Alessia leaned in and kissed him, feeling the security of being beside someone who completely understood her, who saw beyond the secrets and manipulations. And as they pulled away, both felt they were ready to face whatever came next.

That night, they knew they were about to write the final chapter of the story that Lorenzo had started. And this time, the power was in their hands.

# Chapter 61: The Discovery of Pregnancy

Alessia stared intently at the small test in her hand, as if the two lines drawn there had the power to turn her entire world upside down in a matter of seconds. The confirmation of her pregnancy brought a wave of emotions that left her breathless: a mix of happiness, surprise, and a deep love for the life growing inside her. But amidst this whirlwind of feelings, fear intensified. Matteo still didn't know, and with the tension between the families, Alessia knew this wasn't the right time to tell him.

She sat on the edge of the bed, trying to process what this meant. The idea of becoming a mother filled her with an unexpected tenderness, but it also made her fearful for the future. She knew how much her life was intertwined with the dark world of the mafia, and now, being pregnant put her in an even more vulnerable position. Lorenzo, her very own father, might see the child as a pawn, a new piece to be manipulated, and the very thought of that terrified her.

Determined to keep the news a secret, Alessia prepared for the coming days with renewed resolve. Although she wanted to share this moment with Matteo, she knew revealing the pregnancy now would only add to his worries and might distract from their plans against Lorenzo.

The following days were tough. Alessia struggled to keep up with the routine, but Matteo, attentive to every detail, began to notice the changes in her behavior. One evening, during dinner, he watched her with a concerned and observant gaze.

"You've been different, Alessia. Quieter. You seem like your mind is elsewhere," he commented, his voice laced with worry.

She gave a faint smile, trying to reassure him. "I think it's just all the worries with everything we're going through. It's a lot at once."

He nodded but didn't seem convinced. Matteo had always been someone who noticed the smallest nuances, and Alessia knew it would be hard to hide everything from him. But as long as she could protect this secret, she would.

"Are you sure that's all?" he pressed, reaching across the table to take her hand. "If you need anything, I want you to know you can count on me."

That simple, yet caring gesture made her heart tighten. She wanted so badly to share with him this new life growing inside her, but she knew the right moment hadn't come yet.

"Of course, Matteo. And I appreciate you always being by my side," she replied, holding his hand firmly.

He smiled, a brief smile but full of love that seemed to grow with each passing day. And Alessia knew that, when the time came, that child would have a father who would protect it with all his heart.

The weeks passed, and Alessia tried to adapt to the reality of pregnancy while keeping the secret amidst the chaos. One morning, upon waking, she felt dizzy and a little nauseous, struggling to maintain her composure. Matteo was in the office, discussing the details of a new plan, and she took the opportunity to slip away discreetly. She went to the garden and sat on a bench, closing her eyes and trying to breathe deeply.

"Breathe, Alessia," she whispered to herself, feeling the soft wind against her face and unconsciously caressing her belly.

In that moment, she felt a peace she hadn't experienced in a long time. She was determined to protect that life with everything she had, even if it meant carrying the weight of the secret alone. But at the same time, she missed Matteo, the longing for him to know, to share this journey with her. Still, with danger closing in, she knew she had to stay strong and focused.

One night, Matteo entered the room and found Alessia sitting by the window, lost in thought. He approached silently and placed his hands on her shoulders, surprising her.

"You've been distant, Alessia," he said, his eyes searching for hers in the reflection of the glass. "I know things are tense, but there's something else, isn't there?"

She took a deep breath, trying to keep control. "It's just exhaustion, Matteo. I've been thinking about everything we still have to face."

He turned her to face him, his gaze fixed, as if trying to read her soul. "I know you're carrying the weight of the world, but you don't have to do it alone. I'm here for you, and I'll never let anything hurt you."

She nodded, offering a forced smile, feeling the warmth of his touch and wishing she could open up right then. But fear still held her back, and with a gentle caress on his face, she murmured, "I know. And that's what gives me the strength to keep going."

Matteo looked at her with intense eyes, but he respected her silence, holding her in his arms and savoring that moment of calm.

Another morning, while Alessia was walking through the mansion, she felt a slight dizziness and had to steady herself against the wall. Matteo, who had been nearby, watched her and quickly approached.

"Are you okay?" he asked, visibly concerned.

"Yes, I'm... I'm fine," she said, quickly regaining her composure and trying to appear calm.

He studied her for a moment, his eyes filled with a mix of worry and suspicion. "Alessia, you know you can tell me anything, right?"

She nodded, offering a small smile, but feeling her heart tighten. "Yes, Matteo. And when I'm ready, you'll be the first to know," she replied, her words full of truth, though he couldn't understand their full meaning.

Matteo simply nodded, accepting her response with a slight touch of hesitation. And in that moment, Alessia felt the depth of their connection, a trust that went beyond words and secrets.

That night, as Alessia prepared for bed, she placed her hand on her belly, where a new heart was quietly beating. "I'll protect you," she whispered to the baby, a silent promise that echoed throughout her being.

She knew that amidst all the dangers and uncertainties, she now had an even stronger reason to fight. And though Matteo didn't know about this new life, she felt that he was, in some way, by her side, protecting her and their child, even without knowing.

Alessia closed her eyes, determined to keep the secret for a while longer.

That night, silence filled the room, broken only by the soft sound of Alessia's breathing as she looked out the window. Matteo entered quietly, watching her for a few moments. There was something about her, a softness, a vulnerability that he was just beginning to unravel, and he found himself increasingly drawn to this complexity.

He approached her and, as always, broke the silence with his usual teasing, though now there was a touch of tenderness in his voice. "Lost in thought, Alessia? Let me guess, thinking about me?"

She smiled, not taking her eyes off the window. "Don't be so conceited, Matteo. I've got enough things to worry about without you occupying space in my mind."

He chuckled softly, leaning in to whisper in her ear. "Oh, but that's exactly what I do, isn't it? I occupy every space in your mind... and your heart too."

Alessia felt a shiver run down her spine, but she held her ground, not letting Matteo's intensity intimidate her. She turned to face him, her gaze filled with a soft challenge. "I could say the same about you, boss. The truth is, deep down, you can't stay away from me."

Matteo smiled, but there was sincerity in his gaze that almost disarmed her. He stepped closer, his eyes locked on hers, and murmured, "I think I'm finally starting to understand what it means not to want to be away from someone, Alessia."

The weight of his words made her avert her gaze for a moment, a mixture of emotion and desire swirling in her chest. This vulnerable Matteo, the one who could admit weaknesses, was new to her, and yet, it was exactly what made her feel safe by his side.

He tucked a strand of hair behind her ear, his touch soft and careful. "There's something about you that draws me in, that challenges me... even when I want to keep control, you always manage to disarm all my defenses."

She smiled, feeling warmed by his words. "Maybe it's because, deep down, you never wanted to have control over this, Matteo. Maybe you always wanted me to see the real man behind the boss."

He sighed, as if she had touched on something he wasn't ready to admit. "You're the only one who can see that side of me," he murmured, his gaze softening as he held her face, as if she were something precious.

Alessia, feeling herself increasingly surrendering to that connection, teased him with a mischievous smile. "And what are you going to do now, Matteo? You know that if you keep this up, you'll end up losing all control to me."

He laughed, a low, deep sound, and pulled her closer, their lips nearly touching. "I never had control over you, Alessia. And frankly, I'm starting to like it."

The kiss he gave her was filled with a love that was slowly building, a fusion of respect and desire, of provocation and complicity. Both were becoming more immersed in this dance of feelings, and as he held her, Alessia felt that, despite all the secrets and dangers around them, this moment between them was real.

When the kiss broke, Matteo looked at her, his eyes glowing with affection and intensity. "I can face anything, Alessia, as long as you're by my side. That's the only certainty I have."

She smiled, her eyes fixed on his, feeling a deep and overwhelming connection. "Then promise me, Matteo. No matter what happens, we'll be together. With all the secrets, all the truths... we'll face it together."

He nodded, pulling her closer, as if that embrace were a silent promise that, no matter what the future held, he would protect her. And that night, as they both gave in to the silence and safety of each other, Alessia felt stronger and more loved than she had ever imagined.

The decision to keep her pregnancy a secret weighed heavily on her heart, but she knew that, in time, Matteo would understand and support her. For now, she would keep that secret, feeling strengthened by the love they shared.

# Chapter 62: The Deadly Trap

Matteo breathed heavily as he entered the mansion, still tasting the bitter sting of betrayal that had nearly cost him his life. Lorenzo's ambush had left him furious and distrustful, and every fiber of his being screamed for justice and revenge. His eyes burned with a mix of pain and hatred, his body still tense from the fight and escape.

As he crossed the threshold of the bedroom, he found Alessia sitting, lost in thought. Her serene gaze, oblivious to what he had just faced, only fueled his anger further. Without hesitation, Matteo approached, his voice cold and cutting.

"Did you know, Alessia?" His words sounded like blades, sharp enough to make her lift her face, surprised and confused.

"What...? What are you talking about, Matteo?" she responded, her tone uncertain, but immediately aware of the resentful expression on his face.

He stepped forward, narrowing his eyes. "Don't play innocent. I almost got killed today. Lorenzo set up an ambush, and here you are, as if you didn't know anything." His voice was low, but each syllable dripped with venom.

Alessia felt the impact of his words like a blow. Her eyes widened in shock, but also with growing pain. "You... you think I could do something like that? Matteo, I didn't know anything!"

"I don't know what to think anymore," he replied, his voice hardened by rage. "It's obvious you're still tied to Lorenzo. How can I trust you when all the evidence points to the opposite?"

She took a deep breath, struggling to hold back tears. "Matteo, I've given you everything, proved my loyalty time and again! Lorenzo is my father, but I'm not like him. I can't control his actions."

He turned away from her, laughing sarcastically, though there was deep pain in his eyes. "Don't give me that, Alessia. Do you think I can risk my life and the safety of everyone around me with that excuse? You're not welcome here anymore. The trust between us is gone."

His words hit her like a fatal blow. The idea of being banished from his life, especially now that she carried their child, was devastating. Still, Alessia knew there was nothing she could say at that moment that he would believe. He was blinded by pain and anger, and any attempt at explanation would be in vain.

"If that's how you feel," she whispered, struggling to keep her voice steady, "then I'll leave. But know that I'm leaving because you forced me to, Matteo. I would never betray you, but you chose to believe lies instead of trusting me."

He averted his gaze, his jaw clenched, without responding. Alessia swallowed hard, grabbed her few belongings, and, with a heavy heart, walked out of the mansion, feeling as if she were leaving a part of herself behind.

As she walked through the cold night, she instinctively held her belly, seeking comfort in the new life growing within her. "I won't let anything happen to you," she whispered, more to herself than to the baby. She knew that from that moment on, she was alone.

Alessia walked through the dark streets, feeling the cold wind wrap around her body as her tears burned as they slid down her face. Each step away from Matteo felt like an even greater weight on her heart, as if she were leaving a part of herself behind. The pain of the separation was intense, an open wound that pulsed with every memory of the moments they had shared.

As the night wore on, Alessia found herself remembering Matteo's small gestures, those moments when he let his vulnerability slip behind the façade of the mafia boss. She recalled when he would pull her closer after a heated argument, the soft touch of his fingers on her face, his intense and possessive way that, despite everything, made her feel protected. Now, that protection seemed like a distant memory, and Alessia knew her love for him had never been as deep as it was now that she was apart from him.

She stopped in an empty square and closed her eyes, trying to suppress the urge to run back, to tell him everything about the baby and the sincerity of her feelings. But she knew she couldn't. Matteo was blinded by resentment, and to him, any word from her would sound like another attempt at manipulation. His hurt was as strong as his love, and Alessia, though wounded, knew she had to let time heal the wounds that Lorenzo had planted between them.

Meanwhile, Matteo, alone in the mansion, felt the emptiness in every room, Alessia's absence echoing loudly in his heart. He paced back and forth, his mind in turmoil, a mix of rage, guilt, and regret that he didn't know how to process. He couldn't understand why he had felt the need to expel her like that, to hurt her with such sharp words. But every time he tried to rationalize it, the image of the ambush came back, and the fear of being betrayed invaded him once more.

"Why you, Alessia?" he murmured to himself, running his hands over his face. He knew she was the only person he had allowed himself to be truly himself with, the only one who made him feel alive, without the masks of the cruel boss he had to be. And now that she was gone, the pain of her absence was so unbearable that he felt his control slipping from his grasp.

He walked to the window, looking out at the night, and in silence, whispered as if she could hear him. "Alessia... I don't know what to do anymore. I wanted to protect you, but it feels like I'm the one who hurt you the most."

Alessia, already far from the mansion, felt the emptiness spread within her, but she placed her hand gently on her belly, caressing it. "You will be the reason I stay strong," she whispered. And despite the pain in her heart, a spark of hope ignited. Maybe, one day, Matteo would find out the truth.

# Chapter 63: Alone and on the Run

Alessia left Matteo's mansion with a tightness in her chest that felt like it was tearing her soul apart. Every step away from that place carried the weight of love and pain intertwined—a sacrifice she never expected to make. The night air was cold, and the silence around her emphasized the loneliness that now became her only companion. With a small bag containing her essentials and an unshakable determination to protect the child she carried, Alessia made her way to the nearest train station and left for a remote city, far from the reach of the mafia's claws.

After hours of travel, Alessia arrived in a small, forgotten town. It was peaceful, with quiet streets and few inhabitants. She found a modest room in a guesthouse, paid in cash for a few weeks in advance, hoping to stay off anyone's radar who might be looking for her. With her heart still shaken by her forced goodbye with Matteo, Alessia knew she would have to rebuild her life from scratch, without the security and resources she was used to.

On her first night in the new town, alone in her room, Alessia sat on the edge of the bed and felt the emptiness expand in her chest. She placed her hand protectively over her belly. "We'll be okay, my love," she whispered, trying to convince herself of the strength she needed to maintain. "I promise I'll do whatever it takes to protect you."

As the days went by, Alessia established a simple routine, trying to remain inconspicuous. She spent her mornings helping at the small café next to the guesthouse in exchange for food, and in the afternoons, she walked around the town, trying to absorb the new reality she had chosen. At every corner, she looked over her shoulder, fearing that some messenger from Lorenzo might find her, or that Matteo, for some reason, would send someone after her.

The challenges of pregnancy began to manifest: morning sickness, constant fatigue, and occasional pains that caught her by surprise. Without proper care or medical attention, she felt increasingly vulnerable. One particularly difficult morning, Alessia felt a sudden dizziness and grabbed one of the café's tables to steady herself. Clara, the kind café owner, noticed and rushed to her side.

"My dear, you need to rest. You're clearly exhausted," Clara said, genuine concern in her eyes. "Are you sure you're okay?"

Alessia forced a smile, trying to mask her fragility. "I'm fine, Clara, just a little tired. I think it'll pass soon."

But Clara wasn't convinced, and gently took Alessia's hand. "If you need help, don't hesitate to ask, okay? You don't have to go through this alone."

The kindness of the older woman brought tears to Alessia's eyes, and she turned her face away, trying to hide the emotion threatening to spill over. "Thank you, Clara. I... I really appreciate everything."

In her moments of solitude, Alessia found herself remembering Matteo's harsh words, the unjust accusations, and the distrust in his eyes the last time they saw each other. She tried to push those thoughts away, but they returned relentlessly, like a wound that would never heal. Matteo had been the only person in her life with whom she felt completely herself, and now he wasn't by her side to share this journey.

One afternoon, as she walked through the town square, Alessia sat on a bench and watched a few children playing in the distance. She imagined what her child might be like—whether they would inherit Matteo's intense eyes or his teasing smile. Amidst the sadness, a small smile appeared on her lips, and she whispered softly, "I wish you could meet your father... he's such a strong man, even if he's as stubborn as a rock."

She sighed, feeling the tears fall again. "And I... I love him, even if he hurt me. Even if he sent me away." Alessia knew those feelings wouldn't disappear easily, but it was the memory of Matteo that kept her moving forward, even from afar.

That night, back in her room, Alessia lay down and stared at the dark ceiling, where the shadows moved gently with the rhythm of the streetlight outside. She closed her eyes and, for the first time in a long time, allowed herself to dream of the impossible—that one day, Matteo would discover the truth and understand how much she sacrificed to protect what they had built.

But for now, she was alone and on the run, and the only certainty she had was that she wouldn't give up.

In the dim light of the guesthouse room, Alessia allowed herself to relive moments she had shared with Matteo—scenes that replayed in her mind like a painful yet sweet film. She closed her eyes and almost felt his touch, his strong hands holding her face as he gazed at her with that intensity that made her forget everything around her. He was the Matteo she knew—the man behind the mafia boss, the man who, despite all the hardness, showed a vulnerability only to her.

The memory of their heated arguments brought a smile to Alessia's lips, though a twinge of sadness lingered in her heart. Every argument, every provocation, was an essential part of their relationship. "I hate you, DeLuca," she used to say, but she knew that even when those words left her mouth, the feeling was the opposite. The teasing was their way of connecting, of challenging each other. Now, Alessia missed even the fights, the passion that arose in the angry glances they shared, which soon turned into intense kisses.

Far from her, Matteo also struggled with the emotions that insisted on tormenting him. In the silence of the night, in his empty mansion, he found himself thinking about Alessia more than he wanted to admit. Amidst the anger and distrust he felt, there was also a longing he tried to suppress at all costs. He imagined her laughing, mocking his seriousness, questioning his decisions in that provocative way she always did. It was as if, in her presence, he was another version of himself—a version that didn't have to carry the weight of being the ruthless DeLuca boss.

He remembered one time, after a heated argument, when she had looked at him and whispered, with a mischievous smile, "If you were less stubborn, Matteo, maybe I could even like you." He had laughed, a genuine laugh that he rarely allowed anyone to see, and replied with a touch of challenge, "Like me, Alessia? Don't be so obvious. You're already in love with me."

Now, alone, Matteo felt the weight of his own words. He knew he was in love with her, but pride and hurt created a barrier he didn't know how to cross. "I was an idiot," he whispered to himself, his voice heavy with regret. He realized how much he had hurt her, how much he had let himself be consumed by the fear of being betrayed, by the need to maintain control over everything and everyone. Alessia was different. She wasn't a threat, but the woman who made him feel human, who saw beyond the mask he wore.

As time passed, both of them found themselves trapped in a cycle of longing and pain. Alessia, lying in her modest room, ran her hands over her belly, finding comfort in the new life she carried. She felt connected to Matteo in a unique way, as if, somehow, he was still present through that little miracle. "We both love you," she murmured to the baby, caressing her stomach. "Even though he doesn't know yet."

Meanwhile, Matteo continued to battle his own feelings. He knew he had made a hasty decision by sending her away, but pride prevented him from going after her. At the same time, the fear that Alessia might truly be involved with Lorenzo consumed him. It was a battle between reason and emotion, and deep down, he knew he was losing.

At the end of that night, Alessia and Matteo, in separate places, sighed, both consumed by the same longing and desire. She whispered, through her tears, "I wish you could understand me, Matteo." And he, alone in his office, holding a photo of her, murmured, almost like a prayer, "Come back to me, Alessia. I need you."

# Chapter 64: The Net Tightens

With each passing day, Alessia felt the tension growing. Every time she changed her hiding place, the weight of the pregnancy became more evident, and the physical and emotional exhaustion started to take its toll. She knew that Lorenzo was getting closer to finding her, and the fear of him discovering her secret became a constant shadow over her.

Alone in a small, dark room, Alessia leaned against the wall, breathing heavily. The baby moved inside her, and even in the midst of terror, she found comfort in that movement, in the certainty that there was a new life growing inside her, a hope amidst so much darkness. She closed her eyes and whispered, "I will protect you, my love. No matter what I have to do."

Determined to seek help, Alessia tried once again to contact Serena, her trusted friend. She grabbed a prepaid phone she had managed to get in the city, but even as she dialed the number, fear paralyzed her. She knew that every call was a risk; Lorenzo had eyes and ears everywhere.

After a few rings, Serena finally answered, and Alessia felt relief upon hearing her friend's voice on the other end of the line. "Serena, is it you?" she whispered, almost not believing it.

"Alessia! Oh my God, where are you? I've been so worried!" Serena responded, her voice filled with concern and relief.

"I can't tell you where I am, Serena. It's too dangerous. But I need help. Lorenzo is hunting me... and I'm pregnant," Alessia confessed, her voice choking, holding back the tears that threatened to fall.

There was a brief silence on the other end, and Alessia could almost imagine the look of surprise and worry on Serena's face. "Oh, Alessia... I... I don't even know what to say. And does Matteo know?"

She took a deep breath, swallowing the pain that always surfaced when mentioning his name. "No. He doesn't know. I couldn't tell him, Serena. He kicked me out before I had the chance."

Serena sighed, clearly worried. "Alessia, this is too dangerous. Lorenzo will do everything to find you. You need to leave there as soon as possible. Come south. I know someone who can help you hide."

Alessia closed her eyes, Serena's words offering a flicker of hope. But deep down, she knew Lorenzo's network stretched across the entire country, and perhaps beyond. "I'll try, Serena. Thank you... for everything."

Before she could say more, she heard a noise outside the room, and with her heart racing, she hung up the phone, quickly turning off the lights. She approached the window and peeked outside, spotting two unfamiliar men on the street, watching the inn attentively.

Her body trembled with fear, but her determination gathered strength. She had to flee again, despite the exhaustion, despite her body demanding rest. She placed her hand on her belly, whispering to the baby, "Hold on, my love. We're leaving here."

Meanwhile, Matteo spent his nights awake, tortured by memories of Alessia. With each passing day, his distrust and anger faded, giving way to an immense pain and an undeniable need to find her, one he could no longer ignore. Despite everything, he couldn't shake the feeling that he had made an irreparable mistake.

One night, Matteo found himself alone in his office, holding a small photograph of Alessia that he had kept hidden in a drawer. Her face, with that challenging smile, made him remember every teasing word, every intense exchange between them. "Where are you, Alessia?" he murmured, his heart aching. "I sent you away, but I never wanted to lose you."

It was then that Giovanni, one of his trusted men, entered the office, hesitating. "Sir, may I speak with you?"

Matteo nodded, still looking lost in the photo. Giovanni approached, holding an envelope. "We've discovered that Lorenzo has intensified the search for Alessia. He's sent men to several small towns. It seems like he knows she carries something valuable... something he wants at any cost."

Matteo raised his gaze, feeling his blood run cold. "Something valuable? Giovanni, what else do you know?"

The man hesitated for a moment. "We don't have details, but we've heard rumors that Alessia might be... pregnant."

The impact of those words hit like a blow. Matteo leaned back in his chair, his heart racing, emotions swirling in a whirlwind of shock and hope. "Pregnant..." he whispered, trying to absorb the weight of that revelation. "Alessia is expecting a child... and I sent her away."

Suddenly, everything fell into place. Her change in behavior, the moments when she seemed hesitant, the look of pain on her face when he had kicked her out. Matteo felt an overwhelming guilt. He had to find her — and fast.

Alessia, for her part, had moved to a new hideout, an abandoned house on the outskirts of town, but the exhaustion was becoming unbearable. That night, she sat on the floor, hugging her belly, feeling her heart tighten. The loneliness and fear seemed unbearable, and the only thing keeping her going was the desire to protect her child.

"Will he ever know?" she murmured, her voice low and filled with sadness. "Will Matteo ever know that you exist?"

She felt the tears silently falling, a deep pain mixed with the love she still carried for Matteo, despite everything. She wanted to believe he would come, that he would understand the truth and save her from this nightmare. But reality was cruel, and more and more Alessia realized she would have to face this fate alone.

In the following days, Alessia knew she would have to gather all her strength. Lorenzo was close, and her time was running out.

In the dimness of her makeshift hideout, Alessia allowed herself to close her eyes, trying to imagine Matteo there with her. The coldness of solitude was relentless, but in her memories, she felt the warmth of his arms, the intense look that always challenged hers, full of teasing and, at the same time, a tenderness he never admitted. It was hard to accept that now he was so far away, that the protection she once felt with him had been taken away.

Alessia laughed, humorlessly, remembering their heated conversations, the way Matteo could stir up a torrent of conflicting emotions in her. "You're too stubborn, DeLuca," she murmured to herself, "but if you weren't like that... maybe I wouldn't have fallen in love with you." She smiled as she thought about all the times he would roll his eyes or cross his arms in feigned disdain when she teased him. Matteo always said he liked to control everything, but deep down, she knew he enjoyed the way she challenged him, how she always made him yield.

Meanwhile, Matteo, in the mansion, felt Alessia's absence suffocatingly. Every corner of the house seemed empty, lacking her presence to fill it with that vibrant energy only she had. He remembered how she teased him, how she would throw sharp, mocking phrases to destabilize him, and he, no matter how hard he tried to hide it, enjoyed every moment of it.

The night before she left, Matteo remembered how he had held her close, the warmth between them almost palpable. "You think you're too smart, Alessia," he had said, trying to keep a serious tone, but the slight curve on his lips betrayed how surrendered he was.

"And maybe I am," she had replied, her gaze full of challenge. "But let's face it, you like it. You like someone who doesn't bow down to the great Matteo DeLuca."

He had leaned in, his lips just inches from hers. "Maybe I do," he confessed in a whisper, his voice filled with desire and truth. And when their lips finally met, the world around them disappeared. Matteo knew he was a tough man, who didn't easily show his weaknesses, but with Alessia... it was as if every barrier dissolved, leaving him exposed in a way he had never imagined.

Now, alone in his office, Matteo wondered where she was, if she was safe, if she missed him the way he missed her. He felt a sharp pain remembering their last encounter, the harsh words exchanged, words he wished he could erase. "I shouldn't have sent you away," he murmured, his voice choked with regret.

He imagined being by her side, wondering what he would say if he had her in his arms again. "Alessia," he would whisper in her ear, "no matter how much you challenge me, no matter how much you try to run... I will always want you back. Because you're the only one who can see the real Matteo behind the name DeLuca."

Alessia, even at a distance, could almost feel that silent promise. She wrapped her arms around herself, wishing with all her might that Matteo was thinking of her, that he would understand the truth before it was too late.

# Chapter 65: Hidden News

Matteo sat in his office, the first rays of dawn still hadn't broken the darkness that filled the room, and he felt the same darkness inside himself. Weeks had passed since he had kicked Alessia out of his life, but the emptiness she left seemed to grow with each passing day. Her name was on his mind, on the tip of his tongue, like a poison that refused to leave his body.

Rumors that Alessia was being hunted by Lorenzo had begun to reach Matteo through discreet channels, fragmented information he initially ignored. The hurt he still felt, burning like a fresh wound, made him disregard any news of her. But the more time passed, the more he felt a restlessness, a tightness in his chest that he couldn't explain. And even though he wouldn't admit it to himself, the possibility that Alessia was in danger left him anxious, as if each passing second were a race against time.

One night, as Giovanni relayed another set of information about their territory operations, he casually mentioned, "It seems Lorenzo has intensified the search. They almost caught her in a town upstate. She managed to escape... but by a hair."

Giovanni's words hit Matteo like a punch. The image of Alessia running, Lorenzo relentlessly hunting her, brought forth a feeling of guilt he could no longer ignore. His stomach twisted, and he knew he had to seek answers, to understand what had really happened.

"Tell me, Giovanni," Matteo began, trying to control his voice. "About that ambush... do you believe Alessia could have been involved?"

Giovanni hesitated, choosing his words carefully. "Sir, I've always found it strange. Alessia seemed loyal to you. She never struck me as a woman who could be manipulated so easily. But we

346

know how Lorenzo works. He would do anything to manipulate even those closest to him."

Matteo shuddered. How foolish he had been. How could he have believed so quickly that Alessia would betray him? He knew her better than that. He knew her determination, her loyalty, and how much she had fought by his side. And suddenly, he remembered her last words, the look in her eyes as he accused her. There had been real pain on her face, a pain he had refused to see.

With a sudden movement, Matteo stood. "Let's find her, Giovanni. And fast. I won't let her run away again."

Giovanni nodded, surprised by his boss's determination, but understanding that this was more important to Matteo than any power struggle. It was clear that Alessia was the only one capable of touching the boss's heart in a way no one else could.

Meanwhile, Alessia felt more exhausted every day, more pressed by the need to keep moving. The pregnancy, which had been bearable until then, began to weigh on her more than she ever imagined. The pain and the fatigue made every step a challenge, but the thought that Lorenzo could catch up with her was the fuel that kept her going.

She took shelter in an old, abandoned cabin, feeling a slight sense of safety, though only temporarily. She sat in an improvised chair, placing her hand over her belly and whispering, "Hold on, my love. I promise we'll be safe soon."

The anguish grew along with her belly, and in her moments of greatest loneliness, Alessia allowed herself to remember Matteo. She imagined how he would react if he knew about the pregnancy, if he knew that a little piece of him was growing inside her. Deep down, she nurtured a secret hope that he would find her, that he would understand the truth before it was too late. But the cruel reality reminded her that she was alone.

What Alessia didn't know was that Matteo was already on her trail, closer than he had ever been since he expelled her. He searched tirelessly, blinded by the need to understand and to redeem the mistake he had made. It was a primal instinct, a feeling he could no longer ignore.

A few days later, in a nearby town, Matteo followed the lead of an informant who had recently seen Alessia. With each step, his heart beat faster, consumed by anticipation and guilt. His mind was flooded with memories of her, of every moment they had spent together, the smiles, the teasing, the glances that spoke more than any words. He knew he would need courage to face her, to ask for forgiveness, but he also knew that he could never continue without trying.

When he finally spotted the cabin where they said Alessia might be, Matteo took a deep breath. The surroundings were quiet, the sound of the wind the only companion as he approached. With cautious steps, Matteo reached the door, hesitating only a second before knocking.

Inside, Alessia jumped at the sound. Her instincts told her to run, but something held her back. When she opened the door, she found herself face to face with Matteo. The shock was instant, and it took her a moment to process that he was really standing there, before her — the man who had thrown her out, the same man she still loved, despite all the pain.

"Alessia," he murmured, his voice heavy with regret. "I... I came to find you."

She recoiled, her eyes filled with hurt. "Matteo, you have no right to come looking for me now. Not after everything you said, after accusing me of something I never did."

He looked at her, struggling against his own emotions, each of her words hitting him like a blow. "I know, Alessia. I know I was wrong. Lorenzo... he played me, and I let anger blind me. But now

I see how foolish I was. Please... let me prove that I can still protect you."

Alessia stared at him, a tear falling down her cheek. "I needed you, Matteo. I needed you when everything fell apart, and you weren't there."

Matteo stepped forward, extending his hand, but hesitated before touching her face. "Please, Alessia. Let me make up for that. You're the only person who ever showed me a life beyond this darkness. I can't... I can't live without you."

For a moment, she allowed herself to look at him, feeling every word he said, feeling the love and the hurt mix into an almost tangible pain. Without him knowing, she held the secret of a new life growing inside her, something that could either bring them back together — or destroy them forever.

Alessia stared at Matteo, fighting to hide the mix of anger, love, and hurt that consumed her. He was there, before her, with a hardened expression, but with a look in his eyes that now revealed regret — an expression she never thought she would see in the mafia boss who had always been ruthless. Her heart raced, and despite all the pain he had caused her, a part of her longed to feel those arms around her again, to lose herself in the warmth of those eyes that had captivated her from the start.

"You think you can just show up and fix everything, Matteo?" Alessia whispered, trying to hold back her tears. "After sending me away, accusing me of betrayal? I thought you were sharper than this."

Matteo stepped forward, his eyes locked on hers, filled with a desire and guilt he couldn't hide. "Alessia, I know I failed you. I let anger blind me, I let Lorenzo plant doubts that never should have been there. But since you left, there hasn't been a single day I haven't regretted it. I realized what you mean to me... and that scares me."

She laughed, a bitter laugh, trying to ignore the weight of his words. "You're scared of loving me, Matteo? Maybe that's it, after all. Maybe I was never more than a challenge to you, an interesting distraction in your war with Lorenzo."

Matteo reached out his hand, and though hesitating, touched her face, his thumb tracing a soft line along her delicate skin. "No. You were the only person who showed me a life beyond this chaos, someone who saw me for who I really am, beneath all the masks. And I didn't realize it until I lost you. Until I understood that your absence is the only hell I truly fear."

Alessia closed her eyes for a moment, absorbing his touch, the warmth of that hand she longed for. When she opened her eyes, her gaze had softened, but the pain was still there, deep within. "And what do you expect me to do, Matteo? Just forget everything you said? You hurt me in ways that even Lorenzo wouldn't."

He took a deep breath, his eyes fixed on hers, his voice gentle and sincere. "I don't expect you to forget. I don't expect you to forgive me so easily. I just want you to know that if I could go back, if I could undo every word, I would do it without hesitation. I'm here, asking for a chance... one last chance to protect you, to have you by my side."

She hesitated, feeling the weight of the secret she carried, the life growing inside her, the deeper connection that now bound them, even though he didn't know. "Maybe it's too late, Matteo," she murmured, averting her gaze, trying to hide the fragility in her voice.

He took her face in his hands, forcing her to look at him, his eyes full of an intensity she knew all too well. "Don't say that, Alessia. Because no matter how much you reject me, no matter how much you try to pull away, I won't give up on you. I can't. Because you're the only thing that still gives me hope, the only thing that still makes everything worth it."

For a moment, Alessia felt completely defenseless. She knew Matteo was a tough, unyielding man, but here he was, vulnerable, willing to break down any wall for her. Her fingers trembled as they touched his face, sliding over the rough stubble, feeling every detail, as if she wanted to absorb the sensation so she would never forget it.

"You've always had that power over me," she whispered, her voice barely audible. "You challenge me, you drive me crazy... but you also make me feel safer than anyone ever could."

He smiled, that smile that was a mix of arrogance and tenderness. "And you've always known how to destabilize me, how to provoke me until I lose control. Alessia, I'm not perfect, but I'm here... ready to be whatever you need."

Alessia, feeling the weight of his confession, the emotions she carried, leaned in and kissed him, a kiss full of longing, of hope, and of a silent promise that, maybe, there was a way forward for both of them. She felt the world disappear around them, leaving only the two of them, united by something that went beyond understanding. Matteo pulled her closer, and in that embrace, Alessia felt, for a brief moment, that everything was right again.

# Chapter 66: A New Life in Secret

Alessia was exhausted. Every movement, every breath seemed like an effort, and the feeling of being trapped in a cycle of running away was unbearable. The sea, which had now become her home, was like a mirror of her soul: vast, but empty. She tried to find peace, but her life was a constant search for a safe refuge, far from the ghosts of her past. Her body, weakened by pregnancy, and the pain she felt, made her increasingly vulnerable. And in moments of solitude, she wondered if she would ever have a future without fear.

It was in this scenario that she met Marco, a young and attentive doctor who seemed to understand her body's needs in a genuine way. He offered the care Alessia had refused to ask for, and gradually, she began to feel something she hadn't felt in a long time—cared for. Over time, Marco became a comforting presence in her life, someone who didn't make her feel judged or as though there were hidden motives.

"How have you been feeling, Alessia?" Marco asked, his voice gentle and soothing, a stark contrast to the harsh reality of her life. "How has your diet been?"

Alessia tried to smile, but it was forced. "I... I've been eating enough, but the back pain has been bothering me a lot. And the fatigue too."

Hearing this, Marco examined her more carefully, taking measurements and asking her more about how she was feeling. "You need more rest, Alessia. Your body is asking for help, and pregnancy shouldn't be treated so carelessly."

Those words touched Alessia deeply. For the first time in a long time, she felt vulnerable in front of someone who seemed so genuinely concerned for her. In the days that followed, Marco checked in on her several times, offering his help, always with a kindness that she didn't know how to handle. They began talking more, and over time, a cautious friendship began to form between them. Alessia started to feel comfortable in his presence, something she hadn't felt in a long time. But at the same time, she felt lost, as if she were betraying her own heart by letting someone get that close.

Their friendship deepened in small exchanges, like when Marco invited her to take a walk along the beach one evening. "You should get out more, Alessia. The fresh air does you good, and the sea has a way of lifting some of the weight of the world," he said, with his calm and always helpful demeanor.

Alessia hesitated, but the idea of being outdoors without the constant fear seemed appealing. So, she agreed. They walked along the empty beach, the sound of the waves crashing softly in the background. Alessia felt the wind on her face, and for a moment, she almost forgot about the ghosts chasing her.

"Did you know the sea is my only therapy?" Marco asked, looking at the horizon. "When things get tough, I come here, just to breathe."

Alessia looked at him, seeing something genuine in his eyes. This man had no idea how far removed she was from everything he knew. But at the same time, there was something comforting about his presence. Something that gave her a false sense of security, as if, for a moment, she were just a normal woman, without the nightmares of her past.

"I... never knew how to just breathe," Alessia admitted, her voice almost a whisper. "I've always been running, Marco. Always trying to hide from something."

He looked at her with curiosity, a hint of understanding in his gaze. "It's not easy, but we all need to find a way to leave the past behind, Alessia. You deserve a second chance."

Those words struck deep within her. Alessia felt something stir inside her, a feeling she couldn't ignore. She had stepped away from Matteo and all the pain he represented, but now she was faced with another choice: to open her heart again, or to continue living in secret, away from any involvement that could put her baby's safety at risk.

As the days passed, the bond between Alessia and Marco grew deeper. He became her refuge, her support in a life that kept falling apart. She knew that if she allowed herself to feel, she could find a happiness she never thought possible. But the fear that her past would catch up with her and destroy her, along with her baby, prevented her from fully surrendering to the moment.

One evening, while they were walking along the beach, Marco stopped and looked at her with a shy smile. "You know, Alessia, there's something about you... I feel like you have so much more to offer than you realize. Maybe, in the future, you won't have to run anymore. Maybe you'll find something here. Something new."

Alessia looked at him, her heart beating faster than she wanted to admit. She was scared. Scared of falling in love, scared of trusting someone again. But for a brief moment, she wondered if maybe this was the beginning of a new life. A life where she and her baby could be free. Maybe Marco was the first step in that journey. And, for the first time in a long time, Alessia felt that maybe, just maybe, happiness was still possible.

Alessia sat on the porch of her small house, the soft evening breeze brushing her face. The horizon, painted in orange and pink by the setting sun, seemed distant, as if the peace she sought was a mirage, always out of reach. She looked out at the sea, the waves gently breaking on the shore, and for a moment, she forgot the weight she carried. The life on the run, the ghosts from the past, the dangers always lurking... it all seemed less threatening here, in this secluded corner.

She sighed, closing her eyes for a moment. Marco was inside, in the kitchen, preparing something simple for dinner. There was something comforting and secure about him, a stability Alessia hadn't known, and maybe that's why it felt so difficult. She wanted to let go, to allow herself normalcy, but the fear and guilt still crept into every step she took. And yet, she felt a growing attraction to him, something that made her question if she was truly ready to move on.

Marco entered the porch, interrupting her thoughts. He smiled when he saw her, that open and welcoming smile as if nothing could disturb the calm in his life. But in his eyes, there was an intensity Alessia had started to notice. He approached her and, without saying a word, sat beside her. The silence between them was comfortable, but filled with a growing tension they both felt but avoided commenting on.

"I shouldn't be here, Marco," Alessia finally said, breaking the silence, her voice tinged with a regret she couldn't hide. "I should still be running. I can't... let myself do this. Let myself be happy."

Marco looked at her, his gaze intense, and he could see the inner struggle she was facing. He had always known there was more to her than she let on, but something was holding her back from fully opening up. He gently placed his hand over hers, the touch firm yet tender.

"Alessia," he began, his voice soft but with a depth that made her feel something stir within her. "You have the right to live, to be happy, without the shadows of the past. I know it's hard, but you don't have to do it alone. Not anymore."

She felt his hand on hers, and a warmth spread through her body. It was tempting, the comfort he offered, but at the same time, Alessia knew that trusting Marco meant opening a hole in the fortress she had built to protect herself from everything the mafia had once represented. She looked at him, her eyes shining with unspoken pain, and shook her head slowly.

"I can't surrender, Marco. I can't let anyone get close, not like this. Because what I am... what I carry, it's not simple. And I don't want you to pay the price for it."

Marco watched her closely, his eyes softening as he realized the depth of her fear. He had never known what she was truly facing, but something inside him told him she was holding back, protecting herself. He withdrew his hand from hers for a moment, only to move closer, so she could feel his presence in a more intimate way.

"I'm not the kind of man who steps back from what I want, Alessia," he said, his words low, with a mixture of challenge and affection. "And I want you. All of you. No matter where you come from or what you carry. I just know that I won't let you run from me, even if you try."

Those words hit Alessia's heart like a storm. She felt the desire, mixed with fear, intensifying in her chest. The way he looked at her, with an intensity she couldn't ignore, made her feel vulnerable, and at the same time, she wanted to surrender to that vulnerability. But what Marco didn't know was what she carried inside her, the secret that could destroy everything.

"And what if I told you I can't surrender like this, that you don't know what you're asking for?" she asked, her voice hoarse, as she looked at him, feeling a deep pain that kept her from fully giving in.

"I know you're scared. I know you have a heavy past and a future full of shadows. But I'm not Lorenzo, Alessia," Marco replied firmly, his voice deeper. "I'm here, and I want to help you build something different. Something where you don't have to run anymore."

Those eyes. Those words. Alessia felt a growing pressure in her chest, a sense that she was on the brink of a change she couldn't control. She closed her eyes, feeling Marco's hand gently caressing her arm, a possessive yet tender touch, as if he was beginning to mark his territory in a quiet, irreversible way.

And then, the kiss happened. It wasn't planned, it wasn't calculated. It was pure, impulsive, a mix of all the repressed feelings, all the desire and pain, coming together in that instant. Alessia didn't pull away. She didn't want to. Marco's taste was sweet, firm, and she felt as though she was finally being touched by someone who didn't just want to possess her, but understand her. His hand moved to the back of her neck, holding her gently, but with an urgency that made Alessia lose control for a moment.

When the kiss broke, both of them were breathless. Alessia looked at him, her eyes burning with emotion. "You... don't know what you're asking for," she whispered, but her voice trembled, as if the battle within her was lost.

"Maybe I know more than you think," Marco replied, his tone gentle, but with a smile of someone determined not to let her escape.

And in that moment, Alessia knew that her life was about to change forever. She could no longer continue running. She didn't know what the future held, but she knew that, for some reason, she was ready to face it with Marco by her side. Even if her past was a minefield, she felt that, maybe, he was the only one who could help her cross through it.

But somewhere, very far away, Matteo's shadows were still watching, waiting for the moment to intervene. And Alessia knew that by opening her heart to Marco, she was only beginning a new battle, a battle against the ghosts of the past, against the loves and fears that could not be easily forgotten.

# Chapter 67: A New Interest for Matteo

The night was enveloped in a warm, suffocating breeze, typical of a party where business and luxury mingled in a sophisticated, calculated atmosphere. Matteo DeLuca was immersed in the glamour of an event organized to reinforce alliances—a power display disguised as socializing. The laughter and soft conversations filled the room, but he remained distant from it all. The weight of his separation from Alessia still hung over him like a shadow, a sense of emptiness that nothing seemed to fill—not even the business that dominated his life.

He was used to being the center of attention, but that night, the atmosphere of superiority that he so often thrived in offered no comfort. Alessia's words still echoed in his mind. The pain of loss, the regret for pushing her away—it all kept him detached, absorbed in thoughts that removed him from the party, the curious glances, the people trying to pull him into their discussions and power plays.

Matteo was in a tense conversation with one of his closest allies when a striking female figure appeared by his side. She was tall, with dark hair and impeccable posture. Her eyes, deep and observant, were fixed on him with an intensity that immediately captured his attention.

"Matteo DeLuca," she said, a mysterious smile playing on her lips, her voice carrying a confidence that he couldn't ignore. "I've heard a lot about you. But I've never had the pleasure of meeting the man behind the name."

He regarded her cautiously, aware that she wasn't here by accident. "Bianca, right?" he responded, his voice still tinged with suspicion but growing curiosity. "The ally of the Romano family. One of the most powerful women in our line of business, if I remember correctly."

She laughed softly, a low, sensual laugh that made Matteo briefly recall how women often sought him out for the power he represented, not for who he truly was. She didn't seem different, but there was something in her that stirred a sense of challenge within him.

"I'm not just a name in a business, Matteo," she said with a look that made him feel as though she were analyzing him with precision. "And you... well, you're not just the head of the mafia. Or are you? Or is there something more beneath that impenetrable facade?"

Matteo, surprised by her boldness, raised an eyebrow. He knew most people approached him with an interest in power, but Bianca seemed to have something else in mind. She knew how to provoke him, which kept him alert.

"I am what you see, Bianca," he replied, his voice firm, but a rising tension was evident. "But don't underestimate me. What you think you know is probably far from the truth."

She moved in a little closer, fearless, with a confidence that didn't shy away from anyone. "I love men like you, Matteo," she said, her eyes locking with his, challenging him. "You try to be unbeatable, but that's exactly what draws me to you. I'm more than enough to challenge you, if you let me."

He felt intrigued yet uncomfortable. Bianca wasn't like Alessia. She wasn't the type to challenge him with sharp words or the intensity of unrequited love. She was direct, strategic, with a magnetism that wasn't rooted in bitter love, but in a woman who knew exactly what she wanted and how to get it.

"Do you really think you can challenge me like this?" he asked, a half-smile curling his lips, more out of amusement than threat. "I'm immune to these games, Bianca."

She smiled, a clever grin, as though she already knew what he was thinking. "Then prove to me that you're really immune,

Matteo. Because, frankly, I believe you're not as immune as you think. And honestly, this challenge... well, it has something exciting about it."

Matteo felt an odd discomfort. He could sense what she was doing. Bianca wasn't just trying to capture his attention; she was challenging him, and he wasn't used to being challenged in this way. The attraction was palpable, but he didn't want to admit it to himself. He didn't want to allow himself to feel anything for someone who wasn't Alessia.

As Bianca spoke, Matteo felt Alessia's presence, even though she was miles away. The memory of her expression, her look of mixed anger and pain when he pushed her away, infiltrated his mind like a ghostly presence. Bianca was there, offering him a distraction, but no matter how hard he tried, he couldn't shake the thought of Alessia.

Bianca noticed the distraction in Matteo, and it made her smile even more challengingly. "I can tell, Matteo. You're still thinking about her, aren't you? Alessia. The woman who almost destroyed you." She tilted her head, a mischievous smile playing on her lips. "You still love her, don't you?"

He looked at her, surprised by the audacity of the question, but didn't answer immediately. Instead, he pulled back slightly, his gaze distant. "It's not about love, Bianca," he said, his voice lower, but laden with an emotion he didn't want to admit. "It's about a choice I made. And now, I deal with the consequences."

Bianca took another step closer to him, a glint in her eyes. "Then let me be the distraction you need, Matteo. Let me show you what it really means to have control." She took his hand for a moment, firm and sure, as though offering him something he couldn't refuse.

Matteo looked at her, feeling the weight of her words. Something inside him wanted to accept the offer. He wanted to forget the pain, he wanted the ease that Bianca represented. But something, something inside him still held him back. "You're an interesting challenge, Bianca," he murmured, "but I'm not looking for distractions."

She smiled, but now the smile was more subtle, as if she knew exactly where his mind was. "Let's see how long you can resist, Matteo."

He stepped away, feeling the tension ease, but not entirely. What Bianca was offering wasn't what he wanted. Even though she was attractive, challenging, all he wanted was to find Alessia, to know where she was, to understand what had happened. But the reality of his relationship with Alessia was still shrouded in shadows.

As Bianca watched him walk away, she knew she was playing a dangerous game. Matteo DeLuca wasn't an easy man to dominate. But she also knew, deep down, that he was vulnerable. And she fed off that vulnerability in a way she didn't fully understand.

Matteo, on the other hand, was more confused than he had ever imagined. Bianca was a distraction, but Alessia... Alessia was in his heart, and he couldn't erase that. As the party continued around him, he knew there was something deeper, something more important that he would have to face. And it would eventually lead him back to Alessia, someday. He knew that. Even if the path was twisted and full of obstacles.

The night was quiet, but the silence in Alessia was deafening. She stared out at the sea, the soft waves breaking on the sand, and the cool breeze from the coast seemed to offer her some comfort. But inside her, everything was in turmoil. Marco, with his constant calm and unconditional support, proved to be a safe harbor, but something still pulled her toward the abyss of the past. Something in her heart was still tied to Matteo. She didn't know how to let him go, as if the weight of what they had lived together had become so ingrained in her soul that it was impossible to break free.

Even now, in a moment of tranquility, his name echoed in her mind. Matteo. Matteo DeLuca, the man who challenged her, who provoked her, but also the man who loved her in a wild, fierce, and uncontrollable way. He was her obsession, her dilemma, the one who made her question everything she knew about love and loyalty.

She closed her eyes for a moment, remembering how he touched her, how his presence made her body tremble. And at the same time, the way he pulled away, the pain in his eyes whenever he made decisions that hurt them both. There was a constant battle between desire and reason, between the woman she was now and the woman he awakened inside her.

"You're still thinking about him, aren't you?" Marco asked, interrupting her thoughts, his voice soft and patient. He was sitting beside her on the porch, his eyes fixed on her but not pressing her, not forcing her to speak. Marco knew Alessia was distant, knew she carried a weight, but he also saw something more in her, something he couldn't fully understand. But whatever it was, he was willing to help her carry it.

Alessia hesitated, the answer on the tip of her tongue, but she knew she couldn't lie to him. "Yes. I... still think about him. How could I not think about him, Marco?" She looked at him, trying to understand if he could truly understand. "You don't know what he means to me."

Marco looked at her calmly, his eyes fixed on hers, trying to perceive what she truly wanted to say. "I don't know, Alessia. But I know you have the right to live in peace. I'm... not trying to be a distraction. I just... don't want to see you lose yourself in that past that doesn't let you be at peace." The sincerity of his voice made her feel a tightness in her chest, a kind of guilt for being divided.

She looked at him, feeling the softness of his presence, the way he offered her a simple future without the ghosts of the mafia or the secrets. But her mind, still tied to Matteo, seemed incapable of letting go. The desire to be loved by him, to be the only woman capable of softening the hardness of his heart, was embedded deep within her chest.

"I don't know if I can give you what you want, Marco," Alessia said, her voice soft but heavy with weight. "I still have something inside me, something I can't let go. And as much as I want to live a different life... there's something in me that keeps me tied to the past, to him."

Marco leaned in a little closer, his eyes searching hers with a quiet intensity. "I understand that he was a significant part of your life. But Alessia, you don't have to carry this alone. You have a choice, and you can decide what to do with that pain."

She sighed, feeling a warmth in her chest, but also fear. The fear of opening her heart again, of being vulnerable with Marco, when deep down, her heart still cried for Matteo. She stood up from the chair, walking to the edge of the porch, gazing out at the sea as the night deepened.

Marco followed her, remaining silent behind her, feeling the struggle within her. He wanted to do more for her, wanted to be the man who would make her forget everything that had hurt her. But he knew Alessia's past was something he couldn't erase.

"He marked you in a way that no one else has, didn't he?" Marco asked, his voice soft but understanding.

Alessia looked at him, her eyes now filled with silent pain. "Yes. He marked me. And maybe that's what's keeping me from moving forward. Because, as much as I know he hurt me, as much as I try... I can't erase what he means to me."

Marco stepped closer, placing his hand on her shoulder, but not pressing her. "I know it's hard. But, Alessia, you deserve more than living in the past. You deserve a chance to be happy, to live without fear."

The silence that followed between them was filled only with the distant sound of waves breaking on the sand. Alessia closed her eyes for a moment, feeling the softness of Marco's touch, but her heart still beat strongly for Matteo, for that relentless and passionate man, the one who still haunted her thoughts.

But deep down, part of her knew that, if she wanted any chance at freedom, she needed to free herself from the obsession she felt for him. She needed to make a decision. She couldn't continue in war with herself, divided between love and pain.

As she thought about it, a phone rang inside the room, interrupting her thoughts. Alessia quickly glanced at Marco, who gestured he would answer it. When he left the porch to take the call, Alessia was left alone, the weight of the decision crushing her. She knew the time to decide was coming, and the silence of the night seemed to carry all the answers she didn't yet know how to find.

She turned to look at the sea one last time, feeling the wind on her face, the freedom to be whoever she wanted to be. But deep down, there was still a part of her that wished, more than anything, to find a way back to Matteo.

# Chapter 68: Rising Threats

The sun had barely set when Alessia heard the roar of an engine on the narrow road leading to the small house where she was hiding. Her heart skipped a beat, and she ran to the window, peering through the curtain. There, in the darkness of the night, a black truck slowly passed down the deserted street, its headlights lighting the way as if searching for something.

"It can't be," Alessia murmured to herself, panic beginning to take over her body. She knew what that meant. Lorenzo had finally tracked her down. The danger was closer than she had imagined.

With her nerves in tatters, she grabbed her purse, preparing to leave. But when she opened the door, she found Marco, who had entered through the side door without making a sound, as if he already knew what was happening. He looked at her with a grave expression, a mix of concern and determination.

"They're here, aren't they?" Marco asked, already knowing the answer. His tone was soft, but there was a firmness that showed he wasn't asking out of politeness. He was there to protect her, without hesitation.

"Yes, they're here," Alessia replied, her voice breaking. "I... don't know how much longer I can hide. Lorenzo is closer than I thought."

Marco stepped forward, without losing his composure. "You're going to be safe. I'll get you out of here, Alessia. We're leaving now." He seemed determined, leaving no room for argument.

She hesitated for a moment, looking at him. Marco was offering his help, a protection she never expected to receive from anyone other than Matteo. But now, Matteo seemed as distant as the horizon she would never reach. "You don't know what's going on, Marco. What they want from me is more complicated than you think. I can't... involve you in this."

Marco furrowed his brow, his concern turning into something more serious. "I need to know what's happening. I need to understand why you're being hunted. I won't put you at risk without knowing the truth." He stepped even closer, forcing her to look him in the eyes. "If you trust me, Alessia, I can help you."

She felt the weight of those words, the promise of protection, and finally gave in, taking a step toward him. "I... I have no choice, Marco. You'll know everything, but please, understand that my past is far more complicated than anything you've imagined."

Marco watched her carefully. He didn't judge her, didn't question her. He was just there, hand extended, ready to help, asking for nothing in return. "I'll protect you, Alessia. And I'll make sure you and the baby are safe. Now, let's go. We need to leave before it's too late."

With a swift gesture, Marco guided her through the back door, leading her through the dark streets of the city to his car, parked in a remote spot. As they moved away from the house, Alessia glanced back, the weight of fear and guilt mixing in her chest. What had she just done? But as she looked at Marco, feeling the trust he radiated, something inside her began to relax. He was firm, sure of his actions, and the simple fact of being with him gave her a small comfort. She didn't know what the future held, but she felt that, with him, at least she had a chance of finding some peace.

Meanwhile, in another part of the city, Matteo was immersed in the chaos unfolding within his organization. He had been attacked on multiple fronts in the last few days, with allies betraying him and attempts to infiltrate his business. The situation was becoming untenable, and the pressure was immense. Even with all his power, the feeling of losing control bothered him more than he wanted to admit.

"Sir, yesterday's reports indicate that our position is being compromised. They have someone inside the organization," Giovanni said, entering Matteo's office with a serious expression.

Matteo looked at him, his piercing eyes filled with growing irritation. "That can't be. We need to act quickly, Giovanni. We can't let this spread."

Giovanni hesitated before continuing. "There are also rumors about Alessia. We don't know exactly where she is, but... she might be in danger."

Matteo stopped, his eyes now fixed on Giovanni, a sense of anxiety growing in his chest. Alessia. He had tried to ignore her absence, try to move on, but reality always came back to haunt him. He knew that, no matter how much he wanted to deny it, she was still on his mind, her image haunting him in every moment of weakness.

"Forget about the internal investigations for now, Giovanni. Find Alessia. I want to know where she is, now. And if anyone gets close to her..." Matteo said, his voice low, threatening, but also marked by a vulnerability he wasn't used to showing.

Giovanni nodded, understanding the urgency in Matteo's voice. "Understood, sir. I'll gather all the information I can."

Matteo then leaned back in his chair, his fingers pressing against his forehead as he tried to process the avalanche of thoughts. He needed to find her. No matter what happened, Alessia was his, and he couldn't let anything happen to her. Even though the pain of her departure still tortured him, he knew that the guilt he felt couldn't stop him from acting.

Back at Marco's house, Alessia sat in a corner, her hands on her belly, feeling the life inside her. The sound of the silent streets outside made her feel even more isolated. She was in a safe place, at least for now, but she knew her freedom was an illusion. The past would always catch up to her.

Marco entered the room, bringing a cup of hot tea. He set the drink in front of her and sat beside her. "I know you're still scared, Alessia. But here, you're safe. I won't let anything happen to you."

She looked at him, her eyes showing silent gratitude but also deep sadness. "And what happens now, Marco? What will you do? I can't keep asking for help. I can't keep hiding forever."

Marco looked at her, his eyes firm, as if he knew exactly what she needed to hear. "You'll rest, Alessia. We'll figure out what Lorenzo is planning, and when you're ready, we'll make a decision. You don't have to run alone anymore."

Alessia felt his words as a relief. She knew the fight was far from over, but for a brief moment, she could allow herself to have peace. The baby, her, Marco... maybe there was a possible future after all. She didn't know how, but she was willing to try. For him. And for the future growing inside her.

But meanwhile, the specter of Matteo still lingered in her mind, and, unbeknownst to her, the same was true for him. The desire to have her back was stronger than any threat he faced.

Alessia walked through Marco's house, her footsteps silent on the cold floor, her mind distant. The feeling of security was new to her, but there was something unsettling about the peace now surrounding her life. She knew it wouldn't last. Danger was always lurking, and even with Marco, she couldn't shake the constant feeling of running. Running from who she was, from what she had lived, and, above all, from Matteo.

She was there, under Marco's roof, which somehow calmed her, but the emptiness Matteo left still consumed her. His memory was in every thought, every breath. His touch, the way he looked at her—with a desire that seemed overwhelming, all-consuming. But there was also the anger, the disdain he had shown when he sent her away. Even so, something in her mind insisted there was more to that love than the pain she felt. He still loved her, she knew that, but she didn't know how to reach him, how to undo what had been broken.

She sat on the porch, the cold wind brushing her face, her hair fluttering softly around her face. The sea was calm that night, and the city around her seemed silent, as if the world were paused. But her heart raced in sync with the memories and unanswered questions.

Marco entered the porch, noticing Alessia's distance. He approached without saying anything, simply sitting beside her, their shoulders almost touching. His presence was calm, reassuring, and for a moment, Alessia felt that she could rest there, in peace. But peace was an illusion. She knew that, somewhere, Matteo was still out there, and she didn't know how to deal with that. She didn't know if she wanted to go back to him, or if she was simply losing control.

"You're still thinking about him, aren't you?" Marco asked, his voice low but firm. It wasn't an accusatory question, but more of a statement. Marco knew the weight Alessia carried, and he was willing to support her, even if that meant being the silent shoulder behind her pain.

She looked at him, her eyes tired, her chest tight. "Yes, Marco. I think about him. And I don't know what to do with that."

The confession escaped like a sigh, a lament she hadn't admitted to anyone.

Marco looked at her, his eyes soft, but with a hint of something deeper—maybe compassion, maybe understanding. "You don't have to do anything, Alessia. I... I'm not Matteo, but I can show you that you deserve something more. Something without the shadows of the past. I want to be that person for you. I know I can't erase what he did, but you don't have to carry it alone."

Alessia felt a weight sink in her chest, as if his words were a cruel reminder of everything she had lost. She didn't know if she could surrender to this, at least not now. Matteo's words still resonated in her mind, and the desire to give in to him, to give in to what they had, was stronger than any rationality.

"I... I can't, Marco. I don't know how." She swallowed hard, her voice trembling, still fighting the feeling of being torn. "I'm sorry for you. For everything you've done for me. But..." She stopped, the sentence hanging in the air like a sharp blade.

Marco leaned in a little closer, his eyes fixed on hers. He wasn't pulling away, nor pressing her. He was just there, waiting, with a patience that felt eternal.

"Do you think you can push me away like this, Alessia?" Marco asked softly, the smile that formed on his lips gentle but full of quiet confidence. "I'm not Matteo, but if you give me a chance, I'll show you what it's like not to have to run. I'm not the kind of man who will leave you behind. Not after everything we've been through."

She looked at him, feeling the warmth of his presence, the promise he offered without words. There was something in Marco that made her want to believe, to give in to what he offered. But what she felt for Matteo wasn't something that could be easily erased. It was something deeper, something that defied even reason. Matteo had the ability to make her heart race, to provoke an insatiable desire in her that she didn't know how to control.

Suddenly, the sound of a car coming from outside made her turn, and a sense of dread flooded over her. She quickly got up, her heart pounding, knowing that the calm was only temporary.

"They're coming," Alessia whispered, the alertness in her eyes. "Marco, you need to hide me. I don't know how much time we have before they find..."

Before she could finish the sentence, Marco was already on his feet, his face serious, determined. He didn't hesitate, didn't question. He guided her inside the house, where she hid in the back as he prepared to face whatever threat was approaching.

Meanwhile, elsewhere, Matteo was watching the movements of his organization with the attention of a man who knew he was on the edge of war. He could feel the pressure from all sides, with allies turning into enemies and betrayals happening in the shadows. And even with all this happening, his thoughts were fixed on one person: Alessia.

He loved her. He knew that, but he didn't know how to ask for forgiveness. He didn't know how to beg her to come back, to accept him again after everything he had done. The anger, the pride, the pain of seeing her walk away—all of that still haunted him. But he also knew that something was wrong, that there was more at stake than just the words they exchanged. She was in danger, and he needed to find her, no matter what it took.

When Giovanni entered his office, bringing news about Lorenzo's movements, Matteo stood up immediately. He felt the time was running out, and that the hour to act had come.

"Get ready, Giovanni. We won't let them catch us off guard. We'll find Alessia and make sure she's safe. Even if it means destroying Lorenzo," Matteo said, his voice cold, but full of a desperation he didn't know how to hide.

He knew that the shadows of his past, the weight of his mistakes, were still there. But he also knew that if there was any chance for redemption, it was in Alessia's hands. She had always been the only woman capable of making his world spin out of control. And he was willing to fight for her—to fight for them.

As he prepared for what would come next, one thing was certain in his heart: he wanted her back. He didn't know how, but he would do whatever it took to get back what he had lost.

And so, the game between them, between love and revenge, would continue. But one thing was clear: Matteo DeLuca would not give up so easily. Neither would she.

# Chapter 69: A Moment of Weakness

The night was cold and silent, with the clear sky revealing a full moon that illuminated Marco's small house, which had now become Alessia's refuge. She felt strange there, especially when she allowed herself to think about the scars of her past. Marco was home, in the kitchen, preparing something simple. The atmosphere between them was calmer than in the past few weeks, but Alessia still felt like a stranger in his life, as though she were an intruder in a place that should have been his alone.

She sat in the small living room, her eyes wandering out the window. The silence between them was comfortable, but there was a growing tension in the air. It was as if Alessia's past had a weight that she couldn't lift off her shoulders. Marco knew this, and although he had shown understanding up until then, there was something in him that made her feel like he was expecting more—expecting her to give herself in a way she wasn't sure she could.

"Are you okay?" Marco asked, interrupting her thoughts. He was now sitting next to her, looking at Alessia with a gentle expression. The concern was evident, but he knew what she was facing, how much the weight of what she carried still consumed her.

She looked at him, trying to find the right words, but everything seemed too difficult. "I don't know. I... sometimes feel like I'm out of place, like I've lost my way," Alessia replied, her voice soft. "I want to believe I've found something good here, with you. But the past is still consuming me, Marco. I... don't know how to free myself from it."

Marco moved closer, sitting beside her on the couch. He didn't touch her, but there was a comforting presence that made her feel safe. He wasn't pressuring her to open up, but his very presence seemed to have a calming effect. "You don't have to free yourself from your past alone, Alessia. I'm here, by your side, for whatever you need. And no matter what has happened, I won't judge you. I just want you to feel safe. To know that you can trust me."

Alessia looked at him, feeling a tightness in her chest. His words were sincere, and she knew he wasn't just saying them out of convenience. Marco really wanted to help her, wanted to be someone she could trust. But the dilemma she faced made her feel torn. Even amidst that kindness and sincerity, something in her heart still beat unbearably for Matteo. The pain of losing what she had felt for him wouldn't let her go. The loss, the abandonment, the cold words... all of it still haunted her.

"I don't want to hurt you, Marco," Alessia said, her voice trembling. "I don't know if I'm capable of giving myself to this. Sometimes, I think it's just a way to forget. A way to escape this nightmare. And you..." She swallowed, hesitating before continuing, "you don't deserve to be a consolation. You deserve someone who is whole, someone who doesn't carry the weight of a lost love."

Marco watched her closely, his gaze serious, but full of patience. He could feel her inner struggle, the fear of allowing herself to be happy, of giving herself to something that might be uncertain. And although it hurt him, he didn't push her. "I'm not asking you to love me, Alessia. I'm here, by your side, because I care. Because you deserve to find peace. And if this step is difficult for you, then I'll be here, walking with you, without hurry. No need for apologies. Just... trust me."

The silence between them seemed heavier now. Alessia closed her eyes, her heart racing. She could feel the weight of his words, but also something else. Something she feared, something that made her pull away even more. The warmth she felt in Marco's presence was undeniable, but it wasn't the warmth of a deep love, of a desire that consumed her. It was the warmth of a man who wanted to protect her, a man who respected her. Marco offered security, but her heart was still with Matteo, the man who had destroyed her, yet still occupied a place no one else could fill.

It was then, in a moment of weakness, that Alessia allowed herself. The kiss came unexpectedly, an impulse of the moment, a search for a temporary relief from the pain tearing her apart inside. She leaned toward Marco, her lips touching his with a desire she didn't know she still had. It was a soft kiss, yet full of urgency, a search for something that could fill the void, an attempt to feel something beyond the pain and loneliness.

Marco kissed her back gently, but also with an intensity that surprised Alessia. He held her carefully, as if fearing she would break in his arms. His touch was warm, secure, but also showed his concern not to cross boundaries she wasn't ready to give.

When the kiss ended, Alessia pulled away slowly, her face flushed and her breath heavy. The relief she felt was temporary, but it was also accompanied by an even heavier weight, a sense of guilt that consumed her.

"Marco..." she began, but her voice faltered. "I don't know what I'm doing. You... you deserve more than this. I'm not ready to move on. Not the way you want me to."

He looked at her with a calmness that made her pain intensify. "I'm not asking you to give yourself to me, Alessia. I just want you to know that, no matter what happens, I'll be by your side. I won't leave you alone, even when you feel like you don't deserve it." He took a step back, his expression gentle, but full of understanding. "But I also understand if you need more time. I won't force anything. Just... don't pull away from me, please."

Alessia felt a pain in her chest, a knot that made her want to cry, but the tears were held back. She knew she was putting Marco at risk, putting him in a situation he didn't deserve. He was too kind, and she didn't want him to lose himself in something she couldn't give.

"I don't want to hurt you," she murmured. "But I can't keep going like this. I still think about him. I still think about what could have been. And that, Marco... that's not going to change so easily."

Marco stayed silent for a moment, absorbing her words. He wanted more, he wanted to fight for her, but he knew that her battles weren't his to win. And as much as he wished to be the only one by her side, he also knew that, for now, the most important thing was to give her space to face her own demons.

"I won't force you into anything, Alessia," Marco finally said, his voice firm but gentle. "But no matter what happens, I'll be here. I hope that, one day, you'll see me not as an escape, but as someone you can trust."

Alessia looked at him, her eyes filled with silent gratitude. She knew he was sincere, and that only made her feel guiltier for not being able to offer him what he wanted. But deep down, she knew the future was uncertain. She didn't know if she would ever be able to move on completely. And, in the meantime, the love and pain she felt for Matteo continued to dominate her.

That night, as Marco left her with her thoughts and retreated to the other room, Alessia remained alone, her heart heavy with the choice she still needed to make—between the love that burned inside her and the security Marco offered. She knew that, somewhere, the fate of her life was about to be decided. And as the hours passed, she wondered whether she would be able to choose a new beginning, or if she would remain at the mercy of the shadows of the past.

The night was peaceful, but the mood inside Marco's house was heavy. Alessia didn't know exactly what she felt. She had pulled away from Matteo, but the weight of what they had lived still consumed her. Every moment, every gesture from Marco, only made her feel more confused. He was everything she needed—someone protective, someone who cared for her with a tenderness she had never known was possible. But, at the same time, he wasn't Matteo.

She walked around the room, her steps soft, but her heart beating irregularly. When she heard Marco's footsteps behind her, she stopped. He was always there, lurking, as if he knew what she was thinking before she even realized it. Sometimes, that made her feel vulnerable in ways she didn't know how to deal with.

"Alessia," Marco called, his voice deep and soft, but full of a silent urgency. "You're distant today. Where is your mind? I feel you pulling away from me."

She turned to face him, a mixture of gratitude and sadness in her gaze. Marco stood there, his eyes locked on hers with an intensity that made her heart race, but at the same time, made her question whether she had the right to be loved like that.

"I don't know what to do with all of this," Alessia said, her voice low, almost breaking. "I feel your presence, Marco. I see how much you care for me, but my heart still belongs somewhere else. It's not fair to you, and I know that."

Marco took a step forward, his eyes softer now, but still filled with intense emotion. "It's not fair to me, Alessia," he said, his voice deeper, but not out of anger, more out of understanding. "But you don't have to hide from me. I'm not here to replace anyone. I'm here to be the person you can trust, the person who will give you what you need, without rushing, without demands. I understand that your heart is still with him, and I accept that."

She looked at him, surprised by the sincerity in his words. He was willing to wait, to be by her side even though he knew she couldn't give herself right away. There was something in Marco that made her want to open up, but at the same time, she felt the weight of Matteo still in her soul, something that couldn't be erased so easily.

"I don't know what you see in me, Marco," Alessia said, the pain in her words as evident as the love she still carried for Matteo. "I see you, I see what you do for me, and I feel gratitude. But it's not enough to take me out of what I feel for him. I can't just forget, I can't just stop loving him. Even when he hurt me, he... he's still all I know."

Marco took another step, now closer to her, his eyes focused on hers, but with a gentleness she couldn't ignore. "I understand," he said, his hand now on her shoulder, touching her with a delicacy that contrasted with the harshness she knew from the mafia world. "I know you still love him, and maybe that will never change. But what I know is that you deserve something more than what he gave you. You deserve someone who will be there, someone who will make you feel safety and not fear. I won't demand anything from you, Alessia. I just... I just want you to give me a chance. Not to replace him, but to give you something good to lean on, something you can count on when the world around you falls apart."

She felt the sincerity in his words, and for a moment, she felt the temptation to give in. Marco was good. He was the stability she was looking for, but what she felt for Matteo, that overwhelming and complicated love, seemed to be an abyss she couldn't escape. Even in her worst moments, she still thought about him.

"Marco..." Alessia began, but the word died on her lips when he interrupted, his hand now touching her face, forcing her to look him in the eyes.

"I won't pressure you," he said, with a firmness that contrasted with the gentleness of his touch. "But you're not alone. And no matter what you choose, I'll be here. For you. For whatever you need."

The warmth of his hand on Alessia's face made her feel something inside her release, but it wasn't enough to push away the emptiness she felt when she thought of Matteo. The image of him, lying next to her, his hands touching her with the urgency of a passionate man, invaded her mind. The desire he had for her, the love she believed she saw in his eyes... All of that made her feel torn, as if she were betraying something stronger than herself.

When Marco leaned in, his lips touching hers softly, Alessia gave in to the kiss, but not with the same desire. It was relief, a temporary escape. Marco's touch was safe, caring, but something inside her knew that, no matter how hard she tried, she couldn't forget Matteo, nor what she felt for him. It was impossible to escape from a passion so intense, from a man so burning that still dominated her heart.

When the kiss ended, Marco watched her, his eyes searching for some kind of answer from her. Alessia, her breath uneven, pulled away gently, her eyes avoiding his.

"I... I can't do this, Marco," she said, her voice trembling with an emotion she couldn't control. "I'm not whole for you. I'm still broken. And you deserve more than this... indecision."

Marco didn't pull away, but his eyes were sadder now, not for him, but for her. He knew he couldn't force anything, and his acceptance was more painful than he wanted to admit. "I understand, Alessia," he replied with a sigh. "I'm not what you want right now. I'm not him. And maybe I never will be. But, please, don't pull away from me."

Alessia looked at him, feeling a weight settle in her chest. She didn't want to hurt him, but what she felt for Matteo kept her from fully giving herself. "I don't know what I want, Marco," she said in a soft voice, almost inaudible. "I don't know what I'll do. I just know that, no matter how hard I try, my heart still belongs to him."

Marco watched her with a serenity that made her feel even more pain. He knew the path to her was long, but he wouldn't give up. Not as long as she needed someone. Not as long as he had a chance to be the man she deserved.

"I'll wait," he said, with a firmness that was both sweet and painful. "Because, despite everything, I won't leave you alone. And when you're ready, when you decide what to do with your heart, I'll be here."

Alessia didn't know if that was a promise or a goodbye, but the softness in Marco's words touched her deeply. She knew he deserved more. He deserved someone who would love him completely. And she feared that, no matter how hard she tried, the love he offered wouldn't be enough to make her heart heal.

# Chapter 70: The Darkness of the Mafia Draws Near

The night was tense, filled with a threatening silence, as if the world around her was on the verge of exploding. Alessia sat on the bed, her eyes fixed on the window, watching the empty streets outside, as if danger was lurking at every movement. The sound of her own thoughts was deafening, a mix of guilt, fear, and a deep pain that she didn't know how to ease. She knew the mafia was closer, closer than she wanted to admit. Lorenzo wouldn't give up. She felt it in her skin, like a constant pressure on her chest.

The pregnancy, which had once been a symbol of a new beginning, now seemed like an additional burden, something that made her even more vulnerable. She knew her child needed protection, but she didn't know how far her ability to fight would go. The past with Matteo, the love and pain story, blurred with the raw reality of the life she was leading now. With each step, with each choice, she felt like she was losing something—or someone—again.

Then Marco entered the room, interrupting her thoughts. He was more serious than usual, the expression on his face showing that he knew something was about to happen. He approached slowly, and Alessia felt the warmth of his presence, a presence that always calmed her, but at the same time, made her feel divided.

"Alessia," Marco began, his voice grave, straightforward. "I see what's happening. Lorenzo is getting closer. We can't stay here any longer. Not for much longer."

She looked at him, fear rising in her chest, but at the same time, there was a relief in hearing those words. She knew the situation was becoming unsustainable, but the idea of running away, of leaving everything behind, made her feel even more lost. "Where will we go, Marco? How can we escape him?"

Marco came closer, gently placing his hand over hers. "I found a place. A refuge far from all of this. If you trust me, we can leave now. Together."

The proposal was tempting, but Alessia felt the weight of the decision she would have to make. Running away would mean abandoning any hope of finding Matteo again, of understanding what had really happened between them, and more importantly, of forgiving him. She knew he had his flaws, but she also knew he loved her in a consuming way. She couldn't forget the intensity of that love, the way he touched her, the way he looked at her. But, at the same time, what he had done... How could she trust him again?

"I... I don't know, Marco. I can't just run away from my life, from my past. And... Matteo..." The words failed, and she swallowed hard, feeling the weight of everything that was still unresolved between her and the man she could never forget. "I... still love him, Marco. But what he did... I don't know if I can trust him again."

Marco looked at her, his eyes dark but with a patience that seemed eternal. "I understand. But we can't wait any longer, Alessia. Lorenzo won't wait. He will find you, and he won't stop until he gets what he wants. You and the baby are in danger, and I won't let anything happen to you. I can protect you, I want to protect you."

Alessia felt a wave of conflicting emotions. Marco was good, he was strong, and somehow, he made her feel safe. But the idea of leaving Matteo behind, of cutting all possibilities of a future with him, consumed her. She didn't know if she was ready to make that decision, if the risk of distancing herself from him and building a new life with Marco would be something she would regret forever. But, at the same time, she knew that if she stayed, the danger would only increase for her and the child she carried.

"I... I don't know what to do," she murmured, her voice filled with doubt. "How can I run away like this, not knowing if I'll ever find peace? How can I leave Matteo behind, not knowing if he still wants me, if..."

Marco interrupted her, gently placing a finger over her lips. "I'm not asking you to forget what was. I just want you to live, Alessia. For your baby. For yourself. I know Matteo is still on your mind, and maybe he's the only one you can love like that. But you deserve to be happy, to live without fear. And if you can't do that alone, I'll be here. Always."

Those words pierced deep into Alessia's heart. She didn't want to hurt Marco, but the truth was, he was offering her a quieter life, a life away from the shadows of the mafia, a life where she could raise her child in peace. But she knew that by accepting this, she would be abandoning everything she knew, all the promises she had made to herself and to Matteo. It would be the end of a chapter she hadn't been able to finish.

She took a deep breath and finally said, "I'll go with you, Marco. I don't know if it's what I want, but I know I can't stay here anymore. Not while Lorenzo is after us. But I promise you, Marco, I can't give you what you want. I still love Matteo. I can't be the woman you need."

Marco didn't answer immediately. He just nodded, as if he already knew this would be her response. It didn't matter. What mattered was that she wasn't alone. He would protect her, no matter the cost.

Meanwhile, in a world that seemed farther and farther from Alessia, Matteo was dealing with his own demons. His alliance with Bianca was growing stronger, but the shadow of Alessia still haunted him, like a presence that refused to let his heart find peace. Bianca, with her confidence and intelligence, was proving to be a valuable ally, someone who truly knew how to navigate the complexities of power. But there was something in her gaze, a coldness he couldn't ignore. Bianca was not Alessia, and he knew that. No matter how much he tried, his heart still turned to the woman he had lost.

While talking to Bianca about the next steps for the organization, Matteo felt her presence, the calculated proximity. She watched him in a way that was beginning to make him uncomfortable, as if she was waiting for him to give in to something more. She wasn't someone who could easily be controlled, and she knew how to manipulate situations in her favor. He, in turn, was being seduced by her confidence, but not by the woman herself. The emptiness Alessia had left in him was still stronger than any fleeting attraction.

Bianca stepped forward, her eyes fixed on his, and a low laugh escaped her lips. "I know what you're thinking, Matteo. You're still stuck on her, aren't you? The woman who left you."

He looked at her with a mix of frustration and disgust. "I'm not stuck on anyone, Bianca. And you should know that if it were up to me, you would've offered me more than an alliance. I'm not an idiot, and you're not going to use me for your own games."

Bianca didn't flinch, and the way she observed him, as if testing his limits, only increased the discomfort he felt. "I'm not your enemy, Matteo. On the contrary, I can be the partner you need. Together, we can dominate the organization and eliminate any threats. And in doing so, you'll realize you need someone who can control the situation, someone who can give you stability."

He pulled back slightly, his thoughts conflicted. Bianca was shrewd, intelligent, but something about her would always repel him. She wasn't Alessia. She wasn't the woman who had touched his heart, broken down his defenses, and at the same time, put everything at risk. Even now, the thought of being with Bianca seemed hollow, as if he were giving in to a power play, something cold and emotionless.

"Maybe that's what you need, Bianca. But for now, I can't give you what you want. Not while my heart still belongs to someone else," Matteo said, his voice low but firm.

He knew the war inside him was far from over, and that, deep down, he would always be torn between power and love. But something inside him knew that Alessia was more than any strategy, more than any alliance. She was the only thing he truly wanted, and he had lost her. And the pain of that followed him, like a shadow he didn't know how to expel.

Alessia lay in bed, her thoughts a chaotic mix of conflicting emotions. The room was silent except for the distant sound of the city that filtered through the open windows. She stared at the wall, her eyes fixed on an imaginary point, as the reality of her life seemed to spin around her. Marco had become her safe haven, the one who held her when the world was falling apart, but she knew that with each passing day, he was getting closer, more affectionate, and she didn't know how to deal with that.

She sighed, running a hand over her belly, feeling the life growing inside her. The baby she carried was the only thing she still felt she could protect. The sense of guilt consumed her, but at the same time, the love she still felt for Matteo—that overwhelming, impossible love—prevented her from fully giving herself to Marco. She couldn't, not when she still had the taste of Matteo on her lips, the warmth of his touch on her skin.

Marco was kind, and she saw sincerity in every gesture he made, but he wasn't the one she wanted. He wasn't the storm of emotions Matteo provoked in her, nor the man who possessed her with the intensity of a hurricane. She closed her eyes, remembering how he looked at her, how she felt fragile and yet strong under the weight of his passion. And in that moment, the memory of Matteo hit her like a wave.

The sound of the door opening made her lift her head. Marco appeared at the threshold of the room, his expression serious but with a touch of softness that Alessia still didn't know how to interpret. He was there to protect her, and that she knew, but there was something else in his gaze, something that made her uneasy.

"Alessia," Marco called softly, walking closer to the bed, with the same calm demeanor he always had, but there was a tension in his shoulders that she hadn't noticed before. He sat beside her, his eyes now fixed on hers, but without pressure. "You're distant. I can tell. You don't have to hide from me."

She swallowed hard, trying to hide the emotional mess inside her. "I'm not hiding anything, Marco. I'm just... trying to understand what's happening. It's like I'm a piece that hasn't fit yet." She gave a sad smile. "I don't want to hurt you. You've been so good to me, so patient, but I don't know if I'm capable of... of moving on."

Marco was silent for a moment, his eyes never leaving hers. He had sensed the struggle inside her, but he also knew she was divided. And deep down, he knew that as much as he wanted her, she still wasn't ready to fully give herself to him. "You don't have to move on, Alessia. Not in a way that hurts you. I won't force you to do something you're not ready to do. But I want you to know I'm here. And not just for now. No matter what happens, I won't leave you."

His words touched her, but not in a way that made her feel lighter. Alessia felt vulnerable in a way she couldn't control. Marco offered stability, but Matteo... Matteo was a fire. He burned her, made her feel alive and lost at the same time. It wasn't fair to Marco, and she knew that, but she didn't know how to stop thinking about him.

"I..." Alessia started, her voice trembling, but she didn't know how to finish the sentence. The words seemed impossible to speak. She wanted to say that Marco deserved more, that she couldn't continue with him while her heart still belonged to Matteo. But all she managed to say was, "I'm not strong enough to move on."

Marco looked at her, the pain evident in his gaze, but he didn't judge her. "I don't expect you to be strong alone, Alessia. You don't have to be. I'm here for that." He leaned in, his eyes never leaving hers, and she felt the warmth of his proximity, the softness of his touch when he placed his hand over hers. "And when you're ready, I'll be here, not as a shadow, but as someone who will support you, someone who loves you for who you are, not for who you were."

Alessia shivered, a feeling of helplessness taking over her. She didn't know what she wanted. She didn't know if she could let go of her love for Matteo, didn't know if she could trust Marco in the way he deserved. But looking at him now, with sincerity written all over his face, she realized that he wasn't pushing her. He was loving her without asking for anything in return, and that made her feel even more guilty.

"I don't know if I can do this, Marco," she whispered, her eyes down, avoiding his gaze. "I don't know if I can be the woman you need."

Marco moved even closer, gently holding her face between his hands. "Don't try to be someone else, Alessia. Just be yourself. I just want you to know that, no matter how hard it seems now, you're not alone. I'm with you, every step of the way. No matter how long it takes, no matter what happens with this past that haunts you. You'll make it. And I'll be by your side."

Alessia closed her eyes for a moment, feeling his words envelop her heart in a comforting but painful way. She wanted to believe, wanted to surrender to this promise of stability, but her heart still screamed for Matteo. He was still there, in the shadows, in the memories, in the kisses that never faded. How could she move forward with anyone other than him?

It was then that Marco leaned in, the softness of his touch against her lips. The kiss was gentle, unhurried, but with a silent intensity, as if he knew she was fighting against herself. Alessia closed her eyes, giving in for a moment, trying to free herself from the pressure of the past. But as she felt the taste of him, the softness of the affection he offered, a deep pain settled in her chest. It was comforting, but it was also a reminder that she was still torn.

When the kiss ended, Marco looked at her, his eyes now darker, but also more understanding. "I understand, Alessia. I know you're still at war with your feelings. And I won't rush you. I just promise that, if you ever want to come back, I'll be here."

She looked at him, the pain in her chest growing. "I don't know what I want. I don't know if I'll ever be able to look at someone the same way I looked at him. But for now, you have my thanks, Marco. And maybe, my affection. I don't know what else I can offer you."

He smiled, but the smile was sad, full of a patience she still didn't fully understand. "That's more than I ever expected. And for that, I'm already grateful."

And although Alessia knew that the future between her and Marco was uncertain, she couldn't deny that his presence calmed her. But deep down, she knew that as long as Matteo remained a shadow in the depths of her soul, she would never be entirely his—or anyone else's.

# Chapter 71: Alessia's Kidnapping

The night was silent, almost suffocating, when Alessia, sitting in the small living room of Marco's house, felt a strange presence. She knew that the peace she had found, however fleeting, was about to be broken. The feeling of being watched, of being at risk, made her look at the door with a tightness in her chest. Something inside her knew that the tranquility would never last long. She was in enemy territory, and the shadows of the mafia were drawing ever closer.

Suddenly, the front door was smashed open with a violent crash. Alessia jumped to her feet instantly, fear taking hold of her body, but she didn't have time to react. In a matter of seconds, Lorenzo's thugs stormed the place. They were fast, coordinated, and before she could scream or try to escape, she was grabbed with force. The air was knocked out of her lungs as rough hands immobilized her.

"Don't make this harder than it already is, Alessia," a low, familiar voice said behind her. The man holding her shoved her out of the house, her feet barely touching the ground as they dragged her. "Lorenzo wants a word with you. And he's not a patient man."

Alessia struggled, tried to break free, but the grips of the men were like iron. Panic mixed with pain, but something else rose within her — a thread of determination. She couldn't let this end like this. Not now, not when everything was about to change. She had a child to protect.

With each step, she scanned her surroundings, absorbing every detail, looking for a way to escape. They threw her into a dark van, where she was strapped to a seat. The city disappeared behind her as she was taken to a remote hideout, a place where no one but Lorenzo knew where she was. Fear tightened her chest, but she also felt a strange sense of helplessness. She didn't know what else she could do.

The place was cold and dark, with no sign of life, except for her and the thugs surrounding her. Alessia tried to control her breathing, but the panic wouldn't leave her. They shoved her into a small room, an improvised cell, and she hit the floor hard, her knees slamming against the concrete. She quickly rose to her feet, her eyes now fixed on the men watching her like predators.

"Lorenzo will want to see you soon," one of them said, a cruel smile on his face. "He has a few things to discuss with you. And I'd say he's very, very eager to see you in good condition."

She didn't answer. She had no words, no energy to defend herself. The fear for her own life mixed with the pain of loneliness. What did Lorenzo want from her? Why was she here, if not to hit her where it hurt the most? In the heart.

But Alessia's greatest concern wasn't herself. She looked down at her belly, panic growing inside her. The baby. That little life she already loved more than anything. What would happen if she couldn't get out of there in time? And Matteo? Did he still know about the pregnancy? Or did he still see her as a traitor? Alessia no longer knew how he saw her, and the thought that he might have abandoned her for good tore at her.

The door abruptly swung open, interrupting her thoughts. Lorenzo entered, his face impassive as always. His presence was a threat, a dark force that filled the space around them. He looked at her as if she were an object, something he owned, something he controlled. His gaze had no compassion, only a calculated interest, like a hunter watching its prey.

"Alessia," he said, his voice low, almost affectionate, but laced with poison. "I'm glad to see you're doing well. The most important thing is that you're still alive. For now."

She glared at him, trying to maintain her composure, but fear and anger showed in her eyes. "What do you want from me, Lorenzo? I'm no longer your tool. What will you gain from this?

Will you use me to destroy Matteo? Is that what will give you control over something that's already out of your hands?"

He smirked with disdain, his eyes as cold as ice. "Ah, Alessia, always full of words. You don't understand anything. This isn't about destroying Matteo. It's about destabilizing everything he's built. And you'll be the key piece to that. A final reminder of how he failed to protect the one thing he loves most."

His words cut her like a sharp blade. She knew Lorenzo had no limits. He would go to any lengths to weaken Matteo. But using the child she carried as leverage? That crossed every line. She couldn't let this happen.

"You can't threaten me," Alessia said, her voice firm, despite the fear coursing through her body. "I'll fight. I won't let you do this to my child. And to Matteo. You won't win."

Lorenzo chuckled darkly, his expression turning crueler. "Ah, Alessia, always so passionate. But reality is much different. Matteo is too busy with his little lover, and you? You're just a pawn in my game. And when he realizes that, it'll be too late."

The hatred she felt for him burned inside her, but Alessia didn't yield. She couldn't, not now. The thought that Matteo might be completely distant from her, believing Lorenzo's lies, tore her apart. But she knew he still loved her. He just didn't know everything. Everything she had done for him, for them.

"He will come for me, Lorenzo," Alessia said, her voice calmer now, but filled with conviction. "And you will regret capturing me. Matteo won't rest until he finds me. Until he saves me."

Lorenzo looked at her with a sarcastic smile. "You really think he will save you? Alessia, you don't understand the gravity of the situation. And I'll have so much fun watching how much he suffers before he finally gives in. Don't forget, my dear, you are now part of a much bigger game than any feelings you have for him."

Lorenzo's words hit her like a punch. But inside, the flame of resistance never died. She couldn't let him win. Not for Matteo, not for the child she carried, and especially not for herself.

She felt the weight of the situation tighten around her throat, but as she looked down at the floor, she made a silent promise to herself and to her baby: she wasn't going to stop fighting. No matter how dark the path ahead, she would find a way out. She would survive.

The night continued in silence, with Alessia in her makeshift cell, but her mind was far away, calculating every move, every chance to escape. She knew she was in a battlefield, and even without weapons, she would do whatever it took to get out of there — to ensure the survival of her child and, if possible, save the one thing that still connected her to this dark world: Matteo.

# Chapter 72: Matteo's Desperation

The phone rang abruptly, cutting through the heavy silence of the room where Matteo sat alone, staring out of his office window. He hesitated for a moment, eyeing the phone as if he knew the call wouldn't bring good news. With a deep sigh, he answered.

"Matteo..." Giovanni's voice came through the line, low and tense. "Alessia has been kidnapped. Lorenzo's thugs. We're trying to track the location, but... it's bad. They have her."

The world seemed to stop for Matteo. The blood in his veins chilled instantly, and his stomach churned in a way he had never felt before. Alessia. She was in danger. The pain he felt hearing those words was a mixture of rage, fear, and an unsettling sense of helplessness. His heart tightened. How had it come to this? How could she be in Lorenzo's hands, used as a pawn in a dirty game he knew all too well?

"What time? Where is she?" Matteo demanded, his voice colder than he intended, a reflection of the anger burning inside him.

"Lorenzo hasn't made demands yet, but we know he's using her to destabilize you, Matteo. She's probably in one of the rival mafia's hideouts. We've sent some teams to locate the area, but we don't have confirmation yet."

Matteo closed his eyes for a moment, his mind in tatters, but he couldn't allow himself to falter. Not now. Not with her in danger. Despite all the pain, the doubts, and the hatred he tried to bury towards her, he couldn't leave Alessia in Lorenzo's hands. He couldn't.

"Prepare the men. We're going to get her," he said, his voice now firm, with a threatening calm. "And keep this between us, Giovanni. I don't want anyone else to know. The operation must be discreet."

There was silence on the line for a moment, Giovanni likely sensing the tension emanating from Matteo. But he knew what this meant. This was personal. This was no longer about business. It was about rescuing a woman Matteo, despite all his resentments, knew he loved.

"Understood, Matteo. We're ready to act as soon as we have the exact location."

"Stay sharp," Matteo ordered, before hanging up. He looked at the phone in his hand, and for a moment, the silence in the room suffocated him. Alessia was in danger, and despite all the scars he carried, the thought of losing her, of losing whatever was left between them, consumed him in a way he couldn't explain.

He didn't know if she still loved him. He didn't know if she believed the lies Lorenzo had planted, the accusations, the betrayals he himself had imposed. But at the same time, he knew he had to rescue her. He knew that, as much as he hated to admit it, he could no longer live with the idea that she was suffering and he could do nothing. He was torn between the love he felt for her and the wounded pride that still burned within him. The only thing he knew for sure was that he would not let her fall into Lorenzo's hands. The fight she represented for him was stronger than any vengeance or bitterness he carried.

Matteo rose from his chair, his steps long and determined, heading towards the table where the city maps and documents of his organization were spread out. He needed a plan. He needed to act quickly. Rage burned inside him like a living flame, but he knew that logic and strategy had to come first. He couldn't be impulsive, couldn't let the desire for revenge blind him. Alessia needed him, and he wouldn't let her pay the price for his recklessness.

On the other side of the city, Alessia was being kept in a filthy hideout, her arms tightly bound to a metal chair. The cold of the place seeped into her skin, and the smell of mold and desperation filled the air. She tried to remain calm, but anxiety consumed her. The thought of what could happen to her child tormented her, and panic grew with every passing second.

She knew Lorenzo would use her as leverage. But what she couldn't fully understand was how far he was willing to go to hurt Matteo. She missed him. Even with everything that had happened, and the distance between them, her heart still cried out for him. The thought that he might even be considering that she had betrayed him, the thought that he might have completely abandoned her, caused a pain so deep she could barely breathe.

The door opened, and one of Lorenzo's thugs entered, his expression empty. He watched her for a moment before stepping forward.

"Lorenzo wants to talk to you. You're taking too long to understand your situation, Alessia," he said with a cruel smile, before grabbing a chair and sitting in front of her. "I think you'll be surprised by what he has in store for your lover."

Alessia raised her eyes to him, her expression defiant, despite everything that was happening. She couldn't allow herself to weaken now. If she let fear take over, she would lose. "Lorenzo can do whatever he wants with me, but know this: he will never use me against Matteo. He will never bend to whatever you're planning."

The thug stared at her with a crooked smile. "Ah, Alessia, you still don't get it. Lorenzo doesn't need your cooperation anymore. He's going to destroy Matteo, with or without you. You're just a burden he's ready to use. But you haven't realized yet that you're about to lose everything."

The threatening tone in his words sent a chill down her spine. She wanted to scream, wanted to fight, but she knew that would only put her in more danger. She needed to stay calm. If Matteo was really coming after her, she needed to be strong. She needed to survive. For him. For the baby.

As the thug stood up to leave, Alessia took a deep breath, trying to control the emotions that consumed her. She knew the next part would be crucial. Lorenzo's plan was clear — he wanted to destroy Matteo where it hurt most. And as much as she tried to deny it, she knew that this meant she still had a role to play, even if it destroyed her.

She let herself fall against the chair, trying to hold onto her lucidity amidst the chaos. She had to survive. Matteo couldn't lose the battle for her. Not this way.

Back at Matteo's hideout, the men were ready to depart. The planning was being meticulously organized, and the weight of the mission fell heavily on Matteo's shoulders. He knew this mission could be a trap. Lorenzo was a master at this. But he couldn't hesitate anymore.

He turned to Giovanni, his face impassive, but his eyes heavy with an emotion he couldn't name. "Ready?"

Giovanni nodded. "Yes, sir. But you know this mission carries high risk. We can't go in there without absolute certainty that we're not walking into death."

Matteo looked at him, his eyes now intense, with a determination that no one would dare challenge. "If it's death, then let it come. But I won't let her pay for my mistakes. Not now. Not while there's a chance to bring her back."

With Matteo's words echoing through the room, the tension turned into action. He turned, ready for the fight he knew was coming, with only one thing on his mind: Alessia.

He knew he could lose everything, but he wouldn't do anything without fighting for her.

# Chapter 73: A Risky Plan

The air was thick with tension as Matteo prepared for the most dangerous operation of his life. His office, usually a calm strategic space, had transformed into a battlefield, with maps, plans, and photos scattered everywhere. He was immersed in the preparation, carefully plotting each move, but his mind was distant, focused on one single person: Alessia. She was in Lorenzo's hands, and Matteo knew that by stepping into this game, he might be condemning himself, but he couldn't let her be destroyed.

With his most trusted men gathered around him, he reviewed the plan once more. The rival mafia's hideout was heavily guarded, surrounded by multiple layers of security. But Matteo knew the weak points. He wouldn't take the risk without knowing every detail, every move he would need to make. Alessia had to be rescued, and he would do whatever it took.

"This mission has to be clean," Matteo said, his voice firm, with no room for hesitation. "I won't lose her. If anyone fails, we have to be ready to pay the price. No one, absolutely no one, can know about the operation until we have confirmation that she's safe."

Giovanni, his right-hand man and closest confidant, nodded, absorbing Matteo's orders. "Everything's ready, Matteo. Our men are positioned. We just need your signal to act."

Matteo looked at the map in front of him, his fingers tracing the routes he would need to take. Every movement had to be exact. They couldn't afford to make mistakes. Alessia's life depended on it. But despite his focus on the plan, something inside him stirred—a doubt he was trying to push away. What would happen when he saw her again? Would she hate him? Would she trust him? Or would she still love him? Matteo knew his faults were deep, but the need to have her back, to protect her, was stronger than any resentment.

When the office door opened abruptly, he didn't need to look to know who it was. Bianca entered without announcement, her sharp, determined gaze, but there was something else in her eyes—a look of frustration Matteo didn't know how to interpret. She was angry, but there was a hint of pain there too, something he knew all too well but didn't have time to understand now.

"Matteo," she began, her voice cold and controlled, but with a slight tremor of concern. "Are you really going to risk everything for her? After everything that's happened?"

He lifted his head, meeting her gaze. His eyes were hard, but he couldn't hide what he was feeling. "Yes, Bianca. I'm not asking for your opinion. Alessia needs me, and I'm going to bring her back. Nothing is going to stop me."

Bianca took a few steps forward, her eyes locked onto his, now filled with accusation. "You still love her, don't you?" she said, the words bitter as they left her mouth. "You still want her back, even after everything. No matter how much she hurt you."

Matteo stood up, the tension between them palpable. He breathed deeply, trying to keep his composure, but something inside him exploded. He met her gaze, anger rising, but he didn't want to argue with Bianca. Not now. "She didn't hurt me, Bianca. I hurt her. I let the lies and secrets destroy what we had. But that doesn't matter now. What matters is that she's in danger, and I'm going to rescue her. Don't you understand?"

Bianca watched him for a moment, her hard expression softening slightly, but still full of resentment. "I understand more than you think, Matteo. You're going after a woman who isn't the same. She betrayed you, lied to you, and now you're willing to risk your life and your organization for her? For a woman who, in the end, doesn't deserve that loyalty?"

Matteo's anger flared, but he controlled it. He knew Bianca was jealous, but there was something more in her tone, something that wasn't just possessiveness. She was scared. Scared of losing everything he represented to her, scared of being just another woman on the sidelines of his life. But deep down, he knew what he felt. What he felt for Alessia wasn't something that could be erased.

"Do you think she betrayed me?" Matteo replied, his eyes locked on hers, with an intensity that made her fall silent. "Do you think she did it on purpose? No, Bianca. Alessia was a victim of the same lies I believed. She had no choice. And I... I still love her. And I'll do anything to bring her back. If you don't understand that, then you don't know me."

Bianca stared at him, her face hardening, but she said nothing more. The silence between them stretched for a moment before she turned and walked out, leaving without a final word. Matteo stood, watching her leave through the window, his mind spinning. He didn't know how this would end, didn't know if he could ever restore what he had lost with Alessia, but what he knew for sure was that he would do whatever it took. Even if she never forgave him, he couldn't live with the thought of not fighting for her.

The plan was in place. Matteo braced himself for the worst, but with the unshakable determination of a man who knew he had everything to lose. With his men gathered, he made the final adjustments, making sure everyone was in position.

"We're ready," Giovanni said, his voice as firm as the look he gave Matteo. "Everything's in place. We just need your word, boss."

Matteo nodded. He knew this was personal, more than any mission or business deal. This was about rescuing the woman he still loved, despite the scars she had left on him. Despite the lies and the mistakes, he knew she was the only one who had ever made him feel whole. Their love was fierce and tumultuous, but it still existed.

"Let's go," Matteo said, his voice firm. "We're not wasting time. I want her safe, and fast. We're not failing."

With that, they set out toward the location he had identified—a secluded hideout where Alessia was being held. The tension in the air was palpable, and Matteo knew that with each step, the risk increased. But he couldn't stop. Not now. Not while she was in danger.

The journey to the hideout was silent, every man prepared for what lay ahead. Matteo felt the weight of responsibility on his shoulders, but there was something heavier than that—the fear of losing Alessia, the fear that she might not be there when he arrived. He thought of her, of her face, of every moment they had shared together. He remembered the scent of her hair, the smile that always made his heart race, even when they were at odds.

When they arrived at the location, adrenaline took over Matteo. He positioned himself, his gaze stern, but focused. The men were ready, but time was against them. He only had one shot at this. And he wouldn't fail.

With a nod, he initiated the operation. He knew the mission wouldn't be simple, but with every step toward the hideout, his instincts guided him. He was more than determined. He was willing to pay the price for all his mistakes to bring Alessia back into his arms.

As he neared the entrance, with the sounds of action all around him, the last thing on his mind was what would happen after the rescue. The only thing he knew for sure was that, no matter what happened, he was doing this for her. He was doing this to have the chance to start over.

# Chapter 74: The Encounter with the Enemy

The air was thick with tension as Matteo and his men advanced through the shadowy complex, each man immersed in his mission but all fully aware of the risk. The silence of the night was broken only by the heavy footsteps and Matteo's labored breathing as he led the infiltration with a determination that bordered on obsession. Every movement was calculated, precise. They had planned everything with the meticulousness of a surgeon, but Matteo knew that once inside, there was no turning back. This mission wasn't just about rescuing Alessia. It was about revenge, redemption, and above all, it was about a man who was willing to do anything—even risk his own life—to save the woman he loved.

The rival mafia's hideout was vast, dark, and filled with empty corridors that stretched out like a labyrinth. The walls, dirty and worn by time, reeked of mold and decay, further enhancing the grim nature of the place. The sound of gunfire and shouting echoed down the hallways as Lorenzo's men tried to resist the invasion. But Matteo, with a chilling calmness, swept aside every obstacle that crossed his path.

He felt the adrenaline rushing through his veins, but what truly pushed him forward was something deeper. The rage he felt toward Lorenzo and everything he had done to Alessia made him unstoppable. Every thought of her, of her face, of her smile, shattered something inside him. How had he left her so vulnerable? How had he been so blind, so consumed by pain and distrust, that he hadn't seen what was happening? Now, as he faced each resistance, Matteo felt an overwhelming urgency, a compulsion that made him move forward without thinking, without hesitation. He needed to rescue her. He needed to have her back.

"Let's move fast," Giovanni, his right-hand man, whispered, breathless. "We're almost there, Matteo."

Matteo nodded without saying a word. His gaze was fixed ahead, every muscle tense, his eyes blind to anything but the final objective. He couldn't lose Alessia. He couldn't let the weight of his failures and indecisions be what destroyed everything he still felt.

Finally, they arrived at the place where Alessia was being held. Matteo paused for a moment, his heart pounding in his chest. He stood before the door that separated him from the woman who, no matter how much he tried to suppress his feelings, still ruled his heart. He took a deep breath, forcing his mind to focus. The mission wasn't over yet, and Alessia was still in danger.

"Get ready," Matteo ordered in a low whisper, his voice full of authority. "Go in hard. We can't fail."

He turned the doorknob carefully, the door creaking open. When the sight of Alessia appeared before him, something inside Matteo cracked. She was there, leaning against the wall, her hands bound, and her face pale. Her body was bruised, but she still carried that silent strength that had always drawn him to her. She looked fragile, yet unbreakable at the same time. What terrified her the most was the unknown she had to face alone.

Alessia slowly raised her eyes when she heard them enter. Her gaze met Matteo's, and a mixture of relief and distrust overtook her. She knew that even in the most desperate circumstances, he still looked at her with that familiar glint in his eyes. But what did he think of her now? She had hurt him, and he probably believed she had betrayed him. The last thing she wanted was for him to see her as weak, as something he should leave behind.

"Matteo..." she whispered, her voice trembling, but filled with an emotion she couldn't hide. "You... you came."

He didn't respond immediately. His eyes were fixed on her, observing every detail. He saw the bruises on her arms, the exhaustion in her eyes, and the silent pain she was trying to hide. Something in his chest tightened, and he stepped forward. He wasn't thinking, he wasn't reflecting. All he knew was that she was there, and he had to protect her.

"I won't leave you," Matteo said, his voice low but full of determination. He crouched down in front of her and, with a smooth motion, cut the ropes binding her. When her hands were free, he gently held her by the shoulders, his eyes locking onto hers with an intensity that almost hurt. "I promise, Alessia. I got you out of this. And I'll make sure you're safe."

Alessia looked at him, the words stuck in her throat. She wanted to ask why he was there, why he was rescuing her after everything that had happened, but the pain of her own choices stopped her from asking. She felt so much—so much for everything he had done for her, for everything he was still doing. She felt deep gratitude, but also a fear that this rescue might be the last good thing she could ever expect from him.

"I don't know if you can still forgive me," she whispered, her voice thick with unshed tears. "I know what I did. I know I hurt you, Matteo."

He interrupted her, placing a finger gently on her lips. "Not now. Right now, all that matters is that you're safe. I'm not going to discuss what happened. Let's get out of here first. Then we'll talk."

Alessia felt a sharp pain in her chest at those words. She knew he was risking everything for her. She knew that, for him, this wasn't just about saving someone. It was about rescuing something they had lost—something she too wanted but wasn't sure they could ever get back.

But danger didn't relent. The sound of heavy footsteps grew closer, and Matteo knew this wouldn't be an easy escape. "Let's go," he said quickly, pulling Alessia to her feet. He held her firmly but gently, keeping his body close to hers as they moved quickly toward the door. "We're leaving, and no one is stopping us."

Alessia looked at him as they moved through the dark corridors, her body still weak, but the adrenaline helping her keep moving. She felt the warmth of Matteo next to her, and for a moment, the fear lessened. But she knew the battle wasn't over. They still had to escape. And for that, they would need to fight. When they looked at each other, she felt something stronger than pain and fear—a thread of hope. A silent promise that, no matter how chaotic the world around them was, they still had something.

The escape was just beginning. They would have to face many obstacles, but the only thing Alessia knew was that, as long as she was with Matteo, she had a chance. And, despite everything stacked against them, she was no longer alone. She was with the man who, despite it all, was still fighting for her.

"I won't let you go, Alessia. Not anymore," Matteo murmured, his voice low but full of conviction.

And Alessia, with heavy breath, squeezed his hand, feeling that, despite all the adversity ahead of them, he was still the only one who could make her believe that, together, they could survive anything.

# Chapter 75: The Final Confrontation

The sound of boots echoed through the dark, damp corridors of the hideout, mingling with the crackling of splintering wood and the muffled screams of Lorenzo's henchmen. Matteo was at the forefront, his sharp eyes scanning every corner, every movement, his body tensed and prepared for whatever lay ahead. He gripped his pistol tightly, knowing that with each passing second, the risk of failure grew greater. The moment was critical, and even with Alessia by his side, he felt that each step could be his last.

Lorenzo's men emerged from every side, but Matteo didn't hesitate. He moved with the precision of a seasoned warrior, his mind in total synchronization with his body. With every shot, every movement, he advanced, determined to reach Alessia and make sure she was out of harm's way. He saw her at his side, fighting with the same intensity he had, and something inside him warmed. Alessia was no longer the fragile woman he had once imagined her to be. She was strong. She was there, standing with him, sharing the weight of that fight, facing the enemy with courage.

"Matteo!" Alessia shouted, her body agile as she maneuvered through the enemies, taking down yet another of Lorenzo's men. She was relentless, but Matteo could feel that at any moment, she might grow tired. And when that happened, he would have to be there to protect her. He knew she didn't want to be protected, but his instincts wouldn't let him rest. He couldn't allow anything to happen to her.

One of Lorenzo's men charged at Alessia, a wicked smile on his face as he raised a knife. Matteo reacted instantly, rushing toward him, shoving Alessia to the side and blocking the blow with his own body. The impact was brutal. He felt the pain shoot through his shoulder, down to his chest, but he didn't scream. He couldn't afford to lose focus. Grabbing the thug by the throat, Matteo swiftly immobilized him, leaving him lifeless on the ground.

Alessia, now standing, looked at Matteo, her face a mask of concern and gratitude. "Matteo! Are you okay?" Her voice trembled, but she knew he hadn't done that for himself. He always put her first, even when he shouldn't.

He stared at her for a moment, his gaze hard but softened by a trace of tenderness in his eyes. "Not now," he replied with a grim smile. "We need to get out of here. Let's go."

The battle raged around them, but Alessia stayed close to Matteo, not letting any distance grow between them. The path to the exit was treacherous, each step harder than the last, but finally, they reached the door to the hideout and retreated to a safer location, still at risk but at least in a place where they could regroup.

When they finally arrived at the safe location, Alessia collapsed onto the couch, exhausted. She was sweating, her eyes tired, but somehow, she felt a faint sense of relief. They had survived the confrontation, but the weight of the experience, of the loss, still consumed her. She knew Matteo was watching her, but she was so emotionally drained that she didn't know what to say.

Matteo sat beside her, his gaze fixed on Alessia's face. He was breathing heavily, his body still tense, but his mind was elsewhere. He thought about everything they had been through, how he had nearly lost it all. He had nearly lost her. The pain and anger he felt toward Lorenzo, and the events that had torn them apart, seemed irrelevant now. He had her beside him. She was there, alive, though wounded, but she was there. And nothing else mattered.

"Alessia," Matteo said, his voice rough, breaking the silence between them. "I know you're scared. I know what happened between us... it's been harder than either of us ever expected. But I promise you, now... now I'll do everything I can to protect you."

Alessia looked at him, her eyes filled with unshed tears, and felt a deep pain in her chest. She had lost trust in him, but in moments like this, when he spoke with such sincerity, she no longer knew what to feel. She wanted him, but the insecurity that haunted her thoughts was overwhelming. How could she trust him after everything he had believed, after everything he had thought about her?

"I... I don't know if I can anymore, Matteo," Alessia said, her voice faltering. "I was afraid I wouldn't come back alive. I didn't know if I could protect our child, if I could get through this alive."

Matteo froze for a second, the weight of her words cutting through him like a knife. "Our child?" He repeated, disbelief and pain mixing in his tone. "You're... you're pregnant?" He didn't know if the shock came from the revelation or the thought that he had almost lost the chance to know this, to realize what she truly meant. The thought of their child, about to be born amidst all this chaos, consumed him entirely.

Alessia closed her eyes, the pain of the past weighing heavily on her. She knew this revelation wasn't the right moment. She knew that, with everything that had happened, Matteo might not believe her. But he needed to know. She needed him to know. "Yes, Matteo. I... I was afraid you'd never know. I was afraid that if something happened to me, you'd never know that this child is yours."

Matteo remained silent for a long moment, his eyes locked on her as if he was trying to understand what was happening, trying to piece together the fragments that, suddenly, seemed so distant. Shock, pain, anger, and guilt all blended inside him. He had almost lost the chance to be a father. He had almost lost everything. Alessia and the child she carried, his child, were in danger, and he hadn't even known.

He pulled her into his arms with a force that left her breathless, his fingers pressing into her hair. "I... I didn't know," he whispered, his voice full of regret. "I never wanted you to feel like you were alone. I lost you because of my pride, my anger. I... I almost lost both of you."

Alessia felt the pain in his words, the weight of his sincerity, and for a moment, all her insecurities faded away. She didn't know what the future held for them, but in that instant, she felt like there might be a chance. A chance to rebuild, to try again. She pulled back slightly, looking into his eyes, and it was then that she saw the truth. Matteo was willing to fight, willing to make things right. And maybe that was enough.

"I'm not perfect, Matteo," Alessia said, her voice softer, but with a firmness she didn't know she had. "I made wrong choices, but what I want more than anything is for our family to be safe. And if you're willing to try... then maybe we can find a way forward together."

Matteo looked at her, his eyes filled with conflicting emotions, but something within him sparked. The love he felt for her had never disappeared, and now he knew that, no matter what it took, he would fight for her and their child.

"I'll do whatever it takes," Matteo said, his voice now stronger, more certain. "No matter what happens, Alessia. I'll protect you and our child. You're not alone anymore."

They embraced, their bodies joined in a silent reconciliation, a gesture of mutual trust that, though marked by pain, was also filled with a new hope. They had much to overcome, but in that moment, Matteo knew that it was all worth it. The love and loyalty they shared would be the key to overcoming the obstacles ahead. And, even though the future was uncertain, together, they would face everything.

The danger still lurked, and the mafia wouldn't give them peace, but what Matteo and Alessia had found in each other was stronger than any external threat. They had found each other again—and this time, nothing would tear them apart.

# Chapter 76: Love and Sacrifice

Night had fallen over the DeLuca mansion, and the silence seemed deafening. The opulence of the house, with its adorned walls and luxurious furniture, had never felt so cold and distant. Matteo stood before the window of his office, his eyes fixed on the darkness outside. He couldn't shake the image of Alessia from his mind — her expression of pain, fear, with every word she spoke during the rescue. He still felt the weight of everything that had happened. The distrust he had harbored, the hasty judgments, the distance he had created between them... everything he had done seemed irreparable, but he was here, with her, with a chance to make things right, if she was still able to trust him.

In the room behind him, Alessia sat on the couch, her eyes distant but still watching the man who, despite all his flaws, had always occupied a deep place in her heart. What she felt now was a whirlwind — relief for being safe, for being back in her house, but also insecurity and doubt. The wound of betrayal was still fresh, and while the love she felt for Matteo hadn't disappeared, the trust... that was another story.

She knew he still felt guilty. He had rescued her, but he hadn't fully forgiven her. And she didn't know if she was capable of forgiving him. She didn't know who she could trust anymore, but something inside her told her that he was trying. That should be enough, right?

Matteo slowly turned around, his dark eyes reflecting the weight of the guilt he carried. He walked over to the couch where Alessia was sitting and knelt before her. His posture was different now, more vulnerable, more human, something she had never imagined seeing in him — someone who had always been unyielding, strong, and resolute.

"Alessia," he began, his voice low, almost imperceptible. "I... I don't know where to start. I should never have doubted you. When you needed me the most, I let myself be carried away by pride and pain. I saw in you what I wanted to believe, not what was really there, not who you truly were. I... I'm trying to be better. For you. For us."

Alessia looked at him, her chest tightening as his eyes searched hers, filled with genuine regret. She wanted to believe him, wanted to give him the chance he was asking for, but doubt still lingered in the back of her mind. She had suffered, he had hurt her, but at the same time, the love she felt for him hadn't disappeared. He was here, before her, with a sincerity she hadn't seen before.

"Matteo..." she breathed deeply, the words heavy in her throat. "I don't know if I can trust again. I've lived in fear. Fear of not coming back. Fear of not being able to protect our child. And you, you were so distant, so closed off, that I didn't know if I could count on you."

He clenched his fists, feeling the weight of every word she spoke like a sharp blade. She was right. He had shut himself off, had distanced himself out of fear, insecurity, and it had made her feel lonelier than ever.

"I understand, Alessia," Matteo said, his voice hoarse, his pain evident. "I left you alone when you needed me most. And that... that is something I'll never forgive myself for. But I need you to give me the chance to fix this. I know what I did can't be erased, but I promise you, with all my heart, I will protect you and our child. Even if it means giving up everything the mafia represents, everything I am."

Alessia felt the weight of his words fall over her, and something inside her broke. It was no longer about what he had done or didn't do, but about what he was willing to do now. He was here, genuinely, with the promise that he would change, that he would do the right thing. She didn't know if she could fully believe him, but she knew that if there was a chance to rebuild, it would be with him. And maybe, with this new beginning, she could finally trust him again.

She reached out her hand, touching his face gently, his warm skin under her fingers. "I can't promise it will be easy, Matteo. I can't promise we won't go through more pain. But... I want to try. I want to try because you're still everything to me."

Matteo closed his eyes for a moment, feeling the warmth of her touch spread through his body, and for the first time in a long time, he felt whole. He wanted to believe in her, wanted her to believe in him. He wanted that, despite everything, their love would be enough to overcome the mistakes of the past.

"Then let's try, Alessia," he said, his voice firm, but softened by the emotion he could no longer hide. "I will do whatever it takes. Nothing will separate us from now on. I will protect you. And I will protect our child."

She looked at him with a mix of sadness and hope, her eyes shining with a vulnerability he hadn't seen before. "I'm scared, Matteo. I'm scared this won't be enough, that the mafia will still hunt us down. I'm scared that at some point, I'll have to choose between my safety and yours. Between our family and what you represent."

Matteo moved closer to her, his eyes locked on hers. "I will never put you in a situation like that, Alessia. No matter what happens. If the mafia wants to hunt us, let them come. I will face it. Because you and our child are all I have. And now, nothing else matters."

They embraced then, not as two lovers torn apart by the past, but as a family rebuilding the foundations of a love that still resisted the flames of distrust. Alessia felt Matteo's body against hers, his warmth, the silent promise of protection and dedication. She knew there were still dangers ahead, and that the road ahead would be tough, but for the first time, she felt that maybe, just maybe, they could begin to heal the wounds.

"We'll face this together, Matteo. We'll rebuild what is ours, no matter how hard it is."

He held her tighter, his face against hers, his eyes closed as if making a silent promise to himself. "Yes, together. Always."

For a brief moment, the darkness of the night was illuminated by a flame of hope. They knew that the future was still uncertain, that the dangers of the mafia were still lurking, but at that instant, in that embrace, Alessia and Matteo were more united than ever. They had survived the storm, and now, with their child's future at stake, they were ready to fight for what mattered most: the love they shared, the loyalty they were building, and the family they were about to form.

The following morning arrived cold and silent, the kind of silence that seemed to weigh in the mansion's atmosphere. Alessia was in the kitchen, making a simple coffee, trying to hold on to some normalcy while chaos still bubbled outside. What did she feel? A mix of gratitude and fear, the expectation of what this new chapter in their lives would bring, and the uncertainty of what would happen next. The future was out of her control, but something inside her, some quiet force, pushed her to keep going.

She heard Matteo's footsteps approaching before she saw him. When he entered the kitchen, she paused for a moment. He was still there, with that determined, somber look she knew so well, but something had changed. It was subtle, but Alessia could feel it. He was different. More... open. The mask he wore all the time seemed to have been set aside.

"You look well," Matteo's voice was low, but the softness in his words sent a shiver down Alessia's spine. "For someone who's just been through so much."

Alessia looked at him, her eyes meeting his with a challenging but vulnerable glance. "It's not easy, Matteo. But I'm trying. And you?" She moved a little closer, the smell of coffee mingling with the cold morning air. "Do you still think you can save me from everything?"

Matteo smiled, but it wasn't a mocking smile, like she had often seen. It was something gentler, almost as if he was allowing himself to be vulnerable with her. "I know you don't need a savior, Alessia," he said, his eyes fixed on hers. "But I know I can be whatever you need right now. And if you give me the chance, I'll do whatever it takes to fix my mistakes."

A silence fell between them again, but it wasn't uncomfortable. It was as if they were both weighing the words spoken and those left unspoken. Alessia still carried the pain of betrayal, the anguish of distrust, but she couldn't deny that there was something about Matteo that had always drawn her in. Something deeper than the unyielding mafia man. He was there, before her, with sincerity in his eyes, and that was something she couldn't ignore anymore.

She took a deep breath, setting the coffee cup on the table. "I don't know if I can fully trust you, Matteo. What happened... isn't something that's easily erased. But..."

He took a step forward, his eyes locked on hers with an intensity that made her feel exposed before him. "But what?"

Alessia hesitated, her heart racing. She wanted to pull away, retreat, but she couldn't. Something in the way he was looking at her made her resistance start to melt. "But I want to try, Matteo. I want to believe in you. Because deep down, I know you were never fully a monster, like I saw you. And maybe... maybe, with time, I'll be able to trust you again."

Matteo moved closer still, his fingers lightly touching her face, a caress almost reverent. He ran his thumb across her skin, feeling the softness, the warmth. The sensation of having her so close almost disarmed him completely. He had never been this man before. But she... Alessia made him want to be better. She made him want to give everything, even if it meant shedding his pride.

"I never asked you to forgive me now, Alessia," he said in a husky voice, but sincere. "I just... I just wanted you to know that, no matter the cost, I'll do everything to protect you. And our child."

The mention of the baby, which until now had been a weight in Alessia's mind, now sounded like a promise. She felt her heart race faster, a mix of fear and hope filling her chest. She didn't know what the future would bring, but she was ready to face it with Matteo. He had failed her in the past, but he was here now, with her, willing to try. And maybe that was enough.

She looked back at him, her eyes shining with an emotion she couldn't hide. "I'm not an easy woman, Matteo. I didn't expect it to be. I didn't expect you to be so... persistent. But I see what you're doing. I see that, despite all your mistakes, you're here. And that... that means more than you think."

Matteo smiled, and this time, it wasn't a mocking smile. It was a smile that spoke of hope, of a new beginning. He leaned forward, his lips almost touching hers, but he stopped just before. The air was charged with electricity, and he knew what this moment meant.

"Are you sure about that?" he asked, his voice soft, almost as if searching for an answer only she could give.

Alessia didn't say a word. Instead, she closed the distance between them, her hands reaching for his neck, pulling him into a kiss. It was gentle but full of unsaid promises, of regrets, and above all, of a hope they were beginning to share again. When they pulled away, Alessia took a deep breath, her eyes sparkling.

"I never imagined this would happen," she murmured, a tired smile on her face. "But maybe... maybe this is the beginning of something new."

Matteo ran his hand through her hair, the touch soft, but filled with a strength he didn't know he had. "I know, Alessia. And I'll do my best to make this new beginning the best one of all."

The warmth between them was palpable. The mafia, the enemies, the dangers surrounding them... all of that was still there, always a constant threat. But in that moment, nothing else mattered. They had each other, and as unpredictable as the world around them was, that was enough. The future would be hard, but together, they could face anything.

"I love you, Alessia," Matteo said, his voice deep and filled with emotion. "And I'll do whatever it takes to make sure you and our child are happy. Nothing will separate us."

Alessia looked at him, her eyes misty but with a sparkle of determination he knew well. "I know, Matteo. I know."

They stood there together, breathing the same air, their hearts beating in sync, knowing the road ahead would be tough, but for now, they were more united than ever. Love and loyalty would be their strength, and nothing else mattered. They had found each other amid the chaos, and that was all they needed.

# Chapter 77: Exposing the Truth

The morning light filtered into the planning room of the mansion, but the tension in the air made the atmosphere oppressive. Matteo sat at the table, his fingers tapping lightly on the file in front of him, his eyes fixed on the papers scattered around. Alessia sat beside him, carefully examining each detail, every piece of evidence she had gathered about Lorenzo's illegal schemes. The silence between them was deep, yet charged with an energy that didn't need words to be understood. Both of them knew they were on the brink of something big—something that could change the fate of their families, but also something that could end their lives.

"If we do this, there's no turning back, Alessia," Matteo finally spoke, his voice gravely serious. He leaned back in his chair, his gaze still on the documents. "Lorenzo won't stop at anything to get his revenge. And if he finds out what we're planning... the risk will be even greater."

Alessia looked at him, a mixture of determination and fear in her eyes. She knew how fatal this action could be, but also knew they had no other choice. The life of her son and her own safety were at stake. "I know, Matteo. I know what we're facing. But he can't keep controlling our lives. He can't have power over our family."

Matteo sighed deeply, his fingers now gripping the papers as if he wanted to crush all the anger and frustration building inside him. He looked at Alessia, his eyes intense, yet softened in a way he rarely showed. "I don't want to lose you, Alessia. No matter what happens. But if we're going to do this, we need to act fast."

"We already have," Alessia replied, lifting the documents with the collected evidence. "All we need to do now is expose his wrongdoing. The media is ready to receive the information, and the work we've done will ensure that the Romano family is at the center of the investigations. This will weaken his empire, Matteo."

Matteo didn't answer immediately. He knew she was right. The operation was well underway, but doubt still lingered in him. They were about to set something in motion that they couldn't control. The war that followed would be inevitable, but the uncertainty of what would happen afterward consumed him. He shuddered at the thought of what might come next. Alessia was resolute in her determination, but he also felt the weight of responsibility on his shoulders.

"Do you really think this will work? That Lorenzo will fall this easily?" Matteo asked, his voice darker now, though still tinged with admiration for her courage. Alessia had been brave from the start, and now he saw a strength in her that he had always known was there but was now more alive than ever.

Alessia met his gaze directly, her voice firm. "I don't know if Lorenzo will fall, but I know we have to try. And I know that with this, he will lose the trust of many of his allies. The Romano family will crumble from within. No matter what happens, we won't be at his mercy anymore."

Matteo stood up, walking over to the window, his eyes fixed on the horizon. The city seemed calm, as if nothing wrong was about to happen. But inside him, chaos was about to begin. He knew the road ahead would be treacherous, but for the first time, he felt he wasn't alone. Alessia was by his side, and that was enough to make him feel capable of facing anything.

"I'll do this for us, Alessia. For our family," he said, his voice low but full of conviction. "But know this—there's no turning back now. Lorenzo will try everything to destroy us."

Alessia walked over to him, placing a hand on his arm, a simple gesture but full of meaning. "We'll face this together, Matteo. No matter what happens, the future of our family is in our hands now."

Matteo's eyes softened as he looked at her. He felt something warm in his chest—something he didn't want to admit, but that was undeniable. Alessia was his strength, and she made him believe that, even in the midst of all the darkness, there could be light.

"You're right," Matteo replied, almost in a whisper. "Together."

The operation was underway. With the help of trusted allies, the information Alessia had managed to infiltrate into the hands of the media spread quickly. In the following days, reports began to surface, bringing to light Lorenzo's shady dealings involving money laundering, corruption, and ties to international criminal organizations. The storm was forming, and the Romano family was now at the center of attention.

Matteo and Alessia monitored everything closely, their eyes glued to the news as they prepared for what was to come. They were in an improvised office in the mansion, surrounded by papers, laptops, and the sound of phone calls and messages exchanged with their allies.

"Lorenzo's first allies are starting to distance themselves from him," Alessia said, watching the screen of her computer. "The pressure is working. But we can't let our guard down."

Matteo didn't take his eyes off his phone, waiting for the next move. "Yes, Alessia. Lorenzo will counterattack. But for now, we have control. And as long as he's busy dealing with the consequences, we can gain an advantage."

But deep down, Matteo knew this was just the beginning. Lorenzo wouldn't simply surrender. He would react with fury, and they would be at the epicenter of a war that could destroy everything they had built. Matteo looked at Alessia, and for a moment, they exchanged a silent, knowing glance. They both understood the risks. But they also knew that, together, they could face anything.

"Stay close to me, Alessia," Matteo said, his voice dark, but carrying something else. "I'll protect you, but you need to be ready for what's coming."

She smiled, a smile filled with both vulnerability and strength. "I'm ready, Matteo. And I know that together, we can face anything. Everything we've been through has brought us here. And now, we're stronger than ever."

Matteo watched her for a moment, his eyes filled with emotions he rarely allowed to show. Her trust, the quiet strength she exuded, the way she threw herself into their cause without hesitation, made him believe that no matter what happened, they would be able to move forward.

"Together," Matteo repeated, more to himself than to her. "Nothing will tear us apart, Alessia. Nothing."

And in that moment, both of them knew that, no matter the challenges ahead, the bond they had built, the promises made, and the loyalties shared, were stronger than any external threat. They were ready to fight for the future of their family, not just against Lorenzo, but against everything that tried to destroy them. They had each other, and with that, they had the strength to win the war.

The mansion was quiet that night, the soft lights creating a cozy atmosphere, but the weight of what was to come the next day still lingered in the air. Matteo and Alessia were in the living room, but the tension between them was palpable, though there was something else, something they were both starting to realize but hesitated to admit.

Matteo sat in a chair, his gaze fixed on the glass of whiskey in his hand. He wasn't drinking much, but the act of holding it, swirling the liquid inside the glass, seemed to be his only way of staying centered. He felt the weight of the world on his shoulders, the responsibility to keep Alessia and the baby safe, and the fear that still consumed him. He knew the future was uncertain, that the war with Lorenzo could come at any moment, but what haunted him more was the feeling that he had failed in so many ways with Alessia. When he looked at her, he saw the woman he loved, but he also saw the woman he almost lost. The fear that she would distance herself from him again consumed him.

Alessia stood near the fireplace, her body relaxed, but her eyes, though soft, held the gaze of a woman who wouldn't be fooled. She knew how much Matteo was blaming himself. She knew he was fighting against his own insecurities. And while she loved him more than anything, the pain of the mistrust he had shown, the coldness between them that never fully disappeared, still made her heart race for the wrong reasons.

She turned slowly toward him, the sound of the crackling fire behind her, and he noticed her. That familiar feeling of being observed, of being evaluated, hit him hard. They stared at each other for a moment, a tense silence between them, laden with unspoken words.

"You're overthinking it," Alessia said softly, but with a subtle provocation. She stepped closer to him, her legs almost touching his. "I can see you're punishing yourself for something that's already happened. And you know that won't help."

Matteo lifted his gaze to meet hers, his eyes dark and penetrating. He didn't want to hide what he felt anymore, but at the same time, he didn't know how to put it into words. She always disarmed him, always made him feel both small and larger than life. When she was near him, he felt like anything was possible, but also like it was too fragile to be real.

"I know I made the wrong choices, Alessia," he said with a heavy sigh. "I know I've hurt you more times than I can count. But every time you look at me, I'm afraid that this fear, this distance, is all I'll ever get back."

Alessia tilted her head, observing him with a look filled with affection and something else—maybe a touch of silent fury, for the wounds that hadn't healed, but also for his vulnerability. Something in his posture, in the way he surrendered, made her want to fight with him, not against him. She moved even closer, her hand gently touching his face.

"Matteo, you're too stubborn. I can't be both your refuge and your torment," she murmured, her voice low but firm. "But I am yours. And you know that, even when you convince yourself otherwise."

Matteo's eyes softened, and for a moment, he forgot about the world around him. She was there, the woman he always knew could be his, but whom he hadn't known how to care for. The desire he felt for her, the need to have her close, mixed with the urgency to reconnect with her, to finally break the barriers he had built between them.

"Then show me, Alessia," he said with a hoarse voice, the closeness between them making everything more intense. "Show me that we can start over, that we can stop getting lost in our own fears. Because every time I look at you, I feel like I'd do anything to make you believe in me again."

Alessia felt the heat of his closeness, and for a moment, the idea of pushing him away disappeared. She closed her eyes, fighting against the temptation to let herself fall into him. But there was something there, a silent promise that they both needed to make—to not let the past, the failures and mistakes they had made, control them anymore. She wasn't perfect, but with Matteo, she believed she could be better. And above all, she wanted to believe that they could build something stronger than what separated them.

"I can't promise it will be easy, Matteo," she said, finally letting the distance between them disappear. "But if you let me... if you really show me who you are... I'll fight with you."

Matteo smiled, his face softening as he touched her hair. "I won't give up on you, Alessia. Not anymore. And when the dangers come, I'll be by your side."

She looked at him, her eyes shining with an intensity she hadn't noticed before. There, in his eyes, she saw the man who, despite the weight of his own world, was willing to change for her, for their child. And for the first time, Alessia felt that maybe their love was stronger than any war that might come.

Without another word, Matteo pulled her closer, their bodies finally aligning. He kissed her with an intensity that broke all barriers, a kiss that was a silent plea for forgiveness and, at the same time, a promise that, unlike before, they were now together. She surrendered to the kiss, feeling the passion intertwining with the pain, with the unspoken promises.

When they pulled away, both breathless, Alessia smiled softly, her eyes shining with a mix of emotion and fulfillment.

"Now, nothing will separate us, Matteo," she said, confidence growing in her voice. "And if we face the dangers together, then we can face anything."

He smiled, his expression softer, more human. "Nothing. Together, Alessia. Always."

And with that, something more solidified between them, stronger than fear, firmer than any threat that might arise. They had each other, and, no matter how chaotic the world around them became, that seemed to be enough. They were ready to face whatever came — together.

# Chapter 78: The Final Push

The night seemed darker than ever. The DeLuca mansion, usually a symbol of power and security, now appeared to be a fortress on the brink of collapse. Matteo stood by the office window, observing the movement on the property, his body exhausted but still alert. Since Alessia's rescue, he hadn't found a moment of real rest. His eyes, though tired, were fixed on the horizon as if waiting for the inevitable. Lorenzo was not a man who surrendered easily, and Matteo knew that the war with the Romano family was only just beginning.

Alessia entered the office silently, the sound of her footsteps on the wooden floor echoing softly. She was stronger now, more resolute, but her eyes still reflected the tension. She stopped behind Matteo, her fingers lightly touching the back of his neck, trying to ease the visible pain he carried.

"It won't matter, Alessia," Matteo said, his voice dark and weary. "He's going to come after us, to destroy everything."

She didn't say anything immediately but moved closer, placing her hands on his shoulders, feeling the weight of the responsibility he carried. She knew he was right, but she also knew they wouldn't be defeated. Not so easily. "We're ready for whatever comes, Matteo," she said, her voice firm but with a touch of softness. "No matter what happens, we're not alone anymore. We're a family now."

He slowly turned around, his hands gripping hers, his gaze intense. There was pain, yes, but there was also something else—an unbreakable bond between them, stronger than any external threat. "I will protect you, Alessia. And our family. Even if it costs me everything."

She looked at him with a mixture of fear and hope. "You won't lose yourself in this, Matteo. We won't lose what matters most. We're in this together."

Those words seemed to suspend the air around them, as if, somehow, they were finally finding peace amid the chaos surrounding them. But then, the sound of a distant explosion cut through the moment, pulling Matteo back to reality. He felt the shock wave through his body like an electric pulse, and a sense of urgency took over.

"They're here," he murmured, more to himself than to Alessia.

"Let's go, now!" Alessia shouted, adrenaline spiking instantly. "We can't wait any longer!"

In seconds, Matteo and Alessia were running through the mansion's hallways, with Matteo's trusted men by their side. The ground trembled as more explosions echoed, and the sounds of gunshots and screams filled their ears. The attack was imminent. Lorenzo was no longer just threatening them. He was trying to destroy everything, and all that Matteo and Alessia had fought to build was about to be erased.

"Alessia, stay behind me," Matteo ordered, his voice authoritative but filled with concern. He knew she was strong, but the fragility of her pregnancy still lingered, and he couldn't take any risks.

She shook her head, determined. "I won't stay behind, Matteo. You taught me to fight. We'll do this together."

The scene was chaotic. The mansion, usually a place of silence and luxury, had turned into a battlefield. Lorenzo's men had stormed the property, and a fierce fight was unfolding in the corridors and on the stairs. With each shot fired, the tension mounted. Danger was everywhere, just a few steps away, and the only thing Matteo could do now was ensure Alessia's safety. But with every passing moment, he felt the adrenaline consuming him, the pain from the wound he had sustained during the rescue still throbbing, yet he refused to stop. Not while she was there, by his side.

"Watch out!" Alessia shouted, shoving Matteo aside as one of the enemy's thugs approached. She didn't hesitate. She grabbed the gun he had dropped and fired, taking down the enemy before he could attack. Her eyes were filled with a determination Matteo hadn't expected, and for the first time, he saw a woman willing to fight with everything she had to protect what she loved.

When the battle finally seemed to die down, the air was still thick with tension. Matteo was out of breath, his hands trembling slightly, but his resolve was stronger than ever. He turned to Alessia, expecting to find fear or uncertainty, but what he saw was a strong woman, her eyes shining with courage.

"You..." He paused, feeling the weight of reality crashing in on him. "You just saved my life."

Alessia took a deep breath, her heart still racing from the adrenaline, but she smiled sincerely. "We saved each other, Matteo. Together. Don't forget that."

But in that moment, something changed inside him. The sight of her, fighting beside him without hesitation, was all he needed to know that, despite the wounds of the past, they could truly overcome anything. She was no longer just his wife, she wasn't just the woman he loved. She was his partner, his equal.

"I won't doubt you anymore, Alessia," Matteo said, his voice hoarse, laden with emotion. He stepped forward, taking her face in his hands, his eyes filled with an intensity that made the air around them feel heavier. "I promise you, no matter what happens, I'll do whatever it takes to protect you and our child. You are my strength now, Alessia. And nothing will tear us apart."

Alessia stared at him, her eyes brimming with emotion. She never imagined she'd hear those words, especially after everything they had been through. But he was there, with her, in the most dangerous moment of their lives, saying everything she needed to hear. He loved her. He was ready to change. And, more importantly, he was by her side, ready to face whatever came.

"I believe in you, Matteo," she whispered, her voice thick with emotion. "I've always believed. And now, let's end this. Let's win."

But, as they surrendered to the intensity of the moment, a distant sound interrupted their words. The war was far from over. They had just won a battle, but Lorenzo wouldn't rest until he saw them destroyed.

"Let's finish what we started, Alessia," Matteo said, the determination reflecting in his voice. He held her hand tightly, and together, with hearts still pounding from the fight, they moved forward. They knew the future was at stake, but they also knew that, as long as they were together, there was no adversity that could separate them.

The battle was far from over, but Alessia and Matteo were more united than ever. They had survived that night, and that was just the beginning. The real war was yet to come, but now, more than ever, they were ready to face it, side by side.

The night was cold, and the wind howled through the cracks of the open window, but inside the DeLuca mansion, the warmth seemed to come from somewhere else—from the tension still hanging in the air, from their closeness. Matteo and Alessia were in the main room, their eyes meeting with intensity, as if the war they had fought together had only just begun, even after so many battles won.

Matteo stood, watching the fire in the hearth. His shoulders were still tense, his eyes heavy with a weight Alessia knew well. He was distant, but not in the same way as before. He was no longer the relentless man hiding behind his coldness. She knew that, somewhere in there, he was fighting himself, battling insecurities and fears he tried not to admit, but which surrounded him whenever he looked at her.

She, on the other hand, sat on the sofa, her hand resting on her belly. Her pregnancy was more visible now, and the feeling of carrying a new life made everything happening around them seem distant. But, at the same time, she felt the pressure of the decisions they would have to make. They were at war—not just against Lorenzo, but against their own doubts and the past that still haunted them.

"You're thinking too much, Matteo," Alessia said, breaking the silence. Her voice was soft, but with a subtle challenge he knew all too well. "This won't get us anywhere."

He turned slowly, his eyes locked on hers. There was something in his gaze, a mix of arrogance and tenderness he couldn't hide. He was allowing himself to be vulnerable, but also knew that, somehow, she challenged him in a way no one else could. And that, even in the midst of the storm, drew him to her more than anything.

"I always knew you'd say that," he replied with a crooked smile, moving toward her. He sat beside her, closer than she expected. She felt the energy between them intensify. "But you still don't understand that, when I set my mind to something, there's nothing that can make me back down."

Alessia raised an eyebrow, a provocative smile on her lips. "Are you sure about that, Matteo? Would you give yourself completely, for me?"

He looked at her, his eyes darker now, as if weighing his words. He knew she liked that provocation, liked testing his limits. He liked it too. Somehow, they had become two enemies who couldn't stop seeking each other, challenging and testing one another, even when the war seemed to have ended.

"I love you, Alessia," he said so directly that she was left speechless for a moment. He took her hand, holding it tightly, their fingers entwining like it was the only thing keeping them together in the chaos. "I love you, and everything I did, no matter how wrong it might have been, was to protect you. No matter how much I try to deny it, you are the only thing that truly matters."

His words hit her with silent force. She felt the weight of the love he offered, the sincerity in the depth of his voice, even amid the bloodshed and sacrifices they had to make every day. The fact that he was giving himself to her like this, without reservations, breaking the barriers he had always placed between them, made her see him differently. He was no longer just the mafia boss. He was the man she loved. And, more importantly, the man who loved her, despite everything they had been through.

She looked at him, her eyes filled with emotion. "I know, Matteo. I know. And that's why I... I'm willing to fight. Not just for us, but for him too." She gently touched her belly, as if mentioning their child sealed their fate. "Because our family... that's what matters now."

The silence between them was filled with an electric tension. Matteo leaned in closer, his face near hers. He could smell her perfume, feel the warmth of her skin. And, seeing her there, so vulnerable yet so strong at the same time, he couldn't resist. His mouth found hers, without words, just the need to have her close, to feel her presence. The kiss was soft but laden with intensity, making them forget the world around them.

When they separated, both breathless, Alessia smiled, but there was something more in her eyes. It was as if she was revealing more than he could imagine, and, at the same time, giving herself to him in a way she never had before. "Will you protect me, Matteo? Even if everything falls apart around us?"

Matteo looked deeply into her eyes, his hand gently touching her face. He didn't need any more words. He knew what she wanted to hear. "Always. I will protect you, Alessia. Until my last breath."

She took a deep breath, placing her hand on his chest, feeling the steady rhythm of his heart beneath her fingers. "Then we're ready. We can do this, Matteo. Together."

He pulled her closer, now fully aware that, even in the most extreme circumstances, they had each other. And, as the world collapsed around them, as danger closed in from all sides, they wouldn't be alone anymore. Their love was the strength that would keep them firm.

"Yes, together," he whispered, his eyes locked on hers. "Always."

And, in that moment, despite the impending war, the enemies lurking, and the constant threats, they knew that what mattered most was right there between them. Together, nothing could bring them down.

# Chapter 79: Against All Odds

The mansion was silent at night, the soft light from the lamps reflecting off the dark walls. However, the tension in the air was palpable. The atmosphere was charged with expectation, and Matteo, though still feeling the pain from wounds that hadn't healed, was determined to move forward with the plan he had made. He felt this was his last chance to finally end Lorenzo and ensure his family's safety, but the price to pay could be high. What Matteo couldn't see — or didn't want to see — was that the burden he carried could be his greatest enemy.

Alessia, who had noticed the change in Matteo, was by his side, but she couldn't shake the weight of the decision he was about to make. She knew the war with Lorenzo was far from over, but Matteo's insistence on going all the way, without caring for his health, made her wonder if he still believed in the value of his life and their future together.

"Matteo, you need to stop. You're too hurt," Alessia said, her voice filled with concern. She stepped closer to him, touching his forehead, feeling the fever that was starting to take over his body. "I understand you want to end this, but don't kill yourself over it. If you don't take care of yourself, everything we've been through will be for nothing."

Matteo looked at her, his eyes fixed but with a gleam of pain and determination. He had devoted so much to this moment that he could no longer think of anything else but eliminating the threat of Lorenzo once and for all. The physical pain he felt now seemed insignificant compared to what he knew he had to do.

"I can't back down now, Alessia," he said, his voice hoarse but firm. "I know you're scared. I am too. But if I stop now, if I don't go all the way, I'll keep seeing everyone I love destroyed. I can't live like that. I can't let our son grow up in a world where Lorenzo still has power."

Alessia felt a deep pain as she heard those words, but also an overwhelming wave of understanding. She knew he was speaking from the heart, that his words were filled with love and desperation, but what scared her most was the fact that Matteo was sacrificing more than she could bear.

"But what about us, Matteo?" she asked, her voice urgent. "You told me you'd do anything to protect our family. And I believe you. I always have. But you also need to take care of yourself. I can't... I can't lose you now."

He stepped closer to her, his eyes softening but the pain still visible. He held her by the waist, pulling her closer, as if the need to be with her was the only thing keeping him whole. "I won't lose you, Alessia. I won't. This will end him, I promise. I just need one more push, one more chance to put an end to this."

Alessia felt her chest tighten, the love she felt for him and the pain she saw in his eyes were overwhelming. She knew he was willing to sacrifice anything to protect them, but she also knew he was losing himself in the darkness of his own guilt and revenge. And, no matter how much she wanted him to rest, she knew she couldn't convince him to quit.

"Then, let's do this together," she whispered, taking his hand firmly. "I'll be by your side, Matteo. No matter what happens. We're going to end Lorenzo, but you'll do it with your strength, with your intelligence, not with more sacrifices."

Matteo looked at her, his eyes burning with an intensity that almost made her melt. He pulled her closer, and the kiss they shared wasn't just of desire or comfort, but a silent promise that now, they were more united than ever. The weight of responsibility was still there, but the strength of what they had become together made them believe that nothing could separate them.

When they pulled apart, their hearts still racing, Matteo gently touched Alessia's face. "I need you by my side, Alessia. We need to make sure this ends once and for all. You have my word. We're going to win this."

She smiled, though she still felt the apprehension in her chest. "I know. And I'll be with you, Matteo. Not just for our son, but for us. For everything we've been through. And when this is over, we'll have our peace."

And so, in a quiet but profound way, they mapped out their plan. Using the evidence Alessia had gathered on Lorenzo's schemes, they knew they could weaken his position even further. The media was already on their side, with scandals involving the Romano family exploding in headlines, and now the final revelation was just a matter of time.

The operation to destabilize Lorenzo was riskier than anyone could have imagined. They used public support, and the uproar caused by the revelation of Lorenzo's wrongdoings divided his allies. Though the threat to Lorenzo had diminished, they knew the enemy would not give up so easily. They prepared for the next move, knowing it would be the hardest one yet.

Alessia, even with the fear of what was to come, felt a growing strength within herself. She looked at Matteo, now calmer but still with the same determined look in his eyes. He was willing to give everything for her and their baby to have a chance at a better life. This made her love him more than she had ever imagined possible.

"I fell in love with you, Matteo," Alessia said, her voice soft but full of emotion. "And everything we've been through has made me see the truth. I love you, and I know that together, we can face anything."

Matteo pulled her into a tight embrace, his chest pressing against hers with force. "I love you too, Alessia. And I won't stop until we can live the life we deserve. Until Lorenzo never has power over us again."

They stood there, united, breathing the same air, knowing that despite the dangers ahead, nothing could separate them now. Their love, loyalty, and courage to fight for everything they had built made them stronger. Together, they were unstoppable.

The night was dense and silent, with only the sound of the wind tapping against the mansion's windows breaking the stillness. The danger still hung over them, but inside the house, there was a strange sense of peace. Alessia stood on the balcony, her eyes fixed on the horizon, as if searching for something she couldn't see, something beyond the darkness of the night. The tension that had weighed on her shoulders eased with each deep breath she took, but the threats from Lorenzo were still very real. Even with Matteo by her side, even with their future ahead, Alessia knew that at any moment, the world around her could crumble again.

Matteo was behind her, standing in the glass doorway, watching her with a mix of concern and admiration. He felt her distant, more than he would like to admit. She was calmer than he was, but he saw the internal struggle she was still fighting. He felt there was something more behind her strength, something she wasn't letting him see. He didn't fully understand, but he knew that when Alessia spoke from the heart, she had an intensity he never knew was possible.

"You're thinking too much, aren't you?" His voice cut through the silence, low but soft in a way Alessia rarely heard.

She turned to face him, her eyes slightly surprised by the interruption, but there was no anger in her gaze, only exhaustion. Exhaustion from fighting, from living in fear, but also exhaustion from worrying about him, about them, about everything that was to come.

"I'm trying..." she started, her voice heavy with something he couldn't identify. "I'm trying to understand how we got here, Matteo. How everything we've been through was possible, and how much we still have ahead of us. I just..." She sighed before turning fully toward him, letting the doubt and fear show. "I just want you to tell me this will pass. That we'll have a chance to live in peace."

He took a step closer, so close she could feel his warmth, and gently placed his hand on her shoulder. His fingers touched her skin with a tenderness that surprised Alessia. She knew how much anger and pain he carried, but in that moment, he was exactly what she needed him to be: a solid rock, an anchor that made her believe there was still a chance.

"I don't know if this will pass, Alessia," he said, his voice deep and sincere, his eyes locked on hers. "I can't promise there won't be more battles. But I can promise I'll be by your side through every one of them. That no matter what happens, I'll protect you and our son. Always."

Her heart raced as she heard his words. She already knew this, but hearing Matteo finally open up to her, after everything they had been through, made her feel an overwhelming wave of emotion she couldn't control. She had never imagined they would get to this point. She had never thought that, in the middle of violence and war, she would find something as powerful as the love they shared.

"I know," she said, her voice faltering slightly, "I know, Matteo. And that... that gives me strength. You don't know how much this means to me."

He smiled faintly, still with that penetrating gaze, but now with a softness he rarely showed. He moved even closer, his hands now wrapping around her waist. Alessia didn't pull away. They were close enough to feel each other's racing heartbeat, and in the silence that followed, everything seemed clearer. Their past, the lies, the betrayals—none of it mattered anymore. What mattered now was what they were building together. And nothing, not Lorenzo, nor any other threat, could destroy that.

"You know you can count on me, Alessia, for everything," Matteo said, his lips curving into a smile that was both gentle and laden with something deeper. "No matter what happens. We'll get through this together, and when it's all over, we'll have the life we deserve."

Alessia looked at him, her eyes shining with a mix of love and fear, as if, for the first time, she was realizing just how deep the bond between them really was. "You... you promise me this, Matteo? Even after everything we've done and gone through?"

He pulled her closer, his mouth near her ear, and whispered, his voice low and filled with emotion. "I promise you, Alessia. There's nothing more important in this world now than you and our family."

She couldn't help but smile, a smile that came from deep within her heart, a mix of relief and gratitude. But there was also something more, something she knew would be crucial for their future — trust. She hadn't fully given herself to him until that moment, but now, in his arms, she felt like maybe it was possible to truly trust the man he had become.

With her eyes still fixed on him, Matteo kissed her, a soft kiss, but with the intensity of all the emotions he didn't express in words. It was a promise, an affirmation that, despite all the uncertainties, they had each other. And that made them invincible.

When they pulled apart, Alessia touched his face, her fingers tracing the lines of his jaw, her gaze deep, as if she wanted to imprint that moment into memory. "I love you, Matteo," she said, her voice soft but full of sincerity.

He smiled, this time without hesitation. "I love you too, Alessia. And nothing will separate us. Nothing."

In that moment, as the world outside continued to be a battlefield, Alessia and Matteo found a place where their love could blossom, where the pain and scars from the past were slowly healing. They were no longer just surviving — they were living, together, with a strength that only true love could provide.

The battle they would face next would be the hardest of all, but in that instant, as the fire in the hearth crackled softly in the background, nothing else seemed to matter.

# Chapter 80: Love That Conquers Everything

The mansion was calm, a temporary tranquility after the storm. The tension that always hung over them seemed a little more distant now, but it hadn't disappeared. The soft light of the fireplace illuminated the main room, the warmth of the fire contrasting with the cold of the night outside. The two of them sat on the couch, the room silent but charged with an energy that could only be described as a mix of relief and anticipation. They had been through so many trials, so many battles, and now, finally, they were together, living a moment of peace. But Alessia knew, deep down in her heart, that this peace was only temporary. The real fight was yet to come, the final battle against Lorenzo, and the weight of everything ahead could not be ignored.

Matteo was more relaxed than she had seen him in weeks, the stiffness in his shoulders lessened. He gazed into the fire, but his thoughts were clearly elsewhere, still processing the many decisions that awaited them. When he turned to face Alessia, his eyes held a mix of exhaustion and something else — something softer, more vulnerable, that she was beginning to see in him more often.

"I have a proposal for you, Alessia," Matteo said, his voice deep but carrying a tone of gentleness that wasn't usual for him. He moved closer, his eyes fixed on her as if he were weighing his words carefully, measuring each one. "Once we've taken care of everything with Lorenzo, once we've made sure we're safe... I want to leave here. I want to leave the city, leave all of this behind."

Alessia looked at him in surprise, her heart racing faster. She hadn't expected to hear that from Matteo, not now. But at the same time, something in his words touched a deep part of her. She knew he was speaking from the heart, and this sincerity moved her.

They had lived in the eye of the storm for so long, but now he was offering an escape, a possibility to rebuild their lives away from violence, away from chaos.

"Are you serious?" Alessia asked, the doubt in her voice mingled with hope. She wanted to believe him. She wanted to believe they could finally have the kind of life she'd always dreamed of, a future for their child, without the shadows of the mafia chasing them.

"Yes, Alessia," Matteo replied, his voice softer now. He took her hands, their fingers intertwining, and his eyes were locked onto hers with an intensity that she was starting to recognize as his trademark. "I want our life to no longer be defined by fear, by violence. I want us to look to the future and see something beyond the war, beyond the threats. And if we have to leave the city for that to happen, then that's what we'll do. I don't care where it is. As long as it's you, me, and our child. Wherever we can start over."

Those words sank deep into Alessia's heart. She hadn't realized how badly she needed to hear them until that moment. She had feared for so long that Matteo would lose himself in the war, that the hatred for Lorenzo would consume everything, even what they held most dear. But now he was offering her a future. And more than that, he was willing to leave everything behind to be with her, with their family. That sacrifice didn't go unnoticed by her.

"I want that too, Matteo," Alessia said, her eyes shining with emotion. She didn't know what the future held, but in that moment, she felt stronger than she ever imagined possible. "I want a life with you, with our family. And I know we'll fight for it."

They sat there, their eyes meeting in silent intensity. The past was full of shadows, of pain, but the future now seemed brighter, clearer than ever. Alessia knew there was a difficult road ahead, but as long as she was with Matteo, she felt that she could face anything. He had changed. The man she met at the start of their journey was so different from the man beside her now. He was willing to sacrifice everything for her, for them. And she was too.

Matteo leaned in slowly, as if every movement was carefully thought out but, at the same time, inevitable. When their lips met, it was a gentle kiss, but full of all the emotions that had built up between them. It was a kiss of renewal, of unspoken promises, and of a shared future. The intensity of the kiss grew as their bodies drew closer, as if every touch was an affirmation that despite the difficulties, they were still together. It was the promise that they would face whatever came — together.

Alessia gave in to the kiss, feeling the warmth of Matteo's body against hers, and the desire that had built up between them exploded in an overwhelming wave. She wanted him, desired him, and that moment was just for them. She no longer cared about the past, about the mistakes they'd made. They were recreating themselves there, in that moment, leaving behind the scars of a life filled with violence to build something new.

"I love you," Matteo whispered when they finally pulled apart, both of them breathless but with smiles on their lips. "And I will do everything I can, and more, to protect you. To protect our family."

Alessia touched his face, her fingers gently tracing the lines of his jaw, as if trying to memorize every detail of him. "I love you too, Matteo. And we'll make it. We'll have the life we deserve."

He kissed her again, with the same intensity, and for a moment, the world outside disappeared. There was nothing but them, the love they shared, and the promise that they would build something solid, something unbreakable. Peace was within reach, but before they could attain it, there was one last battle to fight. They were ready for it.

When they pulled apart, still holding hands, Matteo looked at her with a softer smile, almost shy, an expression rare in him that

Alessia loved to see. "Now we need to be ready for the final fight. Lorenzo won't give up easily. But we'll end this once and for all."

Alessia nodded, determined. "Together, Matteo. Always."

And as they prepared for the final confrontation, they felt more united than ever. They had found each other, and nothing could separate them now. No matter how difficult the road ahead, as long as they were side by side, they knew they could conquer anything. Their love made them unbeatable, and with that, they were ready to face whatever came.

Night fell over the DeLuca mansion, but within its walls, the atmosphere was far from gloomy. Matteo and Alessia were together, but there was an electric energy in the air, a tension that both warmed and challenged them. He was standing by the window, arms crossed, still holding an air of authority, but something in his eyes had changed. He felt the weight of responsibility on his shoulders, even more now that Alessia and the baby were so deeply involved in everything he had built. But deep inside, the most important thing to him was what he felt for her.

Alessia, on the other hand, sat on the couch, watching him with silent intensity. She knew him well enough to recognize that he was torturing himself with thoughts he wasn't sharing. She felt a mix of curiosity and concern, but also something deeper, something more. He was changing. She knew that. And even with the war and dangers surrounding them, there was a part of her that felt renewed by being with him. Being with Matteo, in a moment like this, despite everything that had happened, was more than she had ever imagined she could have. She had seen the relentless man, the mafia boss, and now she was seeing the man who cared deeply, who allowed himself to be touched by the pain of what they had lived through together.

"You seem distant," Alessia said, her voice soft, but with a hidden challenge. She was approaching him, and he noticed, even before she spoke, that her presence was surrounding him in a way he couldn't ignore.

He slowly turned around, his eyes fixed on her, but with a faint shadow of pain reflected in them. "I'm not distant, Alessia," he replied, his voice deep. "I'm just thinking."

"Thinking about what?" she asked, raising an eyebrow, challenging him with her gaze. It was the usual provocation, the one he knew so well, but this time, there was something different. She knew he was struggling with something inside.

"About everything," Matteo said, stepping forward, his eyes locking onto hers with an intensity he could no longer disguise. "About you, about me, about us. About everything we've built, about everything still to come."

She watched him, her body moving toward him without her even realizing. His words affected her in an unexpected way, stirring something deep within her. Matteo was grappling with the weight of love and responsibility, and she could see it. He was standing there, in front of her, more vulnerable than she ever imagined he could be. And, paradoxically, this only drew her closer.

"You don't have to carry the world on your shoulders, Matteo," Alessia said, now only a few steps away, her voice low but filled with silent intensity. "We're in this together, and that's how it should be. You're not alone."

He took a step toward her, his eyes never leaving hers. The tension between them was almost tangible, and when they were finally just inches apart, he tilted his head to study her face, his fingers lightly grazing her chin. Alessia didn't pull away. His strength, the pain she knew he carried, were part of him, and she would never see him the same way after everything they had shared.

"You know me too well," Matteo whispered, his voice now softer, almost a murmur. "But still, I can't help but lose myself in you."

She smiled gently, the provocation still present in her voice. "Maybe it's because you've always been good at losing yourself. But... I lost myself too, Matteo. And it was in you."

He couldn't resist. With a swift motion, he pulled her closer, his hands wrapping around her waist, and without another word, his lips found hers in a kiss that was more than desire. It was a meeting of souls, of two people who had faced more than they could imagine and who, now, were more united than ever. Their kiss was a silent promise, a guarantee that, no matter the scars or shadows of the past, they were still there, together, facing the future.

When they pulled apart, both breathless, Matteo's gaze still burned with intensity. "I want you, Alessia," he said, his voice husky. "And I want our life. I won't let anything separate us."

She looked into his eyes, her hand gently touching his chest, feeling his heartbeat quicken against her palm. She knew what he was saying. She knew how far he was willing to go to protect what they had. But at the same time, she also knew how dangerous it was to live in this world.

"I know, Matteo," Alessia replied, her voice full of tenderness but also challenge. "And I want you too. But we have to make sure the life you dream for us is possible. No more surprises, no more threats."

He smiled softly but with the usual intensity. "I promise you, Alessia. We'll fight together to make it happen. No matter what it takes."

She moved closer to him again, her eyes fixed on him. "Then let's do it. Let's face everything, together. There's no turning back."

And with those words, the weight of the decision silently settled over them. They were ready. The future was still uncertain, but as long as they were together, Matteo and Alessia knew they could face anything. Their love made them unbeatable. And when the final battle came, they wouldn't be alone.

# Chapter 81: The Inevitable Separation

The house was silent, but Alessia felt a growing pressure in her chest, as if she were trapped in an invisible chain. The days dragged on, slow and endless, without Matteo. He had become more and more distant, immersed in the demands of the mafia, the meetings, the threats, the alliances, and the power calculations. Every time she saw him leave, it felt as though a part of him stayed behind, and she no longer knew how to reach him. The conversations they had used to be intense, filled with promises, plans for the future—but now, they were short, cold, almost as if he were disconnecting from her and everything they had planned. And she no longer knew how to react to that.

Alessia sat in the living room, gazing out the window at the city lights beyond. The cold night air seeped through the glass, but it was nothing compared to the ice she felt in her heart. She loved him. She knew this with all her soul, but he was pulling away from her. And with each passing day, she felt a growing pain. The void between them seemed to expand with every silence, every word left unsaid, every action of Matteo's she wasn't involved in.

She stood up from the armchair, heading to the kitchen, trying to occupy herself with something. But her gaze inevitably fell on the table, where Matteo left his work papers, the documents from his meetings with allies and enemies. Everything seemed more important than her. More important than them. More important than the life they had dreamed of together, away from the violence of the mafia.

Alessia knew that Matteo believed he was doing the right thing. He was trying to protect her, protect them, by staying away from everything that represented danger. But what he didn't see—or what he refused to see—was that by distancing himself, he was creating a barrier between them. She didn't need protection from an absent man. She needed a man who would be by her side, by their child's side.

She didn't want just a distant husband who was sacrificing everything for a future she was starting to doubt. Alessia wanted him to be part of that future, for them to build it together. And, although she tried to resist, doubts began to creep into her thoughts. Did he still believe in the life they had planned? Did he still want that future? Or had he, deep down, given up on everything?

Matteo's footsteps echoed down the hallway, interrupting her thoughts. He entered the room with a tired expression, but upon seeing Alessia, his posture stiffened. Something in his expression told her that he was farther away than ever. She felt a pang of pain, but tried to maintain her composure.

"Matteo," she said, her voice soft, but with a tension that he quickly sensed. "We need to talk."

He sighed, his gaze vacant, tired. "Alessia, not now. I need—"

"No!" She interrupted, standing up quickly. "No, Matteo. I can't keep doing this."

He stopped, looking at her with a mixture of confusion and frustration. "What are you talking about?"

"What happened to us?" Alessia asked, her voice now filled with emotion, her eyes shining with frustration. "You pulled away, Matteo. You pulled away from me. From us. I reached out to you, and you... you just... disappeared. And I don't know how to keep going like this."

Matteo felt a tightness in his chest. He wanted to say something, wanted to apologize, but the words felt too heavy. He knew he was failing. But what could he do? He believed he was doing everything right, that he had to keep Alessia away from the violence, that it was best to keep the problems of his mafia life away from her. But she was right. He didn't know how to get close anymore. He was trying to protect her in a way that was pushing her away, and it was destroying him inside.

"I'm doing this to protect you, Alessia," he said, his voice firm but with an underlying pain. "You know I need to be there. I need to handle all of this to make sure you and the baby are safe. Don't you understand that?"

She shook her head, the tears threatening to fall, but she fought to keep her vulnerability hidden. "I understand, Matteo. I understand more than you think. But I can't live with a man who's always distant, who leaves me alone... forever. This isn't life. And you can't keep sacrificing yourself for something that's not even within your reach anymore."

He took a step toward her, his voice softer, almost desperate. "Alessia, I don't know how to make things right. I... I only know that I want to protect you, I want us to have a future. I can't see anything else beyond that."

"But what about us, Matteo?" She asked, her eyes fixed on his. "What about the love I always believed we shared? Do you still care about me? Or have you become so lost in your mafia life that you've forgotten who's been by your side?"

Matteo felt the weight of those words. He pulled away, as if he'd been physically struck. He wanted to say that he still cared, that she meant everything to him. But the truth was, he was lost, caught in a spiral of responsibilities and conflicting emotions. He no longer knew what to feel.

The silence between them was thick, and for a moment, Alessia felt as if the entire future she had imagined with him was crumbling. She looked at him, trying to find an answer, but the silence he maintained seemed more final than any word.

"Maybe... maybe it's better if we each go our own way," she said, the pain clear in her voice, the words coming out colder than she wanted. But the weight of disappointment made her say it.

Matteo stood frozen. He looked at her as though she had just dealt him a mortal blow. The silence dragged on for long seconds before he found his voice, but doubt and sadness were still there.

"Alessia..." He began, but the words didn't come out as he expected. What he wanted to say seemed meaningless. He didn't know what was happening, but he didn't want to lose her. And yet, he couldn't find the words to convince her that he was still with her.

Alessia, feeling the emptiness spreading between them, turned to leave, but before she could take a step, Matteo grabbed her hand. "Don't go," he said, his voice hoarse, his hand gripping hers tightly. "I don't know what to do, Alessia, but don't ask me to leave you. Not now."

She looked at him, her eyes still full of pain. "You've already left me, Matteo. You just didn't realize it."

Those words sank like a knife into his heart. She was right. He had left her alone, and now, he was trying to find a way back. But was it already too late?

Silence returned to the room, and the distance between them seemed vast, like an impossible border to cross.

The house was quiet, the only light coming from the flames in the fireplace, casting dancing shadows on the walls. Alessia stood by the window, her eyes fixed on the distant city lights. She felt a deep emptiness, as if she had been left behind in a world where everything she wanted most was slipping through her fingers. Matteo had pulled away, and with each passing day, she felt that abyss widening between them. He had become lost in his own inner conflicts, and she didn't know how to reach him.

The silence between them felt louder than any shout. Matteo, sitting in a corner of the room, watched her with his arms crossed, as if trying to gather the strength to speak, to explain himself. But he couldn't. The weight of responsibility for her and the baby's safety still tormented him. He had distanced himself because he believed it was the best thing for her, but in reality, he was distancing himself from himself, and more importantly, from everything he loved most. Alessia felt it, and the pain of seeing him silent, distant, cut deeper than any harsh words could.

She finally turned, her eyes meeting his, and something unspoken passed between them. It was a mix of hurt, love, and perhaps even a little anger. "You don't realize how much you're pushing me away, do you?" Alessia's voice was calm, but there was an underlying tension that Matteo couldn't ignore.

He slowly rose from the chair, as though every movement weighed more than the last. "I'm trying to protect you, Alessia. I thought... I thought you'd be safer this way. Away from the mafia's problems." Frustration was evident in his voice, but there was also a trace of regret he didn't know how to hide. He knew he was failing. But he didn't know how to fix it.

Alessia stepped closer, the usual provocation in her eyes. "Protect? Or run away? Because you pulled away from me, Matteo. You pulled away from our family. I need you by my side, not a man who only lives for war and enemies."

Matteo felt a knot in his stomach. Her words pierced deeply. He wanted to give her everything—the safety, the protection—but what she truly wanted, he no longer knew how to offer. He had let the weight of the mafia consume everything, and now he couldn't see clearly anymore.

"You don't understand. I'm doing this to make sure you're safe. That you and our child don't suffer what I went through, Alessia." The pain in his words was clear, but there was also a hint of pride, of trying to control everything around him, not realizing that by doing so, he was losing what he loved most.

She gave a low, almost bitter laugh and walked toward him, her body so close that the tension between them became palpable. "I don't need your protection, Matteo," she said with a sarcastic smile, her eyes flashing with both anger and desire. "I need you. The man who promised to fight by my side, not someone who hides from what matters most."

Matteo stood silent for a moment, and then, with an intensity Alessia didn't expect, he pulled her closer, his lips crashing onto hers with a desperate urgency. The kiss was fierce, filled with the pain, the frustration of everything he couldn't express. But in that kiss, she could feel everything he wasn't saying: the longing, the regret, the fear of losing her.

Alessia surrendered to the kiss, her hands touching his face, feeling the rough texture of his skin, the tense muscles under her palms. They pulled away for a moment, their eyes meeting with the same intensity, now softer.

"I love you, Alessia. I don't know what to do anymore, but I know I can't live without you."

She looked at him, her voice lower, filled with a mix of emotion and pain. "I love you too, Matteo. But you're losing me. And that hurts more than anything."

They stood there, looking at each other, breathing together, as if time had stopped for a brief moment. They both knew their inner battle wasn't over, but at that instant, there was a chance to reconnect, to rebuild everything that seemed lost. And that, more than any external threat, made them ready to face whatever came next.

The passion between them hadn't died. On the contrary, it was more alive than ever, mixed with the scars and fears they had shared. And yet, Matteo and Alessia knew that their future depended on a simple, but powerful understanding: that despite the challenges, they would always fight for each other.

# Chapter 82: A Glimpse of Betrayal

Alessia felt the pain in her chest like a constant presence. After the last argument with Matteo, she had tried to distance herself, to think clearly about everything that was happening. She knew the situation between them was tense, filled with heavy silences. There were nights when she searched for him, but he was always absorbed, distant, preoccupied with the mafia, the threats, the war that seemed endless. But more than that, what hurt her the most was the feeling of being left behind, as if she was no longer his priority. It consumed her, even though she tried to hide it. She loved Matteo, and it tortured her. But he was changing—or perhaps it was her who had changed, stronger, more fragile, more distant.

It was on a cold morning that she decided to leave. She put on a warm jacket and stepped outside, wandering aimlessly, needing to breathe, to think, to take a moment for herself. The city was calm, the biting wind blowing through the empty streets. The silence around her should have been comforting, but she couldn't shake the weight in her heart. The truth was, she felt like she could no longer deceive herself—something was happening. Something she didn't want to admit, but knew was there, hidden, lurking. The time between her and Matteo stretched like a loose rope, ready to snap.

As she walked through the streets, her thoughts lost in herself, a vision made her stop in the middle of the sidewalk. It was Matteo. He was sitting at a café, talking with Bianca. The two were too close, closer than she wished to see. Bianca was smiling with that enthusiastic expression Alessia knew all too well, and the touch between them was casual, but intense enough to set Alessia's mind racing. Bianca's hand rested on Matteo's arm, a subtle touch, but with an intimacy that made Alessia feel a sharp pang in her chest. As if the very ground beneath her feet was crumbling.

Alessia stood there, frozen, watching the scene without being seen. The cold in her hands seemed to spread throughout her body. She knew she was probably misinterpreting things, that maybe everything was harmless, but the insecurity consuming her left no room for doubt. Matteo was with her, he was always with her, but... Bianca. Always Bianca. Always lurking, always present, always trying to get closer to him, in one way or another.

She closed her eyes for a moment, trying to contain the tears threatening to fall. What she was seeing didn't seem like just a conversation. It didn't seem like a simple friendship or a moment of support. No, it was more. They were so close, almost as if they were in a parallel world where Alessia didn't exist. Her stomach churned, and the feeling of betrayal washed over her. Not physically—she knew nothing had happened between them on that level. But emotionally... Matteo was leaving her for Bianca, in some way. She felt small, powerless, like a spectator in her own life.

The scene continued to unfold before her, and no matter how much she tried to convince herself that she was overreacting, she couldn't. Something inside her had broken. She turned abruptly and walked away from the café, her body tense, her mind a whirlwind of emotions. The pain was unbearable, a tight knot in her throat that barely allowed her to breathe.

She didn't know where she was going, only that she needed to get away. She walked through the streets aimlessly, her heart pounding, each step heavier than the last. Her thoughts were singular: if he was with Bianca, then maybe she had been wrong all along. Maybe she wasn't the one for Matteo anymore, and he had already found something—or someone—that completed him in a way she never could. Alessia felt the desperation rise, the weight of her doubts and insecurities suffocating her. She couldn't stay, she couldn't continue like this.

She returned to the mansion, but instead of seeking out Matteo, she isolated herself in her room. She looked around, at the familiar walls that had once been her home, but now seemed like a prison. Things were different. She was different. And Matteo... Matteo had changed in a way she couldn't comprehend. Or maybe it wasn't him who had changed, but her. Maybe that was it. What they had seemed too fragile now. The promises made, the vows for a future together, felt empty, broken. It was as if the love they had once shared was now a flame dying out, unable to be rekindled.

The sound of footsteps in the distance made her stand up. She knew who it was, but she didn't want to see him. Matteo appeared at the door, and his expression was hard to read. He looked at her, his eyes heavy with a tension she didn't know if she could bear. "Alessia, we need to talk," he said, and the pain in his voice was evident, but not more than hers.

She slowly rose, her chest tight. "There's nothing to talk about, Matteo," she replied, her voice firm but tinged with sadness. She couldn't pretend everything was fine anymore, that things would go back to normal. Something inside her had broken.

"I saw you with Bianca," Alessia said, the words coming out colder than she would have liked. "She's always near you, always insinuating herself between us, and you seem... comfortable with that." She felt the knot in her throat tighten further. "I can't keep going like this, Matteo. I can't live in this game where all you do is leave me behind."

Matteo looked at her, a flicker of understanding passing through his eyes. He stepped forward, but Alessia interrupted him, raising her hand, asking for distance. "I need time. I need space," she said, her voice trembling at the end, as if she herself were breaking. "I don't know who to trust anymore."

The silence that followed was heavy. They stood there, facing each other, but in completely different worlds. Alessia felt completely alone, even with Matteo there in front of her. She felt as though she had already lost everything, as if all they had built together was not enough to overcome the uncertainties that now separated them. And while he watched her, not knowing what to say, Alessia knew, deep in her heart, that she couldn't stay there anymore. She needed to follow her own path, even if it meant leaving behind the man she still loved. She couldn't live with the shadows of betrayal, even if it was just emotional.

"I'm leaving," she said, her words soft, but firm. "I can't stay here anymore."

# Chapter 83: Decision to Leave

Alessia moved through the mansion like a shadow, her trembling hands packing the few things she had decided to take with her. There was no more space for words, for explanations, for broken promises. Every item she placed into the suitcase seemed heavier, as if she were packing not only clothes but the last remnants of a life that no longer made sense. The house, which had been her refuge for so long, now suffocated her. The walls, once welcoming, now seemed imposing and cold, as though they were waiting for the moment to expel her.

She had written a letter—a short, direct note explaining the inevitable. "I need to leave. I can't be a second choice in your life." The small, impersonal handwriting on the paper seemed almost a reflection of everything she felt: pain, anger, and indescribable sadness. She knew Matteo would read the words, but she also knew he wouldn't try to stop her from leaving. Not this time. The trust she once had in his feelings seemed to have evaporated, and deep down, Alessia knew that what she had feared had come true: Matteo was too far gone, and what she had seen with Bianca couldn't be ignored.

She looked out the window; the familiar view of the DeLuca mansion now felt distant, as if it no longer belonged to her. Her steps through the house were silent but heavy, as though each one was burying a piece of the life she had imagined beside Matteo. And despite all the pain that consumed her, Alessia couldn't help the small flicker of hope still beating in her chest. Part of her hoped that he would come after her, that he would seek her out, that something in his heart would stir him to realize the gravity of what was happening. But as the silence stretched on, that hope faded. Matteo didn't come. And she knew he wouldn't. The man she loved was now so lost in his own struggles that he couldn't see the pain he was causing her.

Alessia picked up the suitcase, the letter left on the table, and took one last look at what had once been her home. She was broken, but she couldn't stay anymore. She couldn't live in the shadow of something that no longer existed, of a love she feared she had lost. "I need to go," she whispered to herself, like a prayer. She walked to the door, her steps echoing in the quiet house. The key turned in the lock, and as she opened the door, the fresh night air rushed in, filling the emptiness around her. Alessia hesitated for a moment, feeling the weight of her decision, but then she stepped through the door and closed it behind her.

The cold outside enveloped her like a chilly cloak, and she took a deep breath, trying to hold back the tears. It wasn't just the goodbye to Matteo, but the goodbye to everything she had thought would be her life. The path ahead seemed dark and uncertain, but she knew there was no other choice. She needed to move on. For the baby, for her own survival, for the chance to start over.

Alessia took a taxi and went to a small town a few hours away. A quiet place where no one knew who she was, and where the violence of the mafia seemed distant. She had chosen this place for its sense of anonymity, of a new beginning. But deep down, she knew it would be impossible to erase the past. The longing for Matteo wouldn't disappear. And the love—this deep, visceral love she felt for him—would continue to throb in her chest, like a painful echo.

She arrived in the town and rented a small apartment. Nothing extravagant, nothing that would draw attention. Just a simple place where she could take care of herself and the baby. Life there was quiet, but with each passing day, Alessia felt the weight of loneliness grow. She missed Matteo, but more than that, she missed the trust she had once had in him. The nights were the hardest, when she found herself alone, with the silence around her and the memory of the man she still loved, but who now seemed like a distant shadow.

The days passed, and Alessia tried to adjust to her new routine, attempting to ignore the emptiness in her heart. But there was no denying that Matteo's absence was a part of every moment. She saw him in every street, on every corner. She felt the echo of his touch, his words, and even the silences they had shared. They had been so intense, so passionate, that she wondered if she could really move on without him.

However, while she tried to heal her wounds, something in her heart knew that the cycle between her and Matteo hadn't ended. She felt, deep down, that their love couldn't be erased so easily. But she didn't know if he would be able to find her again. And, more painfully, she didn't know if she would ever be able to trust him like she had before.

One peaceful afternoon, while Alessia was sitting in a local café, gazing out at the sea, she saw something that made her stop. It wasn't Matteo—but the mere fact of being here, away from everything, trying to find peace, still felt like a blow to her own identity. She was running away from everything that hurt her, but the love she felt for Matteo could never be forgotten.

The weight of what she had left behind, what still might be rebuilt, haunted her constantly. She knew she had made the right decision for her own survival, but as she looked out at the horizon, Alessia also knew there was something more at stake: an unfulfilled promise, a love that had never been fully lived. She didn't know what the future held, but the only certainty she had in that moment was that, to move forward, she first had to deal with the pain Matteo had left in her heart.

It was impossible to forget the intensity of what she had felt, of what they had lived. But what would make her move on? What did she really want now?

Alessia walked through the small town where she had sought refuge, the quiet streets contrasting with the turmoil of emotions inside her. Each step seemed to echo in the silence around her, but her heart was far away, still stuck at that mansion, with the man she loved. Matteo. The man who had promised her a future, but who, in that moment, seemed lost to her.

Time had been cruel to her feelings. She tried to convince herself that she was doing the right thing, that the distance between them was necessary for her own peace and for the safety of the baby she carried. But there was something in her chest that never calmed, a deep longing, a silent pain, that only Matteo's presence could ease. She could feel his absence like a constant shadow, as though he were there, but at the same time, so far away.

The memories of him haunted her in the most unexpected moments. His touch, the warmth of his hand holding hers; the way he looked at her, as if she were the only person who mattered in the world. The way he had this possessive yet tender look. She closed her eyes, remembering the last time he kissed her, when she thought they had finally broken through the barriers between them. The kiss had been fierce, but also filled with unspoken promises. She knew he loved her—but something had changed.

She stopped for a moment, looking out at the sea ahead. The gentle breeze brushed against her face, but it didn't ease the heat in her chest. The loneliness, the longing, and the frustration were almost tangible. The life she had planned, with Matteo by her side, seemed to have vanished in the blink of an eye, like sand slipping through her fingers. And the only thing left now was uncertainty. What do you do when the love you feel for someone is mixed with pain and betrayal? When you feel like you can't even trust your own heart anymore?

Meanwhile, Matteo was back at the mansion, sitting in his office, his eyes fixed on the papers before him, but his mind elsewhere. He was tired. Tired of the constant war, the threats from Lorenzo, of being the mafia boss, but, above all, tired of not having Alessia by his side. The distance she had put between them tormented him. Each day that passed, he felt her slipping farther away, growing colder, and it ate at him from the inside.

He knew that what he had done to her couldn't be undone easily. He had pushed her away because he thought he was doing the right thing, that he needed to protect her from his life, from the dangers of the mafia. But in doing so, he had lost her. And worst of all, he had lost her to himself. His pride and stubbornness had created a chasm between them, and now, as he desperately tried to get closer, he didn't know how to reach her heart.

Matteo slammed his hand on the desk, frustrated with himself. He was at war with himself. His loyalty to his organization, to his family, kept him from doing what his heart screamed for. What if it was too late? What if Alessia didn't want him anymore? He didn't know. But what he did know for certain was that he couldn't get rid of her, the love he felt for her. Every minute without her, he felt emptier, more lost. The memory of her smile, the softness of her skin, the strength with which she challenged him—all of it consumed him.

He got up from the chair and walked to the window, looking out at the horizon. What he wanted most at that moment was to see Alessia, talk to her, apologize, beg her to come back to him. But he knew he couldn't just go to her and expect everything to be like before. He needed to do more. He needed to show her that he still loved her, that he was willing to change, to set aside the things that separated them. He needed to show her that, despite being the mafia boss, he could be the man she had always wanted—a man who would do anything for her.

With that thought in mind, Matteo decided he would do whatever it took to win Alessia back. He knew the road would be hard, that he would have to fight not just against his enemies, but against his own demons. But he didn't care. He wanted her back.

However, as he was immersed in these conflicting emotions, the door to his office opened, and Bianca walked in, as always, with her enigmatic smile and the confidence of someone who had always known how to make Matteo feel in control.

"Matteo, are you alright?" she asked, her voice soft and attentive.

Matteo looked at her, realizing what she was trying to do, and how she was always there, trying to infiltrate his life, always trying to take Alessia's place. He felt a pang of irritation, but also a sense of doubt. Bianca was always there when he needed support. She was his ally, but she had never been the woman he loved. She had never been Alessia.

"I don't need you right now, Bianca," he answered, his voice firm, but with a tone of exhaustion he couldn't hide. "I just need... time."

Bianca fell silent for a moment, her eyes studying him. "You're still thinking about her, aren't you?"

Matteo didn't respond immediately, but his eyes betrayed the confusion he felt. "She's gone, Bianca. And no matter how much I want that to change, I don't know if she'll come back."

Bianca gave a small smile, which Matteo knew was another of her manipulation attempts. "You know I'll always be here for you, Matteo. Always."

But even with her words, Matteo couldn't shake the feeling that the only place he really wanted to be was with Alessia. She was still the woman he loved. And maybe it was time to fight for that, for her, once and for all.

# Chapter 84: The New Life Away

Alessia's new life was distant, both physically and emotionally, from everything she had known before. The small, simple apartment in a coastal town was far from Matteo's mansion, and far from the intrigues and dangers that had followed her. But at the same time, this new beginning felt like a burden, more than a real chance at starting over. In a place where she had no luxury of familiarity, Alessia found herself completely alone, and the emptiness in her heart seemed to echo off the empty walls around her.

She spent her days organizing the few items she had brought with her, trying to create a routine for herself and for the baby growing inside her. The pregnancy, which had initially been a promise of a new future, now seemed like a constant reminder of everything she had lost. At night, when exhaustion finally overtook her, she would lie down, and the memory of Matteo would emerge again, more alive than ever. The warmth of his arms around her, the way he touched her with an intensity she had never known, and, most of all, the moments of vulnerability she never imagined seeing in a man like him.

"Did he really love me?" Alessia whispered to herself, eyes closed, slow breath. Sometimes, she wanted to believe that the distance he had placed between them wasn't his fault, but the world he was immersed in. She had seen him with Bianca, yes, and saw the touch, the closeness, but what if it was just a facade, a way to maintain control, like he always did? Or maybe, as she feared, his feelings for her had never been as deep as hers for him.

That painful doubt consumed her. And pride, which had made her leave the mansion and hide herself in a distant corner, only worsened the feeling of loss. Alessia was sure she could never go back now, that she could never expose her fragility, even though the desire to be embraced by him again was overwhelming. The memories of Matteo haunted her, and she didn't know whether to give in to them or distance herself once and for all.

The coastal town, though charming and peaceful, was a prison of memories. She walked through the simple streets, trying to blend in with the people, but with every step, the thought of Matteo resurfaced. Sometimes, while shopping at the local market or strolling through the small shops, she felt that the world around her made no sense without him. Alessia tried to push the thoughts away, to not feel, but the baby inside her and the unrequited love kept her in a constant whirlwind of emotions.

It was on an autumn afternoon, while Alessia walked along the deserted beach, that she found some distraction. A man, perhaps in his thirties, approached her with a friendly smile. He had a backpack and a camera, clearly a tourist, and started talking about the beauty of the town. Alessia, reluctant but polite, smiled shyly in response. It was a small relief, something new for her.

"Are you here alone?" he asked, unaware that the question touched a still-open wound.

"Yes, I am... trying to start over," Alessia replied, trying to control the emotion that threatened to escape.

The man smiled, offering her a sympathetic look. "I know what it's like to start over. I've been through it. Sometimes, you just need a little time and a quiet place."

Alessia nodded, mentally thanking him for being so simple, so harmless. They talked for a few minutes, and although he tried to ask questions about her life, Alessia kept her distance, sharing only what was necessary. When he said goodbye, she felt a mix of relief and guilt. He was not Matteo. He could never be. And her longing for Matteo, no matter how much she tried to bury it, only grew.

Meanwhile, at the mansion, Matteo couldn't escape his own anguish. The decision to push her away, to let her go without fighting for her, gnawed at him. He thought of her constantly, even when surrounded by his men and mafia commitments. But now, with what he feared most, he knew he had lost Alessia. The pain of seeing her leave, of not having fought to get her back, consumed him slowly.

He stood motionless for long minutes, staring out the office window, a soft breeze coming through the glass. The memories of Alessia were vivid. He saw her, fragile and strong at the same time, in his mind. She had been everything to him, and he had destroyed that. His inaction, his need to control the situation with pride and the mafia, had made him lose her.

Matteo didn't know what to do. He knew where she was, had the town and the location of her refuge, but what would he do when he saw her again? How could he repair the irreparable mistake? The voice in his head haunted him: "She won't forgive you." He already knew that.

One night, he went for a walk through the city. He passed the old square where they had once strolled together, the place where he had first let himself be vulnerable and open with her. How he wished to go back to that moment. To feel her warmth, her gentle touch on his skin, as if the world around them didn't exist. But reality was right in front of him, and the pain he felt knowing that she had distanced herself, that he had lost her, made everything feel futile.

In his solitude, he thought of calling her, of trying to reach out to her, but shame stopped him. He knew she didn't want him anymore. The pride, that same pride that had driven her away, now prevented him from doing what his heart truly desired.

On one of his walks through the city, he realized something: he still loved her. He still wanted her. But did she feel the same? Was there any chance of rebuilding what they had lost? Or was it too late?

He was in an alley, near a café they used to stop at, when he saw a familiar figure across the street. Matteo's heart raced, his body paralyzed for a moment. He looked again, and the silhouette was unmistakable. Alessia.

What would he do? How could he approach her now?

He took a deep breath, knowing this would be his last chance to make things right. He knew he couldn't wait any longer.

Matteo stared out the window of his office, the view that had always been familiar now seeming strange and distant. He knew that, within his own mind, the war he was fighting with himself was fiercer than any battle he had fought as the mafia boss. Alessia was out of his reach, and it was eating him up inside. He could feel the loss like a constant presence, a shadow that stretched over his days and nights.

He leaned back in the chair, closing his eyes for a moment, trying to recall the days when she was by his side. The warmth of her presence, the way she challenged him, how he saw himself losing to her, and how, at the same time, she made him want to be better, even though he didn't know how. The last time he touched her, when their lips met, he felt that their lives had something more, something beyond the shadows that surrounded them. But now, everything seemed like a distant dream, a reality he couldn't reach.

And the most vivid memory of all: Alessia in his arms, her eyes filled with trust but also pain. He knew she had believed in him, believed in what he promised, and he had failed. And that failure consumed him. The coldness of his attitude now, pushing her away when he should have pulled her close, felt unbearable. The thought that she might now be living somewhere far from him, with the child he never knew existed, only made the guilt heavier.

The phone rang, interrupting his thoughts, but Matteo didn't want to answer. He just wanted to stay there, alone, with his own ghosts. But he knew he couldn't. He needed to act, to regain control of his life, and for that, he knew he had to face what he had left behind — Alessia.

However, in the town where Alessia was hiding, loneliness also took hold of her. She had tried to convince herself that she had done the right thing by leaving, by cutting ties with Matteo, but her heart was shattered. She walked the streets, trying to settle into the routine, but every step seemed to take her farther from him, and it destroyed her inside. The memory of his touch still burned her skin, and the thought of losing everything she had loved most felt like a sharp blade cutting through her soul.

She didn't know what to do with the emptiness Matteo had left. Sometimes, she believed that if he had come after her, if he had shown that he missed her, maybe she would have given in. But he didn't. And that made her feel like there was no room for regrets, for second chances. She wanted to be strong, but the fear of giving herself to him again, of suffering again, made her pull away from the idea of seeking him out.

That afternoon, while walking through the streets of the small town where she was trying to start over, Alessia found a cozy café and, without thinking much, went in. The aroma of fresh coffee and the warmth of the small shop gave her some comfort, but her heart was still heavy. She sat at a table by the window and ordered coffee, trying not to think about everything she had lost. But as she looked out the window, a familiar movement caught her attention.

She froze. Her eyes locked on Matteo across the street. He was standing there, as if looking for something... or someone. Her heart raced, but she couldn't believe he was really there. "He didn't come after me before, why now?" she thought, her mind struggling against the desire to believe that he still loved her.

Matteo seemed lost in his own thoughts, but there was something in his gaze that made her feel a spark of hope. Maybe he had come to her. Maybe he had finally understood. However, doubt took over Alessia, and she stayed there, unsure whether to go to him or remain in her hiding place, protecting herself from another disappointment.

She took a sip of the coffee, the bitter taste filling her mouth, reflecting on how bitter her life had become since he left her. No, he wouldn't look for her, she thought. Matteo would never come after her if she wasn't his priority.

But Matteo, across the street, couldn't ignore the pain of being without Alessia any longer. The sight of her, there, in his town, distant from him, caused a deep sensation in his chest. He knew he couldn't stay still any longer; he needed to act now. She was right in front of him, and he wasn't going to let her slip away again.

With his heart pounding, Matteo crossed the street and entered the café, his steps firm and determined. He saw her at the table, head lowered, somewhat distracted, as if trying to avoid the world around her. He walked slowly toward her, and when Alessia looked up, their eyes met — shock, surprise, and, above all, the unfulfilled desire still pulsing between them.

"Do you really think you can forget me like this?" Matteo asked in a low, raspy voice, the pain of months without her evident in every word.

Alessia tried to keep her composure, but the heat in her face betrayed her attempt to mask her emotions. "What are you doing here, Matteo?"

"I don't know what I'm doing anymore, Alessia," he replied, sincerity in his eyes. "But I know what I want. And what I want is you. I've always been an idiot, and because of that, I almost lost you. But I won't let that happen again."

The silence between them was palpable, but before Alessia could respond, he reached out and took her hand, holding it with the force of someone who couldn't wait any longer.

"I can't promise that things will be easy, but I promise that, if you let me, I'll never let you go again."

Alessia felt his words like a promise, but she didn't know if she could believe in them again. The love she felt for Matteo was something so strong, but at the same time, the fear of pain paralyzed her.

"Do you really want this, Matteo?" she asked, her voice trembling. "Do you want to risk everything again for us? For me?"

"Yes," he replied without hesitation. "I would risk my life for you and for our child."

It was the answer she had expected, but she didn't know if she was ready to take the next step. Matteo, sensing her hesitation, leaned in closer, his lips almost touching hers. "You don't have to decide now," he whispered. "But give me a chance, Alessia. Just one."

And at that moment, Alessia felt his warmth fill her body, the proximity of his lips causing a whirlwind of emotions. She didn't know what the future held, but something inside her told her that, as painful as it might be, maybe it was time to give herself — and him — one last chance.

# Chapter 85: A Protector in the Shadows

Matteo was lost. Alessia's letter had pierced his chest irreparably, like a sharp blade tearing away something he hadn't even known he still had. Her words echoed in his mind, one after the other, a silent torture forcing him to confront his guilt. He knew he had lost her. She believed he had betrayed her, that his relationship with Bianca meant something more than he had tried to explain, and that had shattered any trust she had left in him. The weight of guilt was crushing, and he felt as though he couldn't breathe with every passing second.

As the pain consumed him, Matteo knew he couldn't let her go forever. Anger and pride had been greater than the love he felt for her, but now, he saw it clearly. He had failed her at crucial moments, and it had nearly destroyed everything they could have been. He stood frozen, staring at the letter, its words blurring in front of his eyes, while his heart bled from the loss.

"I never imagined you would see me like this..."

He closed his eyes and took a deep breath, trying to push aside the frustration. There was no more time to mourn. He knew what he had to do. If she had left him, there was nothing he could do to change that now, but there was still something he could control: ensuring she was safe, making sure the world of shadows he controlled never touched her again. He would do whatever it took to protect her, even if she never knew.

Using his connections in the city, Matteo began tracking Alessia. Every movement she made, every place she frequented, he knew. He watched her from afar, like an invisible shadow, trying to make sure she had the freedom to live without the dangers her life alongside him had always brought. He didn't want to invade her privacy, but he knew that without him, Alessia would be vulnerable to all the dangers she couldn't foresee.

In her new city, Alessia was trying to adjust to her new reality. She felt like a stranger in a foreign place, but at the same time, she felt a rare and welcome peace. The place was quiet, and she was finally beginning to form friendships, though inside, she still felt somewhat lost. Sometimes, she would wake up in the middle of the night with the feeling that something was wrong, but she could never pinpoint what it was. The pain from the past seemed to fade with the routine, but she couldn't stop thinking about Matteo.

What Matteo didn't know was that, even far from him, Alessia still felt connected to him in ways she couldn't understand. The pain of leaving him never went away. Sometimes, when she looked out the window of the small apartment she lived in, she wondered if he was out there, waiting for her, if he had felt her absence. But she couldn't go back. What had happened between them was already marked and engraved in her heart, and she knew she couldn't trust him completely anymore.

She walked the streets, trying to live her life without being consumed by the shadows of the past, but the weight of the decision she had made lingered. The future, which should have been a promise of freedom and a fresh start, now seemed like an unknown path, and she didn't know what to expect. She kept a smile for others, but the loneliness crept into every moment she was alone with her thoughts.

Meanwhile, Matteo watched from afar. He had eyes on her, always, discreetly. In a local café, he saw her talk to new people. He watched from his position, far enough away so she wouldn't see him, but close enough to ensure that no one else knew what was happening. Alessia seemed happy. Or at least, she appeared to be. He knew she was trying to move on, but he could see the internal struggle in her eyes.

Matteo felt a pang of regret as he saw her smile at the others. He wished he were there beside her, wishing he could be the reason for that smile, but he knew he had lost her. She wanted nothing more to do with him, and that was the harsh reality.

But the pain of seeing her so distant made him make a decision: he would protect Alessia from the shadows in which he lived, even if she never knew. He would remain vigilant, continue eliminating any threat that could arise against her, because, in some way, he still believed that deep down, she still loved him. And maybe, one day, when she was able to look at him without pain, he would be there.

Alessia still found herself thinking about Matteo, but there was something that kept her from giving in to those thoughts. He had hurt her, and her trust in him had shattered. She couldn't trust a man who had seemed so distant, so caught up in his own life and the people he was involved with. She thought, perhaps, she was stronger than she had imagined. It was easier to distance herself from everything that had been destructive. And still, something in her heart whispered that maybe she had made the greatest mistake of her life by leaving.

The pain was constant, but she tried to ignore it. What kept her strong was the certainty that, at least, she was protecting the baby, and for him, she would do anything. Even if Matteo never came looking for her, even if he never realized how much she still loved him, Alessia was determined to move forward. She could no longer live in a world of uncertainty and distrust.

But even without knowing it, Matteo was there, in every step she took, in the shadows, making sure she was safe, even if it meant continuing to live with the pain of losing the only love he had ever known.

She would never know, but Matteo's sacrifice was, in a way, the greatest gift he could give. His love was still there, quiet and discreet, protecting her, loving her in silence, waiting, perhaps, for the day when she would look at him again.

Alessia woke up early that cold morning, the sky still cloudy and the city silent. The small, simple apartment was a reflection of the life she was trying to rebuild away from the chaos. She had grown accustomed to the solitary routine, but even so, the emptiness in her chest never dissipated. What bothered her the most was the feeling of living in limbo, not knowing if she was making the right choice by moving forward or if there was still something unresolved about Matteo.

With a sigh, she got up and walked to the window, looking at the street below. Her mind wandered back to the past, to the moments she had lived with Matteo. That man who made her laugh and cry, who challenged her, and at the same time, protected her. He had always had that power over her, a power she hated but, deep down, made her feel alive.

Suddenly, her mind was flooded with the memory of their last glance, that look full of pain and regret. He knew he had lost her, but something in Alessia still wasn't ready to say goodbye completely. Still, she knew she couldn't go back. There were things between them that would never be resolved, and the trust she had in their love was gone, destroyed by the coldness and lies that had piled up over time.

As she dressed, she thought about how much easier it would have been if he had run after her, if he had shown that he wanted her back. But Matteo, as always, had his pride, his impulsive temperament. She knew he would never humble himself for her, not in the way she wanted. What he showed was a possessive, impetuous love, something that no longer aligned with the peace she longed for. She didn't want to be anyone's possession, not even Matteo's.

Outside, the sounds of the city began to intensify. She grabbed her bag, made a quick coffee, and stepped out into the street. With every step, her heart ached, and she tried to convince herself that she was doing the right thing. The place where she lived now, that little refuge, was her new home, but it could never replace what Matteo had represented to her.

Meanwhile, on the other side of the city, Matteo was immersed in his own thoughts. The office was quiet, the only light coming from the lamp above his desk. He had an open file, but his mind was far away, lost in memories of Alessia. He missed her in a way he couldn't describe. What bothered him the most was the certainty that she had abandoned him because of a mistake of his, a mistake he still didn't know how to fix.

Matteo knew her decision to leave had been influenced by many things, but what he couldn't bear was the idea of not being able to protect the woman he loved. Alessia was vulnerable, and he couldn't do anything about it. His heart was at war, torn between the pride of being the mafia boss, the invincible man, and the man who longed for something more, for her. She had been the only one to make him question everything he believed to be right, the only one who had broken down the walls he had built around his life.

The phone on his desk buzzed, interrupting his thoughts, but Matteo didn't answer. He was lost, drowning in his own guilt. Every second without Alessia, without knowing how she was, made his pain grow.

He stood up abruptly, the chair creaking against the wooden floor. He walked to the window of his office, looking out over the city he controlled, but now it felt empty without her. Where are you, Alessia? he thought. And what have I lost?

It was then that a memory flooded his mind: their last kiss. He still felt the softness of her lips, the heat, the urgency. I love her, Matteo thought, his heart tight. He knew it now, but he had never had the courage to admit it to himself until that moment. His pride had always stopped him from being vulnerable, and now it was destroying him.

Alessia walked through the streets of the city, the cold breeze hitting her face. The coffee she had drunk in the morning was starting to kick in, but it wasn't enough to dispel the emotional exhaustion that consumed her. She didn't know what she was waiting for. Maybe for Matteo to find her, for him to somehow realize that he had lost her. But she knew that was just an illusion, that he would never come back.

But her heart still ached when she thought about him, and every thought of Matteo only left her more confused. Why do I still think about him? She tried to distract herself with the movement around her, but the feeling of loss never left her mind.

Then, she saw him.

He was standing across the street, his imposing figure silhouetted against the soft light of the late afternoon. Matteo. Alessia stopped in the middle of the sidewalk, her heart racing. Their eyes met for a brief moment, and the intensity of that look made her feel like time had stopped. She tried to shake off the feeling, but it was impossible. He was there, and something inside her wanted to run to him, to demand explanations, to ask for answers.

But doubt paralyzed her. Did he feel the same? She watched him for a second longer, but then turned, hurrying away in the opposite direction. I can't do this, she thought. I can't be vulnerable again.

But as she walked, a part of her heart knew that, no matter how much she tried to run, something between her and Matteo would never die.

As she moved further away, Matteo watched her from a distance, feeling the same excruciating pain. He wanted to shout her name, run to her, but pride still held him back. He knew that, despite everything, the way back to her wouldn't be easy, and maybe it was too late.

The love between them, intense and devastating, was still there. But what could remain of it when trust had been shattered so many times?

# Chapter 86: The Confession of Love

The cold wind cut through the night's silence as Matteo sped down the road, his mind fixed on Alessia. He couldn't bear the pain of her absence any longer. The weight of guilt consumed him with every kilometer he traveled. For days, he had tried to push aside the feelings he still carried for her, convincing himself that life would be easier without the ties that bound them. But the more he tried, the more he felt something inside him breaking. His pride, the hurts, the doubts—now they all seemed like unnecessary burdens. He needed her. He needed to tell her the truth, open his heart, put his pride aside, and beg for forgiveness.

He stopped in front of the small apartment where Alessia had been hiding, her presence there, even in the most discreet way, made his chest tighten. She was there, living a life without him, trying to move on, perhaps even believing he had left her behind. And, in a way, he had—because of arrogance, broken trust, unaddressed mistakes. But what Matteo didn't know was that, deep down, love had never left him. He had always known that, somehow, Alessia was his reason, his loss, and his salvation.

Matteo got out of the car, the decision already made. He didn't know what the future held for them, but at that moment, there was only one thing to do: go to her and tell her the truth, from the depths of his heart, with no more lies or fears.

Alessia was in her kitchen, preparing a cup of tea when she heard the familiar sound of a car pulling up. She froze for a moment, her heart racing. She didn't want to deceive herself, but something in her chest still tightened when he was near. When she heard the steps approaching the door, she didn't have the courage to open it.

She knew who it was, and somehow, her body sensed it before she even saw him. Matteo. He was there. After so much time, he had finally decided to take the step she had feared. Or maybe not. Alessia knew her pride and anger had driven him away, but deep down, she wanted him to come to her. She wanted to know, at least, if he still felt anything.

He knocked on the door, three firm knocks, as though he knew this was the moment. Alessia took a deep breath, trying to summon the strength not to give in to the impulse to open it immediately. But there was no denying it anymore. She knew the answer wouldn't come from words, but from actions. She needed to see if he was still the man she had fallen in love with, or if, over time, he had become something unrecognizable to her.

She opened the door slowly. Time seemed to stop. Matteo was there, darker and more intense than she remembered. His eyes were fixed on her, and a silent pain hovered in his gaze. She studied him, the conflicting feelings inside her, but before she could say anything, he began to speak.

"Alessia," he said in a hoarse voice, almost out of breath. "I know I don't deserve even a second of your attention. I know I've made mistakes, caused you pain, and that, deep down, I'm the one to blame for our separation. I... I thought I was doing the right thing, trying to keep you away from my dirty, ruined worlds, but in the end, I ended up pushing you away. From us." He took a step forward, and although his posture was firm, his shoulders carried the weight of shame.

Alessia felt her heart tighten, but she couldn't give in right away. She knew she had to be strong. "Do you really think words can fix all this?" she asked, her voice quieter than she wanted. "You made me believe in something that, in the end, wasn't true. I... I can't be the second option, Matteo."

"I know," he murmured. "But, Alessia, believe me, you were never second. I was so blinded by pain and pride that I couldn't see how much I needed you. I loved you all along. I love you now, more than I ever knew how to love someone." He took another step, his face now so close to hers that she could feel his warmth. "I can't live without you. I can't spend the rest of my life wondering what could have been if I had done things differently."

Alessia blinked, trying to hold back the tears that threatened to spill. The pain of everything they had been through was there, in his words, and she didn't know how to respond. But there was something in her chest that was answering him. Something she couldn't control. The love, the same love that had made her blind and vulnerable to him.

"Matteo," she whispered. "I don't know if I can believe you. What's left for me now? What can I do with all of this?" She felt the weight of the words, the emptiness forming inside her, the uncertainty of giving him another chance when the pain was still so fresh.

"I know I'm not perfect, Alessia," Matteo said sincerely, his face now so close that she could see the anguish in his eyes. "But I'm here, body and soul. To fight for you, to fight for us. I won't let you go, not without trying. I love you, and I will show you that every day, until you allow me to."

They stood there, for a moment, in silence, their hearts beating faster. Alessia, with the pain of everything they had been through, looked at Matteo. The man she had loved, the man who had hurt her, but also the man who, with his words, now seemed to want to heal everything.

"I don't know if I can go back," Alessia said, her voice trembling but firm. "But I can try. For us. For the future we can still have."

Matteo smiled, a smile that mixed pain and hope. "I'll be here, every day, to prove that it's worth it."

And then, without another word, he wrapped her in his arms, as if he had finally found the place where he belonged. Alessia, though still cautious, surrendered to the embrace, feeling the love between them reborn, still fragile, but with the promise of a new beginning.

Deep down, Alessia knew that as long as they were willing to fight for what they had, maybe there was a chance for happiness. But for now, she allowed herself to feel the comfort of having Matteo by her side again, and for a moment, that was enough.

Alessia looked into Matteo's eyes and felt the weight of everything that had happened between them, but also a spark of hope she was afraid to hide. She was so close to him, almost touching his skin, and yet, there was an emotional distance still hanging between them, like an invisible wall that needed to come down.

They stayed silent for a moment, the tension between them charged with an energy she didn't know how to handle. She could feel her heart beating fast, her body reacting to his presence in a way that still surprised her. It didn't matter what he had done; the truth was, she still loved him. And that reality hurt more than she was willing to admit.

"Are you saying you want to give me a chance after everything?" Alessia asked, her voice low but with a firmness she tried to impose on herself. Her eyes sought an answer, but she already knew what he would say.

"Yes," Matteo replied, his voice deep and filled with sincerity. "I'm a proud man, Alessia, but... you have to understand that what I feel for you has never been about control or possession. I love you, I always have, even when I tried to run from it." He looked at her, his gaze intense. "I know you're scared, and I know I've caused you pain. But this... what we have... it's worth more than anything I've ever done wrong."

Alessia felt a shiver run down her spine. He was being more vulnerable than she had ever imagined. The strength of his voice, the sincerity in his eyes, were breaking down the walls she had put around her own heart. She didn't want to believe, but his love was so palpable that it seemed impossible to ignore.

"You don't know how much I wanted to believe in this, Matteo," Alessia responded, her voice trembling but with an intensity she couldn't hide. "But... after everything... is it still possible to go back?"

Matteo took a step forward, closer to her. He could feel the tension in the air, but he also saw something more in her eyes. Something he already knew: the internal struggle, the fear of giving in again. The fight for trust.

"If you give me this chance, Alessia, I'll prove to you every day that what we're building is real. It won't be easy, I know. But I will fight for you, for us. I'll protect you... from everything. And the first thing I'll do is destroy the ghosts of the past so that none of them keep us from living the future I know we can have."

Matteo's words were beginning to heal the wounds that, until now, seemed impossible to heal. Alessia didn't know if what he said was just an empty promise or if he was truly willing to change, to give up what he had always been to be with her. But as she looked at him, she knew that his presence, his warmth, his strength, were the only things she really wanted now.

She stepped forward too, closing the distance between them, their bodies so close that Alessia could feel his breath mingling with hers. "Do you want me, Matteo?" she asked, with a teasing smile, but the vulnerability shining through in her eyes.

He looked at her for a second, a smile full of desire and intensity appearing on his lips. "I want you more than anything. Not just the woman you are, but the woman you make me want to be." He ran one hand gently through her hair, his touch affectionate but firm. "I don't want to live without you. Never again."

Alessia felt a wave of emotions wash over her. She was still torn between fear and desire, between what her heart was screaming and what reason was trying to control. But when their eyes met, she could no longer resist.

With a gentle movement, she leaned in and kissed Matteo, first with the tip of her lips, as if testing the waters. But as soon as he responded, the intensity of the kiss overtook them completely. He pulled her closer, wrapping her in his arms with a possessiveness she had always known he had, but now it seemed more comforting than ever. Their passion exploded like a flame igniting, a desire that had been suppressed for so long, but now was released without restraint.

The kiss deepened, and Alessia felt Matteo's hands glide over her skin, touching her as if every inch of her body were his. The heat between them was palpable, and Alessia could no longer deny how she felt for him. Matteo made her feel desired, protected, loved, as if he were the only one who could understand the pain and shadows she carried.

When they finally pulled apart, both were breathless, their hearts racing. Alessia looked at him, her eyes shining. "Do you have any idea how alive you make me feel?" she whispered, her heart pounding.

Matteo smiled, touching her face with the tips of his fingers, his gaze softening. "I knew from the moment I saw you, Alessia. You've always been mine. I just didn't know how to make it work until now."

She smiled, the smile soft but with growing confidence. "Then make me trust you again, Matteo. Make me believe we can start over."

He pulled her closer, kissing her again, more slowly this time, as if he knew every second they spent together now was a victory for the future they were finally ready to build. He loved her, and nothing else mattered. They had the now. And, as uncertain as the future might be, Matteo knew that by her side, he was ready for any battle.

# Chapter 87: The Open Wounds

The days passed slowly, and though Alessia tried to keep herself busy with the new routine and the baby on the way, there was something in the air she couldn't escape. Matteo's touch, his presence by her side—everything felt right—but there was a weight in her heart that she couldn't shake. She wanted to believe Matteo's words were sincere, but the scars from everything they had lived through were still fresh. As if time couldn't heal everything, and the fear of being hurt again kept her on guard.

She was in the kitchen, preparing lunch while the morning sun poured in through the windows, bathing the room in soft light. Her eyes were distant, thoughtful, and the baby inside her, still small, seemed to sense the tension she carried. Alessia felt every movement of the baby like a reminder of what she needed to protect—not just the child, but also her heart. She couldn't allow herself to be vulnerable again, not after trust had been shattered so badly.

Matteo entered the kitchen with quiet steps, his gaze immediately meeting hers. He was still adjusting to this new dynamic, a man different from the one she had once known, yet in some way, he still didn't seem to have the answers for the mistakes they'd made.

"Can I help with something?" His voice was low, as always, with that protective tone she had learned to recognize, but also filled with a gentleness that seemed almost too much for her to bear. Alessia lifted her eyes to meet his, but her emotions were so divided that she barely knew how to respond.

"No, Matteo. It's fine. You can sit down; I'll finish here." She tried to keep the conversation light, but the words slipped away from her hands, as if there was something unsaid between them.

Matteo walked over to the table and, with a sigh, sat down. He watched her closely, knowing that words wouldn't be enough to bridge the space between them. That silence, laden with distrust, still kept them apart. The love was there, undeniable, but the fear of losing Alessia again made him hesitate. He wanted to be the man she had always hoped for, but how could that be possible when he himself was so scarred by the wrong choices of the past?

"I know this won't be easy," he said, finally breaking the silence, his voice soft but with the determination of someone who was willing to fight. "I know I hurt you, Alessia. And you have every right to keep your heart closed to me. But please, let me prove that I can be different. Let me show you that I can be the man you deserve."

Alessia stared at him for a long moment, feeling the pain of the conversation reverberating within her. She knew Matteo was trying, that his actions, though still cautious, were more than empty words. He was putting in more effort than she had expected. And still, something inside her was afraid. Afraid of believing again, afraid of falling into an abyss she already knew so well.

"I know you're trying," she replied, her voice wavering slightly. "But what happened... what I saw... Matteo, I was left alone. You left me alone, and it wasn't just because of Bianca. It was everything. The lies, the silences, the fact that you distanced yourself when I needed you the most."

Matteo stood up slowly, the pain visible in his eyes. He walked toward her with firm but gentle steps, as though he knew that any sudden movement might make her pull away. He placed a hand softly on her arm, touching her with a tenderness that broke his own heart.

"I love you, Alessia," he said firmly, the words vibrating in the air like a silent vow. "I can't change what happened, but I can guarantee that from now on, I'll be by your side. Every day. Every hour. I'll show you, with my actions, that what we've had together is worth more than the mistakes I made. I'll prove to you that the trust you gave me wasn't in vain. I am the man you've always wanted, and I will do everything to be the man you need."

Alessia closed her eyes, feeling the sincerity in those words, but also the resistance still burning inside her. How could she allow herself to surrender completely when the scars of the past still bled in her heart? She didn't know if she had the strength to forgive fully—not yet. But something in the way Matteo looked at her, the reverence with which he touched her skin, began to dissolve her pain, little by little.

She sighed, her hands trembling slightly as she tried to push away the internal battle that raged within her. "I... I don't know, Matteo. I want to believe in you, I really do. But I'm so scared. I'm scared to trust you again, to give myself to you again and... and risk everything."

Matteo watched her with an expression of pain, but also of understanding. He knew words couldn't heal her wounds, but he also knew that if necessary, he would keep fighting for her. He would always do that, until she believed in him, until she believed in the love he had for her.

"I know you're scared, Alessia," he said gently, his eyes never leaving hers. "But what we have is real. And I promise you, even if it takes time, I'll prove that to you. And I'll give you the space you need. I'll be here when you're ready. Always."

Alessia felt the knot in her throat tighten. She was torn, but the sincerity in Matteo's gaze was breaking down the defenses she had built. She looked at him, feeling her own vulnerability exposed. Maybe, just maybe, the pain could finally begin to heal.

She took a step forward, her eyes locked with his. "I need time, Matteo. But for now, I... I think I can try." She took a deep breath, feeling the weight of those words, but also a flicker of hope. "I can try."

And with that, she surrendered to his embrace—a silent hug, but full of promises and dreams still to be realized. They were ready to take the next step. And for the first time, Alessia believed that, maybe, their love could survive, even in the chaos that surrounded them.

Alessia couldn't shake her thoughts of Matteo. Even with the distance, the silence between them, and the wounds still pulsing in her heart, her mind stubbornly kept returning to him, to what had been, to what could still be. Their love, seemingly broken, still hovered like a dying flame, but persistent, waiting for a breath of wind to reignite it.

That morning, she stood on the balcony, the cool breeze brushing her face, while she watched the quiet movement of the distant city. But even in the calm, she felt a storm brewing inside her. She was afraid of what this feeling meant, the pain it could bring, but the love for Matteo, with all its intensity and complexity, didn't seem ready to disappear.

She heard the living room door open, and with a nearly imperceptible breath, she knew it was him. Matteo entered slowly, as though hesitating, as if afraid to interrupt whatever was going on inside her. Their eyes met, and time seemed to stretch, laden with tension. Neither of them spoke, but the air was thick with everything they hadn't said, everything they hadn't resolved.

Matteo took a step toward her, and with each movement of his, Alessia felt her body react. He was still the man she loved, the man she had sworn to leave behind. But the warmth of his presence couldn't be denied.

"I didn't know if you'd come back," Alessia finally said, breaking the silence, her voice heavy with repressed emotion.

Matteo stood a few steps away, still hesitant. He watched her as if trying to understand whether she was truly ready to face him again. The pain in his gaze was undeniable. He knew she had the right to walk away, but his desire to reclaim what they had lost outweighed any fear.

"I never really left," he said, his voice deep and soft at once. "I've always been here, Alessia, even when you thought I left you behind."

She looked at him, feeling his words reverberate in her chest, like an echo of something she knew was true, but still couldn't accept. "How do you expect me to believe that, Matteo?" She paused, her eyes drifting away, as though searching for an answer she knew he couldn't give. "How can I trust you when you left me alone, made me feel like I was just an option after everything we've been through?"

Matteo took a step forward, his expression growing more resolute, as though the pain in his words drove him to cross the distance she tried to impose. "I was wrong, Alessia. And I'll pay for that. It won't be easy, I know. But I'll prove to you that what I feel for you is stronger than the pride that made me pull away."

Alessia's heart was racing, but she still couldn't let go. The fear of being hurt again held her back, the walls she had built between them weren't ready to come down. But something in Matteo's gaze, in the sincerity of his eyes, made her start to question what she thought was a certainty.

"I can't make promises, Alessia," he continued, his voice softer now but more determined. "But I can guarantee that I will fight, every single day, to show you that my love for you never went away. And if you give me a chance, I'll spend the rest of my life trying to make you believe in it."

Alessia felt the internal battle intensify. Love, pain, desire—all tangled together. How could she deny what she still felt for him?

How could she resist the promise of a different life by his side, away from the chaos and violence that had always surrounded them?

She looked at him, her words rising with strength. "And how do you expect me to give you that chance, Matteo? How can I trust again when all I have left is loneliness?"

Matteo closed the distance between them, the intensity in his gaze making Alessia feel fragile. "You give me that chance, Alessia, because I'll show you that by my side, you'll never be alone again." He touched her face with the gentleness of someone who knew every movement needed to be careful, that every touch would count in the rebuilding of what was broken.

That simple action—the touch of his hand on her skin—began to melt Alessia's resistance. She felt the warmth spreading through her, as if her body was finally acknowledging what her mind had been trying to ignore. She wanted to believe, but she was afraid. Afraid to trust, afraid to give herself over again.

"I don't know if I can...," she whispered, her voice breaking with the mix of emotions.

Matteo placed a finger on her lips, interrupting her words. "I know it's not easy, but I'll show you, Alessia. Every day, every gesture. And if you give me this chance, I promise I'll be the man you need, the man you deserve."

Alessia's eyes shimmered, and for a moment, she felt the temptation to surrender. She wanted to believe him, wanted to live by his side, away from everything that hurt her. But something still held her cautious.

"You made me suffer so much, Matteo," she said, the pain in her voice, the struggle still evident. "But I still love you. That's what hurts the most."

Matteo pulled her closer, their bodies now so close that Alessia could feel the intensity of his heartbeat. "I know. And that pain is mine too," he murmured against her skin. "But together, we can overcome this. I'll fight for you. For us."

Alessia closed her eyes, allowing herself to succumb to his touch, to the warmth she so desperately craved, but feared. She knew the road ahead would be hard. But in that moment, as he kissed her with an almost desperate intensity, she felt that maybe, just maybe, their love could survive. Maybe, just maybe, they could start over.

# Chapter 88: The Return of the Past

The sky was dark and heavy, as if it knew the weight of the decision that was approaching. The mansion where Alessia and Matteo had sought refuge, now a place of unsettling silence, was on the brink of a new storm. The past, which for a brief moment seemed to have been left behind, was about to rise again with destructive force.

Matteo sat in the living room, his gaze fixed on a piece of paper before him. The clock on the wall seemed to make time move slower, but his thoughts were racing. The latest news he had received about Lorenzo and his movements had triggered an alarm in his mind. He knew that Lorenzo's final attempt for revenge was forming, and he would need to protect Alessia at all costs.

"I can't lose anyone else," he murmured to himself, the words heavy with a pain that wouldn't go away. The loss of so many allies, the abandonment he felt from everyone who had trusted him, all of that weighed more now, with the impending threat hanging over them.

The door slowly creaked open, and Alessia entered the room. She was different, more serious, her eyes filled with concern. She knew something wasn't right. Matteo, always the strong and decisive man, now seemed more vulnerable, more frail under the weight of responsibility.

She walked up to him, gently touching his shoulder, offering the softness he so desperately needed. "What's going on?" she asked, her voice quiet but firm. "I know you're worried. Don't try to hide it from me."

Matteo lifted his gaze, and for a moment, the world around him disappeared. Alessia, with the strength he had always admired, with the courage he had underestimated, was standing before him, willing to face everything by his side. He sighed deeply and took her hands in his, feeling the warmth of her fingers.

"Lorenzo is preparing a final move," he said, his voice heavy with sorrow. "He knows you're my weakness. And as long as I can't guarantee your safety, he will do whatever it takes to destroy me. I can't allow that. I can't lose you."

Alessia felt a tightening in her chest. It wasn't just the fear of what Lorenzo could do to her, but the fear of what this meant for their future. What she wanted was peace, a fresh start. But their fresh start was once again being threatened. She looked into Matteo's eyes, trying to understand his intentions, trying to measure what he was willing to do.

"Matteo, you can't carry the weight of this alone," she said, her voice trembling with emotion. "I've already lived in the shadow of your mafia life once. And I can't just be a spectator while you try to protect the whole world. I can't... hide again. I can't live with this fear, knowing I'm not the only one paying the price. But I won't let you go alone."

Matteo closed his eyes, feeling a mix of gratitude and despair. "I won't let you go anymore, Alessia. I promise I will do everything to protect you and make sure you and our child are safe. I'll face Lorenzo head-on, but I won't let you stay on the sidelines. Never again. You are part of all of this, and you always have been. Now, we need to fight together."

Alessia swallowed hard, still feeling fear take hold of her body. But she also felt a strength rising within her, a strength she had never known she had, but that she now knew was necessary to survive the war that was about to unfold. She looked at Matteo, pain and hope reflected in her eyes.

"We're in this together, Matteo. And I trust you. But, please, promise me you won't let this destroy us. Promise me you won't lose sight of what really matters."

He pulled her close, holding her face in his hands. "I promise you, Alessia. We'll get through this. Together. I won't lose you. I won't lose what we've built. But, above all, I will make sure you are safe. There is no more room for secrets between us. No more room for doubts. Just you and me."

Silence enveloped them once again, but this time, it was different. There was no longer any distance between them. What had once seemed like a crack was now a bond strengthened by the need to protect what remained of the love that still pulsed between them. Alessia rested her head on Matteo's chest, feeling his heart beat strongly against hers. She felt that, even amidst the chaos, there was something that no one could take away from them.

The life they had lost was still ahead of them, like a distant horizon. But now, together, they were ready to fight for it. And despite all the enemies around them, Alessia felt, for the first time, that perhaps the future could still be theirs.

The wind coming through the window now seemed softer, calmer. Maybe it was just an illusion, or perhaps it was the beginning of a new phase. They didn't know, but they were willing to face anything, even if the past still haunted them. The future was at stake, and there was no turning back.

The day broke gray, with a gentle rain falling over the city. Matteo's mansion was quieter than ever. Every corner seemed to carry the weight of their choices, of everything they had lived through, and the threat that still pursued them. However, inside that house, there was something different in the air—an almost sweet tension, filled with unsaid words, but somehow, words that needed to be said.

Matteo was in the living room, leaning against the window, looking at the horizon. The thought of Alessia consumed him. He knew that the last time he had seen her, she had been determined to leave, and he had done nothing to stop her. Now, the silence between them felt heavier than any words that could be said. He knew he had done the unthinkable, but somehow, his feelings for her had never disappeared. They were so intertwined that he couldn't imagine a future without her.

Alessia was in the kitchen, stirring a cup of coffee with an agitated mind. The memory of Matteo and what had happened between them was constant, but the feeling of loss seemed even stronger. For a moment, she wished everything could be simpler. That life wasn't so complicated, that the betrayals and secrets hadn't come to ruin what could have been their love.

She looked toward the kitchen window, and her eyes met Matteo's. He was there, as always, in silence, with that look that, even without words, said so much. Alessia felt a tightness in her chest. What did he want to say? What did he still feel? She didn't know whether to confront him or simply move on, but something made her hesitate, something that pulled her back.

With her heart racing, Alessia stood up and walked toward him. The approach was slow, but both of them knew what was going on deep inside their souls. She reached him, and for a moment, just stood there watching him, waiting for him to be the first to break the silence.

Matteo turned to her, his eyes fixed on hers as if trying to decipher every emotion running through her mind. Finally, he spoke, his voice low but filled with emotion.

"I never let you go, Alessia." He paused, as if the words weighed on him. "I know I made you suffer. I know I did everything wrong. But you... you never left my mind. You never left my heart."

Alessia felt the words like a sharp blade, each one sinking into her skin with a weight she couldn't avoid. The love he still had for her was obvious, but the doubts remained. She looked at him, and in his eyes, she saw a broken man, a man who, despite his hardness, felt a pain as deep as hers.

"Do you think you can make everything go back to normal, Matteo?" she asked, her voice a whisper but firm. "Do you think you can convince me that everything that happened doesn't change anything?"

Matteo stepped forward, his body so close that his warmth invaded her senses. He raised his hand and gently touched Alessia's face, as if he were touching her for the first time, wanting to engrave the moment in his memory.

"I don't know if I can convince you, Alessia, but I know what I feel. And what I feel for you... is stronger than anything. Stronger than the mistakes, the lies, and the secrets. I love you. And that's what matters."

She closed her eyes for a moment, feeling his touch. Matteo's words echoed in her mind, but the fear still consumed her. She wanted to believe him, she wanted to trust that he was telling the truth, but the pain she felt when she saw him with Bianca was still fresh in her heart. She didn't know if she could give herself to this love again without him hurting her once more.

"And what happens after this?" Alessia asked, looking directly into his eyes. "What happens when Lorenzo, and everyone else, comes back to destroy us?"

Matteo, now so close that their breaths mixed, smiled faintly, a bitter smile, but full of intent.

"I will protect you. I will protect our family, Alessia. And in the end, nothing will separate us. Because you are mine, and I am yours. That's the only thing I know for sure."

The silence between them was heavy, but filled with an intensity that only they could understand. They were there, together, but still with so many obstacles to overcome. Their life would never be easy, no matter how many times they tried, but what was clear in that moment was that, somehow, they were willing to fight for each other, to face the ghosts of the past, and maybe, find a way to move forward.

"Are you willing to fight for us?" Alessia asked, a challenge in her eyes.

Matteo leaned toward her, his hand still holding her face tenderly. "I've been fighting my whole life, Alessia. And now, I'm fighting for you. For us."

And it was in that moment, with their hearts entwined and their eyes fixed on each other, that the world seemed to stop. Nothing else mattered, except being there for each other. The past, with all its lies and betrayals, still haunted them, but the love they shared was stronger. And that, more than anything else, would keep them together, facing all the dangers to come.

# Chapter 89: The Proof of Love

The night was strangely silent, with the sound of rain tapping against the windows and the wind blowing ominously. Inside the house, Alessia tried to stay calm, but she knew something was about to happen. The rustling of the leaves outside the house seemed more intense than ever, and Alessia's heart was racing with every passing second.

She had heard the rumors that Lorenzo, desperate and furious, was planning a retaliation. But in those moments, when fear and anxiety consumed her, nothing seemed to prepare Alessia for what was to come. When the first heavy footsteps were heard outside the house, she knew the battle had begun.

The crash of the door being broken down echoed through the corridors, and the tension set in instantly. She rushed to the phone, trying to call Matteo, but the signal was weak. That's when he appeared, faster than she could have imagined, entering through the front door with a determined look. His face was marked by fury and pain, but he seemed more resolute than ever.

"Alessia, stay inside. Don't go out!" He ordered firmly, his eyes locked on hers as if trying to absorb every second of her presence before heading into the battle.

"Matteo, no... They're here!" Alessia screamed, her voice trembling, but he didn't hesitate. He turned, and with the speed of a predator, went to the closet to grab weapons.

"Stay inside. I'm ending this now."

The sounds of the fight began to echo. The cracking of doors, the heavy footsteps, and, more importantly, the shouts that filled the air indicated that the war was about to unfold inside their own house. Alessia, her heart pounding, looked out the window, trying to see what was happening outside, but nothing could prepare her for what was about to happen.

She heard the sound of gunfire and the thud of one of Lorenzo's henchmen hitting the ground. Every blow Matteo delivered seemed fiercer than the last. She felt, with every crack, every muffled scream, the pain and violence he was facing. But the worst was hearing, amidst all of it, the sound of Matteo being struck.

"Matteo!" She screamed, desperate, running toward the front door. But before she could take another step, he appeared, his exhausted eyes, his suit stained with blood, but still holding the stance of an unbeatable man.

"Alessia," he said, his voice hoarse with pain but with an intensity in his eyes that made it clear he would do anything to protect her. "I told you, stay inside."

The last of Lorenzo's men, defeated, were being dragged out of the house, but Alessia had eyes only for Matteo. He was injured, his face pale, but his gaze locked on hers was the only comfort she needed. She rushed to him, her feet sliding on the wet floor as he staggered, his body giving in to exhaustion.

"Are you okay?" She asked, her voice almost breaking with concern as she tried to wipe the blood from his shirt.

He looked at her, his eyes reflecting a love she never imagined she would see. "I'm fine, but I can't leave you alone anymore. No one, nothing, is going to take you from me."

With trembling hands, Alessia touched his face, her heart torn by the sight of Matteo, a man so relentless, so powerful, now vulnerable before her. "You... you did all this for me," she murmured, tears in her eyes, the pain of fear and loss consuming her.

"For you," he replied, his voice low but full of intensity. "For you and our child. I will never let you go again."

The closeness between them, the words filled with unspoken meanings, created an intimacy so strong that Alessia felt her heart race. The battle still echoed in her ears, but in that moment, all she could hear was the pounding of her own heart. Matteo, despite his irregular breathing, held her hand tightly, feeling the intensity of her touch. He kissed her with a tenderness that didn't belong in the violence around them. Alessia, closing her eyes, surrendered to the kiss, feeling the promise that, with him, nothing else mattered but the two of them, together.

The battle hadn't ended, but that kiss, that moment between them, said everything. The love they shared had become the only force capable of facing whatever the future had in store. When they pulled away, words were unnecessary. They both knew there was much more to face, but nothing would ever be stronger than the bond that now united them.

"I love you, Alessia," Matteo said, his voice hoarse with emotion.

She smiled, despite the fear and pain that still weighed on her, but she felt, in that moment, that he truly was there for her. "I love you too," she replied, with the certainty that, despite everything, the future would be theirs, together, facing whatever came.

Now, with the danger averted and the promises made, Alessia knew the worst had passed. Whatever came now, she and Matteo would face it side by side. Together, they would win the silent war that fate still had in store for them, because, despite the open wounds, the love between them was stronger than ever.

After the violent confrontation and the brief relief of knowing they were safe, the silence in Matteo's mansion became palpable. The house, which had been the stage for so many betrayals and confrontations, now seemed quieter than ever. Alessia and Matteo were in the center of the living room, both exhausted but still with their eyes locked on each other. The weight of the battle was beginning to be softened by the words that were finally starting to be spoken.

Matteo sat on the sofa, his face marked with cuts, his gaze deep but still carrying the strength of someone who had always known how to rise in the face of the greatest challenges. He looked at Alessia, observing the way she was, not only physically tired but emotionally devastated. Her eyes, usually hard and impassive, showed a faint glimmer of vulnerability, something he rarely allowed to show. She, with hands still trembling and heart heavy, stood before him, trying to keep her posture firm, but he could see the pain in her eyes.

"Are you okay?" Matteo's voice was hoarse, but with a soft tone, something he rarely let escape, as if he was finally recognizing that there was something much more important than the battle they had just fought.

Alessia hesitated, looking at him with a mixture of relief and distrust. She knew he was there, that he had fought for her, but the recent past still loomed heavily between them. And, as much as she wished to be honest, the words couldn't come out with the clarity she wanted.

"I'm better now," she said, her voice firmer than she truly felt. "But what about you? You did all of this for me... and you're still here."

Matteo smiled, but it was a smile that mixed pain and tenderness. He stood up slowly, moving cautiously as if every step was heavy, not just because of the battle, but because of the weight of the guilt that still consumed him.

"I couldn't leave you alone, Alessia," he said, moving closer to her. "I'll never let you think you can face this without me."

Their eyes met, and for a moment, the rest of the world disappeared. Alessia felt her heart tighten, his strength seemed to invade her chest, but there was also a fragility there. She wanted to pull away, to keep her distance, but the truth was that love, that feeling that seemed to be her enemy, was stronger than the pain they both carried.

"I know you think I did all this out of pride, but it's not true," Matteo continued, his words softer now, almost whispered. "I did it for you. For us."

Alessia blinked, surprised by the sincerity in his words. It was rare to see Matteo so open, so vulnerable. She knew he had his own demons, but she never imagined he'd expose them like this. She didn't know what to say, but she felt the warmth of his words spreading through her, melting some of the resistance she still had in her heart.

"You... you really think I'll give in so easily?" She teased, trying to mask the emotion that was beginning to overflow. "I spent so long protecting myself from you, and now you come with sweet words?"

Matteo moved closer, his hands finding hers. "Yes," he said, his eyes deep and penetrating. "Because now I know what really matters."

They were so close now that Alessia could feel the warmth of his body, could notice every sigh he made. The words he spoke were harsh, but his touch was gentle, almost reverent. For a moment, she felt a wave of regret for letting things go so far, for being so stubborn, for letting pride and fear dictate her actions.

"Matteo, you left me... you made me believe I was alone, that you didn't love me anymore," Alessia confessed, her voice breaking with emotion. "And that destroyed me. I didn't know what to do, didn't know who to trust."

Matteo looked at her with a gaze so intense it was overwhelming. "I know, Alessia. I was wrong. More wrong than I can count. But I'm here now, and I'm not leaving."

The tension between them dissolved for a moment, and they drew closer, their foreheads gently touching. The world around them disappeared, and in that moment, all that existed was what they were building together. Their story was far from simple or easy, but still, they were ready to move forward, to rebuild what was broken. They had each other, and that, for now, was enough.

"I'll never leave you again, Alessia," Matteo said, with a firmness that left no room for doubt. "I'll fight for you, for our child, for everything we have."

She closed her eyes for a moment, feeling the weight of his words, the intensity of his commitment. She knew the road ahead would still be long and treacherous, but at least he was no longer running away. They would be together, facing whatever came.

"I love you, Matteo," she finally said, her voice soft but filled with certainty. "And now, I believe you love me too."

"I've always loved you," he replied, leaning in to kiss her, this time with all the sincerity of a man who had finally understood what it meant to be willing to sacrifice everything for the one he loved.

The kiss that followed was gentle but full of intensity. It was the promise of a new beginning, the confirmation that what they shared would not be destroyed by anything or anyone. And, in the warmth of that moment, Alessia knew that, with Matteo by her side, she could finally have the life she had always dreamed of—free from pain and violence, but always with the strength of the love that united them.

# Chapter 90: A New Beginning

The house was quiet, more peaceful than Alessia had ever imagined possible. The weight of the past seemed to have been left behind, and in its place was a gentle sense of growing hope. The sun hung low on the horizon, casting a soft golden hue across the sky that illuminated the small village where they now lived. After so many years of fear and pain, this place felt like paradise — simple, serene, and welcoming.

Alessia sat on the porch of their new home, a simple house but one full of promises. The house she and Matteo had chosen together. They had left behind the mansion, the ghosts of the mafia, and the cycle of violence, in search of something simpler, more genuine. Something they could build together, far from the shadow of Lorenzo, the henchmen, and all the storms they had weathered.

Matteo appeared in the doorway, his eyes fixed on her. His steps were slow and gentle, as if he knew this moment needed to be savored without haste. He approached, sitting beside Alessia without a word. The silence between them this time was not heavy. It was comfortable, natural.

He looked at her for a moment, his eyes filled with an intensity she knew well. "I always knew that one day I'd be here with you. But I never imagined it would be like this, in a place like this," he said, his voice full of sincere affection. "I thought we had lost everything. I thought the past would swallow us up, but now... now I see the future."

Alessia gazed at him, her eyes filled with emotion she had tried to suppress for so long. She didn't want to cry for all she had lost, but it was hard to hold back the tears of relief. Matteo, with all the weight of his past, had become the person she had always known he could be. He was no longer the distant, relentless man; now he was the man who fought for her, for their future.

"I love you, Matteo," Alessia whispered, her words filled with undeniable truth. "And after everything... I can see a future with you. A future of peace."

He smiled, his grin lighting up his face but also tinged with nostalgia. "I love you too, Alessia. And I know I can't erase what I've done, or what's happened, but I promise I will do everything I can to make you happy, every day."

Alessia felt her heart race. His words were a balm for the old pain, and she leaned in, placing her hand over his. The touch was soft, but full of meaning. As if, in that simple gesture, she was once again accepting the promise of love he was offering her.

"I know," she said. "I know you'll fight for us, and that makes me believe we can truly start over."

Matteo squeezed her hand, holding the contact firmly, as if the simple act of being there, in that moment, was the assurance he needed that they were ready for whatever would come. The sun continued to set, the golden light reflecting off the little flowers in the garden, on the house they were building. Alessia looked at the house's construction — every brick, every detail, was a metaphor for what they were doing with their lives. They were rebuilding everything from scratch, with time, with patience, and with love.

"So, when do we begin our future?" she asked, a shy smile on her lips.

Matteo looked at her intensely. "Now," he said firmly. "We start now. Because, as long as we're together, nothing else matters. I promise that everything we've done, everything we've sacrificed, won't be in vain."

Alessia felt her heart warm with his words, but something else was growing inside her. There was a growing certainty that what they were building together was not just a new house. It was a new life. And she was ready to live it with him.

Later that evening, Matteo took her to the small garden, where, under the soft light of the moon, he knelt before her, surprise in his eyes. Alessia stood frozen for a moment, her eyes wide with surprise and emotion. He was holding a small box, and inside it was a simple yet meaningful ring. Matteo looked at her, his eyes silent but carrying all the meaning she needed.

"Alessia," he said, his voice thick with emotion, "I know we've had a difficult start. That there's so much we need to face. But more than anything, I want you to know how important you are to me. I want you to be part of my life forever."

Alessia felt a lump in her throat. It was a simple proposal, but filled with promises. She looked at Matteo, her eyes wet, and the answer was clear in her heart. "Yes," she said, her voice firm but full of emotion. "Yes, Matteo. I want this. I want our future."

With a smile, Matteo slid the ring onto her finger. And that night, under the starry sky and the serenity of the little village, they sealed the commitment of a new beginning, a future without the ghosts of the past. The future was finally in their hands. And they were ready to face it together, like never before.

The road ahead would still be difficult, but now, with their love renewed and the promise of a fresh start, nothing seemed impossible.

The night was serene, with the full moon softly illuminating the garden where Alessia and Matteo stood. The peace they had gained in recent days seemed finally to settle between them, but there was still something they both needed to face. Their pasts, the ghosts of a tumultuous and dangerous life, still lingered in the air. Yet, in their hearts, both knew they were ready to move forward.

Alessia, still wearing the ring on her finger, looked at Matteo with a mixture of emotion and a small smile on her lips. She had never imagined she would be here, in such a tranquil place, with the sense of safety she now felt beside him. She, who had spent so much time fighting her feelings for him, now found herself fully immersed in the idea of a life together, without the mafia's shadow lurking at every turn.

Matteo, who until recently had seen himself as the ruthless, distant boss, could no longer hide the love he felt for Alessia. He was used to controlling everything around him, to being the man everyone trusted, but it was with Alessia that he felt most vulnerable, most human. And he knew he could no longer run from this vulnerability.

"I don't know how you do it, Alessia," Matteo's voice was low, heavy with a sincerity he rarely showed. He moved closer to her, his gaze deep. "How do you manage to see the best in me, even after everything that's happened?"

Alessia felt her heart race with his words. She never imagined that this man, so imposing and hard, could have such doubts. But here he was, revealing his insecurities, as though he was finally capable of showing his true self.

"I see you, Matteo," Alessia replied calmly, meeting his gaze. "I see the man you've become. And I see, more than anything, the love you have for me. That's what matters, not what happened before."

The tension that had always existed between them, the coldness and provocations that marked the beginning of their relationship, now seemed distant. There was only a soft quiet and a burning desire to build something solid together. And despite everything they had lived through, here they were, on the brink of a new beginning.

Matteo smiled, a genuine smile that was rare on his face, but now seemed to come from deep within. He leaned toward her, his fingers gently touching her face, as if confirming that she was truly there, by his side.

"I've never been good with promises, Alessia," he whispered, his lips nearly touching hers. "But one thing I can guarantee: there's nothing in this world that makes me happier than being with you, now. Forever, if you'll let me."

The warmth of Matteo's touch, the way his eyes locked onto hers, was confirmation that this man, with all his flaws and mistakes, was finally ready to give her the chance for a life full of love, without fear, without doubts.

Alessia felt her own insecurities melt away. She knew what the world would think of them. She knew that the shadow of the past, the mafia, and the decisions they had made together would still follow them, but it no longer mattered. She moved toward Matteo, her hands wrapping around his neck, pulling him into a deep, intense kiss — the kind of kiss that said more than words ever could.

When they parted, breathing heavily, Alessia murmured, "I was afraid I would never be happy again, that I had let love slip away. But now... now I know I was wrong."

Matteo looked at her with a soft smile, his fingers tracing the ring on her finger. "I'll never let you go, Alessia. And no matter what the future holds, we'll face it together. As it should always have been."

She nodded, feeling a wave of relief and happiness wash over her heart. Finally, she felt that the love they had started to build was no longer under threat. The mafia might have been part of their past, but not of the future they were creating together.

The silence that followed was comfortable. The stars shone above, and the gentle breeze made the leaves of the trees whisper. Danger and threats still existed outside, but inside their little house, they had found a refuge, an unbreakable peace. In the depths of their hearts, both Alessia and Matteo knew that the greatest challenge of their lives would not be what awaited them outside the house, but rather continuing to choose each other, every day.

"Let's take it one step at a time," Matteo said, his voice soft but filled with certainty. "One step at a time, and we'll do it together."

Alessia smiled, cuddling closer to him, feeling the warmth of his body against her skin. "Together," she repeated, with the same certainty. "Forever."

And, as the world outside continued to turn, with its threats and mysteries, inside that refuge, Alessia and Matteo knew they had finally found true peace. Their love, born from the shadows, could finally bloom in the light.

# Chapter 90: A New Beginning

The small house on the outskirts of the city was quiet that afternoon. The soft wind swayed the curtains of the open windows, and the golden light of the late afternoon illuminated Alessia's face as she stared ahead, lost in thought. She tried to find the peace she had been seeking, but despite the calmness around her, she felt a constant weight on her chest.

Matteo was still there, by her side, but his presence, so intensely familiar and comforting, also carried a silent fear. It was no longer the fear of what he might do for her, but the fear that the past would repeat itself. The past that always threatened to destroy them.

She looked at him as he stood up from his chair, with a more serious expression than usual. Even with her heart torn, a part of Alessia couldn't shake the desire that, finally, maybe—just maybe—she could have the happiness she had always dreamed of.

"I know what you're thinking," Matteo said, his voice deep and somewhat tense. He stopped in front of her, his hands in the pockets of his jacket, his eyes locked onto hers with an intensity that she could feel deep in her bones. "But we need to stop living in fear. We can't let the past destroy what we're trying to build."

Alessia looked at him, still hesitant. The love was there, strong and clear, but she knew what that meant. What life with Matteo had always meant. She also knew that there was no going back. With every word he spoke, she became more aware that her life, her heart, were now completely intertwined with his.

"I don't know if I can do this again, Matteo. I don't know if I can risk everything again... if you'll be able to protect me, to protect us, like you promised," she said, with a pain in her voice that she could barely control. The words were a whisper, a confession she didn't know if she wanted to share, but one she had to.

He looked at her with the same intensity, now closer, until their faces were just inches apart. The heat of his body contrasted with the cold wind coming from outside, but he seemed to be the only warmth in her world now.

"I've always protected you, Alessia. Even when you thought I was betraying you, even when you thought I had abandoned you. You were never alone. I've been there, in the shadows, looking out for you." Matteo spoke softly, almost reverently, as though the words he was saying held an importance he could no longer ignore.

Alessia felt a tightness in her chest. She knew he was right, but the pain still consumed her. The pain of betrayal, of lies, of wrong choices. But she also knew that what they had was not ordinary, that nothing about them was simple or easy.

"I... I know, Matteo," she said, her trembling fingers touching his face, gently caressing his skin. "I just wish it were different. That love was enough."

"So do I," he whispered back, taking her hands in his. "But love... is just the beginning. What matters is what we do with it. What you and I do now. What we're going to build."

Alessia felt the sincerity in his words, something stronger than anything she had ever experienced before. It was as though he was finally opening his heart in a way he never had before, something he rarely let show: vulnerability. She knew that despite all the hardness he carried, Matteo was willing to change, willing to risk everything for her, for them.

He pulled her closer, their bodies fitting together in a way that felt natural, inevitable. The physical contact between them had never stopped being intense, but that night there was something more. It wasn't just desire. It was the urgent need to reconnect, to surrender completely to the love and trust that still existed between them, even after everything they had been through.

"I know you're scared. I am too, Alessia," he said, his eyes fixed on hers. "But we have something that no one can take from us. And if you let me, I will spend the rest of my days fighting to make you happy."

His words were like fire, a silent promise that set everything around them ablaze. She felt the weight of those words, and deep in her heart, something began to warm. There was no more doubt. She knew her place was there, by his side. Together. Despite the risks, the threats, the violence, and the pain.

She closed her eyes, her breath heavy as she felt her body pressing against his. It was the same feeling as always—of being home, despite everything. There was no more room for hesitation.

"I can't stay away from you, Matteo," she whispered, feeling the words escape her mouth like a confession, a surrender. "I love you."

And then, as if those words were the key to unlocking everything they were feeling, Matteo kissed her. The kiss was soft but urgent, as if the world around them was disappearing, as if nothing else mattered.

"I love you too, Alessia. I've always loved you."

# Chapter 92: A Cruel Ultimatum

The message arrived without warning, without explanation. Just a cold, direct line. Matteo held his phone in his hands, his eyes fixed on the words that seemed to burn him. *"If you want to keep Alessia and the baby safe, stay away from her forever. Otherwise, the attacks will begin. Their lives will be in your hands."* The threat was clear, straightforward. They knew exactly where to hit: Matteo's weakest point.

Matteo felt the blood freeze in his veins. How could he stay away from Alessia? How could he choose between the love he felt for her and her life? It was a cruel and unexpected dilemma, a test he never imagined he would have to face. He looked out the window, the distant city lights seeming so small, insignificant, as if the whole world had shrunk around him. He didn't know what to do.

But the fear for the baby, for the woman he loved, took over him. He knew that if he didn't act quickly, the violence of the mafia would threaten not just their future, but their lives as well. Deep down, Matteo knew that if he didn't obey the ultimatum, Alessia's suffering would be inevitable.

Alessia entered the room, interrupting his thoughts. She looked radiant once again, but the smile that formed on her lips when she saw him didn't last long. She immediately noticed that something was wrong. Matteo's expression was distant, empty. She had always known him as someone relentless, determined, but now there was something about him that confused her. She went over to him, gently touching his shoulder.

"Matteo?" she whispered, concern in her voice. "What's going on?"

He moved back slightly, the distance between them growing in a way that was almost imperceptible, but Alessia felt the change.

She knew something wasn't right, she knew he was hiding something.

"You're worried. What's going on?" she insisted, more firm now.

Matteo took a deep breath, feeling the weight of his own emotions. He didn't want to involve her in this, didn't want to drag her into another nightmare. But how could he hide something so important? How could he continue lying to her?

He finally spoke, his voice choked. "Alessia... I received a message. A threat. They said that if I stay by your side, you'll be their target. They'll attack you, they'll attack our child. If I don't stay away, no matter what happens... they won't stop." He stopped, fear visible in his eyes. "They're demanding that I stay away from you. To ensure your safety. To make sure you live."

Alessia stood in silence, processing his words. Her heart pounded, but she didn't know if she felt anger, fear, or sadness. Maybe all of it mixed together. How could he make this decision on his own? How could he think that staying away was the best option? She had always known life with him would be full of dangers, but now, that danger was closer than ever.

"Are you telling me you're going to stay away from me?" Alessia's voice was tense, the disgust clear in her words. "That you're going to let the mafia decide for us? That you're going to give up on our life together because they threatened us?"

Matteo didn't answer right away. He looked at her with a tired gaze, as if he knew his decision could destroy them. The dilemma was reflected in his face, his heart heavy with the choice he had to make. "I don't want to lose you, Alessia. I don't want to lose our child. I can't risk..."

She didn't let him finish. "Don't do this to me, Matteo! You don't have the right to make this decision alone!" She nearly shouted, feeling the pain building inside her. How could he think she would let him leave? "We've been through so much already, and now you want... want to abandon us?"

Matteo stepped closer to her, his eyes filled with regret. He wanted to hug her, hold her hands, and make everything go back to normal. But he knew there was no going back. He had to make a decision, and that weight was stronger than any desire. "I just... I want you to be safe. I can't risk anything else. I can't risk your life, Alessia."

"And what are you going to do, Matteo? Abandon me?" She looked at him with tear-filled eyes, feeling her heart shatter. He seemed to have distanced himself, but it was her who was being left behind. She tried to take a deep breath, trying to gather strength. "I can't accept this. I am your life, just like you are mine. There is no safety without both of us."

Matteo closed his eyes, the weight of her words crushing his chest. "If I don't do this... we'll all die, Alessia. I have no choice..."

She stared at him for a moment, the pain visible in her eyes. "I know what you're trying to do. But please, Matteo... don't leave me. Don't let this be another mistake we made. I'm strong, I can fight with you. I won't let you face this alone, not anymore."

Matteo looked at her, his eyes full of conflict, but something deep in his heart finally gave way. He loved her. He knew that, no matter how real the threat was, he couldn't stay away from her anymore. They were stronger together, and he finally understood that.

"I won't leave you. Never again, Alessia," he said, his voice breaking with emotion. "I don't know how, but I'll make sure you two are safe. We'll do this together, and no one will tear us apart."

Alessia moved closer, her expression softening slightly as she touched his face. "I trust you, Matteo. But please, don't make any more choices without me. We're in this together, now and forever."

The two stared at each other for a long moment, unspoken words floating between them. They knew the road ahead would be difficult, but one thing was clear: no matter what the future brought, they would face it together.

# Chapter 93: The Devastating Decision

The house was silent, the air thick with the tension that hung between them. Matteo was in the living room, staring out the window, his eyes fixed on the horizon, but his mind miles away. The rain fell outside, making the world seem even more isolated and bleak. He knew he was about to make the hardest decision of his life. The decision that would cost him everything, but that he believed would ensure the safety of Alessia and their child.

When she entered the room, something in the air shifted. Alessia paused in the doorway, her eyes, normally filled with life and love, now reflecting a subtle fear, an uncertainty she couldn't hide. She knew something was wrong, but she couldn't imagine what he had decided to do.

Matteo turned slowly, the weight of the decision visible in every movement. He looked at her with an empty expression, no longer the flame of desire or the warmth of love that had always united them. He didn't want to do this, but he knew it was necessary.

"Alessia," he began, his voice cold as winter. "You and the baby are not safe here. My presence is putting everything at risk. The mafia will come after you, they'll come after all of us if I continue with this. I can't risk your life anymore. I can't risk the life of our child."

Alessia took a step forward, but she couldn't get close enough. The pain in his words paralyzed her. She knew how much he would sacrifice for her, but what he was saying seemed... unthinkable.

"Matteo, what are you saying?" Her voice trembled, confusion spilling over. "It can't be this. You can't just abandon me like this. We've built everything together! It's not just about safety, it's about us, about the future we dreamed of!"

But Matteo didn't look at her the same way. His eyes were empty, as if he was pulling away, as if he had already decided what he needed to do. "I'm not abandoning you, Alessia. I'm protecting you. I can't be with you anymore. I can't risk everything we've built. As much as it hurts, this is what I need to do."

Alessia felt the weight of his words, a punch to the stomach, a blow so cruel that it made her doubt her own reality. He was lying, she knew it. It couldn't be true. He was saying this to protect her, but deep down, Alessia knew he was convincing himself that separation was the only way out.

"No, Matteo. Don't do this to me," she pleaded, her eyes welling up, her chest tight with pain. "I can't live without you. Not now, not after everything we've been through. Not after... everything I still feel for you."

But he didn't yield. His gaze remained impassive, and he walked away, heading for the door. "I can't be your weakness anymore, Alessia. I can't be the reason you and our child are in danger. You have to go. It'll be safer this way."

Alessia felt his words pierce her heart. The man she loved, the man who had sworn to protect her, was now doing the hardest thing she could imagine: pushing her away. Their love, so intense and unbreakable, now seemed like a shadow, something she might never have again. The weight of betrayal, the bitter taste of seeing him walk away so coldly, all of it felt too real, and all she wanted was to hold him, to stop him from making the biggest mistake of his life. But she knew he had already decided.

"I won't leave," she said, her voice firm, though her eyes were filled with tears. "I won't leave you. Not now."

Matteo turned, finally meeting her gaze. And it was then that the truth became inescapable. He loved her in a way he couldn't even understand, but his hands were tied. He loved her more than anything in the world, and for that reason, he was willing to let her go, so that she could be safe, so that she could have a chance at happiness.

"I can't do this," he whispered, his voice breaking. "I can't watch you suffer because of me."

Alessia took a step forward, and her hands trembled as she touched his face. He couldn't walk away from her like this, he couldn't just turn his back, not after everything they had lived. She needed him, but she also knew that he loved her. The pain he was feeling, the pain he was trying to avoid, she felt it too.

"I love you, Matteo. I love you more than anything. And I will fight for us, for our family. Even if you want to let me go, I won't let you." She whispered, her lips almost brushing his. "I can't live without you. And neither can you without me. No matter what happens, we'll face it together."

Those words were all Matteo needed to hear. He finally closed his eyes, feeling the pain of a love lost, but also the hope that Alessia brought. She wasn't leaving, she wouldn't let him go. And somehow, he knew she was right: they were stronger together.

They were at war with fate, but now, with every breath shared, with every word of love that filled the silence between them, Matteo felt that there was still a chance. The battle wasn't lost. Not as long as he had Alessia by his side.

# Chapter 94: Loneliness and Grief

Alessia looked at the empty crib, feeling the weight of the night descend upon her once again. The silence in the house was deafening. Every sound in the house seemed to echo in her ears, making the emptiness even more profound. She was used to Matteo's presence — his low laugh, his firm steps, the warmth of his embrace — but now, everything was in ruins. Even with the baby sleeping peacefully by her side, Alessia felt isolated in an invisible prison.

What happened? What did she do wrong?

Those questions hammered relentlessly in her mind, creating a thin line between the pain of abandonment and the anger at the uncertainty. No matter how much she tried to deny it, Matteo's words still echoed in her mind, like a curse that prevented her from moving forward: "I can't risk your life anymore."

But he couldn't just leave her, could he?

Alessia stood up and walked to the window, looking out at the horizon without really seeing what was there. The city was calm, but she couldn't feel any peace. Matteo had left, and now she was alone with her baby, trying in every way not to sink into the abyss of loneliness.

"I don't understand..." she whispered to herself, tears welling in her eyes. "Why did he leave me like this? What happened to us?"

She didn't want to believe it was just a matter of safety. There had to be something else behind those harsh words. Something that hurt her even more. Alessia knew he loved her — she was sure of that. But deep down, the doubt was growing. And the fear of not being enough ate away at her from the inside.

On the other side of the city, Matteo watched, hidden in the shadows. His gaze, no matter how distant, never stopped following Alessia. He knew she was suffering, and that pain was a burden he couldn't bear. But at the same time, he couldn't deny that he had pushed her away for a reason: her safety. And the baby's. He had done it to protect them, and now the feeling of loss consumed him.

He felt a deep pain watching the life they had built fall apart. The promises made between them, the dreams of a peaceful future, now were only shadows of what could have been. Matteo felt as though he were adrift in a stormy sea, trapped in a whirlpool of wrong decisions. His soul was broken, but he didn't know how to fix it without destroying what little was left of his relationship with Alessia.

Matteo was alone once again. The emptiness inside him, which he had tried to fill with work, with the power of the mafia, no longer satisfied him. He looked at the organization, his allies, and what had once seemed like the center of his world now felt irrelevant. He didn't care about accomplishments or business anymore. The only thing that mattered was Alessia.

But he knew that the pain she was feeling was his fault. He had pushed her away without giving her a clear explanation, without showing her the truth of his intentions. He still loved her with all his being, but at the same time, he felt that the love she had for him had been diluted by the lie of separation. The pain was in both of them, and he didn't know if he could fix it.

The next morning, Alessia woke to the soft light of the sun streaming through the window. She looked at the baby, still calm in the crib, but her heart was empty. She was afraid to face another day alone. The house, which had once been filled with laughter and promises of a shared future, now felt like a graveyard of dreams.

But, as she looked at her child, Alessia felt a spark of strength. She needed to be strong for him. No matter how much Matteo had left, no matter how much his words had hurt her, she was still a mother. And now, more than ever, she needed to be an example for her son.

With the baby in her arms, Alessia went out into the garden, breathing in the fresh morning air. She tried to focus on the beauty around her, but her heart was still with Matteo. Every flower, every ray of sunshine, seemed to remind her of what she had lost. She closed her eyes for a moment, trying to calm her mind, but Matteo's face invaded her memory.

"I can't go on like this..." she murmured to herself, a mix of anger and sadness in her voice. "I can't be strong for him and keep this emptiness inside me."

What she wanted more than anything was for him to come back, to find her and explain himself. She desperately wanted to believe that his reasons for leaving weren't selfish, but he had chosen to pull away. And she knew that, by doing so, he believed he was doing what was best for her, even if that meant losing the chance to be happy together.

While Alessia lost herself in her thoughts, Matteo was in a place where nothing else mattered. He couldn't imagine his life without Alessia, but at the same time, he felt that the best thing for her was to keep her away from him. The mission he had set for himself was clearer than ever: she needed to be protected. Even if that meant living alone, he would do whatever it took to keep her safe. He didn't know how to do that without hurting her even more, but he knew he couldn't let the mafia's threat destroy what they had.

The days passed, and Alessia found herself trapped in a cycle of loneliness, trying to ignore the memories, trying to move forward for her child. But the pain wouldn't go away. She constantly wondered if one day she would have a chance to understand what had really happened, or if this would be something she would have to carry forever.

With each passing day without news from Matteo, Alessia felt more distant from him, but also more aware that her love for him, no matter how complicated, could never be erased.

# Chapter 95: The Family in Danger

Alessia walked through the garden of her new home, the afternoon sun casting long shadows on the walls of the small cottage where she had tried to rebuild her life. The tranquility she sought seemed more distant with each passing day, and today, more than ever, the feeling of being watched unsettled her deeply.

The calmness she had longed for since fleeing had been interrupted by an invisible presence. Strange men had appeared in the area, and she watched them discreetly, trying to hide her fear. Alessia knew what this meant. She tried to ignore it, but the clues were there, as clear as day. The mafia was still watching her, still seeing her as a threat, even though she had distanced herself. Even without Matteo, her presence was a reminder of her connection to the most feared man in the organization.

"I should have prepared for this," she murmured to herself, a mix of anger and sadness in her voice. It was as if fate, or the curse of the mafia, followed her relentlessly. Her life would never be normal, and that thought terrified her.

She returned to her thoughts, remembering the promises Matteo had made. How he had insisted that she leave, that she stay safe. At the time, she had thought he just wanted to get rid of her. But now, looking at the situation she was in, the truth was clear. He had pushed her away to protect her, even if it meant losing her presence by his side.

The weight of loneliness pressed on her chest, but the greatest burden was the pain of seeing her child grow up in an environment of fear. He didn't deserve this. She didn't deserve this. And despite everything, she still felt the emptiness of not having him by her side. What hurt the most was knowing that Matteo would never understand the sacrifice she had made for him. She loved him, but more than that, she loved what they could have been together —

a life in peace, away from the violence that had always surrounded them.

But the reality was now different. The threat from Lorenzo and the rival families was growing, and Alessia knew she could no longer live in fear. Her child's life was at stake, and she couldn't let history repeat itself. Allowing herself to be intimidated by the past was not an option. If there was a chance to ensure her family's safety, she would have to be brave enough to fight for it.

For weeks, Alessia had kept in contact with Matteo's old allies. She knew he would never openly support her after pushing her away, but there were still those who, in some way, respected what she represented. They helped her unearth crucial information about the new mafia alliance that was pursuing them. The families who had joined forces, aware that Matteo's position in command was now more fragile, were willing to use any means necessary to get rid of him and everything he represented, including the family he had built.

"They won't leave me alone, will they, Matteo?" Alessia asked, more to herself than to anyone else, as she examined the information in her papers. Her heart still clenched when she thought about how things could have been different, but she was stronger now. She knew she couldn't hide forever.

With painful clarity, Alessia knew what she had to do: face the mafia head-on. She couldn't run anymore, couldn't wait for a rescue from someone who, in her mind, had already decided to push her away. She needed to fight for her freedom, for her son's future, and, maybe one day, for a fresh start with Matteo, even though the pain and the fears of everything they had been through still made her doubt.

Matteo was in a hotel in a dark corner of the city, another lonely night. The phone rang, and when he looked at the screen, he saw Alessia's name. His heart leaped in his chest, but when he answered, he realized it was a message. She was in danger. He closed his eyes for a moment, trying to stay calm, but the fear of losing her more haunted him. Matteo's internal war was far from over, and now he knew what he had to do: if she was willing to fight, he would too. But he couldn't let her fight alone.

"I'll end this," Matteo whispered to himself, once again becoming the man he had been before: the mafia boss. But now, he knew his greatest treasure was no longer in his organization, but in the woman and child he had lost. The chance to rebuild something with Alessia was slipping further away, but he would not allow her to face danger without his help. She would not be alone again.

Alessia, in her determination, felt a mixture of relief and fear as she realized that the path she was choosing would require more than physical strength — it would be an emotional battle, a fight for survival and for the love she still felt for Matteo. Even though the mafia was relentless, she knew her real battle would be against her own inner demons. If she was to win, she would have to fight with everything she had left.

She took a deep breath, looking up at the gray sky. "I won't let them destroy us. Not again."

And though her body was exhausted and her heart wounded, something deeper pushed her forward. She knew that, somewhere deep down, there was still a chance for her and Matteo. But now, it was time to fight, more than ever, for the freedom and the family they had both wanted.

# Chapter 97: The Meeting Amidst the Chaos

The sun was beginning to set when Alessia stepped out the door, feeling the weight of the decision she had made. The plan was in motion. The allies were ready, the maps were spread across the table, and the future, though uncertain, felt closer than ever. She could feel the tension vibrating in her veins. The final confrontation was about to take place, and a sense of inevitability filled the air.

She tried to focus on what needed to be done, but her mind was elsewhere — on Matteo. Since he had left her, she had lived with a constant emptiness. Even with all his promises of safety and distance, Alessia had never been able to completely rid herself of thoughts of Matteo. He had been there at every step, in the darkest moments, in the smallest details. Even without his physical presence, she felt as if he were watching her, but she didn't want to admit that. Not anymore. Not after everything that had happened.

But when the henchmen started to move, when the danger became real and uncontrollable, when she found herself once again between a rock and a hard place, something inside her knew that he wouldn't leave her forever. Matteo, with all his strength, with all his pride, would not abandon her.

That was when he appeared.

He didn't come with words or explanations. He simply materialized in the corner of the room, his expression fierce as always, but with a softness in his eyes that she knew so well. Alessia couldn't hide the surprise that flooded her body. His eyes, intense and fixed on her, seemed to carry a ton of regret, but also a depth she couldn't ignore.

"Matteo..." she whispered, her voice trembling, a mix of relief and anger.

He walked toward her, slowly but with an unmistakable authority. When he got close, he stopped and observed her for a moment, as if trying to understand what was going through her mind.

"I know you didn't expect me here, Alessia," he said, his voice lower, graver than usual. "But you need to know that I never left you. I've always been here. For you, for him..." He looked at her belly, which was beginning to show signs of growth, and Alessia felt a sharp pain, but also a wave of unconditional love. "Everything I did was to protect you. To keep you away from danger."

She took a deep breath, the lump in her throat tightening further. But the anger was still there, suffocating. "And you think that's enough? You left me, Matteo. You left me thinking I was a burden, that I wasn't important anymore." She turned her gaze away, the words coming out like poison. "I don't need more empty promises."

Matteo stepped forward, as if his words weren't enough. "I know I hurt you, Alessia. And I know that my distance wounded you in ways I never imagined. But what you don't know is that I spent every second away from you, watching over you, protecting you from afar, because I didn't want to lose you. Because I didn't want you to make the wrong choice. I... I love you, Alessia. And I know the love I have for you is greater than any fear, than any pride."

Alessia turned to face him, her heart pounding in her chest. His words broke through the shield she had built over the past months. She could feel the sincerity in his voice, but the pain was still etched in her soul, like a deep scar.

"I... I don't know if I can believe in you again, Matteo," she said, her voice hoarse, anguish clear in her words. "I want to, but what if you leave me again? What if you disappear once more?"

Matteo moved even closer, now so close she could feel his warmth, his presence, which had always been so familiar. "I won't disappear again, Alessia. Not anymore. I will fight, even if it's the last sacrifice I make. There's nothing between us now except what I can give you."

The silence between them stretched for a moment, Alessia and Matteo's gazes intertwining. It was a moment of mutual vulnerability, where there was no more room for empty words or unkept promises. He knew what she needed to hear, but more than that, he knew what he needed to do.

"If you trust me again, Alessia, we'll face this together," he said, his voice firm but with a touch of softness. "I won't leave you behind."

Those words broke the last barrier Alessia had raised around her heart. She closed her eyes for a moment, feeling the pain and insecurity dissipate in a single act of surrender. When she opened her eyes, there was no more doubt. No more fear. There was only the love she knew had never truly left, despite everything.

"I trust you, Matteo," she whispered, a faint smile on her lips. "But promise me one thing..."

"Anything you want," Matteo replied, with the intensity of someone who knew that promise was not just an empty word.

"Promise me that, together, we'll end this. End this war. End everything that separates us."

"I promise," he murmured, sealing the promise with a soft yet firm kiss. "Now let's end this. Together."

The final battle was about to begin. But now, at last, Alessia and Matteo were ready. Not just to face the enemies, but to live the love they had always deserved, despite all the obstacles fate had thrown their way. And together, they were ready to rewrite their story, one step at a time.

As they prepared for the final confrontation, the tension was palpable. What had begun as a story of hatred and distrust was now transforming into something stronger, deeper. Amidst the echoes of the chaos of the mafia and the ghosts of the past, Alessia and Matteo's love had become their greatest weapon, their strength. And together, they would destroy the enemies and build the future they had always dreamed of.

# Chapter 98: The Confrontation with the Mafia Alliance

The tension was in the air. Alessia and Matteo, now united not only by love but by the need to fight for their survival, were ready. The sound of engines echoed in the distance, announcing the arrival of a new battle. The mafia alliance, composed of various factions that saw Alessia and Matteo's union as a threat to their survival, was finally taking center stage in the war. There would be no more escape, no more uncertainties. They had to end this once and for all.

The mansion, which had once represented a place of refuge and rebirth, was now the battlefield. Alessia felt the adrenaline coursing through her veins as she prepared alongside Matteo. He was by her side, strong, focused, but she knew the pain in his eyes ran deep. He was trying to hide the fear, but Alessia could see the truth in his gaze — the fear of losing her, the fear of failing with the only thing that mattered to him.

"Let's end this, Alessia," he said, his voice low, his eyes intense. He stood beside her, but still didn't touch her, as if wanting to maintain the line between love and war. She nodded without a word, and they moved toward what seemed like the end of everything they had ever known.

The confrontation began before they could truly prepare. Armed men invaded the mansion's surroundings, and the sound of gunfire cut through the heavy air of the night. Alessia ran to a strategic position, moving with precision. Matteo, ahead of her, was an unstoppable force, taking down anyone who tried to stop them. His eyes were focused on the goal — destroy the mafia alliance, ensure nothing would threaten them again.

They were in perfect sync. One movement, one exchange of glances, and they already knew what the other would do. The chemistry between them, forged in pain, loss, and struggle, was now a weapon sharper than any knife. Their partnership was stronger than any obstacle fate could throw their way.

"You're not going to leave me alone, right?" Matteo asked, a shadow of a smile on his lips, as he dodged a bullet and fired back.

"As if I'd let you get rid of me so easily," Alessia replied, a spark of humor in her eyes but also a determination he knew all too well. She was there, by his side, without hesitation, facing the chaos with a courage he never imagined she would have.

The fight continued. The smell of gunpowder and smoke filled the air. Every shot they fired was a promise. Every move was an affirmation that nothing would separate them. Alessia, with adrenaline pumping, felt more alive than ever, even as her body screamed for rest. She wouldn't stop. Not now. Not when she was so close to what she had always wanted — peace.

Matteo fought beside her with the strength of a man who had everything to lose. But no matter how hard he tried, he couldn't shake the constant thought of Alessia and the child she carried inside her. Every move he made was aimed at ensuring they were safe and ensuring that this fight would end, once and for all.

The fight seemed endless. Alessia was beginning to realize that the war they were fighting was not only physical but emotional. Each blow, each move, carried the need to destroy something more — the ghosts of the past, the mistakes made, the promises broken. She looked at Matteo at the exact moment he took down another enemy. He turned to her, and for a brief moment, they shared a deep gaze. He was tired, but there was still a flame in his eyes, a flame she recognized: he loved her. He was fighting for her. And for the first time, she knew there were no more doubts.

"Alessia, stay careful," Matteo shouted, but his voice no longer had the tone of command. It was a request, a plea disguised as a command. He knew the situation was dangerously out of control, but he couldn't lose focus. She couldn't get distracted, not even for a second.

"I'm not going anywhere, Matteo," she replied firmly, her voice cutting through the chaos of the battle. "I know what I need to do."

And she did. She knew that this confrontation was the last one. The final chance to destroy the alliance and finally leave the past behind. They were at the limit, and if they didn't end this now, they would lose everything.

The final move came quickly. Alessia, with impressive agility, took down the leader of the mafia alliance. He was about to fire, but she was faster. The bullet he tried to shoot was deflected by the sound of Matteo's relieved shout. Alessia had won. The weight she had felt was now lifted.

When the last enemy fell, the house was silent. The sound of gunfire ceased, but Alessia's heart still beat loudly, as if the world around her had paused. She looked at Matteo, who was approaching, exhausted and wounded, but with a sincere smile on his lips.

He was hurt, but not enough for her to not embrace him with all her strength. He held her in his arms, feeling her fragility, and for a moment, the weight of the battle, the fear, and the loss dissipated.

"It's over, Alessia," Matteo murmured, his voice hoarse but full of relief. "Now we can have what we deserve. Peace. Together."

She looked into his eyes, and for the first time in so long, she felt that maybe everything they had been through had been worth it. To be here, with him, after everything they had faced. She finally smiled, the tension melting away.

"Yes, Matteo. Together," she replied, and in that moment, nothing else mattered. They were finally ready to live what they had always deserved. Together.

The fight was over, but their love, now stronger than ever, was just beginning.

# Chapter 99: A Request for Forgiveness and a New Promise

The house, now silent after the chaos of battle, was immersed in a calmness that almost felt surreal. Alessia sat beside Matteo, both exhausted and wounded, but with a heavy weight lifted from their shoulders. They had won, together, and peace seemed finally within their grasp. Even with their injuries, the feeling of relief was immeasurable. But as the tension of the fight dissipated, a new kind of tension began to grow between them: the unspoken words, the old wounds, the chills of a love interrupted by fear and insecurity.

Alessia looked at Matteo, who was sitting beside her, his eyes still heavy but with a different kind of light in them. He seemed distant, but at the same time, more present than ever. His body was wounded, but his eyes, those eyes she knew so well, were full of regret. She knew what he wanted to say, but the weight of everything they had lived through still held them back from taking the final step.

"Alessia," Matteo began, his voice rough, almost inaudible, as though every word was an effort. He looked at her with an intensity that made her catch her breath. "I... need to ask for your forgiveness. For everything. For every time I doubted you, for every time I thought you might betray me. For pushing you away, even when the only place I should have been was by your side."

Alessia watched him, feeling his words pierce her heart, but also seeing the sincerity in his eyes. She knew he was fighting his own demons, trying to find a way to redeem himself, but the words never seemed enough. She breathed deeply, feeling the tears threatening to fall, but holding them back. She no longer wanted to cry out of despair, but rather from understanding.

"Matteo, I... I don't know how, but I always knew you didn't betray me," Alessia said, her voice broken but firm. "But what hurt me the most wasn't the doubt, or the fear. It was the fact that you pushed me away, that you left me alone when the storm was about to swallow us. I loved you, and I still do, but you made me believe I was a burden, that I couldn't be with you because of everything that happened."

Matteo closed his eyes, as if her words were a direct blow to his soul. He knew she was right, but how could he fix so much lost time? How could he erase the scars he had placed on her heart? He reached out, touching Alessia's face with a tenderness that almost hurt, his warm palm contrasting with the coldness of the words.

"I know I can't erase the past, Alessia. And I never wanted you to feel like that. I love you, more than I can explain, more than I can say. What happened between us was my mistake, and I was so lost in my own world of fear and revenge that I let you suffer for it. I won't leave you alone anymore, never again," he said, his voice firmer now, but still carrying the vulnerability of what he felt.

Alessia closed her eyes, the pain transforming into something softer, a sense of relief beginning to fill her heart. Matteo was there, with her, saying the words she had needed to hear. She felt the weight of his decision to finally acknowledge his mistake and to be willing to change, and something inside her broke.

"I love you too, Matteo. Even after everything. I always have," she said, the words coming in a deep sigh, as though she could finally breathe without the weight of fear, of doubt. "But I don't know if I can forget what happened, and I don't know if I can trust again... The wound is still here," she said, pointing to her chest, where her heart still beat with an intensity that hurt.

Matteo didn't pull back, even knowing that his words wouldn't be enough. He gently pulled her closer, resting her face against his chest, listening to the rhythm of her heart. The sensation of having her there again, was almost indescribable. He wanted her to know, beyond a shadow of a doubt, that he would never give up on her. He would never leave her alone again.

"I know you need time, and I will give you that time. But I want you to know that from now on, everything I am, everything I have, belongs to you and our child. There is nothing else, Alessia. Only you," he whispered in her ear, feeling the softness of her breath, the way her body seemed to relax against his.

Alessia felt the warmth of his promise slowly seeping into her heart. Even with the fear, the insecurity, and the pain, something was changing. She knew the road ahead wouldn't be easy, but she also knew that their love, renewed and reforged in the ashes of everything they had faced, would be enough to overcome any obstacle. Together, they could rebuild trust, peace, and a future for the family they were creating.

She pulled back slightly, looking into his eyes, and with a lightness she had never felt before, she whispered: "I'm ready to start over, Matteo. With you. Together."

He looked at her with a smile, an expression of relief and love on his face, and without words, just with a gentle gesture, he kissed her. It was a kiss filled with silent promises, redemption, and renewal. The passion, which had never faded, now burned with greater intensity. They were finally ready to write the next chapter of their lives, together.

And, in that moment, in his arms, Alessia felt that, perhaps, she was finally safe. Safe in their love, safe in the future they were building. And as she looked at the baby who would soon come into the world, she knew with certainty that, no matter the challenges, they would be a family, and that was all that mattered.

# Chapter 100: A New Beginning Full of Hope

The small country house was surrounded by green fields and distant mountains, creating a peaceful and tranquil scene. It was the kind of place Alessia had always dreamed of finding, far from danger, far from the violence that had often invaded her nights and days. Now, she could finally breathe freely, without the weight of the mafia, without the constant fear that her every move was being watched. She was with Matteo, the man who, despite all the mistakes and trials, had won her heart in a way that was unique, intense, and true.

Alessia stood by the kitchen window, gazing at the scenery. The sun was setting on the horizon, painting the sky in shades of orange and pink, and she felt a wave of gratitude wash over her. Her life, which once seemed like a whirlwind of chaos and fear, was now transforming into something sweet, serene, and, for the first time in a long time, hopeful. The child she carried in her womb was the promise of a better future, a home full of love, and perhaps, finally, the chance for a peaceful happiness.

Matteo entered the kitchen, smiling when he saw her there, so serene and beautiful. He still couldn't get used to the fact that she was there, with him, after everything they'd been through. He had distanced himself so much, and now, with a new beginning ahead of them, he felt like nothing else mattered, except for their love and the family they were building together.

"You're thinking about the future, aren't you?" Matteo asked, leaning against the kitchen door, watching Alessia with a soft smile.

She turned to him, and for a moment, their eyes met with a silent understanding. She didn't need to say anything. He knew what she was thinking. He felt the same. After all the pain, after all the struggles, they were finally here, together, with a real chance to build something new.

"Yes," Alessia replied, with a deep sigh. "I never imagined it could be like this. I thought we'd be trapped forever in the shadows of the past. But now, looking at you and at us, here... I feel like I finally have everything I've always dreamed of."

Matteo walked over to her, their hands finding each other. "I've done a lot of things wrong, Alessia. I made you suffer, and I can never change that. But I will spend the rest of my life making you happy, showing you every day how much you mean to me."

She felt the warmth of his words and the sincerity in them, but what touched her most was the truth in his eyes, the vulnerability he showed, so rare and genuine. She knew he was giving himself completely, and that made all the difference.

"I know you will," she said softly, her gaze softening. "And, even though I've felt lost and alone for so long, what really matters now is that we're here, together. And you are the man I choose every day, with all your flaws and imperfections."

Matteo pulled her closer, wrapping his arms around her. They stood there, embracing for long minutes, feeling the rapid beating of their hearts, the warmth radiating from their bodies, as if it were a promise that, no matter what the future held, now they had everything they needed.

The small country house became the perfect refuge for them, away from the war, away from the fear. It was in the silence of those peaceful afternoons that they found their new beginning. With Matteo now committed to legitimate business and a life away from the mafia, he could finally be the man Alessia deserved.

On a sunny Sunday, Alessia and Matteo were in the garden of the house, preparing everything for a simple, but meaningful ceremony. They had decided to renew their vows. There was no one around but a few close friends. The flowers in the garden were blooming, and their sweet scent seemed to symbolize the new cycle of their lives.

Matteo wore a suit, but his hair was tousled by the afternoon wind. Alessia wore a simple, yet stunning dress, with fresh flowers in her hair. When she saw him standing before her, she felt like everything around her stopped for a moment. Matteo looked at her with an indescribable intensity, as if he knew this moment would be eternal, engraved in their memory and in their hearts, forever.

"I promise you, Alessia, that I will never let you suffer again," Matteo began, his words coming out low but filled with overwhelming emotion. "I promise to be the man you've always deserved. I will love you every morning and night, in the good days and the bad, and I will protect you, always, until the end of my days."

Alessia felt a tear slide down her cheek, but it wasn't from sadness. It was from relief, from happiness. She tightened her grip on his hand, and looking into his eyes, she said:

"I choose you, Matteo, and I will continue choosing you every day. I promise to love you and walk by your side, no matter what challenge we face. And, if fear ever comes back, I will remember this moment, and I will know that our strength lies in the love we've built. Together."

They stepped closer and shared a sweet kiss, full of promises and deep feelings. It was a kiss that symbolized everything they had overcome, everything they would still face. When they pulled away, still holding hands, Alessia smiled, and with a bright look in her eyes, she said:

"Now, let's build the future, Matteo. Our future."

He nodded, smiling as well, and the two of them walked side by side, ready to begin again. Their love, now unbreakable, was the foundation of the new life they were building, far from the shadows, far from the fear. Now, with the baby in their arms,

Alessia felt she had finally found the home she had always searched for.

And so, with peace finally earned, Alessia and Matteo moved forward. The true battle they had fought was behind them, and now, together, they were ready to conquer the future.

**The End...**

# Don't miss out!

Visit the website below and you can sign up to receive emails whenever Anna Braun publishes a new book. There's no charge and no obligation.

https://books2read.com/r/B-A-JFBTC-ZDMIF

**BOOKS 2 READ**

Connecting independent readers to independent writers.

# Also by Anna Braun